THE BLESSING OF THE BLACK WOLVES

PRAISE FOR JS MURPHY

Mesmerizing

A richly involving story, with twists and turns, wonderful characters, and evocative descriptions that pull you into the place and time. Delightful read - I couldn't put it down!

— V HOWLETT

A Fun Read!

JS Murphy creates a fascinating world that I would love to visit! The story is full of romance, adventure, folklore, intriguing characters and plot twists. A great read for everyone.

— C RICHARDS

JS Murphy is a master story teller

I cannot wait for the second in this series. J S Murphy weaves an adventure in a world of diverse communities. There is an underlying message that pertains so aptly to today's world, a message that illustrates how easily one can misunderstand other cultures, how respect of other peoples is so very important in avoiding conflict.

The story is gripping, fun and intense. The world that J S creates is original and very believable. The characters are vivid and original. I am eager to read the next book once it is released to see how the characters will progress and adapt.

J S Murphy is my new favourite author!!!

Thank You J S!

— D SWIFT

ALSO BY JS MURPHY

The Blessing of the Black Wolves

Raven Seeker

The Road to Mirren-Bar

Black Wolves Series

Crossing Nightfall

East of Nightfall

Willow Girl

The Nightfall Mountain Series

THE BLACK WOLVES SERIES

BOOK ONE

THE BLESSING OF THE BLACK WOLVES

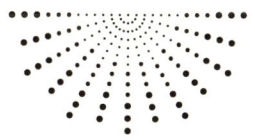

JS MURPHY

EVENTIDE BOOKS

Eventide Books

ISBN: 978-1-989860-03-8 (Paperback) v2
ISBN: 978-1-7771169-1-0 (ePub) v2

Cover Design by Kelly A. Martin

Photography by prometeus (DepositPhotos), arkusha (DepositPhotos), designwest (DepositPhotos),
STILLFX (Shutterstock), alexlibris (Bigstock)

To Peter with Love

THE BLESSING OF THE BLACK WOLVES

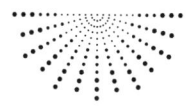

CHAPTER ONE

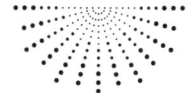

D EATH WAS WAITING.

Laran glanced again at the balcony overlooking the courtyard garden to her right. The man on it had ducked behind an ornate wooden screen, but she could still see the tip of his bow.

And there, across the courtyard on the other side was another bowman, on another balcony. And there, a third, crouched on the roof, almost completely hidden from view.

She was invisible. They wouldn't see her. As a slave her presence there in the courtyard would raise no more interest than the flowers or the ponds below and the death the bowmen sought would happen whether she was there to view it or not.

She didn't care. Let the barbarians murder each other. One less would make no difference to the life she lived now.

Laran attached the buckets of water she'd drawn from the well to the wooden yoke. Hefting it awkwardly onto her slender shoulders, she started toward the wide stone steps leading to the Houses of Du-kar and Morrow. Lord Du-kar awaited her and if she tarried, she would taste his anger. She took a final backward glance at the courtyard.

Surrounded on all sides by the Great Houses of Soldat, it was quiet now in the sunlit dawn, and peaceful.

Not for long, she thought ruefully. Soon the concealed bowmen would kill the probably deserving Soldatian and the walls would ring with the shouts of others just like him. They would fill their balconies, straining for a glimpse of the aftermath of violence below.

Her shoulders and back already ached from the burden of weight. Laran turned away, aware of the first stirrings of a few early morning passers-by.

The bowmen remained hidden, their bows at rest.

Apparently, the dead man had not yet made an appearance.

Male laughter erupted on the steps above as two young men strode into sight from the direction of the House of Morrow. Their heads were down, and the sun shone on the long, shining black hair and white tunics common to Soldat nobility. Both were tall and well-muscled. They wore knee-length boots over loose-fitting trousers and one carried a cloak over one arm, though the day was already warm. Both were still grinning over the remark that had prompted the laughter. The man with the cloak raised a hand in parting and disappeared through a mid-level entrance and into the inner recesses of the Morrow House.

Laran moved over on the wide steps to avoid the remaining man and averted her eyes. Slaves were to remain invisible at all times, a lesson she'd learned the hard way. She had no desire to be knocked down on the hard stone steps.

Even so, when she felt his eyes, she cautiously raised her own to meet them, bracing for a blow as she did so.

It was he! The Smiling Man. The weight on her shoulders suddenly seemed a little lighter.

His eyes were black, his brows a raven arch above them. The jaw was strong and the mouth, still sporting the diminishing grin, was... *By the Holy Ones, Laran, stop staring!* She jerked her gaze away and the young man continued past her, though she felt his eyes once again. He must have turned around to look at her.

She hadn't been invisible to him.

He'd been kind to her once, lifting the heavy buckets from her shoulders as he passed her on the stairs. He'd set them down at the top of the stairs without a word, shooting her a quick glance before striding off on his own business. Du-kar had learned of the interaction. She'd been punished for it.

But she'd never forgotten it. Surreptitiously, she'd begun to watch for him in the early mornings as she made her way down to the well.

She saw him sometimes on his balcony, his hands around a cup of some steaming liquid, watching the garden below as the sun rose. Sometimes a woman and a child joined him there, sometimes it was another young man —the one he was with now, perhaps. He always had a smile and a ready laugh for them.

She began thinking of him as The Smiling Man, his mere existence a kind of solace: proof there could still be joy in the world.

Foolishness. The reality of the man was probably quite disappointing. After all, he was a complete stranger. Worse, he was a Soldatian.

They were a warrior society, these Soldatians, sniping at one another politically at every turn, always on the lookout for personal advantage. She'd been taken from her family and her home, enslaved and brutalized in Soldat.

Ashaii, she thought. Let them murder one another. One less would do the world no harm.

As she reached the upper entrances to the House of Du-kar, Laran's curiosity got the better of her. She glanced toward the adjacent roofline, of which she now had a perfect line of vision. The bowman positioned there had risen in the act of tightening his bow. She sensed rather than saw movement on the two occupied balconies as well.

Her gaze flew to The Smiling Man below.

No! Not this *Soldatian. Any other. Not this one!*

She dropped the heavy buckets. Cold water splashed over her bare feet and legs and poured down the steps. Laran took those steps two at a time, racing swiftly back toward the bottom. The Smiling Man had reached the courtyard and slowed his pace to watch the antics of two young children who pursued a large puppy helter-skelter around the garden while their nursemaid watched, laughing.

The first arrow hit him in the thigh. Shocked, uncomprehending, he staggered once, and then stood a moment, trying to understand what was happening. Laran's tackle took him down and the two of them crashed into a flowerbed.

"What in the Seventh Layer?" he shouted. He wasn't smiling now. The second arrow pierced his tunic and scraped across his shoulder.

He realized the girl in the flowers beside him had probably saved his life. He tried to ignore the pain in his thigh to rise and pull her with him to safety. She was small and light, and the lower entrance to the House of Morrow was only steps away.

But another arrow caught him squarely in the throat and he fell on his back to the ground, choking and clutching frantically at the imbedded shaft.

Laran scrambled to her feet, got behind him, grasped him under the arms and tried to drag him behind a short stone wall. By the Holy Ones, he was heavy! An arrow whistled past her face and another tore her clothing as it passed close to her skin.

After what seemed an interminable time, she dropped down behind the wall to the ground beside him and grasped his face with two hands.

"Look at me!" she hissed at him. He was struggling for air, each laboured breath making an awful bubbling sound in his throat. His body was rigid and his back arched with effort. Blood trickled from the corner of his mouth. "Look into my eyes," she ordered.

He locked wide, panicked eyes with hers.

"The pain will be great," she told him. She squeezed her own eyes shut just a moment to concentrate her will. When she opened them again, she took hold of the arrow and, with all her strength, pulled it free while the wounded man writhed in agony.

He was choking again, drowning in his own blood, unable to draw the breath he needed.

"Watch me," Laran ordered again. "Watch my eyes." She stared into his and tried to will him to continue looking at her. His focus was slipping now. She placed her hand on the sides of the gaping neck wound and whispered words of comfort while he struggled.

The bubbling, choking sound of his breath gave way to a strained whistle as air began to trickle through his damaged windpipe. Still he choked, but less and less now. His labouring chest rose and fell less fitfully. His focus returned. His arched back relaxed as he began to draw great lungfuls of air. His wide ebony eyes still held hers.

Laran saw the creeping darkness at the edges of her own vision. Exhaustion was stealing her senses, though she could hear movement all around them now, could feel feet pounding into the courtyard.

As The Smiling Man's life returned, her energy ebbed. Her hand began to fall away from the neck wound, but she willed herself to keep it there. *Almost,* she thought. *Almost there.*

Du-kar. He'd beat her to death for this. She'd never see her family again. *No!* She wouldn't think of the consequences of what she'd done. She couldn't. Not now. Her hand dropped from the neck wound.

Darkness filled her vision now. Her body seemed to sag and she was vaguely aware of her head bouncing lightly on the wounded man's chest. She barely heard the now steady beating of his heart as she drifted into unconsciousness.

* * *

SHEFTU MORROW LAY still a moment longer. As his breathing eased, the pain in his upper leg seemed to intensify. One hand rose in wonder to touch the head of the unconscious woman on his chest, the other reached down to probe the shaft of the arrow protruding from his thigh.

By the Souls of the Dead, what had happened here? He'd been dying, that much was certain. *Hadn't he been?* Yes. Dying. He'd been unable to breathe, his neck pierced by an arrow. He placed his hand on his bloodied throat but felt nothing. No torn flesh, no hole, no wound. No pain. He turned his head. An arrow lay, its tip red and wet, on the ground beside him.

"My lord?"

A small contingent of Morrow soldiers stood guard over him now, and one knelt on the ground beside him. The attack had ceased.

"My lord?" he asked again. The soldier looked aghast. Blood covered his wounded lord from neck to thigh. And what in Soldat was this Du-kar slave woman doing lolled over him? She, too, was covered in blood— the lord's, it seemed. Frowning, the soldier began to push Laran's unconscious form aside.

"Gently," Sheftu told him hoarsely. He grasped the hand offered him and staggered awkwardly to his feet, clenching his teeth against the pain in his thigh, and throwing his arm around the nearest soldier for support. "Carry the girl inside, Reedin," he rasped to his captain. He stared down at her. "Bring her to my chambers. I want a bed prepared for her there. Call for the physician."

"But, my lord," the kneeling soldier said hesitantly, "she is Lord Du-kar's."

Sheftu became aware of more activity as his men scoured the rooftops in search of his assailants. "I know," he acknowledged softly. There'd be the Seventh Layer itself to pay for bringing the girl into the House of Morrow. The two houses were not allied and there was no love lost between them.

He looked at his men. Their presence had undoubtedly ended the attack. He released his hold on the supporting shoulder to stand on his own a moment. He placed one hand to his heart and inclined his head slightly in thanks. Then he grasped the soldier's shoulder once more.

Someone wanted him dead, that much was obvious. Who? And why? If not for this girl, he would be.

Reedin carried her now in his arms. Sheftu glanced at her unconscious form. As was customary for slaves, her hair was short but, strangely, light brown in colour. It curled softly over her brow. Her eyes, he knew, were large, slanted slightly, and, even more strangely, golden. Dark earth, presumably from the flowerbed, smeared her cheek and blood, his own he thought, coated her hands and chest. She was small, not much over five feet, and very pretty.

This was the girl he'd passed on the steps earlier. He'd seen her before. He'd admired her lithe form and the way she carried herself like a queen in slave's garb, admired, too, the graceful way she moved though her feet were bare and her burdens often great.

She'd saved his life, healed him somehow. But that was impossible. She couldn't have.

He felt his throat once again. Smooth, unmarked. And bathed in blood. He drew the back of his hand across his lips and stared at the streak of red.

He renewed his hold on the supporting shoulder and continued to limp painfully through the entrance of the House of Morrow, glancing continuously at the girl who'd somehow beaten back his death.

CHAPTER TWO

LARAN AWOKE SLOWLY. The bed was soft, the bedding softer. She was at home in her own chambers, the trailing ends of a nightmare fading away. Even the terror of that dream was ebbing, the soothing voices of birds at her window becoming more distinct. There were other voices in the background now, too, speaking quietly.

In Soldatian.

Her eyes flew open. An old man, long black hair threaded with silver, inky eyes moist and red rimmed, leaned over her. A stranger. He'd been the source of those quiet words. A young woman hovered in the background, eyes wide with sudden alarm. Both wore the garb of a Soldatian household.

But not Lord Du-kar's. No, not his!

Laran threw back the bedclothes and leapt to her feet. A wave of dizziness threatened to overtake her as she backed away from the strangers. She leaned heavily against a wall, vaguely aware of the foreign texture of thick tapestry at her back and even thicker carpet beneath her bare feet.

She glanced quickly at the window. No exit presented itself there, though the windows were wide open to the late spring air. The customary dark Soldatian draperies had been removed for the season and filmy gauze hung to the sills now, but it wasn't the snow-covered peaks of her homeland she saw beyond. No. Between the grey stone buildings of the noble houses, she glimpsed the wide, yellow plains of Soldat.

The terror of her nightmare took hold once more. *No! Not a nightmare!* This was not her place. These were not her rooms. And these were definitely not her people.

A sob rose up in her throat. She was still here. Still in Soldat. Still the captive slave of a barbarous lord, still a thousand miles from her mountain home, and still separated from the family that loved her.

And she was going to die most cruelly. Lord Du-kar would see to it.

Tears slid down her cheeks now and she brushed them angrily aside. In all the many months she'd been enslaved, she'd not let anyone see her cry; she'd not allow it now.

The old man's hands were raised, palms toward her in a universal gesture of pcacc.

"Do not fear," he told her, but the rest of his words were lost as she turned in place and sprinted for the doorway. Pushing heavy fabric aside, she plunged into the next room.

The man she thought of as The Smiling Man lay on a couch within, one leg bandaged white and elevated. The moniker seemed ironic now: his face was pale and pain had drawn a deep line between his brows. His laughter had been erased. The cushion on which his head lay was draped with an untidy disarray of shining black hair, and one arm had been thrown over his eyes to block the light of the advancing day.

She stopped dead and stared at him. In the other room the old man had raised an alarm, but it seemed he was reticent to enter this chamber.

Perhaps The Smiling Man was the Morrow Lord. He seemed too young, but...

The Smiling Man was dropping his arm. He awkwardly raised himself to a sitting position, wincing as he did so.

Laran cast about for a way out. She saw the open door to the balcony, gauzy fabric blowing in the breeze at either side, and shuddered. The young lord would be an easy target out there. So would she if she made a run for it. The balcony was two stories above the courtyard and there was no succour there for her regardless.

There was no succour for her anywhere.

Behind her in the next room, she heard the arrival of the lord's guards. Fear coursed through her. *Trapped.*

"What...?" She swallowed audibly. "What do you want with me?" she asked the young lord. She divided her attention between him and the door between the two chambers. On the other side she could hear his guardsmen querying his command.

"Do not fear," the young lord was saying, his voice deep and hoarse, his words an echo of the old man's. "No one will harm you here."

Laran desperately wanted to believe him. She searched his coal black eyes for the truth but saw only the continued reflection of pain from his leg wound.

"Believe," he said as though reading her thoughts.

Despite her obvious distress, the girl's voice had been quiet and even. The faint accent was unusual and gave it an almost musical timbre.

Sheftu tried to rise to his feet, but sank back down on the couch, gritting his teeth rather than crying out.

She could help him, and she saw that he *knew* she could help him. He didn't ask. Perhaps he feared *her* now.

"What do you want of me?" she asked him again. The dizziness was returning, and her head began to pound. It was becoming difficult to stand up straight.

"You are hurt?" he rasped, alarmed at her sudden pallor.

"Tired," she mumbled.

"What you did," the young lord began, "does it fatigue you so?"

"*Ashaii,*" she answered in the language of her mountain home. She was unaware of the lapse.

12

Sheftu was silent a moment. "What do I want?" He looked into her golden eyes. "I ask no more than you have already given," he began. "But you will want something of *me*. Something for what you did. Will you not?"

She looked into his handsome face, blinking heavily. The line between his brows was still there and the pain in his dark eyes was still pronounced, but there was gentleness in his expression.

"What *do* you want?" he asked her again.

She hadn't had a plan, hadn't done what she did for a price, but, by the Holy Ones, she wanted something now. *I want you to smile at me,* she thought. *I want to hear your laughter. I want to feel that reassurance of joy still in the world.*

"I want to go home," Laran whispered.

She sank down on the couch beside him, only vaguely aware of the intimacy of doing so. She reached out, her hand seemingly moving of its own accord, and touched his neck where he'd been wounded. She heard his sharp intake of breath and felt his body go rigid in surprise.

The last remnants of pain in his throat faded away.

She moved her hand to his thigh. She could feel his stygian eyes boring into her.

The pain in his leg receded. She could feel that. The damaged limb began to heal. The young lord exhaled in relief and the pain cleared from his eyes, leaving some unnamed emotion in its place. She couldn't decipher it. Couldn't even try. Her body sagged. She slid off the couch onto the thick carpet.

Sheftu frowned in confusion at the young woman sleeping on his floor. He swung his leg off the couch, tested it, put his weight on it. Free! It was free of pain. He looked down at the white bandage. He knew he'd see smooth skin beneath—healthy tissue unmarked by the arrow that had pierced it.

He stood in wonder, whole, then bent to pick the girl up. He tried to whisper words of comfort as she'd done for him, though he doubted she could hear them. He glanced at the door between the two rooms where the frantic physician and his assistant waited.

He'd keep what the girl could do to himself for a time. He feigned a heavy limp as he moved into the antechamber. Two Morrow guardsmen stood at the door now. Six others waited without.

Sheftu placed the sleeping girl in the bed that awaited her there and covered her to the shoulders. He glanced at the physician's assistant. She was a young woman, perhaps of an age with the slave girl. "Stay with her, Landi," he told her. His deep voice was no longer hoarse.

He held up two fingers to indicate that two guards were to remain at the door.

"Protect her," he told them.

The slave girl was a treasure. If Du-kar understood her value, he wouldn't have left her to toil for the kitchens drawing water. Good. His chances of acquiring her were far greater if Du-kar did not recognize what had happened there in the courtyard.

Sleeping, she looked like a child. Her skin was fair. The fringe of light brown lashes beneath her closed eyes matched her brows and the soft curly cap of her hair. The smudge of dirt on her cheek had been removed. Her full lips were soft and slightly parted in a soundless "o". He wanted to trace them with his fingers. He wanted to trace all of her.

No. He'd respect her. The Seven Gods knew he respected what she could do, what she'd done for him! He'd repay her somehow.

He couldn't deny his fascination, though. He'd keep her close for a time. But to do so, he had to acquire her from Du-kar. He rubbed the back of his head a moment in thought.

That would be a trick.

Sheftu nodded to the waiting physician, then turned and affected a limp back into his own chamber.

The old man followed him in clucking his tongue and softly admonishing his lord not to put weight on his leg unnecessarily. He helped the young man elevate the once-wounded limb and, shaking his graying head, clucked his tongue again at the imprudence of the young.

Lord Sheftu restrained himself from leaping off the couch to go in search of those that would have murdered him. Instead, he looked at the curtained doorway to the antechamber where the slave girl lay and made a decision.

CHAPTER THREE

L ARAN STRETCHED OUT luxuriously. The physician's assistant, Landi, had arranged a bath. It was warm and lightly scented. The towel at her fingertips was soft. Sunlight poured into the bathing room through a carved wooden screen, dappling the water. Reflections danced up the walls and winked on and off on the ceiling. Her eyes closed in pleasure and she wriggled her toes at the bubbles near the edge of the oval pool and thought of the young Morrow lord whose rooms adjoined this one.

I ask no more than you have already given, he'd said. Laran was unconvinced. She'd yet to meet a Soldatian male whose word she could trust, though she desperately wanted to trust this one. *Trust must be earned.* That's what her father said.

Shadows moved across her closed eyelids as Landi walked through the sunbeams to the edge of the bathing pool. Laran could sense her standing above her, staring down at her as she lay in the pool.

Mere slaves were not accorded such privileges. That had been Landi's comment. The implication of those words hung in the fragrant air ominously. Laran knew she would be forced to deal with any expectations on the young lord's part soon enough. She kept her eyes closed and resolved to enjoy these last brief moments of contentment.

"Go away," she instructed Landi.

Landi sniffed haughtily. "And just what did you *do* for the young lord for the privilege of bathing in his pool?"

Saved his life. Healed his wounds. "Go away, Landi!"

Landi ignored her. "I was a slave once, you know."

Laran opened her eyes. "You were?"

"*Aey*, and so were most of the servants you see here in the Morrow House." She moved about the bathing room running her fingers along the intricate screen carvings. "The Morrow Lord and his family do not believe in slavery. When slaves are purchased, they are expected to give five years of service and then they are freed."

"Freed?" Laran sat up in the pool. Landi had her full attention now.

"*Aey*." Landi was warming to her story. She sat at the edge of the bathing pool. "Slaves that steal or cause trouble are sold, but if they perform loyally and well, then five years of service will see them freed. Or employed. The Morrow Lord offers most of us the opportunity to stay if we wish. Some do. Some don't. I did. And now I am assistant to the physician," she boasted. "Or at least I was until *you* came."

Landi looked down at Laran pointedly. "But I have *never*," she continued, "seen a slave invited to use the young lord's bathing pool. So." Landi leaned in conspiratorially. "What *did* you do for the young lord?"

Laran frowned. "You are being impertinent."

"Impertinent?" sputtered Landi. She straightened her back. "Well, and just who do you think you...?"

But Laran had closed her eyes once more. She sank below the surface of the pool, her soft curls suspended around her head like a light brown halo. She could hear bubbles rising in the water as she disturbed the bottom of the pool, could hear her own movements amplified. She heard the beating of her heart and imagined she heard the rush of blood in her veins. She could no longer hear Landi.

She opened her eyes wide against the water to see silvery strands of sunlight lazily piercing the surface. It danced lightly over her pale skin.

She saw the large, shadowy form of a man standing in the doorway of the bathing room, his body moving in and out of focus as the surface of the pool was disturbed.

She sat up abruptly and cast about for Landi. *Gone!*

The man, a stranger, was leaning against the doorframe, shining black hair pulled back in a queue, and a wide grin on his boyish face. He was tall and well-muscled like The Smiling Man. He'd been with him on the stairs! Had it only been yesterday? The bulge under his tunic gave evidence to the fact that he'd been there long enough to see... everything.

"Well, well," he intoned. "Aren't you a pretty surprise?" His grin widened. "Glad to see my cousin has finally..."

His words stopped as the slave girl rose slowly to her feet and straightened her back. Water rushed down her nude body in rivulets and one breast gleamed wetly in a shaft of light, but she lifted her chin and pointed an arm imperiously at the door in which he stood.

"Get out!" she ordered.

Provos took a step back. The command had rung with authority and he had to resist the urge to do as he'd been ordered. After all, despite possessing the haughty bearing of a queen, a small queen, the girl's hair was short and strangely light in colour. That marked her as a slave and an outsider. He continued staring instead, still grinning in enjoyment.

She was completely naked. She was also beautiful, proud, and... familiar somehow.

His memory stirred, widening his eyes and wiping off his grin just as a hand reached around from behind him and jerked him out of the doorway.

* * *

"WHAT IN THE Seventh Layer of Darkness!" Provos shouted at his cousin. "It's The Elf! Isn't it? The one you called The Elf! Tell me you *bought* her from Du-kar, Sheftu! Tell me you didn't..."

"Not exactly," Sheftu interrupted. "It's kind of… ah… complicated."

"Complicated!" Provos shouted. "You *stole* her? You *know* Du-kar has been looking for an excuse, any excuse to come down on the House of Morrow."

"She's special, Provos."

"*Aey*, Cousin. I *saw* how special she is." His grin returned but just as quickly dissolved. "And it's not like you to think with your cock."

Sheftu stared at his cousin a moment, evaluating how much truth there was to his words. He couldn't deny the girl aroused him and he'd told Provos as much after they'd passed her on the steps the first time.

"Someone tried to kill me," Sheftu told him softly. Provos' eyes widened again.

"*What?*"

"After you and I parted yesterday. The girl, there," he nodded toward the bathing room, "saved my life."

"She… Are you *insane?*"

Sheftu nodded thoughtfully. "*Aey*. Maybe."

The young woman stood in the doorway of his chamber now, hastily but fully dressed, wet hair damp and curling around her face. Water made points of her brown lashes and spiked one of the curls on her brow. Her slanted golden eyes, her diminutive stature, even the short light hair had given rise to the nickname.

"Elf?" she asked.

Despite her casual question, her slight body was braced for flight. Sheftu frowned. Du-kar had a reputation as a brutal son of a bitch. Perhaps she feared the same at his hands.

He forced a grin despite his cousin's censure.

"*Aey*," Lord Sheftu said. "Elf." Provos stared at his cousin in disbelief.

"By the Seven Gods," muttered Provos. "You court disaster. You must return the girl *now*! Before more damage has been done."

But Sheftu was shaking his head, and the girl watched him carefully from the doorway.

His grin, though it had been at her expense, seemed to mark a return of the good humour she associated him with. And, although being referred to as an "elf " did not sound overly complimentary, she supposed he would not be any better disposed to The Smiling Man, the nickname she'd given *him*. She smiled back at him.

Provos looked from one to another in undisguised horror.

"She's a *slave,* Cousin, and Du-kar's property at that. You cannot..."

"I," Laran turned her golden eyes on Provos, "am no man's *property.*" Her smile had disappeared. "And most certainly not *that* one's." She raised her chin once more.

"Go away, Provos," Sheftu told him. "I wish to speak to our little elf alone."

Provos stared a moment longer, then turned on his heel and strode out the door, brushing by her and swearing softly as he did so.

"I meant no disrespect with the "elf " comment," Lord Sheftu told her, smiling once more.

He was speaking to her as an equal. She had remained visible to him.

"And," he continued, "if you wish me to return you to the House of Du-kar, I will."

"No!" Laran said quickly, her golden eyes wide. She took a step into his chambers. "I will stay here." She looked desperate. "With you." She said this last in a very small voice.

"You fear him? Du-kar?"

"I fear no man." Laran's chin rose proudly once more, but her gaze faltered.

"Yes," she amended softly. "I fear him."

She took a deep breath and looked into the young lord's eyes. They were, like most Soldatians', jet black. But unlike any man's she'd seen before him, they were also beautiful.

"I have courage," she told him. It seemed important he believe her. She wasn't sure why. "And strength." Her face clouded. "But Lord Du-kar..." She stared at the carpet at her feet, ashamed. "He steals them from me," she whispered.

Sheftu felt a surge of anger. Just what had the bastard done to "steal" her courage and her strength?

"You had no shortage yesterday morning during the attack," he said quietly.

Laran looked up at him, surprised, and pleased, at the compliment. "Tell me again: why did you save my life?" he asked her.

Haven't we had this discussion? He was waiting expectantly.

"You are The Smiling Man," she finally told him as though that explained it all.

"I don't understand."

Laran shrugged, not willing to explain further. He was a symbol that joy still existed, that kindness still prevailed, and if he died, then for her, so did joy. He'd been her only thread. That thin filament of hope she'd clutched so fiercely would become too fragile to hang on to.

"I would repay you for what you did for me," Sheftu prompted. His voice was deep and even now, the last lingering trace of damage having been healed.

Home. I want to go home! Laran felt her stomach clench. She wanted to tell him again what was in her heart, but she was certain of his response. Symbol or not, he was only a man. And a Soldatian.

He wouldn't help her. Not with that. Perhaps he couldn't.

Sheftu tried again. "Do you wish to live here, away from Lord Du-kar? Do you wish money? Protection?"

Laran looked down at her feet. Longing for the family she loved kept her mute.

"You wish to go home."

He had *heard. And he'd remembered.* Was he toying with her? "You... you would send me home?"

"If that is what you wish."

"It is!" She felt a surge of elation. *Can I believe him? Does he mean it?*

She crossed the room, stepped close to the young lord, tilted her head back and searched his beautiful eyes.

"What kind of man are you?" she asked him quietly.

Sheftu frowned. "What do you mean?" The girl did not *act* like a slave.

"Are you honourable? Do you *mean* what you say?" Her eyes never left his. "Can I trust you?" He was staring down at her, his expression unreadable. She took a step back, suddenly unnerved. "I... I have met others whose smallest gesture of kindness comes with too high a price."

Those eyes! Golden like the treasure she is. "I mean what I say, Little Elf. You can trust that I will do everything in my power to return you to your home." He was quiet a moment and then he smiled. His teeth were straight and white, his lips sensuously formed. His dark eyes crinkled at the corners. They shone with mischief.

"As to whether there is an additional price, that remains to be seen." His smile broadened to a grin.

"There can *be* no additional price, my lord," Laran answered, her face serious. "Do you still wish to help me?"

Sheftu's smile faded away.

"*Aey*," he answered quietly. "I do."

Eyes shining, Laran placed one hand over her heart and rested the other on his chest, over his.

He looked startled and Laran jerked her hand away.

"Forgive me," she said. "I only meant to show my gratitude. It is a common custom where I am from." She met his eyes again.

They were as black as the tarns of her mountain home, the brows like the wings of ravens. His straight, shining hair lay loose on his shoulders and she found herself yearning to touch it, to feel its smooth texture.

She took another step back and swallowed. *Careful,* she reminded herself. *The man is a stranger raised among others just like him. I know nothing about him. Despite his assurances, I dare not trust that he has no agenda of his own.*

Sheftu continued staring down at the girl, his expression sober. Provos was partly right. He would have to be certain his physical response to her did not influence his actions. She looked fragile with her slight build, fair skin and wide golden eyes. She appeared to have no artifice and she did not guard her expressions. But appearance of fragility and innocence aside, she'd been strong in the face of danger. She'd risked her life to help him. Whatever the reason, he owed her. He'd help her. He'd see her returned to her home.

He'd keep his doubts about his success to himself.

And he wouldn't, as Provos suggested, think with his cock.

"I am Lord Sheftu Morrow," he told her. "Second son to the Morrow Lord." He watched for her response. She didn't seem to be impressed by his status nor did she seem to be intimidated. She did, however, remain wary.

"All that you see here," he continued, gesturing widely, "belongs to my father and to my brother after him. I am Lord here now, guardian of the House of Morrow until their return. I've made an enemy as you've seen and I'm not certain how that will play out."

Laran stood absolutely still. She fervently hoped he wouldn't ask *her* any questions. Well, why would he? She was only a slave after all.

"My own resources do not equal what you see here. I tell you all of this so you will understand. As a second son, some things I cannot influence. Others..." He paused a moment, "I can." He looked at her pointedly. "I will."

"Now," he stared down into her eyes, "tell me who you are, who your family is, where you come from, and how you believe I can help you return to them." He leaned against a tapestry, crossed his muscular arms across his wide chest and waited.

CHAPTER FOUR

L ARAN STIFFENED. SHE wanted to trust him. She'd kept her secrets for a long time and wanted to tell the young man everything.

I don't really know him.

She looked up into his face. He was still leaning against the tapestry, still waiting for her answers.

Best to guard the truth for a time yet, she told herself. After all, she didn't want to become a political pawn or, worse, an excuse for war.

A portion of the truth: hadn't that been her father's counsel? Give your enemies a portion of the truth but safeguard the balance. She had to give him something. How could he help her if he had no information?

But her thoughts were becoming jumbled. He was watching her with a curious expression and his eyes really were… beautiful. He was very handsome. She was suddenly aware of his strength, of the breadth of his shoulders, of his stature, even his scent. He smelled clean and faintly of… fresh air.

By the Holy Ones, Laran, you are doing it again! He is Soldatian. Admire if you must, but do not trust! At least not entirely.

She straightened her spine and took a deep breath. "You've heard of Mirren-Bar?" she asked him quietly.

"*Aey*," Sheftu laughed. "Would you have me believe you are from the mythical city of Mirren-Bar?"

"That you do *not* believe," she told him, frowning, "does not make it untrue." Sheftu continued leaning casually against the tapestry.

"It's said," he mused, "that its walls have been carved into the cliffs of mountains so high only the gods have seen their peaks." He grinned at the tall tale. "Its residents are said to have eyes of gold." He glanced at her, suddenly off-balance. "They are said to possess the power of…" He straightened, dropping his arms from his chest and stared.

"Healing?" Laran asked softly.

His ebony eyes widened at the full impact of the statement he'd been about to make. He was silent a moment.

"Are you saying it's *not* a myth?" He sounded skeptical despite the living proof before him.

Laran shook her head. "Thirty thousand people live within the walls of Mirren-Bar. There are two hundred thousand more living in greater Mirren."

Sheftu was silent a moment as he digested that. "Should I believe this story?" he asked quietly.

Laran frowned. "It is not a myth! Why would I tell you such a thing if it were untrue?

Sheftu rubbed the back of his head.

"And your family?"

Careful, Laran. "My father is Captain Tishane of the King's Guard in Mirren-Bar. If I could get a message to him my family would know that I still live."

Sheftu nodded thoughtfully. "This place," he began, "this non- mythical city of yours, is said to be carved into the mountains west of Barraid."

"That is so," Laran said.

"Soldat and Barraid have enjoyed an uneasy truce the past few years, but it's tenuous at best, volatile at worst. Still," Sheftu said, "perhaps we can get a message through Barraid to your family." *Somehow.*

Could it be true? Was the girl actually from Mirren-Bar?

"Captain of the King's Guard," Sheftu said thoughtfully. If she spoke the truth, if there was a King's Guard, then Mirren had a ruler, and Laran's father, this Captain Tishane, held a high position under him.

Laran nodded, ashamed of the deception. The young lord seemed sincere in his desire to help her. *Trust must first be earned.* That's what her father said.

"Returning you to your family will not be easy," he continued slowly, though he could see she understood that. "It must be accomplished within the laws of Soldat." *Aey, within the law for the sake of my family, for the sake of the Morrow House, and for my own sake. And if it doesn't work?*

Sheftu tried not to give in to his doubt in that regard. The alternative was worrisome.

Laran's eyes had glazed with troubled thought. *Within the laws of Soldat! And Lord Du-kar? What of him? He lived by his own laws.* He would never willingly let her go.

Sheftu put his hands on her shoulders to reclaim her attention. His body's response to the contact was immediate and so, he thought, had hers been. *Interesting,* he thought.

Laran took yet another step back, and then another. Lord Sheftu's touch had shot through her like lightning. She looked at his hands, now resting on his hips. They were strong and surprisingly rough for a privileged young lord. She wondered at the kind of work that occupied them. Her shoulders still seemed warm where he'd placed them. She imagined those fingers lightly tracing her face, her throat, and then dipping down to...

She shook her head forcefully to dispel the notion.

"Your name?" he was asking her brusquely. "What is your name?"

He sounded irritated. *With me?* Perhaps with himself. Perhaps he'd felt the same shock at his touch that she had. Perhaps he didn't welcome it. *Well, neither do I!* She was not some wanton Soldatian maid. She raised her chin.

"Laran Tania," she told him. She blinked. She hadn't intended to tell him her family name! She couldn't seem to think with the man so near.

But he wouldn't understand the significance of the Tania name regardless, and with any luck, he never would.

CHAPTER FIVE

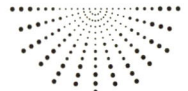

L ARAN ROSE LAZILY, enjoying the softness of the bed linens beneath her. For the first time in many months, she'd awoken to cautious optimism and not to near-immobilizing fear of what the day might bring foremost in her waking thoughts.

She could feel it, though, the fear, uncoiling its tendrils as though the very thought of its absence could stir it to life.

A ray of sunlight filtered into the room through the filmy window coverings, but no breeze moved them as yet. She looked about the antechamber. The thick tapestries, the soft rug, even the dark, heavily carved bed were foreign to her.

In Mirren-Bar the lines of the few pieces of furniture in her rooms were clean and simple, the wood light and finely grained. At this time of year, no carpet covered the white stone floors, no hangings hung in front of the floor to ceiling windows obscuring the view.

And what a view! Even here on the Soldatian prairie, imagining the sight of those jagged peaks and the blue, blue sky beyond was a comfort. Laran could almost hear the rush of water as it cascaded into the valley below. She could almost smell the scent of cool, clean air blowing off the snow. Yes, she thought, imagining her home brought her comfort.

And a sense of longing so deep it almost hurt.

She glanced at the doorway to the young lord's sleeping chamber. She wondered if the child she'd seen on his balcony was his own. Was the woman his wife? Perhaps she merely shared his bed. Landi would know. When she saw her again, she'd ask her. Not that it mattered.

So. If it doesn't matter, why is the thought disturbing? Remember his heritage. He is Soldatian!

Still, she admitted to herself, she wanted to peek within, to catch sight of him while he slept. She wondered if he slept alone.

She wondered if he slept naked.

Stop that! There are weightier matters to consider. But she crept to the doorway just the same, and silently parted the heavy fabric.

He was alone. White sheets were draped over his legs to his waist, exposing the bronzed expanse of his upper body. His belly was flat and ribbed with muscle, his chest broad and smooth. His shoulders were wide and his arms were well muscled. Black hair framed his handsome face. His expression was... sweet. He looked completely at peace. His eyes, she knew, beneath the closed lashes, were truly beautiful and...

He opened them and looked directly at her.

Laran quickly withdrew into the antechamber, her cheeks burning with embarrassment.

"Laran." His voice was deep and soft.

She pretended she hadn't heard it. She glanced about, and then climbed back into her own bed. *No. What if he came through the curtained doorway looking for her?* She climbed back out.

"Laran," he called again, a little louder this time.

Laran pushed the heavy drape aside and entered the room, her eyes averted from the bed.

"I apologize," she said. "I did not mean to intrude." *Well, actually, I did. I just didn't mean to get caught.* She nearly smiled at her own thoughts and slid her gaze to the young lord who was still abed. She blushed to the roots of her hair.

Lord Sheftu was staring at her. His eyes carried an expression she'd seen too often in other Soldatian men, and seemed to stroke her from face to toes. He began to rise, pushing aside the bedclothes.

"My lord," she gasped. She wanted to look at him, at *all* of him, but she averted her eyes once more. An urgent sensation was snaking through her belly. *Not fear.* No. Not that.

Sheftu saw her reaction and frowned. He wanted her. She appeared to want him.

"Are you afraid of me?" he asked her softly.

He was standing now; Laran could see that in her peripheral vision. His height and stature seemed to fill the room. She shook her head.

"No," she told him. *Should I be?*

She straightened her back, raised her chin, and looked directly into his eyes. Her gaze began to stray down to his naked chest and beyond, but she snapped her attention back to his face.

"I do not fear you," she answered truthfully. "But..." She paused, thinking of the words she must say. "My people, the Mirren, do not become intimate with one another on casual acquaintance. We reserve that intimacy for marriage. It is a gift to both partners.

Here," Laran continued, "in your world, in Soldat, that gift is all I have. And that makes it even more precious. Do you understand?" She stared hard into his eyes so he could see how serious she was. "It's not that I don't find you..."

"Enough," he growled.

He didn't look angry, Laran thought, though he sounded it. What he *looked* was disappointed.

"I understand all too well," he told her gruffly. Then he, too, elevated his chin. "You believe I am not worthy of this gift of yours."

Laran was appalled. He could bed her by force if he had a mind to. She didn't want to, and hadn't meant to, offend him.

"I only meant to explain…"

But he turned his back on her to reach for his clothes. He pulled them on, one by one, as she watched, fascinated. There was a ridge of muscle running down his spine that she longed to touch. His back was broad but tapered down to a slim waist. His buttocks looked hard beneath the bronzed skin and they flexed as he moved.

He turned back to her fastening his trousers. His gaze had softened.

"Perhaps one day you will change your mind," he said quietly. "And in the meantime, we go to the courts."

"The courts?" Laran's eyes had widened. "What? Why? To petition my release? No! Lord Du-kar will never agree to… *Both* of us?"

"*Aey*. I have already petitioned Du-kar and he has accepted my offer."
"Your… offer?"

"To purchase you."

"To…?" *What?* Laran was incensed and profoundly insulted. She'd believed the young lord was different. Clearly, he was not.

"You," she spat out, "can give Du-kar, that miserable excuse for a human being, as much money as you wish. He will never release me. Even if he did, *you* will not *own* me! No man will!" She sought the most contemptuous edge to her voice she could muster. "My *lord*."

Sheftu's brows shot up.

"Hold your temper, Little Elf," he said quietly. "I have no need of another slave in my household." He tried to look into her eyes and not down at her breasts. They were nearly visible through the thin sleeping gown and jiggled as she stamped her feet in anger. She *defi ly* didn't act like a slave.

"If you *belong* to me," he told her, "Du-kar will no longer have power over you. If you *belong* to me, it will be easier to find a way to return you to your home. And if you *belong* to me and I am murdered, you will gain your freedom within five years regardless. I will see to it in writing."

"Oh," Laran murmured. Five years. *Murdered.* She stifled a quick vision of him lying in the courtyard, his throat pierced and bloodied. Her stomach lurched. "Just so long as you understand that you won't really…"

"And," Sheftu continued as though she had not spoken, "if you *belong* to me, I will have a better chance of being the recipient of that precious gift you hold." He grinned lustily.

"The Smiling Man, indeed," she muttered. She turned on her heel and pushed aside the fabric to re-enter the antechamber.

"What?"

But her response was delivered in a language Sheftu was unfamiliar with. His grin widened then faded away as he thought about the hours ahead.

Du-kar had demanded a fortune for his little slave girl, a price beyond reason, and Sheftu had complied. He'd stipulated, though, that the transaction be finalized before the courts and Du-kar had agreed. By law, he and Du-kar would have to appear before the Justice, and so would Laran.

Sheftu was uneasy. Du-kar was not to be trusted. As Morrow Lord in his father's absence, Sheftu had opposed Du-kar in his bid to re-invade Barraid despite the existence of a treaty. He'd garnered hard-won support from the majority of the noble houses, effectively putting an end to Du-kar's plans. Du-kar had been furious. He stood to lose a great deal of money. He'd lost face. And he'd promised retribution.

Aey, and perhaps that retribution had come in the form of attempted murder.

Now Laran seemed certain that he would not let her go despite their agreement. Then again, the matter was being brought before the courts to counteract any deceit Du-kar tried to visit upon him or the House of Morrow.

The plan remained in place. Sheftu wanted Laran. He would have her. He'd *need* to own her before he could fulfill his promise to her.

* * *

LARAN PACED THE small room anxiously.

When Sheftu pushed through the curtain between the two rooms, he was dressed in the white tunic she remembered, his dark, loose-fitting trousers tucked into high leather boots. His shining hair was brushed and hung loose about his shoulders.

He looked confident and at ease.

She looked down at her own clothing—at the white floor length Soldatian tunic she wore, at the fine leather sandals that peeked out beneath. She felt like an imposter.

"My lord," she began, "truly, Lord Du-kar will never let me go. He… he has plans for me." *Terrible plans.*

"It will be before the courts, Laran," Sheftu told her. "The Justice will finalize the sale. He cannot claim rights to you after that."

"I am afraid," she whispered. Her golden eyes were huge with fear.

Du-kar would hurt her if he got his hands on her again. He'd enjoy it. He'd hurt her and then he'd kill her.

"Must I go? Can I not remain here?" She was ashamed of the near panic she felt.

"The law says otherwise." Sheftu frowned. "You will have my protection and the protection of my men, Laran. Once inside the courts, the Justice will have her own men to keep order. You will be safe."

But he was becoming more and more uneasy.

Perhaps, Sheftu thought, looking at the terror in the girl's face, he should have acted outside the law. Then he thought of his father, the Morrow Lord, and knew he must begin this particular journey within it.

CHAPTER SIX

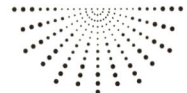

THE TENDRILS OF terror unfurled as Lord Du-kar glanced, seemingly casually, in Laran's direction. She knew, *knew*, he wouldn't willingly let her go despite the agreement he'd made with the young Lord Sheftu.

Now they stood, the three of them, in the centre of an opulently decorated courtroom, her only anchor the presence of The Smiling Man beside her. She tried to concentrate on him, to *feel* his strength and confidence. With Du-kar so near, her own had ebbed away.

The Justice, an elegant woman in her fifties, looked down at the trio with undisguised impatience, then over their heads at the unprecedented number of armed men in the room, five on both sides, the maximum allowed. *Over the simple sale of a slave?*

She looked significantly at her own men stationed behind her and to the sides of the courtroom.

"I am well aware," the Justice began, "that the Houses of Morrow and Du-kar are not on friendly terms, but *surely* such a simple transaction need not require the ratification of the court?"

Laran swallowed audibly. She darted a glance up to Du-kar and caught him staring at her malevolently. He was possessive and vindictive and he would be furious that she'd interacted with another lord, especially this one, and even more so that she'd dare to leave the House of Du-kar for his.

She wondered if he was furious, too, that she'd foiled the attempt on Lord Sheftu's life. She couldn't know for certain that Du-kar had been behind the attempt, but she, too, had been made aware of the animosity between the two Houses.

Du-kar dragged his eyes from the little slave girl to address the Justice.

"Lord Sheftu," he began, his voice dripping with disdain, "has made an error. I have not agreed to the sale of this slave, nor do I intend to sell her."

Sheftu's expression did not change, though inwardly he seethed at the duplicity of the Du-kar lord. He kept his eyes forward, fastened on the Justice.

"Lord Du-kar's memory has failed him, Lady Justice. Money has changed hands, a great deal of money, and I have an agreement signed by Du-kar himself last night." Sheftu nodded at one of his men to bring the document forward.

Du-kar snatched it away from the man and tore it up, dropping the torn pieces to the floor at his feet. He stared at Sheftu, and so did the astonished man he'd taken the document from.

"The slave belongs to me." Du-kar reached over and grabbed Laran by the arm. He jerked her roughly toward him.

"Get your hands off her." Sheftu's voice was deceptively soft, but his calm composure had slipped, and his anger was there in his face for all to see.

"Enough!" The Justice was incensed. Around her, her men shifted. "Enough, I said!" The slave girl was young, and small, and Du-kar's grip on her slender arm was clearly painful. She was afraid of the man: that much was certain.

But Du-kar tightened his grip and whispered something harsh in the girl's ear. She paled, struggling harder, and then suddenly stood still.

Laran looked up at her captor as anger overwhelmed fear. She punched at the much larger man with the fist of her free hand, catching him squarely in the nose.

Du-kar bellowed in fury and released his hold. He swung his fist at her face.

Laran ducked. Sheftu sprang forward, swung his own fist and smashed it into Du-kar's jaw, knocking him down. He stood over him for a moment breathing hard. He wanted to kill the son of a bitch. Had his fist connected with Laran's face, he would have killed her.

But the court guards were already in motion. Two restrained Sheftu from behind, a man on each arm, and a third held a sword to his throat.

Du-kar climbed, staggering, to his feet, his eyes on Sheftu and promising vengeance.

Sheftu debated trying to shake the guards off, striking out at Du-kar again, and taking Laran out of there. Du-kar's men had their weapons out and aggression in their eyes. If Sheftu acted now, there would be hell to pay and any number of his men hurt. The sword at his throat bit into his flesh.

The expression in Laran's wide golden eyes tore at his heart.

"Enough!" the Justice shouted again. She was on her feet now and her eyes flashed with fury at the disrespect shown to the court by the Lords Morrow and Du-kar. She sighed heavily.

The law was the law. Though the Justice did not condone the mistreatment of slaves, her own principles would have no bearing on the conclusion of this dispute, nor would the deplorable behaviour of the men in her courtroom.

"Lord Sheftu," she began, "if Lord Du-kar wishes to keep his own slave, he mostly certainly has the right to do so. As the court did not ratify this 'agreement', whatever the reason, it is not binding. The money must be returned. This slave will continue to be considered the property of Lord Du-kar."

Du-kar was watching him smugly. He leaned in close. "Have you learned nothing, young Lord Sheftu?"

Sheftu tensed in fury. The court guards tightened their holds on Sheftu's arms in anticipation. The sword at his throat pricked him in warning and

Du-kar watched a thin rivulet of blood track down the blade with apparent satisfaction.

"Perhaps," Du-kar sneered, "another lesson is in order."

"Another *lesson?*" Sheftu snarled from behind the sword tip. "So, then, it *was* you who tried to have me murdered!"

Du-kar glanced at The Justice who had registered surprise at Lord Sheftu's words. *No matter.* It could not be proved. He sneered contemptuously and signalled his men to leave the courtroom.

"Hold!" The Justice turned her attention to the young lord. "Do you have an accusation to make before the court, Lord Sheftu?"

Sheftu's eyes followed Du-kar's, but the older man had narrowed his gaze and directed his attention to Laran. The threat was obvious to all, including the Justice.

"No," Sheftu said softly. Laran would pay the price if he spoke out. He couldn't chance it. Wouldn't. But by the Seven Gods, he'd send Du-kar through the Seventh Layer of Darkness if he had to drag him down himself.

Laran looked up in terror at the Du-kar soldier who held her.

She was dead. She'd never see her family again. She turned her head to see The Smiling Man once more. Still held firm by two court guards and immobilized by the blade at his throat, he was enraged. There was no joy there. There was no joy anywhere.

Du-kar's soldier was easing his hold to allow Du-kar to fasten his big hand around her arm once more.

No! She twisted away from the two men and sprinted for the entrance arch. From somewhere outside of herself she could hear Lord Sheftu yelling. His voice was strained and anguished. *Was he in pain? Had Du-kar managed to get his hands on him?* He'd enjoy hurting him. She knew that.

She stopped dead, turned back and prepared to defend The Smiling Man instead, but found her way blocked and every avenue of escape closed.

Du-kar was striding towards her angrily. He overpowered her quickly.

The Justice frowned. "Release the girl, Lord Du-kar." Du-kar eyed her guardsmen, who, with the exception of the three who had immobilized Lord Sheftu, were suddenly focused solely on him.

"It appears she has re-thought her inclination to run," the Justice continued. *Though she has demonstrated considerable spirit.* "Has she even understood the purpose of these proceedings?" She didn't expect an answer and turned away.

"I understand it, Lady Justice," Laran replied quietly in a strange language.

Sheftu, still restrained, had made eye contact with his men, who awaited his command. Du-kar's men shifted uneasily at the continued focus of the Justice's guards.

"Hold," the Justice ordered once more. The change in language had startled her. She raised her hand to quell the nearly palpable threat of violence in the room. She stared at Laran.

"Come forward," she ordered.

Du-kar reluctantly released her. Laran, rubbing her arm, approached the formidable Justice.

"Lady Justice," she began again in that strange tongue, "Lord Du-kar will kill me. Please, if there is something I can do..."

"How is it you know the language of the Sowth?" the Justice asked, ignoring Laran's plea. "And how," she demanded, "did you know that *I* would understand it?"

"I speak many languages," Laran told her. She'd begun to tremble. *No!* She straightened her back, elevated her chin and concentrated on standing bravely. "And I knew yours by the small tattoo you carry on your left hand. It is the mark of the Sowth ruling class."

The Justice was silent a moment as she digested that. The girl was educated. Not many in Soldat would have recognized the symbol and she hadn't discussed her heritage in all the years she'd been a citizen. Hadn't considered it wise. Soldat did not look kindly on outsiders.

"How many languages?"

"Eleven spoken and written, and two others besides which I can speak but not yet read and write."

The Justice raised her hand again as Du-kar began to protest. Lord Sheftu, she noted, was watching the interaction intently despite the sword at his throat.

"Thirteen languages," she said thoughtfully, then switched tack entirely. "Have you seduced the young Lord Sheftu?" the Justice asked bluntly.

Laran's eyes widened. "No."

"Then," the Justice leaned closer to Laran, "why has he risked losing face and credibility by bringing this 'sale' to court? Look at him. He is practically vibrating. He has every intention of fighting Du-kar for you, does he not?"

Laran turned to look at him. It was true: The Smiling Man was not smiling now. He had violence in his eyes.

"His heart is kind, Lady Justice. There is no more to it than that. He knows Du-kar's reputation."

"As do I." The Justice sighed and leaned back in her chair breaking the intimacy of their conversation.

Once more the Justice raised her hand, but this time she rose as she did so, to silence them all. She addressed Laran once more in the language of the Sowth.

"The law is clear and I am a servant of that law. You will be returned to Lord Du-kar." She rose. "In two days' time, I will inquire of you. Perhaps…" The Justice shrugged, then delivered a similar speech in Soldatian, minus the last half-spoken thought.

Du-kar fastened his hand around Laran's arm once more while behind them Sheftu let out a strangled oath and struggled against the restraining court guardsmen.

Tears sprang into Laran eyes, but she blinked them away. She tried to look behind her to take a final glance at The Smiling Man, but he was blocked from her view.

In two days' time, I will be dead.

CHAPTER SEVEN

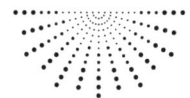

"YOU ARE WEARING a path in the carpet, Cousin," Provos said. Sheftu stopped pacing a moment to look at him.

"I was ten thousand kinds of a fool, Provos," he muttered. "A *fool* to believe that Du-kar had even a shred of honour." He picked up a vase, stared at it as though it were entirely to blame, and then hurled it against the wall. "A fool!" he repeated, furious with himself.

Provos jumped out of the way, glaring at his cousin. He brushed ceramic shards from his sleeve.

"What in the Seventh Layer of Darkness has this girl done to bewitch you so?" he demanded. "She is a *slave*, nothing more!"

Sheftu dropped into a chair, sprawled, and rubbed a hand over his face.

"She is special," he finally said.

"*Aey,*" Provos answered dryly, "we've had this discussion. And again I say, she is a *slave*, Sheftu. Du-kar's slave. Leave off this obsession."

Obsession? Is that what this is? He could almost see the expression in those wide golden eyes as Du-kar hauled her, *hauled her,* out of the courtroom. It tore at his heart. *Obsessed. Aey, perhaps.*

And perhaps there was more to it than mere obsession.

He looked up at Provos, the resolve in his eyes clear. "I need to get her out of there."

Provos only stared in response.

"How do you propose to do that?" he finally asked.

"When night falls," Sheftu told his cousin, "I will enter the House of Du-kar and I will find her."

"You will be discovered, Sheftu. If his men don't kill you outright, Du-kar may himself. You still don't know for certain who tried to have you murdered."

"It was he," Sheftu told him. "He all but admitted it to me. Even so." Sheftu stared at the open balcony doorway in the direction of the House of Du-kar but saw nothing. *Had Du-kar already brutalized her? Had he killed her?* The thought made his chest hurt and he jumped to his feet.

"Laran. Her name is Laran. I... I care about this girl," he told Provos. "She matters. There is something about her, something..."

"Special," Provos repeated dryly. He hesitated, wondering whether he should speak his mind.

"The Lady Tanile broke your heart," he finally said.

Sheftu jerked his head around to retort, but Provos held up a hand to silence his cousin.

"Let me finish!" he insisted. "And don't deny it. Not to me. Tanile broke your heart and you have been alone ever since. When I first saw the little slave girl in your bathing pool, I thought you'd finally decided to take another woman to bed. I was *relieved*." He shook his head at the irony.

"You said she saved your life, Cousin," Provos continued. "Are you confusing gratitude with... what? Affection?"

Affection. "I promised to send her home. Unlike that bastard Du-kar, or the Lady Tanile, I *do* have honour and I *will* keep my word. And," Sheftu continued softly, "I cannot stand by and let him hurt her."

Provos sighed deeply.

"All right," he said grudgingly. "What time tonight do we march to our deaths?"

Sheftu rose from the chair and grinned at his cousin.

CHAPTER EIGHT

"FOLLY," PROVOS MURMURED to Reedin. "Utter folly." From his vantage point he could see both the upper and lower entrances at the back of the House of Du-kar. He shifted uncomfortably as sweat trickled down his neck.

The soldier's whispered response came out of the dark of the alley in which they hid.

"This slave woman, she is important somehow?" "Somehow," Provos grumbled.

She was a catalyst; that much was certain. If Sheftu were successful tonight, he would have broken the law and brought trouble to the Morrow House. If he were *not* successful, it would mean he'd been discovered, and the outcome would be the same. Or worse.

Perhaps far worse.

Provos' limbs ached with inaction. Either way, he meant to help his cousin. Either way. But by the Seven Gods, let it be soon!

* * *

SHEFTU SLID INSIDE the open doorway and looked around. It had taken him the better part of an hour of reach the recesses of the Du-kar House where he imagined the servant's quarters would be. He'd encountered little activity at this time of night, though there'd been people about. He saw one now, a woman of middle years standing against a stone wall ironing. *Ironing! At 2:00 am?*

He swallowed and prepared to approach her. It was time. He couldn't search every room and he couldn't search all night. He'd need an idea where to look.

"My lady," he whispered though the woman was clearly a servant.

She cried out in shock to see a man there, dropping the iron to the floor. Another woman rushed through the adjoining doorway.

"Marid, did you burn yourself again?" she scolded.

Marid looked back at the shadows Sheftu had retreated to. She could barely make out his silhouette, could barely see the shake of his head. She frowned and glanced at the other woman, clearly wondering what she should do.

"Ah, no. Well, a small touch against a finger. Startled me is all. Didn't even leave a mark. See?" She held up a finger.

"Tsk," her friend said. "Have a care, then. If you burn Lord Du-kar's tunic, you'll pay a higher price than a burned finger!" And with that she turned away, leaving Marid alone in the room. *With the stranger!*

Her stomach lurched.

"What do you want?" she hissed.

Sheftu emerged from the shadows again and this time the woman gasped as she recognized the young Morrow Lord.

"What are you doing here, my lord?" she whispered. "If Lord Du-kar finds you here…"

"A small slave girl with golden eyes and light brown hair," Sheftu interrupted. "Laran, her name is. Do you know of her?"

Marid darted a glance at the doorway. "I have heard of such a one." "Can you take me to her?"

Marid's eyes widened. "No! I daren't." She glanced again at the doorway then seemed to come to a decision. "Wait here," she told Sheftu, then disappeared through the doorway.

Sheftu swore beneath his breath. He faded into the shadow again and fervently hoped the servant would bring him the information he sought and not the Du-kar guardsmen.

Marid returned on running feet, tugging the woman who'd come to her rescue only moments earlier.

"What are you up to?" the woman demanded crossly. "You know I have work to…" She stopped dead in her tracks, breaking Marid's grip. "What? What? What is happening here?" she whispered, thoroughly alarmed at the sight of the man awaiting them.

"The slave girl, the little one with the strange eyes and hair. He is searching for her. He means to help her." Marid looked at him. "You *do* mean to help her?"

Sheftu nodded.

The second woman lifted her arm, still shocked, and pointed to the doorway through which she'd come.

"Please don't tell anyone we helped you," Marid begged. "Please. Lord Du-kar…"

"You have my word, mistress." He was elated. *I've found her!* "Is she all right?" The other woman shook her head. "No," was all she said.

CHAPTER NINE

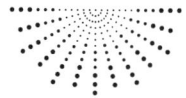

NOT ALL RIGHT. *Please, gods, let her be alive!* He had to find her. He had to!

Sheftu sprinted down the hallway. There were others in service to the Du-kar household who had seen him now. How many of them would be willing to raise an alarm? How many would turn their backs rather than watch him die for this transgression? And where in the Seven Layers of Darkness was Laran? Which doorway?

He stopped abruptly and so did the ancient woman rounding the corner in front of him. She wore the garb of a Du-kar slave, her brittle hair shorn and piled atop her head like a pallet of white straw. Her mouth opened and closed like a fish, and finally she sputtered a number of words in an unfamiliar language while backing warily away.

Sheftu held both hands out in front of him, palms toward her. "Do not fear me, Old One," he told her quietly. "I am seeking a young woman, a slave like you," he told her. He glanced behind him, leery of being overheard. He hoped she understood at least a few words of Soldatian. He held one hand out now, palm down at the height of his upper chest.

"She is very small, perhaps this high," he told the old woman. "Her eyes are golden." The old woman stared at him blankly. "She looks like an elf," he muttered lamely, dispirited. He glanced behind him again.

When he turned back to the old woman, she'd brightened. "Elf?"

"Or a fairy," Sheftu said, encouraged. "Very pretty, like a fairy. Have you seen her? Do you know where she is?"

"Yes, yes," she nodded vigorously. "Come, come." She took his hand in her withered grasp and hobbled as quickly as her aged limbs would allow. "Come, come," she said again. Stopping, she pulled at him and pointed silently around yet another corner to this seemingly endless corridor.

"Two man," the old woman whispered holding up two fingers. "Much knife." She gestured at the sheathed knife at Sheftu's hip. "Very dangerous for you," she told him finally. Then she pushed him gently. "You go. Go to fairy girl. Go to Mirren-Bar."

Sheftu registered the old woman's comment. *Mirren-Bar!* The place must indeed exist. And the old woman had known Laran was from there. He filed his surprise away to be examined later. He'd need to focus on the task at hand and the guard at the end of the corridor.

The guard was large, well over Sheftu's six feet in height, and looked to be about fifty pounds heavier. He appeared utterly bored. He was leaning haphazardly against a closed doorway examining his nails.

Sheftu swallowed, gathered his courage, and then strode purposefully around the corner towards the guard. "There has been a change in plans," he told the man. "Lord Du-kar has sent me for the woman."

But the guard only snorted. He straightened to his full height and drew the short sword hanging at his waist. By the time Sheftu reached him, he was turning his head to shout, presumably for the "two man" the old woman spoke of, who must be nearby.

Sheftu cracked his fist into man's cheekbone, catching him by surprise. He staggered back two paces but didn't fall. Sheftu tackled him around the waist, dodging the swinging sword as he did so.

He was heavy, much heavier than Sheftu had imagined, and his tackle did not have the desired effect. The guard crashed into the adjoining wall but kept his feet. His sword arm was momentarily pinned behind him, but he lashed out with his other fist, connecting with the side of Sheftu's head and sending him reeling.

Sheftu tried to shake off the vertigo the blow caused. The guard was fast for a big man. He'd have to go at him low and lethally. He withdrew his knife from its sheath.

He'd never killed a man before, but one thing was clear. He was going to have to kill this one. He crouched, knife in hand, ready to spring.

The guard was prepared, knees bent, sword upright, blood lust in his grin and confidence in his eyes as he surveyed his adversary. Clearly a nobleman—possibly even the young Morrow Lord—the man was not much over six feet tall, six inches shorter than he was himself, and lighter. He was insufficiently armed. He looked brave enough but so had many of the men whose lives the big man had ended. His grin widened and his eyes narrowed as he prepared to move in for the kill.

Sheftu saw the narrowing eyes and ducked low, thrusting hard with his knife hand as the sword swung in an arc above his head. The guard shrieked as Sheftu's blade sank into his thigh and out again. He lowered his sword to grasp his leg and immediately understood the folly of his actions. Sheftu swung his fist again, hitting him square in the mouth and this time sending him sprawling onto the stone floor.

Alerted by the noise, the second guard tore around the corner at a run, teeth bared, sword raised. Sheftu dodged back, felt his feet tangle, and fell backwards onto the first man's prone body. The second guard stabbed down mightily with his sword.

Sheftu rolled slightly. The wounded man under him screamed again as the sword meant for Sheftu bit deep into his shoulder. As the sword was raised a second time, Sheftu kicked out at the second guard's knees, leapt to his feet, and thrust his knife into the man's throat.

The second guard went down grasping frantically at his neck, choking and writhing on the floor. Sheftu regarded him passively for a moment, watching the blood bubble out of the wound and slide down the corners of his mouth. *This was the way I lay dying.* He wondered if this man had been involved with the attempted murder.

He turned his attention back to the first guard, but the big man appeared to be incapacitated by his wounds. He had elevated his head, but still lay prone. He was whimpering in fright.

Sheftu turned from him in disgust and thrust through the doorway the big man had been guarding.

Laran lay on the stone floor within, her back to the door. Her clothing had been ripped from her and what little remained hung in tatters. Most of her back and her buttocks were bared. Her hands had been bound in front of her. Sheftu could see the marks of Du-kar's grip on her slender arms, could see, too, the bruises on her shoulders and the long abrasion marring one buttock. The soles of her bare feet were dirty. They were pressed together, the toes curled slightly as if to protect them. There was a shallow cut on one instep.

He closed his eyes and took a deep breath. He felt as though his heart was breaking. His chest hurt. Horror was snaking through his belly and anger was close behind. He couldn't allow it take over. He had to keep his wits about him.

He knelt at Laran's side. One of her eyes was purple and swollen and both eyes were closed despite the noise of the violence outside her door. Her breathing was regular. She was sleeping. Or unconscious. He touched a bruised shoulder gently and spoke her name in a soft voice, surprised that his own was not shaking.

She came awake with a start and curled her body protectively. Her undamaged eye was wild with fear, but she too had the embers of anger banked within.

"It's me," he said, aware that those two words could not possibly portray the comfort or confidence he meant to offer.

But the result was immediate. Laran struggled upright, one golden eye large and slanted intriguingly, the other swollen shut.

"He will kill you," she whispered. "You must go! Please, I couldn't bear that. I couldn't…"

Her words stopped when Sheftu drew his knife to cut her bonds. It was stained with blood. She looked deeply into his eyes and read the horror of the last few moments.

Sheftu stifled a sudden chill. He couldn't allow himself to relive the event. He wouldn't! If he did, he would be undone and they were not out of danger yet. Not even close.

He stripped off his tunic and placed it over Laran's head. She gingerly raised her arms to receive the sleeves. One small, round breast was exposed. When he helped her to her feet, the tunic fell to her knees and so would she have had Sheftu not caught her about the waist. He bent and lifted her into his arms.

"I should have listened to you, Little Elf," he told her. "You knew Du-kar would not let you go." *And I will not allow that son of a bitch to keep you.*

Laran wrapped her arms around Sheftu's neck and nestled her head against his bare chest. It hurt her swollen eye, but he was solid and warm, and the brief contact was worth it.

Soon they would both be dead.

Sheftu glanced at the door apprehensively. There was no balcony outside of this room. He'd have to go through it.

CHAPTER TEN

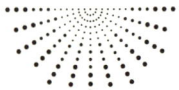

THE SHOUTS OF men disturbed the night. Provos was almost relieved. It meant an end to what had seemed an interminable wait, though the shouting could only mean one thing. His cousin had been discovered.

He signalled his men to leave their cramped positions in the alley. Du-kar's soldiers were coming—a lot of them by the sound—and Provos wanted to be ready. He hadn't seen his cousin escape through either of the entryways he could see from his vantage point, but clearly the wait was over. Only a few moments more. He stared intently through the darkness, trying to wish away the shadows.

There! He could just barely make out the dark form of a man running hard. The man stopped a moment to get his bearings and Provos could see by his silhouette against a backlight that he had glanced behind him.

He was carrying something. The girl! This was his cousin!

"Sheftu!" he hissed and stood out in the centre of the street in order to be seen. "This way!"

Sheftu's breath released explosively. He hadn't been aware that he'd been holding it.

"Provos!" he said. "They're on my heels!"

"*Aey,* so I hear. There they are! Run, Cousin. We have your back."

Sheftu did so. He was getting tired now. His flight from the House of Du-kar had not gone smoothly.

"Put me down. I can walk now. I can *run,*" Laran was insisting again. "And I know where we are."

Sheftu released her and set her on her feet. "Follow me!" she urged.

"What? No!" Sheftu had a plan. Following the little slave girl was not in it. Around the corner another contingent of Du-kar soldiers appeared, this one on horseback. They'd managed to get in front of them. That wasn't in the plan, either.

Sheftu grabbed Laran and flattened them both against a wall and back into the shadows.

"This way," she said again. She took his hand and tugged.

They were effectively trapped. He'd need time to think of a way out of this. He allowed her the lead for the moment but stopped them both dead in their tracks at the sight of the ornate stone entrance in front of them.

"Through there!" Laran whispered, tugging on his hand again. Two heavily armed Court guardsmen blocked the entrance arch to the Courts.

"Lady Justice!" Laran said to the guardsmen. "We've come to see the Lady Justice. Hurry! She is expecting us."

What? Sheftu stared at her a moment, then glanced back at the street behind them. This was *not* the refuge he would have chosen. It was the Justice, after all, who'd handed Laran over to Du-kar.

Du-kar's horsemen rounded the corner and thundered toward them. The lead horseman pulled back on his bow and let loose an arrow presumably meant for Sheftu. It struck one of the Court guardsmen in the chest. The man looked down at the arrow in amazement then crumpled to the ground, silent.

Sheftu was not. He shouted at Laran to run and pushed her through the arch and past the remaining guardsman, who had been shocked into inaction for the moment, before he, too, began shouting. Previously unseen others suddenly appeared in inner doorways, tugging on weapons, pulling up boots and running towards the archway, spilling around Laran like current against a mid-channel rock.

She turned and sprinted barefoot into the Courts.

"Lady Justice!" she called. "Lady Justice!" The woman was in a position of considerable power and influence. There had been a connection between them, just for a moment. However slight that connection, the Justice was their only hope.

At the archway, Du-kar's soldiers had dismounted with weapons drawn and a few bows still at the ready, even though here the quarters were close. The threat of Du-kar's anger if they did not return or kill their quarry was a powerful motivator.

Sheftu positioned himself in the centre of the Court guardsmen. They did not understand the reason for the attack. They didn't care. One of their own was down and the Justice threatened. They retaliated fiercely, most only vaguely aware of the Morrow Lord fighting with them in their midst.

Sheftu fought for his life and for Laran's. The Court guardsmen were far outnumbered and one after another went down in agony and bloody defeat.

Two of Du-kar's men grabbed Sheftu from behind and a third thrust a sword at him. He jerked violently aside, and the sword pierced the arm of one of the men holding him. He wrenched his own arm free, twisted and punched at the Du-kar soldier holding his other arm, but before Sheftu could move away, the sword plunged into his lower back.

Sheftu arched backward, gasping in pain, then fell to his knees. He stared at the darkness beyond the doorway in which he'd thrust Laran and imagined the blow that would end his life.

But it was Provos at his side now, thrusting his shoulder under Sheftu's arm and half dragging him through the archway. He was barely aware of Laran issuing urgent commands and wondered vaguely at Provos's willingness to obey them. Perhaps he felt he had no choice.

He didn't.

Sheftu's vision was clouding. He was losing blood; he knew that. His legs were leaden. His heart was pounding and his breathing was strained and shallow. Maybe the blade had pierced his lung.

Inside the Courts now, he could make out Laran speaking to the Lady Justice in the strange language they shared. She kept glancing his way, worry and fear clear in her eyes. Perhaps they spoke the language of Mirren-Bar, though the Justice looked nothing like Laran did. But perhaps Laran wasn't typical of her people. Perhaps she...

His legs gave way and Provos lowered him gently to the ground. His cousin was talking to him softly, but Sheftu couldn't understand his words any more than he could understand Laran's. Consciousness drifted just out of reach and was slipping away.

"I will do your bidding," Laran was promising the Justice hastily in the Sowthern tongue. The formidable lady had been in the process of raising her arm to call over the guards behind her. Outside, the bitter sounds of violence were growing weaker. The gates had been closed, sealing them in. A score of Court guardsmen lined the wall behind them.

"I will go where you send me, even if it is back to Du-kar and my death. You have my word." Laran looked over at Sheftu anxiously.

The Justice hesitated. This slave girl was more than she seemed. "I have questions. I will know who you are. Where you've come from. To start."

Laran nodded. "I will answer." She glanced again at Sheftu who lay still and pale now on the stones, a spreading pool of blood beneath his back. His eyes were open. She could see the faint rise and fall of his chest. Her stomach twisted with urgency. If she couldn't get to him soon, it would be too late. She looked back at the Justice in desperation.

Could she trust this woman with the truth, with *all* of it?

But by the Holy Ones, she couldn't think! Couldn't strategize. *Not now.* Laran wanted only to put her hands on The Smiling Man, to restore his life once again.

"I need fifteen minutes to help Lord Sheftu. Please Lady Justice, fifteen minutes and then I will tell you what you want to know, go where you want me to go."

The Justice looked over at the young lord and at his kinsman beside him. The kinsman looked desolate. It was unlikely the young lord would survive.

And just what did this slave girl think she could do to stop the March of Death?

"I will send for my physician…" the Justice began.

"No!" Laran's anger bubbled to the surface. "I will care for him myself. Now!" She turned her back on the Justice and scrambled to Sheftu's side.

The Justice frowned at the girl's impertinence, but held her hand up to stay her guardsmen.

The young lord would die. His kinsmen would grieve. The slave girl would be returned to her master *after* she had answered the questions put to her. That was the way of things.

And so be it.

CHAPTER ELEVEN

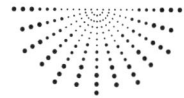

"LOOK AWAY," LARAN told Provos.

"I cannot," he told her. His eyes were wet with unshed tears. He loved his cousin; that much was certain. He held Sheftu's head in his lap.

The Justice watched the interaction from across the room. Her guardsmen and the very sanctity of her Court had been attacked. Lord Du-kar was responsible. She had much to ponder.

"Then do not interfere, Provos,"

Laran said softly. Provos frowned. "What are you...?"

"I'm going to help him," she said softly. Sheftu's eyes were closed now. She tried to roll him over, but he was too heavy. She slid one hand under his tunic and along his bare, bloodied back until she found the gaping wound. And there, bent over his body awkwardly, she held it.

She felt Provos stiffen with indignation, but she blurred him from her mind.

The healing began. She could feel it. Severed arteries and muscles began to knit. The flow of blood eased. She was aware of tissue becoming whole, of lungs beginning to fill.

Sheftu stirred. He took a deep breath. His vision began to clear and the pain subsided slightly. He saw his cousin's grief-stricken face above him and Laran's battered face beside him.

"Watch me," she was telling him softly.

He watched the battered face, saw the golden eyes, one wide and beautiful and slanted like a cat's, one purple and swollen nearly shut. He saw the strange, light-coloured hair and the spikes that unshed tears had made of her lashes. He saw the brows which swept like bird's wings and he saw the energy drain from her body as it was restored to his.

"Stop!" he ordered her. He put a hand to her chest to push her away. She looked startled and sat back heavily on the floor. She was very pale now. She raised a red-wet hand to finish what she'd started.

"No, Little Elf. You've been hurt." His voice was weak and sweat stood on his brow when he struggled to sit up. "Keep what remains of your energy. I can heal the rest of the way on my own."

Sheftu pushed to his feet shakily and winced heavily at the pain still remaining in his wounded back. He glanced at Provos, who remained on the floor looking up at him in disbelief.

What kind of trick is this? Provos thought. His cousin had been moments away from death. Moments! He'd have sworn it.

Sheftu reached down for Laran's hand and pulled her to her feet, clenching his teeth as he did so. He looked for the Justice and found her standing ramrod straight across the room, her eyes wide and clouded with... what? Awe?

"I saw you with a woman and a child, a small boy," Laran was saying to Sheftu. "On your balcony."

He frowned. *Why was she asking about them now? They needed to find a way out.*

He looked back toward the archway, hidden now from view.

"My brother's wife and their child," he answered her distractedly. *Could they fight their way through the other entrance?* Not likely. Standing was taking all of his strength and he could feel it ebbing.

"Do you love them?"

Sheftu turned back to her, a new knot of fear unfurling in his chest. *Why this question? Why now?* He glanced again at the Justice who was listening, but Laran seemed not to be aware. She was blinking heavily, exhausted.

He focused on her eyes. "I love them," he told her.

"And Provos? Do you love him?"

Sheftu glanced at his cousin who was standing now. He appeared rooted to the spot. He was staring at Laran with an expression of incredulity, but looked briefly at his cousin to hear his answer.

"Yes," he answered her, somewhat embarrassed. He half expected a derisive comment from Provos, but his cousin had been shocked silent. "Laran, why are you...?"

"Could you... ever love someone like me?" she whispered. A tear rolled down her cheek now and she bit her lip. A sob threatened to rise but she swallowed it down.

He placed both hands on her shoulders gently, aware of the terrible bruising there.

"There *is* no one else like you," he told her softly. He meant it as an endearment, but he could see the hurt in her face. Two of the Justice's men appeared on either side of her.

"No," she told them flatly. Her eyes never left Sheftu's. "I am not ready to go yet. I will finish what I began." She stepped closer to Sheftu, but he took her hands in his and shook his head.

"Back off," he told the guardsmen without looking away from her.

"If you do not allow me to finish," Laran told Sheftu, "you will be in pain for many months, and weak with injury." She was standing straighter now, her chin elevated. Her voice was no longer wistful but resolved, though fatigue was still evident in her face.

Laran glanced at the Justice's guards. "I have given my word that I will do as Lady Justice bids," Laran continued quietly to Sheftu. "And so I will do as I must."

Sheftu stared at her. *She believes she goes to her death at Du-kar's hands. That is why she spoke of love!*

Sheftu shook his head again and looked toward the Justice who still had not moved. "The girl stays with me," he told her in no uncertain terms. "I'll not allow her to be taken again."

The Justice raised one brow. "And how do you propose to stop me, young lord?" Her voice sounded almost tremulous now with none of the coolly confident authority he'd heard in it the day before.

Sheftu straightened as much as his wounded back would allow. "I have no wish to fight you and your men, Lady Justice, but I, too, will do what I must."

She looked at him skeptically. "And you, barely able to stand?"

"And still I would fight," he told her. He tried to remain unwaveringly tall. Laran was watching him carefully.

"The girl has made me a bargain, young lord," the Justice told him. "Her cooperation in exchange for time and leniency for you." She was quiet a moment. "I see now that it was a better bargain than I could ever have imagined."

Sheftu frowned and stepped forward aggressively. Provos moved to his side.

But the Justice only sighed. "Come with me," she commanded. She had regained her formidable presence. "All three of you." She waved her guards aside. "*If* you can walk on your own, young Lord Sheftu." She made it sound like a challenge.

When they reached the Justice's antechamber, she swung the door closed behind them and rounded on the trio.

"Now, lay yourself down before you fall down," she ordered Sheftu. He was breathing heavily and the sweat, which had appeared on his brow, ran down the side of his face now and pasted his black hair to his neck. Clearly, he was still in considerable pain.

"*Can* you help him, young woman?" She sounded skeptical as though what she had just seen and heard in the outer courts had all been a lie.

Laran nodded. "If he will allow it." She, too, looked as though she would not have her feet for long.

Provos looked from one to another and back again. "Then, by the Souls of the Dead, Laran, never mind what he says, just do so!"

"You cannot escape, and you cannot help if you have no strength," she whispered to Sheftu though the Justice was only a few steps away.

Sheftu said nothing. The pain in his back was robbing him of speech and will. The truth of her words was evident.

Laran stepped close and Sheftu's arms went around her to pull her to him in an embrace. One of her hands rose to the back of his neck in what felt like a caress, the other sought the injury on his back. She looked up into his beautiful raven eyes and he stared down into hers.

Provos and the Justice watched in stunned silence as Sheftu drew his breath in sharply. His body went rigid for just a moment, then slowly began to relax as the pain gradually left him. His eyes cleared. His stance grew stronger, surer.

Laran felt Sheftu's strength return to him. Her knees were weak now and if it were not for Sheftu's embrace, she would have collapsed to the floor. She could no longer hold her head up to watch his eyes and she rested it against his chest. She felt his embrace tighten, felt his chin as it rested on the top of her head, heard his whispered thanks in her ear.

Her hand slipped from his back.

"I could," Sheftu whispered, still close to her ear. "I *could* love someone like you."

The brief moment of joy she'd felt on hearing the words dissolved. It was only gratitude after all. Sleep claimed her.

Sheftu reached down to place his arm beneath her knees, his other under her shoulders. He straightened, Laran in his arms, battered, courageous, and fast asleep. He looked over at Provos and at the Justice.

"Do not try to send her back to Du-kar," he told the Justice. His voice was strong now. Firm. "I will die to protect her. I will die and so will you before I let you take her. I swear it."

61

The Justice looked up at him. "Do not compound your trouble with threats against me, Lord Sheftu. I can clearly see that the girl is…" She seemed at a loss for words.

"Special?" Provos asked, astonished. He glanced at his cousin and smiled ruefully. His smile broadened to a grin and then he laughed outright. "*Aey*, Cousin, I readily admit it." He was suddenly jubilant. "The girl is special."

Sheftu grinned back at him despite the danger they remained in. He looked again at the Justice.

"Go," she told him. "All of you. The girl owes me answers. She has given her word and one day I expect to have them. But in the meantime, Lord Dukar cannot be allowed to destroy one so beautiful and so extraordinary. And destroy her, he would." She brushed by them to approach the back of her offices. Drawing a curtain aside, she indicated the doorway hidden behind it.

CHAPTER TWELVE

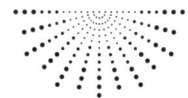

LARAN GLANCED BEHIND her apprehensively, the slight movement nearly unbalancing her on the narrow wooden gangplank. The muddied water below slapped at the ship's hull and an oily slick moved languidly on the chop.

"Careful," Sheftu said quietly at her back. He reached a hand out to steady her.

He'd been steadying her since her first sight of him.

She felt an overwhelming surge of guilt at deceiving him.

"I have something to tell you," she told him abruptly. She turned to look up at him and he grabbed her elbow once again.

"Will it make a difference if you tell me in an hour? Or a day?" He, too, glanced behind him and over the crowded jetty below.

"No. But…" she began.

"Later, Little Elf. Let's get on board and out of sight until the sails are set." He steered her off the gangplank, across the wooden deck and past the furrowed sails. "Our room is aft," he told her.

"*Our* room?" she asked, scandalized.

He looked down at her. Her curls, riotous now, seemed to dance in the sunlight as though they had a life of their own. "With the exception of the captain's quarters, I'm told there *is* only the one room. Provos and the others will sleep below deck with the crew. I'll not leave you unprotected all night while I lay sleepless in a hammock with twenty other men a deck away. Propriety be damned."

"They will think me a whore," she protested.

"What do you care what this lot thinks? *You'll* know the truth. *You'll* know whether this *gift* of yours remains yours to give. And *I'll* know if you decide to share it." He grinned lustily.

Her eyes widened. "I explained…"

"Now don't say something you'll regret," he suggested good-naturedly, but he acquiesced, still grinning. "Worry not, Laran. I'll stay on my side of the bed. There'll be plenty of room."

They both glanced aft towards a small wooden structure. It was the only one above deck with the exception of the wheelhouse. Sheftu reached for the embedded iron ring to pull open the door.

"Oh," Laran said dismayed.

The room was barely more than a shed, cramped and windowless, with a bed barely wide enough for one.

"Ah," Sheftu said. He rubbed the back of his head. "Let's find a place for our belongings." He looked around at the spartan accommodation. "Or perhaps not." He threw the pack that held his few possessions on the narrow bed and tried not to contemplate the undoubtedly long night ahead.

"Sit. Tell me what you considered so important you'd stop on a thin gangplank to say it."

Laran sat gingerly on the narrow bed beside him, pushing at the mattress with her hands. *It seems comfortable enough.* She looked up at Sheftu. His presence dominated the entire room. She *couldn't* allow him to sleep there with her though the prospect was… intriguing. Something uncurled in her belly. *More* than intriguing. *Stop that!*

On the other hand, his words held some wisdom. She'd seen the way a few of the sailors had looked at her as she climbed aboard, as though she were a tasty morsel suddenly set out amongst a starving crew. The gaze of one in particular had seemed to threaten violence and rape. She shuddered. If Sheftu didn't trust them, she wouldn't either.

Ashaii. He'd *have* to stay there with her.

The fabric of his tunic brushed against her bare arm. She felt a tiny thrill race down her spine. By the Holy Ones, how she wanted to touch him! Wanted him to touch her. Wanted...

She wrenched her mind away to answer his question. What *had* she been going to tell him? Oh. *That!* Well, how could she tell him while they sat there, in that tiny room, so close to one another she could almost taste... She groaned.

"Perhaps it can wait," she mumbled.

Around them they could hear heavy footfalls on the wooden deck as the ship was cast off. The shouts of men competed with the creaking of the rigging and the soft whirl of blocks and tackle. The little room slanted slightly as the wind caught the massive sails and their journey began down the wide and roiling river.

"We're underway," Laran said unnecessarily.

Sheftu nodded thoughtfully. *So far so good.* It appeared that they hadn't been pursued. With luck, their hasty departure from the Soldat capital had gone unnoticed, and would continue to go unnoticed for a few days. There had been little time to gather supplies and no time to draw the money that would have eased their journey. Their resources were few. But for Provos, Reedin and two Morrow soldiers, they were on their own, and heading toward the border with Barraid.

Where Soldatians were despised above all others.

Sheftu pushed that thought to the back of his mind. He needed to think. He needed to find Provos and Reedin. He needed to devise a strategy to keep Laran safe and to survive the landing in the Barraidi border town, not to mention the long journey across the breadth of Barraid itself.

And who knew what sort of reception waited in Mirren?

The whole venture was perilous, uncertain, and almost certainly doomed to failure.

"You are grinning," Laran said. She was staring at him speculatively. Was he actually looking *forward* to the journey ahead?

"*Aey*," Sheftu answered, unable to contain it. He had always loved an adventure, and this was the mother of all of them. He was eager to continue. *Eager.* Doubtless there was something wrong with him.

"A character flaw," Sheftu said. "One of many." His grin widened.

Despite the well-placed misgivings of his cousin, he'd be surprised if Provos didn't feel exactly the same way.

CHAPTER THIRTEEN

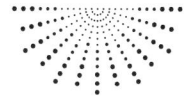

T HE EARLY MORNING sun made diamonds of the wide river beneath the ship and warmed Laran's upturned face. Her heart was filled with excitement.

She was going home. *Home!* And leaving Du-kar and Soldat behind her.

Sheftu was still abed, his stomach and his disposition soured by the movement of the ship.

Or perhaps it wasn't seasickness that soured his disposition.

There had been little sleep for either of them that first night. Laran had finally given in to her misgivings and crawled into bed, wedging herself against the wall. Sheftu had remained on top of the thin blanket, fully dressed and uncovered.

She'd been acutely aware of his presence, of his every slight movement, of every intake of his breath. The press of his body on the bed caused her to roll against his side though she'd tried to brace herself to avoid doing so.

He'd lain awake as well. She could feel the tension in his body, and by the Holy Ones, she had definitely felt the tension in her own! She longed to touch him, to trace the line of muscle running down his spine. She'd seen it the day he'd turned his back to her to dress.

She'd like to have followed the faint curve of his narrow hips with her fingertips, to outline the wide shoulders with her palms, to trace the smooth arc of his biceps…

Would it be so terrible to let him touch her, she wondered? To touch him back? He seemed to respect her. She respected him. And by all that was sacred, she wanted him!

Now, leaning against the ship's rail, her short cap of light curls blowing around her head in the warm breeze, she tried to wrench her thoughts back to the present, to relish once again the feeling of freedom. *Home.*

She couldn't wait to see her family again. She couldn't wait to feel the cool mountain air on her face, to hear the night birds singing outside her window, to ride her horses through the narrow passes and out into the wide avenue of hanging valleys.

Ashaii. She shuddered. *And that's how I was taken. One ride too many, too far from home.*

She could hear the raucous laughter of a deck hand. Though the hour was early Provos, Reedin and the two soldiers who had accompanied them were already engaged in a noisy game of cards with sailors who probably should have been sleeping when the opportunity presented itself.

If they were captured, Reedin and his men might fare all right, but even the formidable Lady Justice would not be able to help Laran and the two Morrow nobles now. If they were found, Laran would die; she knew that. Perhaps Sheftu and Provos would be jailed. The House of Morrow would be shamed, perhaps worse. She didn't know the intricacies of Soldatian law. She fervently hoped she'd never have to.

Laran felt a presence at her back and she turned swiftly, alarmed. There was a man standing there, staring down at her. He grinned at her, his teeth yellowed and ghastly. He was huge.

This was the sailor who'd watched with such menace as she boarded!

By the Holy Ones, had she not been through enough?

"What," he breathed down at her, "is a pretty little piece like you doin' out here all alone?"

She tried to move away, but the sailor hemmed her in with big, meaty fists planted on either side of her, his arms as efficient a barrier as the ship's rails.

Laran cast about for a weapon. The sailor had the customary long knife tied to his belt, but pinned as she was, she couldn't reach for it and she couldn't see around him.

The shore boat! Hadn't it been stowed to the right of where she'd been standing? It had oars. If she could just...

"Where are your men folk when you need them, eh? Playin' cards and sleeping off a bender maybe?" He smirked. Though the day was young, liquor seemed to ooze out of his pores and his breath reeked of it.

He knew where Sheftu was, where Provos and the rest were! He'd followed her up here.

"Let me by," she demanded. He was only inches away. She didn't want to touch him, and she knew trying to push past him would be futile regardless.

"Now!" she ordered. *Please. Oh, please leave me be!*

"Sure," he said agreeably. "Right after you an' me have a little fun." He pushed one knee between her legs and pressed his heavy body against hers bending her backwards over the rail.

She glanced behind her but there was only the river below. He was too big, too strong. *Use your wits, Laran.* That's what her father would have said. *If your adversary outweighs you, use your wits.*

She relaxed suddenly. Smiled up at him beguilingly. The sailor grunted. "*Aey,* an' tha's better," he muttered.

She wrapped her arms around his neck. Raised herself on tiptoe and stretched to reach his lips.

And bit him ferociously.

He screamed, released his hold and jumped back a step. Laran straightened against the rail, darted to the side and ran, but the sailor lunged and grabbed hold of her once again. Pulling her closer with one hand, he struck her across the face with the other.

Laran thudded to the deck. Her vision clouded but the pain in her mouth kept her anchored. She shouted at him in the language of Mirren-Bar and one of a group of sailors who had gathered to watch the entertainment stepped out, his face lit by surprise.

"Hillman!" he called to his inebriated shipmate. "Leave off. Let her go."

But Hillman only glared at the smaller man. "She's mine, Santago. Get your own." His rage was nearly palpable as he dragged his free hand across his torn lip and looked down at the blood on the back of it.

"Let her go or die," a deeper voice said ominously.

Hillman looked up, sneering. Here was the young lord, pale from seasickness or hangover, with hands as undoubtedly soft and white as his body probably was. He was tall, and he looked strong, but men of privilege seldom were.

"Make me." He'd enjoy killing the noble and then he'd have the woman with or without Santago's blessing.

But Santago stepped up to him first and Hillman's eyes widened. Though his fellow shipmate was considerably shorter, he was a formidable fighter and now he was pushing his curly brown hair off his face. It was a gesture Hillman knew well. Santago was about to do violence and Hillman was the target. The big man's gaze darted back and forth between him and the young lord who was clearly furious, his obsidian eyes narrowed.

With the distraction, Laran gained her feet and backed across the deck and away from Hillman. Sheftu reached for her and pulled her behind him, but she didn't stay there. Unnoticed, she dashed to the shore boat and tugged an oar free of its restraint.

Santago's interests had lain solely with the Mirren girl. Now that she was no longer in danger, he directed a wicked smile at Hillman and gestured grandly towards Sheftu.

"Have at 'im," he said softly to his shipmate.

Hillman grinned evilly, put his head down and charged Sheftu.

Laran yelped in alarm. She couldn't let Sheftu be hurt again. Not again! *And not because of me!* She maneuvered across the now crowded deck intending to launch herself at Hillman, but it was Santago now who grabbed her around the waist.

"Stay still, girl," he hissed in the language of her home. "Hillman will end the Soldatian and you will be free."

Laran stared at the sailor in surprise. His eyes were flecked with gold and slanted. His curly hair was light brown. He was smaller in stature than the men of Soldat though he appeared solidly muscled. He was Mirren!

His language and his appearance proclaimed him so! Here was a man of her own country, a man who…

End the Soldatian? No!

But Sheftu was already engaged in deadly combat with the horrible Hillman!

He was fast, her Smiling Man. All thought of coming to his rescue evaporated as she watched him, mesmerized. He was magnificent! Skilled and agile despite his bout with seasickness, his beautiful eyes were narrowed, calculating, and he wore a half-smile on his face.

By the Holy Ones, he was enjoying himself! She remembered the anticipatory grin of the night before as he contemplated their journey. Here was a side of The Smiling Man she'd not understood before. It was probably dangerous, and she wasn't certain she liked it. She rested one end of the oar on the deck.

A series of vicious blows finally knocked the much larger sailor to the deck. Sheftu glanced at the water below and resisted the urge to heave the son of a bitch over the railing.

He turned his back on the fallen man to seek Laran and found her staring at him incredulously, an oar gripped vertically in one hand, another sailor at her back. A small man, he stood only a few inches higher than Laran, and his cap of curly brown hair proclaimed him her countryman. He placed his hand on her arm possessively.

Sheftu frowned at him and started forward, but Laran held up her free hand to stay him.

She turned toward Santago. "I *am* free," she told him quietly in Mirren. "Lord Sheftu is returning me to my home."

Santago snorted derisively. "Hah! Free. So you do not share his quarters? His *bed*? Does he not *own* you?"

She straightened her spine.

"Though it is no business of yours, sir, I tell you this: my honour is intact. The Soldatian is a gentleman. He has been my protector. He has respected my choices." She pushed a finger against Santago's chest. "Now remove your hand before he suspects that you do not!"

Her tone was imperious and Santago looked at her strangely. She seemed familiar, as though he'd known her all his life. How strange that he couldn't put his finger on where he'd....

Santago paled and he dropped his hand. His eyes widened and his mouth opened and closed as though he wanted to say something but couldn't. He stepped back a respectful distance then fell to one knee.

"Tania," he gasped. "You are Tania." He touched his head to the deck.

Oh no! Laran looked over at Sheftu in dismay. He was staring, confusion evident in his handsome face. So were the other sailors. Behind them she could see Provos, Reedin and the two Morrow soldiers, eyes wide in amazement.

"Stand," she hissed at Santago in Mirren. "Stand, before all here understand who I am. Tell all who ask that you have made a mistake, that you mistook me for a noble woman of your country, that the truth is something else altogether. Do you understand?"

"*Ashaii*," Santago whispered, his eyes averted. "Please. My apologies. I thought you were but a Mirren maid, that *he*..." Santago jerked his head toward Sheftu, "had bedded you and kept you. I thought I was helping..."

"I know," Laran conceded. "But he doesn't know who I am." She looked up at Sheftu. "And yet," she added softly, "even so, he leaves his home and his country to return me to mine." She locked eyes with Santago.

"Lord Sheftu has my friendship and my respect. I would demand the same of you where he is concerned."

Santago looked at the young lord dubiously.

"*Ashaii*," he said again, nodding. He climbed to his feet and bowed low. "As you wish. I am yours in all you say."

Laran walked toward Sheftu, who was still frowning at Santago, and placed her hand in his. He looked down at their entwined fingers in surprise.

"What...?" he began.

"Thank you," she said quietly, cutting him off. She shifted the heavy oar in her other hand.

Santago watched Hillman climb silently to his feet and stare at the Soldatian lord's back. As Santago debated whether to act, Sheftu saw the direction of his eyes. He released Laran's hand and turned swiftly, tensing, his muscles readying. He dodged the descending arc of Hillman's knife.

Laran was faster yet. She side-stepped Sheftu's restraining arm and darted between the two men while simultaneously swinging the lower end of the oar up so it could be gripped in both hands. She thrust the now horizontal bar upwards into Hillman's ribs.

From somewhere outside of herself she heard Hillman grunt. She heard Sheftu swear, heard Santago's shout, heard the cheering of the other deck hands, but her focus remained true.

Further enraged, Hillman turned his full attention to Laran. Fleeter of foot than the big sailor, she ducked the slash of his knife, and lunged around him to strike him between the shoulder blades with the oar. Hillman shrieked in fury, his voice high and furious and Laran moved swiftly to face him again. She delivered another blow to his temple. The sailor staggered backwards, tangled his feet on a coiled line and crashed onto the deck.

Laran stood over him, knees bent slightly, oar balanced and ready, watching for his next move.

Sheftu stood absolutely still, though his knife was unsheathed and his body tensed. *Here was another surprise.* He took in every nuance of Laran's body

73

language, calculated every possible move that Hillman could make. He'd act when he had to. He'd leave no chance for Laran to be hurt.

But the little elf knew how to wield that oar! She'd been trained, probably with a staff, and was a formidable force. If she weighed more than 100 pounds he'd be surprised—Hillman must outweigh her by 150 more.

A part of him wanted to pull Laran away, to finish the bastard once and for all, but another part wanted to see what would unfold.

Besides, distracting her now would be unwise.

He was grinning again, he could feel it, though he knew it was misguided.

Hillman shot one leg out to knock Laran's feet out from under her, but she jumped the swinging limb and brought the oar down onto his shin.

Santago was watching in horror. He was aware of the readied tension in the Soldatian lord, aware, too, of his own, but a move against Hillman now could distract Laran and cause her death. She was Tania! She *must* not be allowed to die.

After all, the reward for her return would be enormous.

Hillman shrieked again, jumped to his feet favouring the one leg, and threw his whole weight at Laran. She dodged to the side, brought the oar up and cracked it against his nose as he passed. He went down again. And stayed down.

Santago saw his opportunity. He signalled three other deckhands to take hold of his fallen shipmate's arms and legs.

Sheftu pulled Laran behind him once more, then watched warily as Hillman stirred, suddenly suspicious of Santago's intent. The big sailor began to struggle, kicking one of his shipmates away and staggering to his feet once again, one hand covering his bleeding nose. He swung his long knife with the other, at Santago now, but the smaller man was swift. He plunged his own knife into Hillman's side.

Santago turned to stare with open hostility at Sheftu as Hillman fell.

Still Santago stared. When he tore his eyes away, he bowed reverently to Laran, who stood slightly behind Lord Sheftu. He signalled the three deckhands to re-take the fallen man's arms and legs. Alive or dead, they threw him over the rail and into the roiling river.

Laran ran to the rail to look over the side, but Hillman had already disappeared beneath the muddy surface. She took a deep breath and turned to look at Sheftu, but he had his eyes on Santago and then on Provos, who'd come up beside him.

The two cousins exchanged a look but said nothing. Shock, anger, and something else, sparked behind both sets of dark eyes.

CHAPTER FOURTEEN

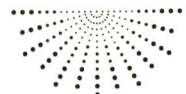

"**W**HERE IN THE Seventh Layer of Darkness *were* you?" Sheftu demanded of his men. He was furious and Reedin swallowed audibly.

"My lord," he began, "I…"

"You will give me an excuse for playing cards while the girl moves about the ship unprotected? For playing a *game* while she is *attacked?*"

Reedin wisely said nothing and had the grace to look, and to feel, ashamed.

"You," Sheftu ground out, "are here to protect her. To help *me* to protect her." He was furious with himself as well and closed his eyes a moment to control his anger. "See that someone remains close to her when I am not," he finally said. He turned on his heel and left them. Reedin gestured with one hand to his two men.

"Go," the Morrow captain sighed. "Watch carefully. See that nothing else befalls her. Watch, too," he added, "that our lord stays whole and safe. Here," he motioned around him, "a man such as he may become a target."

* * *

"OR WHAT?" LARAN asked softly. Provos was angry with her. "I must tell you who I am or *what*?" She knew Provos was only concerned for the safety of his cousin, perhaps for *all* of them, but his tone made her bristle.

By the Holy Ones, she was tired—tired of violence, tired of fear, tired of waiting for the next blow to fall. And tired to the bone of deception. She was honest by nature, and open. Here, outside of her own country, she had to guard her tongue, her every action.

She yearned for peace, for security. She yearned to be surrounded by the people who loved her.

"Well?" she demanded.

Provos struggled to soften his voice. She was still healing from Du-kar's brutalization. He could see that her mouth was swollen where that bastard Hillman had struck her. In a strange land surrounded by strangers, she probably felt very much alone.

He tried to swallow his frustration, but anger still flickered at the edges.

"Or nothing," he conceded. "I am not in the habit of threatening women. And I can see how the daughter of a Captain of Guards might have been trained to handle a staff, but are we expected to believe that this sailor, this Santago, mistook you for a Mirren noble woman? Or that the Mirren *kneel* before their nobles? That they touch their heads to the floor in reverence to their *nobles?*"

"Our customs are different from…"

"My cousin will know you've lied to him, Laran."

Laran was silent a moment. She dropped her gaze to the floor. "It is not my intention to hurt him, Provos," she said quietly. *No. Never that.*

Provos had seen the way Sheftu looked at the girl. He loved her. After what happened with the Lady Tanile, he wondered if his cousin had even realized it.

Had Laran? Did she care? Had she used his feelings for her to manipulate him?

"Then tell me the truth."

She shook her head stubbornly. *I cannot.* "I will tell Lord Sheftu when the time is right."

Provos frowned. *When the time is right.* "Then you as much as admit you've lied?"

When Laran remained silent, Provos clamped his mouth shut.

Not her intention to *hurt* him? Intended or not, his cousin would soon be immersed in it.

"See that you do," he said finally. "He is risking his life, his livelihood, even his family's well-being for you. As am I." He mumbled this last under his breath. "See that he understands the risks fully. You owe him that."

Laran nodded miserably. Her life had been charmed—a loving family and a beautiful home, a country she loved, and prospects for a happy future. She'd been fulfilled.

She'd been a fool.

It had all crashed down around her the day she had been abducted. And now the one person she could rely on, the one person who brought her hope in a hopeless world, that one person would probably despise her.

She'd lied to him.

It was unforgivable. And she couldn't stop now.

"Provos?" she asked his cousin quietly. "If he believes I've lied, how will he feel?"

Betrayed. He will feel betrayed. Provos told a lie of his own. "I do not know what is in his heart."

Laran turned away and tried not to imagine those beautiful ebony eyes turned cold against her.

CHAPTER FIFTEEN

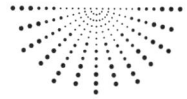

R EEDIN WAS DOGGING her.

In the close quarters of the ship, he made no attempt at discretion and now that she'd stopped dead in the narrow below-decks corridor, he nearly walked into her back.

"Lord Sheftu has ordered that you are not to be left alone," he told her by way of apology. "He has instructed that when he is not with you, one of us must be."

Laran looked up at Sheftu's captain and sighed. Now that she had both Sheftu's *and* Santago's protection, it was doubtful there would be another incident. Santago, despite his smaller stature, seemed to command respect among the other sailors. Sheftu most certainly did. Even those who had mistaken him for the sort of man who had others do his dirty work realized now that he was not to be trifled with.

She doubted the others could be either. Provos, Reedin and his men were, like their young lord, tall men, well-muscled and well-trained. All five wore their confidence in their own abilities like armor.

Her privacy was not her main concern at the moment. She had yet to see Sheftu after the fight with Hillman. Perhaps he wouldn't *want* to see her. Perhaps he really did understand now that she had lied to him. Perhaps he, too, was tired of violence and hurt and wanted peace. Perhaps helping her home was too great a burden.

Perhaps he would leave her with Santago now.

She stopped dead in the corridor once more and Reedin nearly collided with her back again.

Perhaps she'd never see Sheftu again after the ship docked in Barraid.

Her heart felt swollen and empty, too heavy for her chest. Never to see The Smiling Man again… The thought made her ache.

"Leave off!" she told Reedin irritably without turning around.

She climbed to the outer decks once more, wedged herself into a corner, and leaned against the rail where she could watch the water below and the land pass by on either side. She knew Reedin was nearby, but she couldn't see him.

The great yellow plains of Soldat were becoming a memory. Here the land rolled gently into grey-green gullies and rounded hills and the sparse trees took on more height. A herd of grazing black deer jerked their heads up as the ship slowly appeared around a bend in the wide river. They darted away, scattering, and within moments they, too, were only a memory.

In two days Barraid would be in sight and their river journey would be at an end. If Sheftu intended to continue on, once across the border, he and his men would be in considerable danger. Their height and clothing, their black hair and bronzed skin would mark them as outsiders. The citizens of Barraid had no love for the war-like Soldatians.

What must the young lord be thinking now? That he should never have left his home? That he should never have given his word to the little Mirren slave girl? Did his heart ache for his family now, just as hers did for her own?

He appeared at the railing a few feet away. Laran peered around the corner she'd wedged into. Reedin was already turning away, ducking through a hatch door on his way below-decks.

Sheftu rested his arms on the rail and stared out over the water. His shoulder-length black hair blew back from his face and he breathed deeply of the moist river air. He exuded power and strength.

He didn't acknowledge her presence.

Laran edged a little closer to him. They stood side by side now, neither addressing the other. She peeked up at him furtively, but he still looked over the water, his expression thoughtful. *But not hostile.*

"Are you all right?" he finally asked, his eyes still on the changing scene before them.

Laran's gaze jumped to his profile. *No accusations!* Perhaps he believed that Santago really *had* mistaken her for another! Even if that were so, she'd have to tell him the truth eventually. Perhaps he'd understand. Perhaps he'd...

"Laran?" he asked again, frowning.

She did not want to say goodbye to The Smiling Man. Tears stung her eyes and the burden of her fears suddenly pressed heavily upon her, threatening to overwhelm her.

I will *not cry. Not now after all this time! And definitely not here where Sheftu can see.*

But Sheftu was turning towards her. He put his hands on her shoulders and looked into her eyes. She'd begun to shake.

Laran was appalled. She did *not* tremble. She was stronger than that. She was...

Strong arms enfolded her. He held her closely against him and one hand rose to stroke the back of her head. She felt safe there. Right. She could hear the beating of his heart.

She loved him.

No!

No. She didn't. Of course she didn't. She couldn't. He was Soldatian ! Her family would never approve. And she... she...

I love him.

And he didn't love her back. Even if he did, when he discovered the enormity of her lie...

She began to sob against the wide expanse of his chest.

"It's all right, Little Elf," Sheftu said quietly. His big hand threaded through her hair. She could feel the heat from his palm on the back of her neck. "It won't happen again. I swear it."

He didn't understand. He thought she cried in shock at Hillman's attack. He rested his chin on the top of her head and moved his other hand against her back. "I'm sorry," he whispered.

Laran pulled away slightly to look up into his handsome face.

"Me, too. I'm sorry," she echoed. She wiped at her nose and eyes with the sleeve of her tunic. "I'm sorry I didn't tell you..." She stopped herself abruptly. *Would* he continue on to Mirren-Bar? If he didn't, he wouldn't need to know what it meant to be Tania.

"I'm sorry that you had to... do what you did," she told him. "I'm sorry you were hurt again."

He looked surprised.

"I'm not hurt." He raised a hand to the angry bruise on his cheekbone. "Not much." He grinned.

When she raised her hand to his face, he grabbed it in his own.

"No. It will heal. And it will be a reminder to be more careful with you."

Laran broke free of his arms. She leaned against the rail beside him once again and stared out at the passing hills and gullies.

"I'm not the delicate little 'elf' you think I am, Sheftu. I can protect myself."

"So I saw," he said. Laran heard the smile in his voice and glanced up at him. He looked... proud of her. *Proud?* It filled her with pleasure that it might be so.

He was grinning at her now. "Who trained you?"

She looked out over the river. "My father thought it important that we know how to protect ourselves."

"We?"

"My sister and I." She risked a swift glance at his face to see if her admission registered, but he was still grinning. "And you, Lord Sheftu?" she asked him. "How did *you* become such an efficient fighter?"

"I, too, have trained," he said simply. "Fighting and riding: these are the boyhood pursuits of my people. I still train every morning. Or did."

His eyes turned cold. "That son of a rabid dog hit you. It was all I could do not to kill him outright," he admitted grimly.

"And still he died," Laran said.

"*Aey.* So he did. Thanks to your new protector. Santago, is it?"

Laran took a deep breath. *Here it comes. He will demand an explanation now.*

"He has approached me," Sheftu told her. "He plans to jump ship at the Barraidi border. He wants to accompany us to Mirren-Bar. I am sending Reedin and the others back to the Soldat capital. Provos will refuse to go. I will allow Santago to come." He looked at her a moment to gauge her reaction. There was something about Santago that bothered him, something he didn't trust. Or was it simply jealousy? It galled him that it could be so, but he realized now that he wasn't above it.

"That will make four of us," Sheftu continued. "Two Mirren, which should help. Provos and I will try to alter our appearance to blend in a little better, but there's not much to be done about our height."

"Then… then you plan to stay with me? All the way to Mirren-Bar?"

Sheftu nodded. "Did you imagine I would abandon you to the protection of a lone sailor, a man we've only just met?" He could see that she had. He frowned.

"Before we left so hastily, I arranged for a message to be sent to your family through Tishane, Captain of the King's Guards." He hesitated. "Your father."

He glanced down at her, but she hadn't moved—she just stared out at the passing landscape.

"I told him we were traveling by river to Barraid. I requested safe passage at the border of Mirren."

She jerked her gaze up to his.

"You did?" she asked in a small voice.

"*Aey.* I will see you returned to your family. Then, with your father's influence, Provos and I will return to Soldat." *Provided you've given me no reason to stay.*

He turned his head lest she read the direction of his thoughts.

Laran sighed and rested her head against his shoulder and Sheftu's arm slid around her. He held her close.

"You seemed to enjoy it." Her voice was soft, but it sounded like an accusation.

"What...?" Oh. The fight with Hillman.

She'd made no comment on his plan to travel without Reedin and his men, on his intention to allow Santago to accompany them, on his declaration that he'd continue all the way to Mirren-Bar with her. She'd made no comment on his message to her family though she'd been adamant one be sent. She'd made no comment on his plans at all, such as they were.

Perhaps she doubted their success. Perhaps she needed time to think. Laran Tania did not appear to be a woman who'd follow a man blindly and without input.

He wrenched his mind back to her question. *Had* he enjoyed the fight? He'd wanted to kill the man for striking Laran. Then again, he'd been brimming with sexual frustration and uncertainty. The fight had been a welcome release.

"Perhaps," he acknowledged, smiling grimly. "Perhaps I did enjoy it. It seemed to cure my sea-sickness."

Laran's thoughts were in turmoil. And so was her heart. Would Tishane receive Sheftu's message? Would he know what to do with it? Would her father send a contingent of soldiers down to the border to ensure safe passage into Mirren-Bar? Surely he wouldn't risk a border war with Barraid to send them further! And Sheftu and Provos?

They would be in grave danger the moment they left the ship.

The Smiling Man had asked her nothing about what he'd seen there that afternoon.

CHAPTER SIXTEEN

"YOUR HAIR! OH! It looks... ah... You *both* look very... ah... I don't believe I've ever seen...." Laran stopped trying to come up with an appropriate response and pressed her lips together.

Sheftu eyed her, one brow raised. "I feel like a damned fool," he grumbled.

Provos laughed. "You look adorable, cousin. As do I." He waggled his brows up and down lasciviously. He stuck his fingers in Sheftu's now short hair and rumpled it vigorously.

Sheftu swatted his hand away and grunted. "Provos here hacked it off with his knife, then hacked off his own."

"Hacked?" Provos feigned insult.

"The bleach," Sheftu added, "was Santago's idea. Little bastard's probably *still* laughing."

Laran stifled her own laughter. A head taller than her own countrymen and solidly built, these two had wide shoulders and bronzed skin. Her own people were smaller in stature with fair skin. Soldatian eyes were black and shaped strangely, almost level in their faces, much like the Barraidi. The eyes of the people of Mirren-Bar were golden and tilted upwards at the corners.

These two would stand out no matter *what* they did to their hair. Besides, poker straight, haphazardly cut, and nearly white-blonde with the odd black streak, it looked nothing at all like the light brown curls of her countrymen *or* the darker hair of the men of Barraid.

She grinned openly. *No amount of bleach could hide the handsomeness of this pair of kinsmen, either. Look at them!*

Sheftu grimaced, but a slow smile began to spread across his face as he looked at Provos. He burst out laughing.

"*You* look like a damned fool!" he told his cousin.

Provos ignored him and turned to Laran. "Santago told us the women of Mirren-Bar do not cut their hair after they reach maturity, that they pride themselves on their long hair."

He reached out and gently touched Laran's short curls.

Beside him Sheftu felt a surge of jealousy so strong it shocked him. *What's the matter with me?* He rubbed the back of his head, felt his own shorn locks, and scowled.

"It's only hair," Laran assured Provos softly. "I still have my life and even more importantly, I still have my honour."

"Your honour?" Provos prompted, his voice flat. He must be waiting for her to dispel the lie he knew she'd told.

Not yet.

Laran nodded. "I was afraid," she admitted. She looked down at her feet. Her voice grew quieter yet. "My pride... I *had* to put it aside in order to survive." She glanced up at him quickly, and then just as quickly looked away again.

Provos had been watching her as she spoke, a question in his eyes.

"No countryman of yours ever saw me cry," she explained. *At least not before yesterday.* She looked up at Sheftu. He was frowning. "And... and I..." Laran swallowed, suddenly self-conscious. "I... I never begged. Not once. Not even when..." She took a deep breath. "I never gave up," she finished, acutely embarrassed now.

Provos was staring at her, aghast.

"So, you see…" *By the Holy Ones, stop talking, Laran. It's too much! Too much to tell, too much to hear.* But she felt powerless to stop the rush of words. "If I see sympathy or distaste for my short hair in the faces of my people, I will remember."

She averted her eyes from both of them now. "And… and I will be proud."

"Anyway, it's only hair," she murmured. These two were Soldatian. It was their people who had enslaved her, who had brutalized her. She glanced over at Sheftu again.

But he'd turned away, unwilling to let Laran see his anguished reaction to her words. She'd been through the Seventh Layer of Darkness and back.

That it was so hurt him more than his wounds ever had.

And why was that? Other slaves suffered. It was… unfortunate. Why was it so hard, then, to hear of her *suffering?* He wanted… no, he practically *hungered* to kill that sadistic bastard Du-kar for his part in it all.

Before he'd met this little slave girl, he'd never killed a man. Well, he'd killed one now, wounded another, was complicit in the death of a third and wanted desperately to murder a fourth. He'd been jealous: jealous of Santago, jealous even of Provos, his trusted kinsman and friend. It wasn't reasonable. *What in the Seven Layers is the matter with me?*

The first glimmering of truth hit him hard, and denial snapped at its heels.

He owed Laran a debt: she'd saved his life. In return he would bring her back to her family. He liked her, he respected her, and, by the Seven Gods, he most definitely wanted to bed her.

There was no more to it than that.

There could *be* no more to it than that. *A reason to stay in Mirren-Bar?* What had he been thinking?

"What? What are you thinking?" Laran was asking. Sheftu was watching her now, though he seemed to be seeing something else entirely. She couldn't read his expression.

He focused on her face. *I'm not in love with this girl!*

She hadn't spoken the truth about her family; any fool could see that. Doubtless, the lie would have served him better. After all, the second son of a noble, even a Soldatian noble, might be considered a suitable match for the daughter of a Captain of the King's Guards.

The truth was likely much less palatable.

A match! Sheftu shook his head to clear it. What *was* the matter with him?

"What is it?" Laran demanded again. Why *had* she told them so much?

He decided that it was easier to contemplate mortal danger than his own thoughts and emotions where Laran was concerned.

"We will reach the border in the morning," he told her, switching tacks. He turned to his cousin.

"Provos, reconsider. It will be dangerous…"

"We will discuss this no more, Sheftu. You'll need me. I'm coming."

"We haven't discussed it *yet*! You've refused to."

"And so be it," Provos said.

Sheftu only nodded, resigned. The truce between Soldat and Barraid had done little to ease the sense of enmity between the two countries. Soldat had expanded its borders, taken Barraidi territory and killed its citizens. His people were hated there.

Though he worried for his cousin's well-being, he couldn't deny that having Provos at his side would be both a relief and a comfort. The two had been nearly inseparable since boyhood.

Sheftu would pray for success in returning Laran to her family and he would pray for his cousin's safe return to Soldat. As for himself?

That remained to be seen.

CHAPTER SEVENTEEN

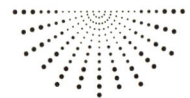

LARAN SAT UPRIGHT and rigid on the narrow bed. She watched the heavy door, and waited. Her hands were clutched in her lap in anticipation of yet another night, another *long* night shipboard and spent in close quarters with Sheftu.

It didn't seem to be any easier for him. Perversely, that made her feel better, though it shamed her to admit it.

He wasn't sleeping well. When he thought *she* was, he quietly slipped away and out of the cabin. She'd listen for the almost imperceptible rustling of his clothing as he slid down the outside of the door to a seated position, and for the soft thump as he rested his back and head against it. She slept better then, though she doubted he did.

Now, the guttering oil lamp threw dim light and shadow around the tiny room as the ship rocked. The sounds of movement and voices as sailors shouted to one another from the rigging and moved aft to secure the sails permeated the thin walls of the cabin.

A gale was blowing and the roiling surface of the great river was crested with dark waves. White foam blew off those running peaks to spray across the charcoal water.

Sheftu had yet to enter the tiny cabin, but she could already feel his presence dominating the room, could almost smell the fresh air scent that seemed to cling to him. She imagined his arms around her and holding her close as he'd done the day she'd cried. She imagined the heat and solidity of his wide chest...

By the Holy Ones, Laran. Leave off!

She positioned her feet more securely on the cabin floor to keep herself from sliding, seated, off the narrow bed as the movement of the ship intensified.

The wind was picking up and thunder echoed through the river valley, though lightning remained invisible there in the windowless space. The sideways tilt of the ship intensified as the mammoth sails, reefed now, were filled by the squall.

The rusty iron door pull rasped from the outside. She could hear Sheftu bidding Reedin, who stood without, good night. He thrust a hip through the wooden portal, and then nudged it closed again the same way. His hands were full, his legs braced against the movement of the ship under his feet.

He grinned at Laran, still seated on the bed, and held a jug of amber liquor and two glasses aloft.

"Wild night," he said. "Our last on the ship. And one step closer to your home." *One step closer to the perilous landing in Barraid as well.* He decided to keep that last sentiment to himself. "Whiskey," he told her, "to celebrate." He shifted his feet and braced his legs wider as the ship fell in a seemingly endless dive then rose again swiftly.

The storm was a distraction. By the Seven Gods, he needed a distraction! He didn't think he could face one more night alone with Laran in the confines of the aft cabin.

Honour was important to her, she'd demonstrated that: her own as well as that of those around her. Damned if he'd lose sight of his now! He'd more or less promised he would respect her decision. And he would. He would try. No. He *would*. He sighed deeply despite the celebratory announcement he'd delivered so jovially.

91

Laran frowned. *Whiskey! A full jug of it.* And if The Smiling Man consumed a great deal, what would happen then? Was he a good-humoured drunk? Or an ill-tempered one? Would he become violent? Her stomach lurched at the thought. She couldn't fight him off. He was too big, too strong, and the cabin too small.

No. She didn't believe that of him. And besides, he wouldn't purposely put her in peril by consuming liquor if that were the result.

Perhaps he thought she might give in to him if she, too, imbibed. *Maybe she would!* She wanted to. By the Holy Ones, she wanted to.

"No thank you," she said. She was still sitting rigidly on edge of the bed.

Sheftu raised a brow and, ignoring her, poured the amber liquor into both glasses. He cast about the room for the chair he knew did not exist, but neither chair nor space to put it in had miraculously appeared since he'd last searched. He sat down beside Laran on the narrow bed, placing a hands' breadth of distance between them. He planted his feet firmly to keep his seat in the teetering space.

"Come," he urged her softly. "Sharing a glass with me won't hurt you."

"Would you?" she asked him.

"Would I what?"

"Would you hurt me? If you were drinking?"

Sheftu stiffened, his eyes widening in surprise. "No! By the Souls of the Dead, Laran, I swear I would not hurt you. Not if I drink too much, not ever!" *Not even if I am so damned frustrated I feel I can't bear it another moment!* "Not ever," he repeated quietly.

"Oh," she whispered. She'd been almost certain of the answer and hadn't meant to be so blunt.

They stared at each other in silence a moment while the ship pitched and rocked. Sheftu tipped his glass back and swallowed it in one gulp. Outside the wind grew fiercer and the ship tilted wildly in response, unseating them both. Sheftu grabbed for the bottle one-handed and placed the other against Laran's chest to keep her from falling against the forward wall. He snatched it back again, discomfited.

He poured another glass and swallowed its contents down, too.

"How about you?" he finally asked her. "You a nasty drunk? Am I in danger?"

Laran laughed, as much as a relief of tension as in humour.

"Maybe," she told him, positioning herself back on the edge of the bed. "I've never been drunk before."

The renewed shouts of crewmen could be heard over the now steady rush of the squall as they lowered the main sail entirely.

"Now might be a good time," Sheftu muttered. He picked up Laran's glass from the floor and filled it again.

Laran reached for it and, she, too, swallowed it in one gulp. She gasped and sputtered. "How do you *do* that without choking?" she demanded.

"Practice," he told her. He poured her another.

The wind rose to a howl and something tied to the outside of the cabin banged relentlessly against the wall. Crewmen still shouted to one another and the ship suddenly righted itself as the huge gust died away for the moment. Sheftu slid down to the floor beside the bed, leaned against the cabin wall, and extended his arm to Laran. She slipped down beside him effectively wedging them into the only remaining floor space.

The side of her body where it pressed against his felt as though it might burst into flames at any moment.

"Won't fall now," he grinned at her. She grinned back and held up her glass. He groped for the bottle, found it, and poured them both a swallow. Outside, the gale raged once again. A thunderous boom sounded directly overhead and a blaze of lightning flared blindingly in the slim space beneath the door. The ship slanted crazily, and quickening air burrowed noisily into every open avenue. Gravity pushed Laran's body heavily against Sheftu's as the slope of the floor tilted to one side.

By the Seven Gods, Sheftu thought. This was more of a distraction than he'd bargained on. He sought a safe topic, anything to avoid thinking about the pitching ship and the soft contours of Laran's body against his.

"I was nearly married," he told her.

Laran squirmed away from his side to look into his face.

"Last year," he continued. "Her name was, is, Tanile. Lady Tanile." He looked down at Laran. *Why bring her up? What is the matter with me?* She was watching him closely but hadn't asked any questions.

Lightning blazed again, a slash of light, and gone, beneath the heavy wooden door.

"I, too, was nearly married," Laran finally told him. "The man to be my husband has been my friend and confidant since childhood. I don't know if he's waited." The thought should have broken her heart.

It didn't.

A weight descended on Sheftu's chest that had nothing to do with the press of Laran's body as the ship rose and fell.

Sheftu was silent a moment. "You love him?" he finally asked.

The crash of waves against the hull was escalating. She could barely hear the shouts of men above it.

"Yes. He is my friend." She glanced up into his eyes. She saw she had his full attention despite the roar of riotous sound rising all around them. "But," she told him wistfully, "it is not as I had dreamed it."

The ship lurched again, and then righted violently.

"By the Seven Gods," Sheftu murmured, alarmed. He tried not to show it. He looked down into Laran's face. Her golden eyes were huge.

They were effectively trapped. Leaving the cabin for the heaving deck now would be lethal.

Might as well brace and wait for the storm to pass.

Or the ship to sink.

He swallowed. "What was it you dreamt?" he asked her. His brow was furrowed and Laran could see she no longer had his undivided attention.

Perhaps the movement of the ship was making him ill again. He didn't look frightened.

But he must be! She bit her lip. *He has courage.*

The ship rolled drunkenly.

I will find my own courage. I must!

A crewman yelled, his voice rising in pitch but diminishing in volume until it could be heard no more over the roar of the storm. He must have fallen, *fallen,* down the slanted deck and into the seething river below. Laran shuddered and grabbed Sheftu's arm. She held tightly.

"I... I've dreamt of the kind of love that rages like the lightning storm outside," she told him as steadily as she could. She took a deep breath. "Jagged and bright and beautiful. I've dreamt of being dazzled. Jodpul does not dazzle me. Nor, I think, do I dazzle him."

Jodpul. Sheftu felt an unreasonable urge to kill the non-dazzling son of a bitch.

The ship leapt out of the water then smashed down at an impossible angle before leaping skyward again. Water coursed through the narrow gap under the closed door and raced toward them in a foaming, grey flood.

Outside, the mast split with a shriek of ripping timber. It's enormous weight crashed down against the roof, crushing the sidewall of the sheltering cabin on its way to the shuddering deck.

On the adjacent wall, the door burst open. Rain and water washed over them in great, cold drifts and tore Laran's hand from Sheftu's arm. The ship dove deep into the inky waves. Through the doorframe a burst of flame illuminated the sheer rock outcropping on the shore directly in front of the bowsprit.

The ship struck with an earsplitting crash, throwing Laran against the wreckage of the sidewall.

"Sheftu!" she cried. But he was nowhere to be seen. *Where was he? Where?*

Had he been pinned beneath the rubble of the cabin wall and the splintered mast? She scrambled through the torrent of rain and the wash of waves to tear at the debris in an attempt to free him. She glanced beyond. *Or had he been thrown out and into the river?*

The ship tipped nearly vertically in the water.

Laran spun and lunged awkwardly back toward the narrow bed which remained wedged into the ruins of the cabin, but the steady pour of water, unchecked now, tore her hands from any purchase she might have found. Her body spilled out over the tilted floorboards, her groping fingers no match for the force of gravity and her own body weight. She felt herself sliding painfully down the now steep slope of the deck towards the black water below.

"Sheftu!" she screamed.

Pain flared hot as her body hit an obstacle and then tumbled out into open space. The churning river reached up for her and pulled her under its cold, agitated surface and down, down to its empty heart.

CHAPTER EIGHTEEN

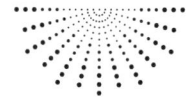

CAN'T BREATHE! THE current held Laran in its icy grasp and she flailed against it blindly as she struggled for the surface. *Can't die here. Not here! Fight!*

Her head broke through and she dragged in a huge lungful of air. The shadowy ship loomed ominously above her, tilted at an impossible angle. Fire had broken out on deck and flaming objects were hitting the water. One struck her soundly on the head, driving her under once again. When she re-surfaced sputtering and choking, something landed solidly against the back of her neck.

A body floated by, face down in the water.

"Laran!" called a voice, deep and frantic. "Laran!" it called again. She turned in a full circle, her legs pumping to keep her afloat. Sobbing, she strained to see through the jet-black night.

Above her the huge spectre of the dark ship hammered against the rocks over and over again. It groaned as though grieving its own demise and began to slide into the river. Flames rained down onto the water where they flickered briefly and were extinguished.

The panicked hand of a drowning sailor reached out for her. He grabbed her shoulder and tried to climb on top of her and out of the water.

To where? Where could he go? She fought the hoary edge of her own panic as the man pushed her in his frantic efforts to climb, forcing her head below the surface once again.

The current seemed to latch onto her legs. Resisting the draw of the flood, she gathered them beneath her and kicked out hard at the sailor, then suddenly relaxed, allowing the surge to separate her from the dying man.

She sank below the waves. The panicked hands fell away and a new one reached for her hair and hauled her up.

"Laran." Sheftu had her now. He had a long cut across his forehead, and it bled freely down his face and into the foaming waves. His shortened hair was plastered to his face, the strange white and black colouring the most visible part of him. Even in the gloom she could see that his beautiful dark eyes were intense. He drew her close, holding her upright with one arm. With the other he stroked strongly away from the sinking ship.

"You all right?" he shouted. His voice was strained but steady.

Laran nodded. She squeezed her eyes shut a moment, letting him tow her away through the dark night and watery peaks.

"Tired now," she told him.

"*Aey.* We'll let the current take us where it will," he told her. "Come. Swim horizontally toward the shore. We can make it." He looked into her frightened eyes though he could see little more than the glistening orbs. "We can make it!" he assured her.

Laran nodded again and looked beyond him as he released her. Burning debris flared in a few places, but the night was pitch. She was cold.

How far was the shore? They'd moved away from it. A brief vision of the sheer rocky outcropping she'd glimpsed through the cabin door before the ship struck it intruded on her will. Even if they made land, could they survive it? The river had thrown the ship against the solid wall of the cliff without mercy. She glanced back at Sheftu, but the guttering flames were dying away and though there could only be a few feet separating them, she could no longer see him. She felt her fears mount higher.

"Stay with me?" she implored.

"I will," he said. She felt his hand on her arm and saw his dark silhouette now against the dying embers of smoldering debris.

"And you, Laran? You'll stay with me?"

"I will," she said solemnly. *I will!*

If they were to die there tonight, they'd die together. They'd die trying to live.

The storm was moving away, but the river hadn't learned of its desertion yet. The black waters continued to thrash and the moon remained concealed.

"I'll stay with you," she said again as they struck out through the chilling crests.

CHAPTER NINETEEN

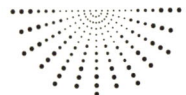

"BY ALL THE gods, what is *that?*" The Barraidi hunter nudged his companion. "Down there."

The companion shouldered his bow and squinted through the trees to the river's edge. "Bodies," he said. "Maybe from the wreck." He started down the slope. "The dead don't need their valuables, Kincane," he called behind him.

Kincane hesitated a moment, then followed his friend down to the beach.

The bodies were entwined: a man and a woman. Had they drowned in each other's arms like that? The man was big. The water was lapping at one of his booted feet, but he was beyond caring about that now. His shoulders and chest were wide and the woman he'd held against him in life was very small in comparison. Kincane bent closer. Her hair was curiously short, light brown in colour and curling about her face.

"Mirren," he said. His companion nodded.

"*He* looks Soldatian." The companion spat contemptuously onto the muddy beach at his feet. "*Raven Seeker,*" he sneered.

"Well, he's beyond his borders now," Kincane sneered. "Way beyond." He booted the corpse in the back.

* * *

A SUDDEN EXPLOSION of pain jerked Sheftu awake. He leapt up, confused. At his feet, Laran climbed stiffly to her own and pushed unruly curls from her eyes. She cast about apprehensively.

Two heavily armed men stood not three feet away, their expressions incredulous. One was stepping back to swing a large hunting bow from his shoulder; the other was standing stock still in shock. Both were staring at Sheftu.

"The... ah... cadaver seems to have revived," Kincane's companion observed.

Barraidi! The men spoke to each other in Barraidi. The storm must have driven the ship beyond its borders before it sank.

Her memory stirred. Had she crawled, literally *crawled*, out of the water on her hands and knees? Sheftu's strong arms had encircled her from behind: she remembered that. The two of them had fallen to the muddy beach, cold and utterly spent. Sheftu had gathered her in close and she'd wrapped her arms around him. They must have spent the remainder of the night asleep where they'd collapsed, exhausted, on the riverbank. She glanced up at him.

Now he stood warily, his muscles tensed and his fists clenched. An angry scrape trailed across his forehead and blood stained one shoulder. His wet tunic was soiled and plastered against his chest. His boots and trousers were coated with mud. His face betrayed no emotion as he stared back at the Barraidi.

Here was a new peril. The two strangers were darker of complexion than Laran was, though neither as bronzed nor as tall as Sheftu. Their long shirts were skins and fell to mid-thigh. Their legs were encased in leather, but their arms were bare. A series of tattoos circled their biceps like rope. Ankle length boots, the stitching on the outside, protected their feet.

Laran stepped in front of them, one hand on Sheftu's chest, the other raised palm outwards toward the two hunters. She could feel the subtle change in Sheftu's body as he shifted. *He's readying to push me out of the way,* she thought. She summoned a smile and spoke to the men in their own language.

"We are strangers here," she told them in Barraidi, "and marooned. Our belongings, perhaps even our friends, were lost last night in the storm."

"Shipwrecked?" Kincane asked. His stance was calm but guarded. His companion remained braced for violence and stared at Sheftu malevolently.

"And this Soldatian?" Kincane's voice turned thick with loathing and his eyes slid, narrowed, to Sheftu's. "What of him?" He thought of the bodies they'd seen earlier that morning and wondered why, if there was any justice, this one hadn't numbered among them.

"The river was hungry last night," Kincane continued, sneering, "but even *she* spits his kind out." His hand moved to rest on his long hunting knife. "Soldatians are not welcome here."

"He... he is not from Soldat," Laran told Kincane hastily. "He... he is from Marabee, far to the south."

"Marabee?" Kincane sounded dubious.

"Yes. Their people look a little like Soldatians but..." She looked up at Sheftu. "Their hair... it's... ah, different," she finished lamely.

Kincane grunted and shook his head. His companion lowered his bow slightly.

"The woman is lying," he said. Kincane nodded and grunted again. Sheftu remained immobile, watching and trying to decipher the turn of the conversation.

"Will you help us?" Laran asked him. "We are cold and hungry."

Kincane took a few steps back, watching for the Soldatian's reaction. When he remained still, the hunter turned and walked away. His companion backed away more cautiously.

"We have little to spare," Kincane told her over his shoulder. "And none at all for the likes of *him*. We will leave what there is at the edge of the woods for you, Mirren. Do not approach until you know we've gone or the

Soldatian will die. Understand that there will be no tears shed." He disappeared into the trees and his companion followed.

"I understand," Laran whispered. She glanced at Sheftu. Even she had underestimated the force of Barraidi hatred for Soldat. She wondered if he understood just how much danger he was in.

The expression on his face as he watched the Barraidi walk away made it abundantly clear that he did.

She tried to muster another smile. "They will be leaving us a few supplies," she told him.

Sheftu looked down at her. Her face was streaked with dirt, her clothing soaked and muddy, the long tunic stuck damply to her legs. One foot was bare. She was swiping light brown curls from her eyes again and she looked... beautiful.

Staying alive long enough to deliver Laran to her family in Mirren-Bar was beginning to feel less and less likely. He'd known his countrymen were hated in Barraid, but the hunters' reactions had driven that fact home tenfold.

He was going to need a miracle.

And Provos? Had he survived? Was he alone in Barraidi territory? Were Reedin and the others with him?

He reached a hand out to touch Laran's face.

This woman, he thought, *this woman will mean my death.* He wondered why he didn't feel the urge to run back toward the border, his country, his family, and his comfortable life as the second son of Soldat nobility.

He searched his tunic for a clean spot to wipe the streaks of mud off her face but failed to find one.

CHAPTER TWENTY

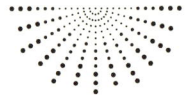

NIGHT WAS FALLING hard in Barraid.

Sheftu swatted absently at the occasional biting fly. He was bare from the waist up, having given his tunic shirt to Laran to wear so she could dry her own tunic by the fire. She was staring down at her one bare foot, lost in thought. He wondered if she was afraid. He knew she was still chilled. *Aey*, and so was he. He moved as close to the meagre flames as he could.

A quarter loaf of bread, a handful of dried meat, and a piece of bruised fruit Sheftu didn't recognize had made up their dinner. A tattered blanket, a small, rusted knife, some fire starter, and, curiously, a women's ornately carved hairbrush, made up the balance of the supplies the hunters left them.

They had moved inland and away from the river to minimize the possibility of chance encounters, but the fire was small just the same. No sense risking being seen.

But Provos, if he lived, would never find him here. Sheftu frowned at the fire. Where *was* his cousin? *Had* he survived? Was he hurt and alone in hostile territory?

They'd return to the riverbank at first light and continue the search they'd begun that afternoon, but if they didn't find him, they'd have to move on, avoiding the roads and other people, through the Barraidi wilderness toward Mirren.

They'd need better provisions first, including a good knife, a bow, and warmer clothes. How in the Seven Layers would they manage that? They had no money and Sheftu dared not show himself in public. He glanced at Laran again and this time she met his eyes.

Almost glowing in the half-light, those golden eyes seemed to see right through him.

"Why didn't you marry the Lady Tanile?" she asked him.

Sheftu was silent a moment. "She didn't want me," he told her roughly.

How could that be? How could any woman not *want this man?* The thought made her uncomfortable. *How many women were waiting for him back in the Soldat capital? How many women had he...?*

"She used me," he continued. "Used me as a steppingstone to marriage with a *first* son, a man who would soon inherit an enormous estate, a man with political power and social status. I had none of these things."

His voice was soft, but his eyes were bitter. The woman had hurt him.

"I'm sorry," Laran told him quietly.

He looked at her. "Are you?" he asked. It sounded like a challenge.

No. She dropped her eyes. "Perhaps not entirely," she admitted. She stared into the fire, then darted a glance at his face to gauge his reaction. He was staring at her, bemused.

"And Jodpul?" Sheftu finally asked. "You will be devastated if he has not waited for you?"

Laran murmured the same answer. "Perhaps not entirely."

She felt the heat rising in her cheeks and was thankful he couldn't see it. "Why is that, Little Elf?" Sheftu watched her closely now.

"I told you, he does not dazzle me. And… and I have a… a fondness for you," she said softly.

Fondness.

"So. You like me, then?" he forced a wide grin. "Even though I am Soldatian?"

"Even though." She grinned back. She waited for him to tell her he was fond of her as well, but he reached for her instead, wrapping a bare, muscular arm around her shoulders.

"We will keep each other warm tonight. And in the morning, we will find Provos and begin our journey to your home."

Laran nodded and nestled close to his side, his solid presence a comfort. And discomforting. His bare skin was cool and smooth and curved with muscle she longed to stroke. She felt the familiar tug on her insides she always felt around him. He wrapped the tattered blanket around them both and rested his chin on the top of her head.

She has a fondness for me. The thought filled him with despair. Sometime during the long night on the muddy beach, as he awoke, slept, and awoke again in fitful starts, he'd finally admitted to himself what he knew for a certainty now.

He loved her.

CHAPTER TWENTY-ONE

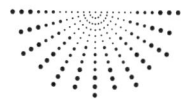

L ARAN LAY, CURLED against the cold, on the bed of dry leaves and slender branches piled near the inadequate fire. Bare from the knees down in Sheftu's too-big tunic, she pressed her legs together to preserve warmth and pulled the thin blanket tightly around her. She watched, through a fog of chilled breath, as Sheftu moved about the clearing, still naked from the waist up, feeding small sticks to the hungry flames. Her own tunic, draped over a rock on the other side of the fire, was still wet.

When Sheftu was satisfied that the blaze was neither too small to warm them nor so large that it might attract attention, he moved behind Laran on the leafy nest and lay down on his side behind her. He gently unwound the blanket from beneath her and draped it over his own shoulders.

He pulled her against him.

She tried not to notice the sudden intake of his breath as he did so.

Now he lay, one arm beneath his head, the other wrapped around Laran and holding her close with splayed fingers to her upper chest. He covered her bare legs with one of his own and pulled the thin blanket around his naked back and over her torso.

The hard ridge of his erection pushed at her lower back.

By the Holy Ones! The sensation of cold faded away as she grew acutely aware of every plane, of every angle, of every touch of his unyielding body against hers. The arm that held her to him rested in the valley between her breasts, and his fingers, which were splayed across her upper chest, radiated heat. Arm, thumb and little finger touched the swell of her breasts and every breath seemed to push those soft mounds against him. Something inside of her *yearned* to push against him.

One of his long, powerful legs pressed against the back of her bare knees, the other straddled her upper leg. For warmth. *Ashaii. For warmth.*

Just as she'd tried not to notice the sudden intake of his breath as he'd pulled her against him, she tried not to notice the uneven heaviness of his breath now. She tried not to notice her own. She closed her eyes.

She tried not to notice the press of her buttocks, soft against his hard lap.

She tried not to notice the almost imperceptible movement as he caressed the swell of her upper breast with his thumb or the slight dip of his hand as his fingers brushed softly against one nipple. She tried not to notice her own body's treacherous response as she moved involuntarily against his hand.

The ache deep within her grew overpowering and she moaned softly.

"Laran," Sheftu whispered in her ear. "Do you want this? Do you want me?"

He'd only meant to keep them both warm. He'd thought he could handle the contact. He hadn't thought far enough ahead.

By the Souls of the Dead, could he stop if she refused him now? *Yes,* came the answer. But the Seven Gods knew he didn't *want* to stop.

His hand moved down her chest to stroke her flat stomach and the flames within her ignited a response so intense she felt she might faint.

"*Ashaii!*" she gasped. "*Ashaii.*"

You are the one, Sheftu. The one I have waited for, the one my gift was meant for. She twisted in place to face him and he pulled her against him once more, this time face to face. He touched his lips to hers, gently at first and then with mounting pressure.

Her breasts pressed against his wide chest now and she insinuated her hand between their bodies to stroke the ridged muscle of his stomach. Her hand drifted lower to touch the hard, velvet-smooth shaft of his erection and he sucked his breath in again.

Sheftu's big hand was moving down her back to the soft curve of her buttocks. He placed his hand on them and pushed her against him, grinding his erection onto her stomach. Her breath caught and she felt she was back on the ship once more with the bottom falling out of her world and waves, black and hot this time, cresting over her head.

His finger caressed that secret core of her and she cried out.

"Fear not," Sheftu murmured. "I will be gentle. And slow. I'll not hurt you, I swear it."

She took his face in both of her hands and, panting, looked into his hooded eyes. "I do not fear you, Sheftu. I want you. Only you. Only you."

Something broke inside of him and he rose up over her, placing her on her back beneath him. Her arms circled his neck and she tried to pull him down to her. He wanted to possess her, to make her his own. He loved her. By the Seven Gods, he loved her!

When he entered her, she froze. "No," she breathed. "You are too..."

"I will be gentle. It will be all right." He was speaking through his teeth, his breathing ragged. He didn't want to be gentle—he *wanted* to thrust into her, deeply, strongly, and at once. He ground his teeth with effort, looked into her eyes, and all rough desire melted away.

He was in serious trouble.

He wouldn't hurt her, but *he* was going to be hurt, he understood that. And still, he'd give up his home, his country, even his life for this small woman, this denizen of the once mythical Mirren-Bar.

She began to move tentatively under him, and then suddenly lifted her hips off the bed of leaves, effectively immersing him to the hilt. She cried out again, then relaxed, wrapping her legs around his hips. They found a rhythm together and together they plunged off the high crests and into the watery depths of pleasure.

He is mine, Laran thought in wonder, *and I am his. And when he learns the truth?* She squeezed her eyes shut. He wouldn't want her anymore. He'd hate her.

CHAPTER TWENTY-TWO

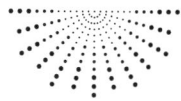

S HEFTU WADED THROUGH the thick underbrush at the edge of tree cover, and then finally broke through to the long yellow grass leading down to the riverfront. He glanced behind him at Laran and frowned.

"You are limping," he accused when she appeared on the bank beside him.

She balanced on her one shod foot, raising the offending appendage for inspection. "Sliver," she said of her bared foot.

Sheftu scanned the open landscape carefully, one hand raised to shadow his eyes. Accustomed now to the cool shadows of the woods, the glare of early morning sunshine was almost painful. It slanted across the river and shattered the rippled surface into blinding fragments of light.

He moved his gaze back to Laran and grunted. "Let's have a look."

She plopped down to sit on a rock and Sheftu knelt on one knee before her, taking her bare foot into his lap and squinting at it.

"I see it," he murmured. He briefly contemplated the rusted knife but discarded the idea, trying to work the splinter out with too-big fingers and short nails instead. Laran flinched silently and tried to jerk her foot away, but he held it tight. "Got it!" He held the tiny piece up triumphantly.

"Oh." Laran bent close to peer at it, amazed that something so small could have hurt as much as it had.

Sheftu stared at her a moment. She seemed to grow more beautiful with each passing hour. Sitting there in the long, yellow grass, sunlight shimmering in her unruly hair, her long tunic dry now but torn and dirty, a smudge on the tip of her nose... *Aey.* Beautiful. Still on one knee, still holding her bare foot, he smiled into her golden eyes.

"Laran," he said softly.

It sounded like an endearment and his deep voice caught at something in her heart and pulled. She didn't smile back. She couldn't. She felt paralyzed. He was big, strong and handsome. He was kind and courageous. He was risking his life to help her. His eyes were... dazzling. *He* was dazzling. Here was the man she wanted!

He was Soldatian.

She was in serious trouble.

She'd have to protect him somehow, keep him safe. The Barraidi would kill him given a chance, any chance at all. She knew that now.

The Smiling Man. She raised her hands to either side of his face in a gesture he was beginning to recognize. Her lovely cats' eyes crinkled at the corners now and she smiled back at him shyly. She leaned in towards him. He touched his lips to hers and sudden warmth spread through her right to the tips of the toes he still held in strong hands.

Sheftu groaned. She was sweet to the taste and her lips were soft. The kiss had been tender. He broke contact and looked into her eyes for confirmation. *It was still there.* He knew the value she placed on bestowing her "gift" and he'd been afraid that in the morning's light she would regret having given it to *him.* But she still appeared to desire him.

Laran's breath quickened, but she placed a hand against his wide chest. "Sheftu, wait! There is a... a truth you must know."

"Later," he murmured, his lips only inches from hers. Dark desire flickered in eyes like soot, half-hooded beneath thick, black lashes.

He released her foot, drew her off her rocky perch and lifted her, placing her feet gently on the rock she'd be sitting on. Now they were face to face, their lips still only inches away. He closed the distance.

"Wait!" she said against his mouth. She pushed him away. "You may not *want* to kiss me when you hear what I have to say," she told him.

"You clearly have *no* idea how much I want to kiss you, Little Elf." He let his hands run down her arms. He felt the tremor in her limbs and saw the hunger flicker in her golden eyes. He leaned in to touch her forehead with his.

"This 'truth' of yours—you don't really want to share it, do you?"

Laran shook her head, felt him shift, and felt his lips brush her neck. She arched the column, giving him more surface to touch. She could feel the sigh of his breath, warm against the cool of her skin. "But, you… you need to know…"

But Sheftu was shaking his head.

"Let this truth of yours be your gift now, Laran," he said into her hair. "Like the other, it means nothing if not given freely." His hands were moving toward the small of her back. He angled his head and pressed his lips against hers. She felt as though she might melt against him.

He jerked his head up and peered intently over the open grass and along the riverbank.

"What is it?" Laran asked in alarm.

"Provos!" he said.

"I heard his voice!"

Laran stood on her toes on the rock, her hands on Sheftu's shoulders for balance, straining to see across the waving yellow grass.

"Someone is calling your name!" she exclaimed.

Two figures appeared above the muddy bank, one considerably larger than the other, both plunging through the waist-high grass and calling out. They were too far away to make out, but the voice was familiar. It was Provos! It had to be!

"I'm going to circle closer to have a look," Sheftu said. "Stay here, out of sight."

"Wait! I'll come with…"

But he was gone, faded back into the woods from which they had just emerged.

Stay here? She felt annoyance rise up in place of ardour. Did he imagine he could order her about because they'd been intimate? And why was she not happier that Provos had found them? After all, she *wanted* Provos to be safe. She didn't want Sheftu to worry for him or grieve his death. He loved him. Besides, she trusted Provos and there were not many of his countrymen she could say that of.

She raised herself from her rocky perch once again to peek out over the waist-high grass. Upriver, Sheftu had burst out of the woods and was running toward the two figures on the beach. Laran heard his jubilant shout. The larger of the two men gave a whoop, raced toward him, and embraced him mightily. Relieved male laughter carried on the breeze. The second figure was undoubtedly Santago. He stood apart, watching the interaction between the two Soldatians. Sheftu gestured downriver towards her with his arm. She plopped back down on the stone.

Her time with Sheftu was finite—she'd known that.

And she was deeply ashamed of the disappointment she felt at having to share him now.

* * *

"OF REEDIN'S MEN," Provos was telling them, "I only saw one. He was heading towards the Soldat border in company with three sailors when I came across him. None of the four had heard or seen anything of Reedin." He shook his head. "I hope he made it," he added softly.

"As do I," Sheftu acknowledged. He turned to Santago. "You still wish to accompany us to Mirren-Bar?"

The smaller man nodded but fastened his eyes on Laran. "As you wish," he told her in Mirren, ignoring Sheftu. "I am yours in all you say."

Laran glanced up at Sheftu. He was frowning at Santago and so was Provos.

"So be it," she told the smaller man in the language of their home. To Sheftu and Provos she added, "A man who is not, ah, Soldatian may prove to be valuable."

"*Aey,*" Sheftu said. "Might be at that."

Something about the Mirren sailor, something over and above his apparent deference to Laran, still troubled him. The lines between Sheftu's brows deepened as he tried to fathom just what it was that bothered him about the smaller man.

"Sheftu," Provos said, "there is talk of a great army amassing on the Mirren side of the Barraidi border. Seems to be a lot of speculation, but no solid facts as to why." He turned to Laran and raised a brow in question.

Laran paled. *It couldn't be for her!* No, of course not. That was absurd. Her father would never risk conflict with their Barraidi neighbours by sending men into the already war-torn and impoverished country. Barraidi political sensibility teetered on a sword's edge as it was.

"Sheftu has requested an escort across Mirren," she ventured. "Perhaps there are already men on the Mirren border awaiting our arrival." She swallowed, warming to this probable truth.

"Doubtless stories of a 'great army' are exaggerated," she continued. She looked up at Sheftu. He was nodding slowly, digesting this news and her take on it.

"*Aey,*" he said. "Doubtless." He glanced at Santago, who wore a speculative air.

"Getting to the Mirren border alive will be a trick," Provos observed. "These Barraidi seem not to be overly inclined toward friendliness."

Sheftu snorted at the understatement.

CHAPTER TWENTY-THREE

"WEAPONS," SHEFTU BREATHED in surprise. He sorted through the contents of the bags Provos and Santago had kept slung over their shoulders. "And knives. Blankets! Rope. Cloth. Fire starter. And food!" He nodded in approval of the four jars of preserved fruit.

"And money," Provos told him. "Nearly 100 Barraidi lirar. The Mirren has it." He cocked his head toward Santago, who was speaking earnestly with Laran. She didn't look pleased at his words. "All of it, in fact," Provos continued. "Grabbed it up and stuffed it in his shirt."

"Where did it all come from, Provos?" Sheftu asked.

"Some of it, like the jars of fruit, washed up on shore near the wreck, some of it *that* one scavenged off the dead." Provos eyed Santago with censure. "It didn't feel right, cousin."

Sheftu nodded thoughtfully, his gaze on Santago and Laran. "But we need these things if we are to survive the trip through Barraid."

Laran's voice rose suddenly. Her final three words, spoken in Mirren, were unintelligible, but the tone was negative and anything but subtle. She stood suddenly, elevating her chin. Santago rose to his feet as well. Anger flashed briefly across his face: there and gone. He bowed to Laran and moved away toward the embers of the fire making a show of warming his hands though the afternoon was mild and the fire nearly extinguished.

Laran glanced at Sheftu and Provos, who were both watching her curiously. She offered a tentative smile, then turned away quickly offering no explanation. She made herself busy by draping the wet cloth and blankets over the sparse bushes still lit by the sun.

Provos muttered something about secrets under his breath.

"Boots," Sheftu said. "Our little elf here needs boots." He looked down at Santago's feet, which were considerably smaller than the two Soldatians' though not as small as Laran's.

Santago saw the direction of his gaze and grunted in annoyance. He grabbed a short spear from the small pile of weapons and began to walk downriver. "I'll be back," he threw over his shoulder.

"Gone to rob the dead again, no doubt," Provos said. He shivered involuntarily. He wasn't a superstitious man, and he couldn't deny the practicality, but scavenging from the corpses of their drowned shipmates made him uneasy.

"Don't much like that one," Provos admitted quietly to Sheftu. Sheftu nodded but said nothing.

The two of them bent to stow their scavenged possessions for the long journey ahead.

CHAPTER TWENTY-FOUR

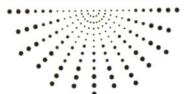

LARAN STOOD AT the edge of the bluff, dawn making a golden nimbus of her softly curling hair. The angled light shone through her tunic and outlined her lower body in amber. Her back was straight, her head was thrown back, and her eyes were closed. She held her arms straight out from her sides as though she imagined wings with which to soar off this edge of the world to the valley below.

From his vantage point on the trail beneath, Sheftu could see the press of cloth against that lithe form as the breeze raced up the slope to push at her tunic. The garment fluttered against her legs and wind lifted the long hem to reveal the rough, ankle-length Barraidi boots beneath.

Santago said he'd found them together with the waist-length deer skin jacket Laran wore now over her dress, but the items were unlikely to have been worn by one of the dead sailors and even less likely to have been washed up in the wreckage of the ship. He fervently hoped the little Mirren hadn't killed a Barraidi passer-by for them.

Was he even capable of such an act? It was disturbing not to know for certain.

"I am envious of the wind," he told Laran when he reached her. His voice was deep, warm and seductive.

She opened her eyes, saw his wide grin and followed the direction of his gaze down the visible curves of her body. "The wind makes me feel good," she told him, laughing. *And so do you.* She looked up at him wistfully.

He was looking out, now, at the rolling, wooded hills and the streams that threaded through them like silver ribbons. Beyond the hills, the land began to rise and enormous boulders lay on the ground in places. Beyond that, jagged rock seemed to thrust up through the earth like massive swords. There, low clouds hugged the serrated contours of the rock, veiled the higher hills and almost obscured the snowy peaks of the Mirren mountains in the distance.

"It's beautiful," he murmured. He moved behind her and wrapped his arms around her still gazing at the scene before them.

Laran leaned back against his chest and signed contentedly. "You can see Mirren when the clouds lift," she told him.

"*Aey,*" he said thoughtfully, but it was Santago he strained to see as the smaller man traversed the valley trails below. He'd be an hour into his journey now to the town just barely visible in the distance. The land was considerably rougher ahead and they'd need information to find the best route through to Barraid's mountainous border.

With luck Santago would return with bread and milk, too. And perhaps some sweet Barraidi tea. And eggs. Sheftu tried to tear his thoughts away from his stomach.

"If we were high enough, we could see the sea beyond that," Laran continued.

"The sea?" Sheftu asked, suddenly fascinated.

"*Ashaii,*" she said. He could hear the smile in her voice. "I love the sea. My sister Shell and I spent half our childhoods on its shore—the sound of it at night as we slept, the scent of it in the early mornings as we raced down the beach, these are the things I miss most. Sometimes we found fantastic things there, too, strange and beautiful animals, and always it changed. The sea has moods, just as we do." She twisted to look up into his face. "Does that sound foolish?"

"No," Sheftu answered. "I would like to see this sea of yours."

119

"I will show you!" Laran said. "The mountain passes will still be snowed in, but if you stay in Mirren-Bar for a few months, we could…" She stopped abruptly and turned back towards the view, suddenly embarrassed. "Ah, well, then again, perhaps you wouldn't want to stay," she said quietly.

Sheftu was silent a moment, then wrapped his arms more tightly around her.

"I would," he answered. "Take me to this sea of yours, Laran."

Laran relaxed in his arms and smiled at the sunrise, elated. *I will. I will take you there.*

Sheftu dipped his head to press his lips to her hair.

"After four days of travel," he said, "it will be good to stay put for a while. Maybe do a little more hunting. Those rabbits didn't last long."

Behind them in camp, Provos pulled on his jacket to ward off the chill rising with the mounting breeze. He rolled up his blanket and put away the remains of their meagre breakfast.

He'd watched his cousin wrap his arms around Laran. Watched, too, as she nestled against him, obviously comfortable despite the intimacy of the gesture. He heard the quiet timbre of their voices as they spoke to one another. Something had happened in his absence to break the tension between them. They slept chastely and separately, he noted, though close together, and twice when he'd awoken first, he'd noted their fingers entwined as they slept.

Provos sighed. Disaster approached. He could feel it.

"Do you think your family will be worried for you?" Laran was asking Sheftu.

He shrugged. "Perhaps. If so, hearing about the wreck and the drownings from Reedin's man will not allay their fears."

"Will you tell me about them, your family?"

Sheftu shifted, though he kept his arms around her, still facing the vista. "My brother, Tyson, is five years my senior. He and my father have been visiting Morrow holdings south of the capital. By now they will have heard of my clash with Du-kar, of the attempted murder, of my departure from the Morrow House. Perhaps they will have heard about the little slave girl at the heart of it all. Doubtless they will wonder."

"Oh," Laran murmured. *And what would they think of Sheftu's involvement with 'the little slave girl'?* Doubtless they were horrified. She bit her lip.

Sheftu paused a moment.

"There was another brother, a babe," he continued softly, "but he died in childbirth and so did my mother." He was silent a moment. "I miss her," he said softly.

Laran's heart ached for him. "What was she like, your mother?"

"She used to sing. All the time. In the garden, as she dressed, even walking the halls of the Morrow House—all the time. She had a beautiful voice."

"And your brother, Tyson?"

"He married and has a son of his own. You saw them on the balcony. His wife, Marna, can be funny. She has a wicked sense of humour. She's good for him. As first son, he has responsibilities. He takes them seriously. He can be… intense."

Laran twisted again to look up into his face. He smiled at her, a little sadly she thought. Her smile in return was genuine and warm. It crinkled her eyes at the corners.

Sheftu tried to imagine her as an old woman. She'd be more and more beautiful as she aged, he thought. Perhaps she'd become plump. The thought made him grin.

"You are grinning. Are you thinking of your brother's wife? I always wanted to be funny," she said.

"You've had your moments," Sheftu assured her.

She laughed and turned her body in his arms to face him. She wrapped her arms around his waist and rested her head against his chest.

"And Tyson?" she said against his tunic. "You are not very close?"

"Provos became the brother of my heart, Laran. He is my brother still." He looked over his shoulder at his cousin and found him staring at them. Provos looked away self-consciously and began to arrange their bags for travel though they were already set out and ready to go.

Laran wriggled out of Sheftu's arms to stand beside him. She took his hand in hers and looked out over the vista again, but this time saw none of it.

"I have been very lucky," she told him slowly. "My family is very close.

My mother is a painter, a *wonderful* painter. Even as a small child I can remember the passion she felt for her art. She'd often disappear for days at a time to paint, but we never felt neglected. She was always so happy afterwards." Laran smiled at the memory.

"What did your father think?"

"He never minded. He was so *proud* of her. Sometimes he looked as though he could burst with it."

"My sister, Shell," Laran continued, "is two years younger than I am. She is beautiful. Wait until you see her! She sings, too, like your mother perhaps, and when she does, people stop what they are doing to listen." She smiled at the thought.

"My father is a very serious man with many responsibilities, but his heart is warm. He…"

"It is time we made our way down to the valley," Provos interrupted quietly. He moved up beside them. "Santago will be halfway to town by now. We have camp to set up and fish to catch while we await his return." He smiled at both of them. "Come," he said. "The sun is climbing."

Sheftu turned to pick up his share of the belongings and handed Laran hers. He glanced at Provos, who was standing at the edge of the bluff, his eyes on the scene below.

"There," Sheftu said pointing towards a grassy headland at the sharp turn of the stream below. "That's where we will set up camp. It's a landmark easily recognizable from both directions. Santago will meet us there."

Provos nodded. His disquiet was escalating. He tried to shake it off, clapped his cousin on the shoulder, and then set off down the path.

CHAPTER TWENTY-FIVE

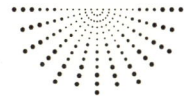

E STALLA RE-ADJUSTED THE cloth carrier on her chest. She was careful to keep the babe within asleep. A little thatch of dark hair and a tiny, pale brow was all that was visible beneath the soft cloth. She smiled at her daughters, four-year-old Seren and five-year-old Alam, already barefoot at the edge of the stream.

"No deeper than your knees," she told them as she readied her coiled fishing gear. The girls had heard those words so often that Alam rolled her eyes. Seren giggled and stepped out into the stream. She stared down at her bare toes, visible in the clear water, and wiggled them against the muddy bottom.

A man stepped out of the woods and Estalla sucked in a breath in shock. He was facing away from them for the moment, but she could see that he was tall, broad shouldered and muscular. His hair was straight and nearly white with broad jet-black streaks. It was cut haphazardly and its length brushed the neck of his garment. He wore a tunic shirt over loose trousers and knee-length boots.

Soldatian garb.

When at last he turned to face them, the sun shone straight into his face. His eyes seemed to absorb the light. Black. They were black!

He was Soldatian!

Estalla screamed. Fear immobilized her for a moment, but maternal instincts quickly took control. She threw down her fishing gear and moved quickly toward her two daughters who were staring at the stranger in fright. She turned them in the opposite direction.

"Run!" she hissed. "Run!"

But another Soldatian man, drawn by her scream, ran, *ran*, out of the woods and into the open, though he stopped short when he saw them.

Terror unfurled in Estalla's chest. The second man was even closer than the first and just as big. She and her little family were between the two of them. There was nowhere to run! She gathered her daughters close and stepped backwards, into the stream.

Provos saw her course of action and moved forward in alarm. "No!" he called out. He raised his hands, palms out, towards her. "Don't!"

But the terrified woman was still moving backwards, her eyes wide with fear. One of the little girls started crying as the water reached her thighs and threatened to unbalance her.

The Soldatian closest to them retreated and the first man, looking right at them now, did the same.

Estalla saw the men put distance between them and took a final step, trying to summon both strength and courage to wade downstream with her daughters and away from the two Soldatians, but one foot caught in the tangled waterweeds and she fell backwards, letting go of the girls. She tried to arrest her fall so as not to immerse the babe still tied to her chest in his cloth carrier.

Estalla floundered helplessly, one hand on the carrier, one hand below her in the water trying for purchase. Her tangled foot kept her rooted to the muddy bottom, but the stream pulled at her, tugging the rest of her body away from the bank, away from her daughters. Unbalanced, pulled by the flow of the water, she thrashed about in a vain attempt to put her free foot beneath her and to keep the carrier, and the babe within, out of the water.

Provos loped toward her, waded in and pulled her to her feet, then moved away quickly again. He spoke softly, calmly, trying to reassure the woman but it was clear she was still afraid. She bent to disentangle her trapped foot from the weeds and divided her terrified gaze between Provos and her daughters, just out of reach on the bank of the stream.

Provos met his cousin's eyes and in silent agreement they turned their backs to move towards the woods and away from the stream and the little family.

"Ow!" Provos cried.

Something struck him in the back of the head. He turned quickly to see the older of the two girls pick up another rock. He frowned and shook his head at her, and she dropped it immediately. He reached behind his head and his hand came away bloody. He muttered something under his breath and glanced at the girl's mother.

She was aghast. Fear turned to panic. She thrust her oldest child behind her to protect her from the Soldatian's imagined wrath and grabbed at her younger daughter, pushing her, too, into deeper water behind her. Estalla fell to her knees on the edge of the stream, bowing her head and speaking rapidly in Barraidi. It seemed she was begging him to spare the child who'd injured him. She began to sob, clearly believing her case to be hopeless.

"Do not fear," Laran called out to the distraught young mother quietly in Barraidi. She walked down the stream bank towards her. "These men will not harm you."

When the woman only stared in disbelief, Laran continued.

"Look at their faces. You see? They have no wish to hurt you or your children."

Estalla darted a quick look at Provos, and another at Sheftu. Their skin was bronzed. Their brows and lashes were jet-black. So were their eyes! They were undeniably Soldatian. But the Mirren's words rang true. They did not appear to want to harm her.

Estalla climbed shakily to her feet.

"W... what are you doing with them?" she asked Laran. "They are Soldatian!"

"They are bringing me to my home in Mirren from Soldat. We've been traveling through the Barraidi wilderness for many days now." She approached the young mother.

"If your countrymen learn of their presence here, they will kill them," Laran said quietly.

"You are certain they mean no harm to me or my children?"

"I am certain."

"They will not follow me if I leave?"

Laran shook her head. "I promise," she said.

The first Soldatian spoke quietly to the Mirren woman in his own tongue and Estalla shivered. She had hoped never to hear the language spoken here, so close to her home.

"He asks if your husband or other Barraidi are nearby?"

Estalla hesitated, clearly wondering at the wisdom of answering truthfully. Finally, she shook her head.

"No," she whispered, her eyes rounding in dread once again. "We are alone." *All alone!*

Laran nodded again. "Do not fear," she repeated quietly.

Estalla looked at the young man who had helped her from the water. He was holding fishing gear, she realized, much like her own. He had drawn no weapon; he was making no threatening moves. The other Soldatian was listening quietly to their exchange. She couldn't tell if he understood any of it.

She swallowed audibly. "You are going to meet the Mirren soldiers then?" she asked Laran.

"Soldiers?" Laran asked, surprised. "You've seen soldiers? *Mirren* soldiers? Here?"

The Barraidi nodded, still eyeing Provos warily.

"My husband saw them—perhaps fifty altogether. Everyone in town, everyone *everywhere* is talking about them. No one knows why they are here." She looked at Laran curiously. "Are they here for you?" she asked.

Could they be? "Perhaps," Laran admitted slowly. She felt a surge of excitement. "Where are they?"

"They… they were setting up camp in the hills north of town. They've been traveling south. My husband thought they might be here tomorrow."

Tomorrow! Laran grinned in anticipation and turned to Sheftu and Provos to relay the news in Soldatian.

When she turned back to the Barraidi mother, she had already gathered up her children and was walking quickly away. She cast a final, apprehensive glance over her shoulder at them before she disappeared from sight around the bend in the stream.

Sheftu had watched her go.

"Other Barraidi armed with more than just fishing gear may learn of our presence now," Sheftu said. "I know we agreed to meet Santago here, near the headlands, but I say we move on."

"*Aey,*" Provos said, frowning. "After we've established a new camp, one of us can take up a post near here to watch for him."

Laran nodded. To risk being found by a group of revenge-minded Barraidi now, when they were so close to the Mirren soldiers, would be the height of folly.

Provos looked at his fishing line in disappointment. "I'd like to have tried for a good, fat trout," he lamented.

CHAPTER TWENTY-SIX

LARAN NEARLY COLLIDED with Sheftu's broad back when he stopped dead at the edge of a large clearing. They'd been walking single file down a narrow deer path through the wooded hills for over an hour searching for an alternate campsite.

Provos was last on the trail. His sense of unease had not diminished. He looked over his shoulder for the twentieth time, though he was certain they hadn't been followed and the trail was all but invisible. He climbed over a moss-covered log and shouldered the final branch out of the way before he, too, stopped dead at the edge of the clearing.

Here the sun shone in yellow bands from a charcoal sky heavy with ponderous storm clouds. The horizon was limited by the wide, roughly circular opening in the forest, and a faint rainbow seemed to illuminate most of it. A creek ran the length of the meadow, falling several feet through boulders in the otherwise grassy landscape, providing the water music they'd been hearing the past few minutes as they maneuvered through the dark woods. Two deer at the far edge of the clearing regarded them impassively, then slowly sauntered into the sheltering trees to disappear from sight.

"It's beautiful," Laran said softly.

"It is," Sheftu agreed, awed. "We're far enough away from the headland here, and the path to a camp would not be obvious."

Provos nodded. Laran was still staring at the meadow in delight, her golden eyes lit with pleasure. Sheftu turned to smile at her expression, clearly enjoying her reaction.

"Cousin," Provos said. "I'll rest here a moment, take some water, then return for Santago. I wouldn't want to have to try to follow that trail in the dark. If Santago returns late, we'll bed down near the headland, out of sight. If he doesn't return at all, I'll stay until morning."

Sheftu frowned at his kinsman. "Santago can spend the night at the headland on his own. One of us can return for him at dawn."

But Provos was shaking his head. "I have a bad feeling about this, Sheftu," he admitted. "Better we gather up the Mirren and be away from the area entirely by tonight if we can." He began rummaging through their belongings, taking two blankets, a bow, arrows, and one of the jars of fruit.

He held up the jar, grinning. "Incentive," he told them, but his grin faded at the look on Sheftu's face.

"Worry not, Cousin," Provos said. "If Santago doesn't return with enough daylight left to find the trail, or doesn't return at all tonight, I'll bed down in the woods where I won't be seen. I won't be lighting a fire."

He swung the bag holding his few belongings over his shoulder and turned away, looking back only once to raise his arm in farewell. "Have a good evening," he said softly.

Sheftu's eyes widened. Provos had already vanished, but he could hear him moving away down the path. His cousin had volunteered to return for Santago in order to give him time alone with Laran! He stifled the urge to go after him. After all, Provos' plan had merit. The sooner they gathered up Santago and removed themselves from the area in which they'd been discovered, the better.

"Do you think he will be all right?" Laran was asking. Sheftu nodded slowly. "*Aey.*"

"You don't think he will lose his way, all alone on that tiny, twisting path?"

"No," Sheftu told her. "Where the path disappears, Provos knows to mark his way. He was last on the path: he will probably already have done so on the trip here."

The faint rainbow faded away and the bands of sunlight retreated, leaving only the charcoal sky behind. Fat raindrops began to fall, splashing circles into the creek and wetting the long grass of the meadow.

The tall Soldatian and the small Mirren grabbed their belongings and ran back to the haven of the trees.

"Let's build a shelter, Little Elf," Sheftu said. He glanced about as he spoke. In the clearing the quickening rain pelted the ground, flattened the long grass, and drowned out the music of the creek. Above them the closely-knit branches of the dense woods provided a temporary umbrella, but already long streams of liquid were pouring off the ends of limbs and into the undergrowth below.

"There!" Laran called. The roots of an upended tree made a small cavern. Dripping ferns hung off the edges but the ground beneath was dry.

Sheftu threw their bags inside, ducked at the entrance and drew Laran within. Rain hammered now against the root roof and bounced off the needled ground in front of them. Sheftu pulled Laran close, then nestled in against the one hard earthen wall at the core of their refuge.

CHAPTER TWENTY-SEVEN

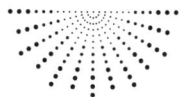

PROVOS TOOK UP an uncomfortable position in sight of the headland. The woods were not far from the stream bank, but he could barely distinguish stream from bank in the rainy deluge, let alone spot a lone man waiting anywhere along the way. Doubtless Santago had taken cover and was waiting out the storm just as he was.

He sighed. Daylight, such as it was, was fading to darkness. He was wet and chilled, and it would be a long, cold night without the comfort of a fire to warm him. He briefly thought about building a small one. After all it was unlikely anyone would be looking for them now, in this weather. He discarded the idea. Better to fashion a nest for a bed with a branch covering, wrap up in the two blankets, try to sleep, and wait for morning. He was tired enough.

And, by the Seven Gods, he was hungry! He stared at the coveted jar of fruit, and then pried off the top to dip his fingers inside. Might as well get *some* pleasure out of this ordeal.

* * *

SANTAGO ROUNDED THE bend in the stream. The headland was close. He tried to swipe the water out of his eyes, but the rain was relentless. He was soaked through and distinctly unhappy. By the Holy Ones, this storm could ruin his plans! He swore crudely in Mirren but didn't worry that his voice might be heard. *Nothing* could be heard above the cacophony of the water.

The rain was beating, *beating*, down on his body and the stream he followed was swollen over twice the size it had been that morning.

A small, uprooted tree smashed its way along the watercourse, tearing submerged bushes off the bank in its wake. The water was muddy and swift.

He hoped those Barraidi bastards were still behind him and watching his progress.

* * *

LARAN POKED THE small fire at the edge of their shelter with a stick. Occasionally a wayward gust blew rain inside splattering the already wet wood and threatening to extinguish the stingy flames, but it remained stubbornly lit through it all.

She scooted back to Sheftu, seated and leaning against the back wall of the root cavern. He opened the blanket wrapped around his shoulders to receive her.

"And how do you imagine your father will react to two Soldatian men arriving home with his daughter?"

"I honestly don't know," Laran admitted. "I *imagine* you will be welcomed and received with gratitude for bringing me home."

"And your mother? The rest of your family and community? Will they be scandalized when they find out you have been alone with us all this time?"

"Possibly," she said quietly. She stiffened against him. "But I have nothing to be ashamed of! And neither do you!"

Sheftu frowned. He knew well how a community could react to transgressions outside of the societal norm. He hoped she would not suffer because of them.

And what of the fact that she was no longer a virgin? Would that non-dazzling son of a bitch Jodpul be unwilling to wed her now?

Sheftu ground his teeth and hoped it was so. "Laran," he began. "I..." He hesitated. *I love you.*

"What is it?" Laran asked, looking up into his face. The firelight cast his features in gold. His eyes glittered like obsidian.

But he only shook his head. "Nothing," he finally mumbled. *Coward*, he admonished himself.

"What about your father, Sheftu? How will he react when he knows what you have done?"

"My father," Sheftu said, "is fiercely proud of his Morrow heritage and holds the honour and prestige of the Morrow House first among his priorities. Certainly higher than the wishes of his son. He will not be pleased to hear that I have left the Morrow House to return a slave girl to her homeland. And he will be even less pleased to hear that I have fueled the flames of Du-kar resentment in doing so."

Du-kar. Laran tensed at the very thought of the man. Memories of his cruelty flooded her senses and she felt herself pull away from Sheftu.

He leaned down to whisper against her hair. "That part of your life is over, Little Elf. Du-kar has no part in your future. Don't let his memory spoil a single moment of it."

She nodded stiffly. Sheftu was right. *Du-kar has no place in my life, no place in my heart.*

"What was it you did that angered him so much he tried to have you murdered?" she asked Sheftu.

"He had a thousand men of his own and nearly two thousand more from two other noble houses poised to re-invade Barraid and take more territory. I won enough support from the remaining noble houses to stop him in the senate. He lost credibility. And a great deal of money."

"Why, Sheftu? Why did you care?" She felt Sheftu shrug slightly.

"We had a treaty," he explained simply. "It wasn't right."

It was ironic, he thought. The Barraidi would never know how close they'd come to being re-invaded. They'd never know the role he'd played in averting another war. Given an opportunity, they'd gladly kill him for the unforgivable sin of being Soldatian.

Laran thought back to Sheftu's statement about his father. That he cared more for the status of the Morrow House than he did for the well-being of his second son clearly hurt him.

"I'm sorry," she whispered.

"For what?"

"I'm sorry if I have caused problems for you with your family."

Under the blanket his arm dropped to her waist and squeezed in a one-armed hug. "I fear I'm about to do the same for you, Little Elf."

Laran had a sudden sense of foreboding. Perhaps Sheftu was right. Perhaps there *would* be problems with her family. He was Soldatian. Would he be distrusted? *Despised?* Would they separate the two of them? Send him away?

She wiggled out of his embrace to kneel on the hard ground beside him. She placed her arms around his neck and kissed him gently at first and then with mounting fervour as apprehension about their reception solidified.

"Who knows what tomorrow may bring?" she said solemnly.

Urgency flooded through Sheftu, coupled with a nearly overwhelming sense of loss. He wrapped his arms around Laran and returned her kiss almost desperately. When she lay back against the earthen floor, he rose over her. Together they gave and took of each other with rising passion tinged with the fear of an unwanted future apart.

'Tomorrow,' the Barraidi mother had said of the Mirren soldiers. 'My husband thought they might be here tomorrow.'

Fringed by ferns, lit by fire glow, the visible world shrank to the confines of the tiny cavern under the overhanging roots. Darkness descended in the rain-soaked woods.

CHAPTER TWENTY-EIGHT

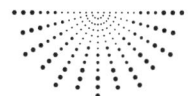

P ROVOS STIRRED IN his leafy nest. Daylight was beginning to work its way through the branches covering his burrow. He sat up slowly, shaking needles and tree bits from his hair and pushing branches and blankets aside. He scratched absently at an insect bite on his neck and tried to ignore his hunger.

Rain was still falling in these Barraidi woods, though there in the scrub trees, penetration through the dense foliage was minimal. Keeping low, Provos moved quietly to the edge of tree cover and peered through the underbrush where he had an unobstructed view of the headland and surrounding territory.

Some two hundred feet down the stream bank, Santago sat alone in the rain staring morosely into the water, his back to a rounded boulder, a fishing line, presumably the one dropped by the Barraidi mother, dangling from his hands.

Provos rose slowly and carefully scanned the area for movement. *Nothing.* It was absolutely quiet but for the splash of rain on the leaves. He stepped out of the woods and into the open.

"Santago," he called softly as he moved closer.

Santago jerked his head around and half sprang to his feet with a curse. He dropped the fishing line. This time it fell into the stream and was swept away in the muddy torrent. The little Mirren straightened.

"Provos," he breathed, obviously relieved. His gaze strayed beyond him and over the headland. "Where are the others?"

Provos, too, looked behind him and over the headland, but still nothing moved in the rainy landscape.

"Away," he said. "Come. I'll show you the way."

The Mirren hesitated. His hair had been plastered to his head by rain and rain ran down the wavy strands in rivulets over his face. He rubbed at it in annoyance and glanced again at the headland.

"All right," he said without enthusiasm.

"What did you learn?" Provos asked him as they walked away from the stream bank.

"There are two main routes through the mountains to the Mirren border," Santago replied from behind him. Though unseen, he patted his jacket pocket. "I have a map, here."

Provos nodded. "Good." He'd reached the entrance to the narrow deer path. "Anything else?"

"Brought food. Bread mostly, some apples, a little milk. Wine." Santago frowned at the woods. "Where are we going? Is it far? I don't see a trail."

"Not far," Provos told him. "We were spotted by a Barraidi family yesterday and decided to make camp away from the headland. The trail's all but invisible the first time you take it, but I've marked the way in places." He pushed branches aside and strode confidently into the trees.

"What else did you learn?" Provos asked.

"Nothing," Santago replied glancing over his shoulder once again. "Nothing else."

Provos stopped walking. He turned to stare at the little Mirren.

"Nothing?" he asked softly. He thought of the Barraidi mother's translated words: *'Everyone in town, everyone* everywhere *is talking about them.'*

Mirren soldiers, here in Barraid! And *this* Mirren doesn't mention them. *Why?*

"Nothing else," Santago repeated.

He met Provos' eyes and took a step back, alarmed at the Soldatian's expression.

"What?" he growled. He looked behind him again.

Provos, still watching Santago, widened his stance and slowly withdrew the hunting knife he wore at his waist. His free hand shot out and grasped Santago around the neck. He pushed him against a tree, and squeezed. With the other hand, he brought up the hunting knife, pierced the Mirren's tunic and pricked the skin over his heart.

"What are you playing at?" Provos snarled.

"What...?" Santago choked. "What're...you...talking...about?"

Provos leaned in close and spoke through his teeth.

"Mirren soldiers, you little bastard. At least fifty. Camped north of town."

Santago was using both hands now in a failing attempt at loosening Provos' grip. His eyes were rounded in fear and surprise. The sounds of choking suddenly ceased as his airway closed entirely.

Provos released him abruptly but kept his hand on his throat and his knife against the Mirren's chest.

Santago sucked in an enormous, wheezing breath and shook his head as vigorously as he could from the confines of Provos' grasp.

"You think I betrayed you?" Santago rasped.

"Did you?" Provos demanded.

The Mirren stopped trying to pry Provos' grip away and dropped his hand to pluck frantically at his shirt, withdrawing a knife of his own. He stabbed awkwardly at Provos' midsection and was rewarded when the Soldatian loosened his hold in shock.

Finally able to break Provos' hold, Santago slashed at him again, this time leaving a bloody trail across his bicep.

But the larger man quickly took the upper hand once more, this time pressing his knife to Santago's throat.

"What are you playing at?" Provos repeated. Pain sharpened his sense of urgency. He couldn't let anything happen to his cousin, here, so far from their homeland. And Laran! She would be completely vulnerable without them.

He let the tip of his blade sink into the Mirren's skin. "Speak," he ordered.

Santago suddenly relaxed. He smiled at Provos.

"Marked the trail, did you?" he said. His smile broadened to a grin.

Provos' eyes widened in sudden understanding and he turned quickly. Five Barraidi stood behind him on the narrow trail now, one with bow drawn and sighted not eight feet away. He felt Santago dart swiftly to the side.

Provos tensed. He, too, dodged to the side and the arrow, fired at close range and meant for his back, speared right through his shoulder from the front. The momentum carried him back a foot and pinned him against the tree he'd held Santago against. Pain flooded his upper chest and arm as he tried to jerk free, but the arrow was imbedded in the trunk and effectively held him in place. He reached behind him frantically with his other hand to pry the arrow loose, but the man with the bow had already sighted a second arrow. He let it fly.

It struck Provos in the chest.

He looked down at the protruding arrow in horror. *Sheftu,* he thought. *Sheftu, they are coming for you!* But the words remained unspoken. There was a curious black border on his vision and the sounds of rain and men's voices were diminishing. He was vaguely aware of Santago striking him in the jaw with his fist, but he felt nothing.

Provos' head sank onto his chest and his body crumpled beneath him. His weight tore his staked shoulder and dragged the arrow out of the tree as he fell.

The earth was cool and wet against his face and soft between his clenching fingers. His fears for the lives of his cousin and the girl with him faded as the black border on his vision grew. He sank into the soil and was enveloped.

CHAPTER TWENTY-NINE

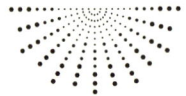

LARAN AND SHEFTU woke slowly, their limbs entwined beneath the blanket. The soft light of a new morning shone hazily into their refuge.

"Still raining," Laran said. "I love the sound it makes against the roof."

Sheftu looked up at the roof of their root shelter. It had kept them dry, and they'd kept each other warm.

"We got lucky, finding this." He rolled onto his side and caressed her cheek with one finger. Today was the day they expected to meet the Mirren soldiers.

Apprehension spiked through him and his pleasure at awakening there, with the woman he loved, was tarnished. He tried to shake it off.

"Perhaps Du-kar did me a favour," he told her quietly. "Had he not tried to have me murdered, I would not have met you."

Laran shivered at the unbidden image of Sheftu lying in the courtyard near the Morrow House, choking and writhing in agony, an arrow through his neck.

"Sheftu," she whispered in dismay. "I couldn't bear to lose you, even then, when I did not know you. You were the bringer of hope," she tried to explain once again. "When you smiled and laughed, and I saw you do both often, it reminded me that there might be joy in *my* world again someday, too."

She put both hands on his face and gazed into his beautiful raven eyes. "I didn't realize then that *you* would bring it to me." She was quiet a moment.

"I love you," she told him simply.

Sheftu's smile faded away in surprise. He stared in disbelief. Laran withdrew her hands abruptly.

"Don't worry," she said moving away. "I ask no more than you have already given. Is that not what you told me once?"

He sat up in the tiny cavern, feeling dazed. He looked down at Laran as though seeing her for the first time. His smile slowly reasserted itself, changed to a grin, which widened, and then finally he laughed outright. Still laughing, he grabbed her by both shoulders.

"You are a surprising woman," he told her. "A beautiful, courageous, surprising woman. I didn't think…" He hesitated, searching for the right words. "I am honoured that you could love me."

Honoured? Laran was disconsolate. *He was honoured she could love him.* He'd meant it as a compliment. That he didn't *return* her love was clear.

She'd been a fool.

Her chest began to hurt.

Sheftu was watching her carefully, saw the hurt in her eyes, saw the sudden sheen of tears.

He lowered his head to kiss each eye gently. "What is it? I've said something wrong." But Laran was shaking her head.

"It's only… I had hoped you could love me, too," she whispered.

Sheftu's eyes widened in surprise. "I *do* love you, Laran. Did you not know? By the Seven Gods, I swear it. I love you!" He laughed again, elated, and so did she.

"You love me!" She threw her arms around his neck and kissed him fiercely. "You love me," she repeated happily.

He pushed her away gently, still grinning. "The sun rose nearly two hours ago. Provos and Santago will soon be here." He glanced out into the dripping forest. "I'm surprised they are not here already."

His gaze returned to Laran. His expression was tender, his hands on her shoulders gentle. His beautiful black eyes crinkled at the corners as he smiled, his pleasure in her evident.

"Will you stay with me, Little Elf?" he asked her quietly. "Will you be mine?"

"I *am* yours, Sheftu," she told him, her voice solemn. "I've *been* yours since the first moment I saw you on the stone steps—I just didn't realize it then." She was quiet a moment. "Do you remember, Sheftu?"

He nodded, his face suddenly as serious as Laran's tone. "I do," he answered. "I remember."

He dipped to touch her lips with his. His hands roamed over her slender back and he drew her against him. His body's response was immediate.

And so was hers. The imminent arrival of Provos and Santago was forgotten.

But Laran pulled back to look into his eyes.

"I can't believe you love me," she said in amazement. "In Soldat, I was just a slave, nothing more."

Sheftu shook his head. "You," he said, his gaze locked with hers, "wore slave's garb and performed slave's tasks but you were never 'just' a slave." He was silent a moment as he thought out what he wanted to say.

"On the ship," he continued, "you told us you had to put your pride aside in order to survive. It endured, Laran. It surrounds you like an aura. It was likely the reason you attracted Du-kar's attention, the reason he wouldn't let you go. He wanted to break you and couldn't." He frowned, angry with himself for bringing up Du-kar, but he wasn't finished yet.

"Even struggling with a load far too heavy for you on those stone steps," he told her softly, "you carried yourself like a queen. Though you had little control of your own life, you demanded honour of yourself and those around you." He shook his head in wonder.

"No, Little Elf. *Never* were you 'just' a slave. Not to me."

Tears sprang into Laran's eyes once again and spilled down her cheeks, but instead of blinking them away, she let them fall.

"I thought myself unlucky," she told him. "Unlucky to have been abducted, unlucky to have been enslaved, unlucky to have been mistreated." She saw the ache in his eyes that it had been so, and she placed her hands on either side of his handsome face.

"But I was wrong," she whispered. "I would have endured it for you. For you I could endure anything."

He looked down at her in silence, distressed at her last statement. He drank in her beauty and her happiness. *In him!* That his admission of love had brought her happiness astonished him.

"Your family…" he began.

"Will grow to love you, just as I do. Give them time, Sheftu. It will be hard for them at first."

He nodded. *For mine as well.*

"And Jodpul…"

"He will understand," she interrupted again. She moved her hands away from his face and looked down at her lap. "Though, if he *has* waited, he may not be happy."

Sheftu frowned at both the reality of Jodpul and the fact that Laran found it troubling.

"What are you not telling me about Jodpul?" he asked.

Laran took a deep breath. "We grew up together, Jodpul and I. Though we have not yet officially Promised to one another, our eventual marriage was a life-long expectation. When we were children, we even play-acted the wedding we knew to be in our futures. It was an alliance that pleased both families for different reasons." She bit her lip. "He may not be happy," she repeated worriedly. *And his family will be furious.*

"Perhaps it is too soon to concern ourselves," Sheftu said quietly. "Perhaps our meeting with the Mirren soldiers and our preparations in case they are *not* here for you should be our first priority."

"*Ashaii*," she said distractedly. Her thoughts were obviously still in Mirren-Bar. She sat back.

"Sheftu?" she asked hesitantly. "When did you know?"

"That I loved you?" he asked. He smiled into her eyes. "Perhaps it was the moment in the courthouse when you spoke of love, when you asked if I could love someone like you... I told you I could. I do."

He gathered her gently to him and sat back against the back of the root cavern once again. The rain had begun to sound like music; the droplets slow in cadence now and varying in timbre.

"On the ship I knew for a certainty," he continued, "though still I fought against it. And then on the riverbank, when I realized how close I had come to losing you—this is when I finally admitted to myself what I had known almost all along."

"But why?" Laran looked up him. "Why could you not admit it? Was it because I was a slave? A foreigner? Your cousin warned you about getting involved with me. Was it because you knew it would be too difficult for you and your family?" She tried not to let the hurt she felt show in her voice. She pulled away from him suddenly, sure she understood the reason now. "It was too dangerous! You knew it would be dangerous because Dukar had claimed me!"

Sheftu frowned at her. "No," he told her shaking his head.

"My appearance, then," she guessed. "We Mirren find beauty where Soldatians do not. I would not be considered a pleasing woman in your country."

Sheftu laughed. "You would be considered a "pleasing" woman in any country, Little Elf."

"Then why, Sheftu? Why could you not admit to yourself that you loved me?"

He rested his head against the hard surface of the root cavern and listened to the slow cessation of the rain. It would continue to splatter against the roof of their shelter for some time as the trees above shed rainwater. He wished they could stay there, alone, for the rest of the day. He would make love to her again, this time slowly. Very slowly. The thought quickened his breath and a slow ache thrummed in his groin. He tried to turn his thoughts back to her question.

"You had been taken from the family and the home you loved and enslaved in my country," he told her. "You'd been hurt. Abused. You had no love for Soldatians. *I* am Soldatian. Why would you love me in return, Laran?"

Laran bit her lip but said nothing. *How could I not?*

"And then, after Tanile... I did not want to give myself to anyone. Truth be known, I didn't think I could."

Tanile! Laran hated the woman for hurting Sheftu.

"I could never use you like that," she told him earnestly.

He smiled once again. "You may use me as you please, so long as your love is at the core of it."

It was a concept she hadn't considered before. "We will use each other," she acknowledged. "And I will protect you, Sheftu. I won't let anything happen to you."

He grinned.

"Isn't that what I should be promising you?" His grin faded and he spoke seriously. "And I do. I *will* protect you, Laran, from physical harm, from unhappiness. I will keep you safe."

He looked into her eyes, willing her to understand what he also knew for a certainty now, that as much as she proclaimed herself his, so, too, did he proclaim himself hers.

He tightened his embrace and they sat in silence a few moments listening to the sounds of the dripping woods.

"Where *is* Provos, I wonder?" Laran said worriedly.

Sheftu shrugged. "Perhaps he slept past first light." His gaze slid out into the forest. "They should be here any minute." He dropped his arm from her shoulders and moved away, the air suddenly cold between them.

"If I am going to hunt, I'd better go. If the contingent the Barraidi mother spoke of is not here to provide escort, we'll need meat for the hard journey through the mountains."

He frowned as he contemplated that and shrugged out of the blankets. He draped them around Laran's shoulders. Her features, declaring her happiness only moments ago, now pronounced her unease.

"Stay warm," he told her, smiling. "I'll not travel more than an hour away. If I am not successful, I'll return then regardless."

"Wait," she told him firmly. "I'm coming with you." She began to rise. "Laran, one of us must stay here to meet Provos and Santago."

She saw, reluctantly, the logic in his words. She was likely a better bowman than he, though he wouldn't know that yet, but he was far better at tracking and finding game. She sat back down in the tiny cavern, her golden eyes troubled.

"Return to me quickly, Sheftu."

He ducked at the entrance to their sanctuary and straightened on the other side.

"*Aey*, Little Elf. I'll take care. You do the same."

She scrabbled to the entrance to watch him stride off through the rain-soaked woods in the direction of the clearing.

The Smiling Man. Her *Smiling Man.* She shook her head at the strange twists and turns of fate and sat back to stir the embers of their fire back to life.

He loved her!

She felt as though her heart might burst with joy.

Joy! Sheftu had returned it to her. And soon he would help her return to the arms of her family.

Dread stilled her hand and settled over her like a shroud. She hadn't told him what he needed to know.

I will tell him the truth the moment he returns. The very moment! She fervently hoped he'd still want her when he understood what she'd kept from him.

CHAPTER THIRTY

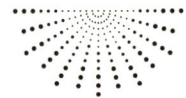

"LORD SHEFTU!" SANTAGO called. And then in a different tone altogether, "Laran Tania!"

Laran could hear his voice drifting through the trees. They must be in the meadow! She threw off her blanket, pulled on the short Barraidi jacket Santago had found for her, and shambled in an awkward half-crouch out of the root cavern.

"Santago," she shouted. "Wait there! I'm on my way!"

She raced out into the drizzling woods and into the grey light of the clearing, waving at the little Mirren. He approached her, his smile open and friendly.

"Where is Lord Sheftu?" he asked looking around.

"Hunting," Laran replied. "He expected to return in an hour, and it must be close to that now." She peered behind his back.

"Where's Provos?" she asked in return.

Santago grinned good-naturedly. "Also hunting," he told her. "Guess we'll have no shortage of meat for the journey."

Laran nodded. "What did you learn?" she asked, her words an unknowing echo of Provos'.

But Santago didn't answer. He was looking at her closely. She looked different somehow, more at ease. Happier. He stiffened suddenly and pushed his curly hair off his face. His brows descended over his gold-flecked eyes and the expression in those eyes turned dark.

She'd dishonoured Mirren-Bar! He could see it in her. She'd let that Soldatian bastard put his hands on her; she'd probably let him bed her!

He'd bet every Barraidi lirar he'd stolen off that hapless corpse that it was so!

"What is it?" she asked in alarm. "What's happened?"

Santago stifled a snarl. *No matter,* he told himself. The Tania would not learn of her dishonour until *after* she had been returned by the contingent of Mirren soldiers searching for her. He would have collected his reward by that time.

And the Soldatian lord would be dead and rotting in the Barraidi woods along with the corpse of his kinsman.

"Gather your belongings," he said. His carefully modulated voice carried a hint of venom and Laran was unnerved.

She placed her hand on his arm. "Santago, has something happened?" she asked again.

He looked down at her hand as though it was soiling his best tunic. "Clearly," he muttered grimly. He removed her hand from his arm disdainfully. "Gather your belongings," he ordered raising his voice slightly. "We're going back to the headland."

Laran stared in bemusement and not a little fear. Santago's sudden change in demeanor from smiling friendliness to what appeared to be barely restrained violence was inexplicable. And now he was issuing orders?

"Santago," Laran began slowly, "I will remain here until Lord Sheftu returns. It won't be long." She blinked at his expression.

He wanted to strike her. She could see it in his eyes; in the way he held his body.

"I don't understand what has upset you so," she began. She took another step backwards. "Is it that we did not camp at our agreed upon site on the headland? We encountered a Barraidi family there yesterday, and…"

Santago grabbed her arm and yanked her hard enough that she nearly lost her footing. He all but dragged her six or seven feet toward the deer trail.

"Unhand me!" she shouted. "You forget yourself, Mirren!"

"And will you tell me you did not forget *yourself*, that you did not forget your place as Tania? Will you stand there and tell me you did not allow that filthy *Soldatian* to dishonour you?"

"What?" Laran sputtered. She tried to wrench her arm free of his painful grip but failed. He continued dragging her toward the woods.

"I have done nothing wrong!" She tried to plant her feet, to dig her heels in to stop him. "And by the Holy Ones, who are *you* to question my actions, Santago?" She jerked sideways trying to free herself, but he tightened his hold, cutting off her circulation.

"You are hurting me," Laran gasped.

But Santago only pulled her after him as he brushed aside branches to enter the deer trail. Unable to keep her balance, she tripped over a log and would have fallen but for his agonizing hold on her arm. She steadied herself and aimed a hard kick at his shins, but the soft Barraidi boots did no damage.

Santago glared at her.

"Let…me…go!" she demanded with as much authority as she could muster.

The little Mirren stopped short, his eyes aimed above her head, his hostile expression turning darker yet.

"What are you doing here, Trand?" he hissed in Barraidi, his voice dangerously soft. "I told you to wait at the headland."

Laran turned her head to see four rough-looking Barraidi men appear on the trail behind them. They took positions lounging against trees, but they looked anything but casual. A fifth, a man with long, knotted hair, straddled the path, effectively blocking the route back to the clearing, his arms folded across a massive chest.

"And so you did," Trand agreed readily enough. He turned to his companions. "What do you think, my friends? The Mirren here didn't mention a woman. Looks like he wanted her all to himself, yes?"

He didn't sound annoyed with Santago. What he sounded was… excited.

All five were looking at her hungrily now and one licked his lips in coarse anticipation. Laran felt the blood drain from her face.

"By the Holy Ones, Santago," she breathed. Still held in his vice-like grip, she moved as far away from the men as his reach would allow. Her voice dropped to a whisper. "Let me go."

The Barraidi were laughing, pushing one another playfully in companionable competition, evidently to see who would get Laran first.

"Please, Santago," Laran implored. "Let me go now. Let me *run!*"

The man with the knotted hair addressed Santago with a twisted smile. "Don't look so worried, Mirren. We'll do as we were hired to do. Truth be known, though, we'd 'a killed both Soldatians for free." He laughed and so did his cohorts.

"Now," Trand said, his good humour vanishing suddenly, "give us the woman."

"That wasn't part of the deal," Santago said angrily. "She's coming with me back to the headland."

"Time for a new deal," one of the other Barraidi said. He rubbed his crotch lewdly and grinned a brown-toothed grin. He moved forward and latched his meaty hand onto Laran's other arm. He looked down at Santago threateningly.

"Let go of her, little man," he ordered.

The Mirren sailor was watching the brown-toothed man, clearly debating his next move. The Barraidi was big, outweighing the smaller Mirren by at least fifty pounds. So did his companions.

Santago relaxed suddenly and smiled. He half-turned to Laran. "Not likely you're a virgin anymore anyway," he sneered in Mirren.

And with that he abruptly let go of her arm leaving her to the Barraidi.

Oh no. By the Holy Ones, no! Sheftu! Come for me, Sheftu!

But no! He mustn't come! *They'll kill him, sure.*

Laran tried to wrench her arm free once again, but the brown-toothed man slid his eyes sideways toward her. They were narrowed with implied threat.

"See that the Soldatian dies as agreed," Santago was saying. He turned his back and began to walk away. "I go to meet the Mirren contingent," he called over his shoulder. "And Trand, do not allow your men to kill the woman. She is valuable."

Trand grunted his disdain.

"Valuable," leered the brown-toothed man, his gaze raking over Laran suggestively. "Won't be once we're done with her," he muttered, laughing cruelly. He pulled her against him.

Santago stopped on the trail and turned to face them once more. He looked impassively at Laran who was being held against the Barraidi's chest, his continuing grip on her arm obviously painful. She looked very small in comparison to her captor. Her golden eyes were huge with fear and her face was pale.

"See that she is returned to the headland when you are done with her. And, Trand," Santago warned softly. "You'd better hope Mirren soldiers do not see you defiling her." He turned and disappeared into the trees.

Laran's heart pounded against her ribcage. *Santago had betrayed them! He'd hired these men to kill Sheftu and Provos. Was that why Provos hadn't come to the clearing? Was he already dead?*

By all that is sacred, I cannot allow Sheftu to be next!

Laran stifled a sob. The Barraidi's hold on her arm was excruciating now, and all efforts to free herself were futile.

152

If your adversary outweighs you, use your wits. Her father's words resounded in her memory. *How? What can I do? What?* She glanced over at the leader of these men, Trand. When he bent over, she glimpsed a small leather sheath tucked against the small of his back. It was barely visible under his waist-length jacket. A *ceilid!* Not more than three inches long, the ceremonial dagger was integral to every Barraidi male over the age of twelve.

The brown-toothed man must have one on him somewhere.

Laran let her knees give way, let herself go slack in the Barraidi's agonizing grasp, closed her eyes and let her head loll forward. The brown-toothed man swore at the unconscious female he believed he held and dropped her roughly to the ground. He rolled her half over with his foot, then aimed a frustrated kick at her mid-section.

Laran remained unresponsive, though the sudden explosion of pain in her ribs was nearly overwhelming. She felt herself on the teetering edge of blacking out in reality and fought with every fibre of her being to remain absolutely still. And alert.

"Mirren," Trand scoffed. "One run away and one fainted. And didn't we all grow up hearing tales of how tough they are?" He snorted. "Seems those tales were exaggerated."

He glanced at the brown-toothed man who was winding up for another boot at Laran's mid-section. "Leave off, Frenel. You can't kick her awake." He laughed again, this time at his own joke.

Frenel stared down at her in disgust. "She'll be no fun unconscious," he grumbled.

"Strip her," another's gravelly voice said. "Let's see what she's kept us waiting for."

There was a chorus of ascension and a rough hand reached for the neck of her tunic. And yanked.

CHAPTER THIRTY-ONE

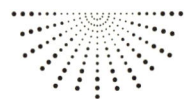

S HEFTU WAS SMILING in anticipation. Though he'd only been gone the better part of an hour, he'd had success with his hunt and time to relive their admission of love for one another.

Laran loved him!

His smile widened. His life, so uncertain only a few hours ago, suddenly seemed blessed. That this remarkable, beautiful woman could love him was astonishing. And she *did* love him. He shook his head in wonder.

By the Seven Gods, how he loved her in return!

Grey clouds hung low over the trees as he thrust through the knee-high heather and low brush of the clearing. Bird song was re-asserting itself in the drenched woods now and overhead a red-tailed hawk left its refuge to begin the hunt interrupted by the torrential rains of the day before.

"Laran," he called quietly.

Drops of water spattered the back of his neck as he pushed foliage aside to see into the fern-fringed shelter provided by the uprooted tree.

"Laran," he said again. He frowned at the blankets. Was she was lying beneath, perhaps curled on her side and sound asleep?

No. She wasn't there.

He straightened to his full height and glanced about the woods surrounding the root cavern. *Where is she?* He stooped once more to look inside the shelter. Her jacket was missing, but everything else was still there, including the remaining weapons and the food-stores. *She can't be far away.*

He looked down at the two geese he held and reluctantly dropped them to the earth near the root cave.

He retraced his steps to the clearing, climbed into the low branches of a large tree at the perimeter, and surveyed the meadow and its circle of surrounding forest from on high.

There were no movements in the misty landscape but the fluttering of tiny birds and the graceful pursuit of a chestnut marten, its sinuous body undulating with the uneven terrain, it's prey unseen.

Provos and Santago would surely have returned by now. *Where are they?*

The euphoria Sheftu felt only moments earlier faded away. Concern for Laran's safety took root. And grew.

"Laran!" Sheftu suddenly shouted. He remained out of sight but continued to watch, and listen, carefully.

Nothing! No answering shout, no good-natured wave from the other side of the clearing. Nothing at all.

I shouldn't have left her! I should have stayed until Provos returned.

Sheftu's stomach lurched. He climbed down from his perch and dropped the remaining few feet to the ground.

He searched the forest behind him and the clearing before him one more time, his eyes and ears straining for a hint of Laran's or Provos' presence.

He ran his fingers through his hair in agitation. Something was definitely wrong. He could feel it.

Wrong!

He set off at a run for the deer path leading back toward the headland. With the exception of the game trail he'd followed hunting, it was the only known avenue of travel out of the area of the clearing.

* * *

LARAN FELT THE eyes of all five Barraidi as one among them tore at her clothing. She kept her own eyes closed, her body limp, even when she felt the rip of the fabric covering her. Terror snaked through her and she began to doubt the wisdom of feigning unconsciousness. At least the horrid Frenel, the brown-toothed man, had released his hold on her arm, allowing her *some* hope of escape.

Now, though, she could hear the men closing in around her, *all* around her. *Wait. Perhaps not* all *around her!* The muted light easing through the thick woods was brighter on one side, her right. Perhaps no one stood there!

The long tunic split, the sound of ripping cloth drowned by the gleeful cheer of one of the men, presumably the one doing the ripping. He stopped tugging on her clothing and must have risen.

Laran remained unresponsive, her limbs lifeless. She peeked through the slits of her eyes to see a man standing above her, one hand raised, the remnants of her torn tunic dangling from his hands like a trophy. He was grinning and yelling something at the other men and his companions laughed and began to turn their attention back to the small woman lying, vulnerable, at their feet.

Laran jumped to her own and kneed the man standing over her in the groin. Still holding the torn fabric aloft, he shrieked in pain then hit the ground with his side, making an effective, though momentary, barrier on the narrow deer trail.

As he fell, Laran spied the *ceilid* tucked into the small of his back. She seized it, spun on her heel and plunged down the deer trail to her right in the direction of the headland. Behind her, *close* behind her, she could hear the furious shouts of the Barraidi as they all but trampled their still shrieking companion in their enthusiasm for the pursuit.

Laran sprinted down the path. Her lead-time was slight. She smacked branches out of her way with her bare arms, unaware of the cuts and scrapes left by the sharper twigs of dead boughs. She leapt over tree falls and splashed through muddy sections, straining, always straining for the markers Provos left in the muted light of the dripping woods.

She *couldn't* lose her way now, not now when any delay would mean her capture.

As she darted around the wide trunk of a rough-barked tree, she skidded to a stop so suddenly that she lost her footing and slid several feet, her momentum carrying her to within an arm's reach of Santago.

The Mirren jerked his head around in surprise, and Laran scrambled back out of reach, her feet sliding out from under her on the muddy trail. She splashed down hard on her buttocks, her hands in the wet muck behind her. The *ceilid* skimmed away.

Eyes wide and focused on the traitorous Santago, one clenching fist closed on a rounded rock. Santago smirked and moved closer to her. Laran reached a muddied hand toward him as though requesting assistance and the Mirren leaned down to grab her hand. As he pulled her to her feet, Laran brought her other fist up and smashed the stone against his temple.

Santago staggered back, howling in outrage. He balled his own hands into fists. Laran ducked low, dodging his blow. She snatched a short, stout branch off the ground, closed both hands around it, and smashed it against Santago's knees as she rose. He attempted to leap back out of range, but one of his battered knees crumpled beneath him. As he strove to regain his balance, Laran straightened, twisted around him and walloped the back of his head.

The branch broke. Santago went down.

Behind her, Laran could hear the Barraidi. *Only a few feet away now!* Still out of sight but just behind the wide tree trunk, they thundered down the path, fury evident in their voices. *Run!*

She cast about for the *ceilid*, saw it glinting dully in the half-light at the edge of the path, and snatched it up.

She ran.

Santago, a prone and bleeding obstacle on the path, gave her pursuers little pause. One of the men was gaining. Laran could feel him close on her heels, even imagined she felt his breath on the back of her neck.

Run, she admonished herself again, though her gait faltered slightly as she registered what she was seeing ahead.

Provos, an arrow protruding from his chest, lay, lifeless, at the side of the path near the end of the deer trail.

The hoary edge of panic rose in her throat.

She burst out of the woods and into the open. Light flooded her eyes, temporarily blinding her, but she kept her feet moving just the same. *There!* To the left was the actual headland, to the right the path by the creek the Barraidi mother had taken. Laran swerved to the right.

Trand crashed into her from behind, landing heavily upon her, driving the air from her lungs, and crushing her against the rocky ground. When he rose to his knees, she scrambled out from under him, but, breathless and weakened as she was, he grabbed her by one leg and hauled her back. She twisted around to kick at his chest and landed a solid blow. He grunted and released her.

Still gasping for air, she jumped to her feet and pitched into the swiftly moving creek, trying to submerge her body and lose herself in the current. But Trand, swearing loudly, saw her strategy, loped downstream and jumped in, wading waist deep into the flood to grab hold of her once again.

He dragged her out of the water, up the creek bed, and over to the long yellow grass of the headland. He threw her to the ground and stood above her, legs apart and fists balled.

"Mirren *bitch,*" he snarled.

Laran sat back in the grass, terror gelling her muscles and making her mute.

Don't do this, she silently begged. *Please let me go.* A sob welled up in her chest as the rest of the men caught up to them. *No.* She wouldn't give in to tears, not for the likes of *these.* She put one hand out to try to forestall them.

"My people," she began shakily, "will reward you well if you deliver me to them, safe. Unharmed."

Trand stared down at her, his brows lowered over angry eyes.

"That," Laran suddenly realized, "was what Santago was going to do! It must be! *He* wanted to bring me to the Mirren soldiers for the reward! *You* could have it now!" she added desperately.

She looked around at the Barraidi assembled above her. All were winded, and two looked furious. The others looked eager. They were staring at her openly, lustfully, and one made a crude gesture when she met his eyes.

"Shut up," Trand ordered. He began to unfasten his trousers.

No! Laran swung one leg out sideways in an attempt to topple him, but his stance was wide and his weight too much for her. She rolled to her stomach, gathered her legs beneath her, and thrust herself forward, crashing into one of the men who, instinctively trying to dodge her, moved slightly to the side. She careened past him and he made a grab for her, catching her by the hair and pulling her backwards.

Instead of recoiling, Laran allowed herself to be pulled against the man's chest. She brought both arms down over the back of her head and stabbed at the hand wrapped in her hair with the tiny *ceilid*. When the man's grip suddenly went slack, she wrenched her hair away and launched herself off the man's chest.

Free! She'd gained her freedom once more! She ran as swiftly as she could, for the headland this time, but Frenel was faster now. And stronger. He caught up to her, grasped her around the waist with a muscular arm, and punched her in the side of the face with his fist.

Laran fell backward onto the rocks striking her head. She didn't feel it.

Her vision clouded grey, darkened, and then turned black. She barely heard the shouts of her captors before the descending silence became absolute.

CHAPTER THIRTY-TWO

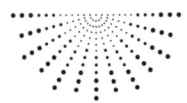

S HEFTU STOPPED ABRUPTLY on the deer trail, arrested by the sight in front of him. Facedown on the path ahead lay Santago. He was out cold. Or dead.

Sheftu dropped his bow and knelt at the Mirren's side, noting the blood seeping into his curly hair from a wide cut on the back of his head. He rolled him over carefully. A livid bump in the centre of Santago's temple was beginning to swell.

"Santago," Sheftu said, shaking the shorter man gently. A sense of urgency was escalating, and it was all he could do not to slap the insensible man.

Santago stirred, moaning. He looked up at Sheftu with unfocused eyes, and then started in surprise when he finally recognized the Soldatian lord. He tried to sit up but his attempts were clumsy and awkward.

"Let me help you," Sheftu said, placing his arm under Santago's back to elevate him. "What happened here?"

Santago touched the back of his head then paused to inspect the blood on his fingers. He willed his mind to sharpen. *Think!* he told himself. He looked up at Sheftu and recalculated his course of action.

"Barraidi," Santago told Sheftu. "Barraidi hunting party. Must have knocked me out."

"Laran?"

"Haven't seen her," he told Sheftu. His eyes closed and his head rolled back on his shoulders.

"Santago!" Sheftu said. He shook him harder now. "Where's Provos?"

"Don't know," he told Sheftu groggily.

Sheftu eased his arm out from behind him and Santago slumped back onto the wet ground. Sheftu rose, apprehension for Laran and his cousin foremost in his mind. He looked down the trail toward the headland. *Are they there? Could they be?*

Let them still be alive!

"I'll be back for you," he told Santago. He slung his bow over his shoulder once again and shrugged the pack he still carried on his back into better position, and then set out down the path at a run, leaving Santago slumped on the trail.

Bright grey light insinuated itself into the woods as he drew nearer the headland. He stopped moving just inside the tree line, intending to situate himself where he could look out at the open terrain without being seen.

But that tactic, and all thought, was effectively erased from his mind.

Provos lay to one side of the path, an arrow protruding from his chest. He was utterly still. Blood bathed his neck and one shoulder, soaking his upper chest in scarlet. He did not appear to be breathing.

Provos! No! By the Seven Gods! He can't be dead!

Sheftu tried to smother the urge to go to his kinsman. He tried to push Provos from his thoughts altogether, but a curious numbness had taken hold of his body and was dulling his mind. Shock was setting in. Overwhelming grief was close behind.

No. I can't give in. Not now! I need my wits until I know Laran is safe.

He finally wrenched his attention away and dropped to his stomach. He eased to the entrance of the path on his belly and took a position in the underbrush just short of the long grass.

Provos. His cousin's body drew him like a magnet. He glanced behind him once more, staring at the bloodied chest. He willed it to rise and fall but saw no sign of life. *Nothing.* The impaling arrow remained inert.

He jerked his head around, aware now of the shouts of men in the near distance.

There! He could make out three Barraidi, rough-looking men draped with a variety of weapons and moving together towards two more of their kind. Something struggled against the chest of one of those two. Sheftu strained to understand what he was seeing.

A small figure suddenly propelled itself away from the man and rushed into the open. Sheftu had a fleeting impression of brown curls and bare, white legs as the figure dashed up the grassy bank toward the headland, one of the Barraidi in close pursuit. And gaining.

Laran!

Fear coursed through Sheftu and turned his guts to liquid. He leapt to his feet, slinging the bow from his shoulder and reaching behind him for the arrows attached to the sheath on his pack. He slid one across the cording, took quick aim, and let it fly.

As he strung the second arrow, he'd already planned his next move. Yelling, *roaring*, in anger, he sped towards his adversaries.

Only vaguely aware of the uneven ground under his booted feet or the lash of the long grass against his bare hands, Sheftu's concentration was solely on the scene playing out on the headland now. As he'd strung the first arrow, his intended target had reached Laran and yanked her roughly off her feet. The Barraidi had drawn back his free arm.

When the arrow hit him, the man had already struck her in the face with his fist and she was falling to the rocky ground. Sheftu saw the man jerk backwards, flailing at the arrow lodged just out of reach in his back.

Fury and fear coursed thick and hot through Sheftu's body and threatened to overpower him, but he tamped it down. He needed to think! Surprise had been his only ally and that was gone now.

The arrow-shot man thrashed wildly with his hands behind him trying to dislodge the arrow. He screamed for help in his own language.

But Frenel's four companions were already on the move. They were sprinting through the long grass, racing toward Sheftu, their weapons ready. One, the leader perhaps, bellowed an order and Sheftu heard the word "Soldatian" in the Barraidi command. It seemed to spur the men on, and they shrieked out their hatred as they ran.

The distance was closing between them.

Sheftu's second arrow, let loose as he advanced, struck one of the men in the abdomen and that Barraidi suddenly stopped yelling and crumpled to the ground, silenced.

Sheftu contemplated moving back into the trees, using them for cover, and trying to pick off the Barraidi one by one, but fury made him bold.

He threw the bow aside as he neared the three remaining Barraidi. He withdrew his short sword from its sheath with one hand. He palmed his hunting knife with the other.

They came together in a crash of weapons and bone, blood and shouted obscenities.

A knife scored Sheftu's chest, leaving a swath of pure fire in its wake, and a sword plunged into his upper thigh. But the Barraidi had underestimated their adversary.

Sheftu felt no pain. Fear was no longer a factor. Two thoughts drove him forward: he would kill these bastards for what they had done. He would survive to help Laran.

He spun on his heel, drove his short sword into Trand's throat, and stabbed backwards with his knife hand. He felt resistance against the smaller weapon as it pierced a Barraidi shoulder. The knife-wounded man jumped back out of harm's way, grasping his bloodied shoulder and crying out in his own language.

Trand fell to the ground, eyes wide with shock, blood bubbling from the gaping wound in his neck. He grabbed at it with both hands, his legs thrashing.

The third Barraidi abruptly ceased his assault, his eyes first on his fallen leader who was still now, and then on his wounded companion. He looked around for the others, but the only indicators that they'd ever been there were the indentations in the long grass where their bodies now lay. The Soldatian was a formidable enemy. Continuing the attack suddenly seemed unwise.

The Barraidi backed up slowly, both hands in the air now, palms forward. He mumbled something conciliatory.

Sheftu snarled his disdain and started forward, blood on his hands and staining his tunic and upper leg. The shoulder-wounded man seemed to see Sheftu's wounds for the first time and grew more confident. He urged his companion on, his tone cajoling.

He lunged at Sheftu abruptly.

Sheftu blocked his knife thrust with his arm and slashed the short sword across the man's midsection. The Barraidi stumbled to his knees, the expression on his face one of total surprise. His eyes rolled up and he fell, face-first, to the ground, dying.

His companion turned and ran.

Sheftu started after him but abandoned the chase almost immediately. He thoughts were on Laran now. *Where is she?* He felt fear clutch at his belly again.

Where?

He looked upstream and saw her a short distance from the creek bed. She lay unmoving in the shorter grass of the rocky headland. She was all but naked. Souls of the Dead, please let her be alive!

Dread kept the pain of his wounds at bay as he sprinted up the terrain towards her. Behind him he heard the thunder of horses and the shouts of men.

Soldiers had appeared on the outskirts of the headland, though it was doubtful they'd spotted him yet.

"Laran," Sheftu said softly as he reached her. She was lying on her side, one arm over her face, the other above her head. Her tunic had evidently been torn from her. It hung in shreds, barely covering her. Her bare legs were streaked and muddy. A long abrasion marked most of one thigh and small cuts and bruises, purpled and swollen, peppered her arms.

He rolled her over gently. "Laran," he said again, his voice ragged and breaking. "Wake, Little Elf."

One side of her face was swollen and bruised. It was barely recognizable. She remained motionless.

On his knees, Sheftu stripped off his bloodied shirt, wadded it and placed it under Laran's head. In the near distance he thought he could hear Santago's voice, but his concentration was on Laran now.

He placed two fingers to her neck to feel for a pulse. *Nothing.* He stared down at her chest. Was it rising? He thought he saw it rise! He moved his fingers slightly, pressing on her throat once again. *Live, Laran! By the Seven Gods, live!*

He felt the cold tip of a sword on his bare back and slowly rose. He turned around.

A well-armed Mirren soldier of middle years stood behind him silently, his eyes on Laran, his face a mask of horror. When his gaze slid to Sheftu, something else kindled in his golden eyes. *Rage.*

It was sheer rage.

Behind the man a growing flank of Mirren soldiers filled Sheftu's vision and began to surround him. Those that could see Laran looked aghast and one by one their eyes fell on Sheftu hard. From somewhere far outside of himself he wondered if these men thought *he* was responsible for the abuse so evident on the body of the Mirren woman before them.

He turned back to Laran, the mounting number of Mirren soldiers becoming less of a concern in his mind. He bent over Laran, trying once again to feel a pulse. He'd breathe life back into her body if he had to. He'd…

The sword bit into his back, and Sheftu felt blood roll down his skin to soak into the fabric at his waist. Nearly sick with a sense of impending loss, he tried to ignore it. *Laran*, he thought numbly, *live! Live for me, Laran.*

"Get up!" the sword-bearer hissed. His voice was heavily accented. The sword bit more deeply.

"She's hurt," Sheftu told the man without turning around. He knew it sounded foolish. "Do you have a physician? She's hurt!"

Four sets of strong arms jerked him up from Laran's side. They dragged him away and into the tall grass.

"No!" he was shouting, alarmed. *Why were they not helping her?*

Another Mirren, a little taller than the rest, his handsome face framed by silver curls and his expression intense, pushed his way into the circle of men. The Mirren soldiers deferred to him immediately, moving aside in unison. When he reached Laran, he cried out inarticulately and dropped to his knees on the ground beside her. The circle of soldiers closed around them and Sheftu could no longer see him.

The first soldier, the sword-bearer, broke away from the group and issued orders to the men holding him. His voice was seething with anger. The men forced Sheftu's arms behind him, intending to bind him.

"What are you doing?" he shouted. The pain of his wounds was beginning to assert itself and, weakened and exhausted now, he felt his mind beginning to dull.

Should he fight these men? He was considerably larger than most of them. But they were Laran's people. They were Mirren! Surely it was obvious that it wasn't *he* that had hurt her?

He allowed himself to be bound, his hands behind his back, but he remained standing, naked to the waist, bloodied, and still staring at the circle of Mirren who shielded Laran from his view.

Mirren! A sudden realization widened his eyes. Did any among them have the power of healing? Was the man the soldiers had deferred to a Healer?

Like Laran? *Was he helping her?* What in the Seven Layers was happening there?

The sword-bearer approached him, staring up at him ominously. "Tishane?" Sheftu asked him. "Are you Tishane?"

The man looked startled.

"I am Sheftu, second son to the Lord of the Morrow House. It was I who sent you the message." Sheftu's eyes skimmed above his head to the circle of Mirren soldiers surrounding Laran. "Is someone helping her?" he asked.

But Tishane only gestured to one of his men, who ran off immediately to do his captain's bidding. He returned moments later with Santago in tow, a gruesome lump decorating his forehead.

"Santago!" Sheftu said. He'd never been so pleased to see the little Mirren. "Explain to these men…"

But Santago ignored him and spoke directly to Tishane in Mirren, his explanation long, his gestures and speech seemingly punctuated by damning rhetoric. The eyes of the soldiers within earshot had turned to granite as they listened. They stared at Sheftu malevolently.

"What are you doing, Santago?" Sheftu asked him softly. He frowned. Was the little sailor spinning lies? Was he *betraying* him?

Santago bowed to Tishane and moved away. The sailor threw a backward glance at Sheftu, sneering contemptuously, then stalked off, his usual gait marred by a painful limp.

"Tishane," Sheftu said, eyeing the man. "Captain! Is Laran going to be all right? Is someone helping her?"

Tishane stared up at his Soldatian captive, enmity narrowing his golden eyes.

"She is dead," he told him slowly.

CHAPTER THIRTY-THREE

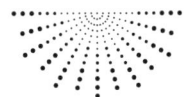

"PAPA?" LARAN ASKED. There was a strange glow at the edges of her vision and the image of the man in front of her was wavering and hazy. She blinked heavily. It *looked* like her father. But it couldn't be.

Why can't I think?

She tried to look around her, tried to elevate herself to a seated position, but the wavering image of her father put a hand on her chest and gently pushed her back down. His words were tender and kind, his voice warm and soothing and she half-smiled at the comfort offered.

Still, something stabbed at her consciousness and she tried to will her mind to sharpen.

Sheftu. A sudden surge of fear honed her wits. *Sheftu! Was he safe?* "Papa?" she asked again. She tried to squint the man into focus.

"It is I, my daughter," the man replied quietly. He sounded sorrowful. "Rest, now," he told her. He brought her hand to his lips and kissed it softly. "You are with your own people now."

"Am... am I home?" *What is the matter with me?* Her mind was clouding again. *Why can't I think?*

"Soon, Laran. You will be home very soon now. Your mother and sister await you."

"I've missed them," she murmured, her sense of self and the world around her muddled. What was it she needed to know?

The Tania nodded silently. "They will be overjoyed to see you." He hesitated a moment. "As I was," he added quietly.

He hadn't given up. He'd searched exhaustively, every lead a dead end, every thread of hope severed, until the morning they'd received the message from Soldat. She still lived! His daughter was alive and returning to Mirren-Bar!

He'd known it was foolhardy for a man in his position to accompany his men into Barraid, but how could he not? He wanted, no, he *needed* to see his daughter with his own eyes. He *needed* her to understand that no matter what she had been through, she would be welcomed back into the arms of her family with joy, with celebration, and with love.

And then a lone Mirren sailor had approached the contingent with news: Laran Tania was only a day's travel away. The Tania's initial jubilance was corrupted by dread as he learned from Santago that his daughter was in the hands of two Soldatian kinsmen, unscrupulous men who had enslaved and abused her time and again in Soldat, men who'd raped and terrorized her on the perilous journey through Barraid.

These were men whose ignoble intention to return her was prompted solely by the money they imagined would be their reward.

They had learned differently.

The Tania knew that second sons of Soldatian lords did not inherit their family's estates. They were frequently cast aside and impoverished when their elder brothers became lords of the noble houses. It was not unimaginable, then, that this young Lord Sheftu and his kinsman, a man even farther away from inheriting from the Morrow Lord, might hatch such a scheme.

The corpses of murdered Barraidi hunters littered the landscape where Laran had been found. The sailor, Santago, had led his men to the bloodied body of a Soldatian, which lay just inside a wooded trail. This, Santago told them, had been the kinsman.

The kinsman was the lucky one, the Tania thought darkly. His eyes turned cold.

The other, the second son, the young Lord Sheftu, would not be as fortunate.

"Papa," Laran said weakly. "Where is Sheftu, Papa?" "Fear not, my daughter. He will never hurt you again."

"What do you mean?" she mumbled in confusion. She blinked heavily, trying to focus, trying to remain awake.

"He no longer lives, Laran."

Laran's heavy eyes opened wide.

"Dead?" she whispered. *No! Oh, no, please, no!* Her eyes filled with tears and spilled down her face. "No," she said aloud. She shook her head only vaguely aware that it no longer pained her to do so. She tried to sit up once again.

"His b...body," she stammered. Grief was surging through her, an unstoppable torrent. "I... I need to see him." *It must be a mistake! Perhaps he is just hurt. Perhaps I can heal him!*

The Tania tried to reassure her.

"He is dead and gone, my daughter. Long gone. His body was tossed into the flooded creek and will be at the bottom of the great river by now."

His expression softened in distress as he watched his daughter. She was weeping softly even as her eyelids closed. She was succumbing once again to the sleeping draught she had been administered. Tears continued to leak from her eyes and she began to sob in her sleep, the sound heartbreakingly mournful.

Clearly the Soldatian had traumatized her.

Though her body had been repaired, only time would mend the damage to her spirit. With luck she would remain insensible in healing sleep until they arrived in Mirren-Bar.

CHAPTER THIRTY-FOUR

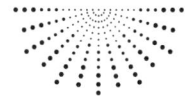

THE JARRING BLAST of pain across his chest startled Sheftu out of fitful sleep. A Mirren soldier stood above him, contempt shadowing his face. He was holding a short whip.

"Get up, Soldatian," he ordered.

Sheftu looked down at his chest. The shallow knife slash he'd suffered at the hands of the Barraidi had begun to scab over, but the lash had opened it again. Three thin lines of blood flowed freely down his naked chest and across his ridged stomach to soak into the fabric of his trousers.

He struggled to climb to his feet but the wound in his thigh was becoming more and more painful. His balance, hindered by his bound hands, was off, and his movements were slow and awkward.

He gasped in renewed pain as the lash hit him again, this time across his shoulders as he rose. He felt his skin tear open, felt his blood run down his back, liquid and warm. The lash fell a third time.

Sheftu straightened to his full height, a full head above his tormentor, and glared at the shorter Mirren, fury glinting in his obsidian eyes. The smaller man, though clearly at an advantage, backed up a step in alarm before coming to his senses.

After all, the soldier reasoned, the Soldatian's black eyes held no real power despite appearances to the contrary. And, although the Soldatian looked decidedly large and powerful, he was still bound and at their mercy.

There would be none.

The soldier knew what the Soldatian had done to Laran Tania—he'd seen the aftermath. By the Holy Ones, when they'd arrived, he'd already removed his shirt and had been bending over her. He'd been readying to defile her.

The soldier had been told, they all had, to give their prisoner no quarter. The Soldatian would find no sympathy among the Mirren contingent.

"We reach Mirren-Bar today, Soldat," the soldier told him icily in accented Soldatian. He resolved not to look into the bottomless eyes again. "Let's see how well you fare there." He sneered and prodded him in the back with the handle of the whip to get him moving.

"He will receive the same *kindness* he showed the Saharani," a second soldier interjected. He stood directly in Sheftu's path and stared up into his face. "You are going to wish you'd never been born, Soldatian," he said softly.

Saharani. Sheftu looked down at him wondering what that meant. The Mirren flinched when he met Sheftu's eyes, then seemed to remember himself and straightened to his full height. He was not much taller than Laran, the top of his head even with Sheftu's broad shoulders.

Sheftu clamped his mouth shut and moved around the man, one painful step after another. He'd given up trying to defend himself, trying to explain that whatever tale Santago told them had been a lie. He *hadn't* harmed Laran.

He couldn't.

And he sure as the Seven Layers hadn't killed her.

Grief rose up in his chest once more. It choked him. It *became* him. There was nothing left *to* him but anguish and pain and anger.

He continued to plod ahead, every step excruciating. He wondered if the wound in his thigh had become infected.

Bound as he was, he did not look forward to enduring another agonizing day in the inflexible back of the wooden cart he would be tied into, every rut and ridge in the rocky ground bruising his back, his arms and his legs as his body hit the rigid sides time and time again.

They told him he would wish for death before they were done with him. It was possible. Although he did not want to die, life held little attraction for him now.

Provos and Laran were gone. Their demise had been unspeakably violent. And he'd been responsible.

He should *never* have allowed Provos to accompany him into Barraid. He'd thought of it as an adventure. An *adventure*! He'd been a selfish fool.

And Laran? He'd loved her. He'd failed her.

He'd promised to protect her and then, thinking she was safe, he'd left her alone and at the mercy of the disloyal Santago.

Even if it were true, even if he *did* wish for death in the days to come, he would not *allow* himself to die. He would survive! He would track Santago down.

He was going to kill him.

The soldier herding him onward shoved him against the stationary cart, and Sheftu wearily angled his body to slide inside. His guards appeared to be wary of him despite his inability to strike out at them.

He raised his stygian eyes to those of the soldier tying him into the cart and stared directly at him. When the smaller man glanced up and met Sheftu's gaze, he fumbled and backed up a step. At the goading of his companions, he came back to finish the task, this time avoiding his captive's stare.

This was interesting, Sheftu thought. These golden-eyed Mirren found *his* eyes disconcerting. Was it the shape, so different from their own? Perhaps it was the colour, or rather, the lack of colour. Perhaps they associated the blackness of his eyes with the perceived blackness of his heart.

His heart didn't *feel* black. It felt... empty.

CHAPTER THIRTY-FIVE

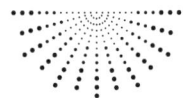

"COME NOW, RANDIDE," Estalla prodded her husband, grinning. "Have you no curiosity? Don't you wish to *know*?"

Randide laughed in spite of his misgivings.

"Leave off, wife. I'm here, aren't I?" he grumbled good-naturedly. Still, his eyes swept every inch of the headland including the scrub and trees at its border. He adjusted his bow on his shoulder and checked for the tenth time that his knife was in position, the sheath open.

"Don't know how I let you talk me into this. I saw enough Soldatians during the war to last me a lifetime. I have no need to search out two more!"

"But these two are different, Randide," Estalla told him as they walked. The little path near the creek was nearly visible now. "They could have harmed us, but they did not! The little Mirren woman they were with told me to look at their faces so I would *know* they meant no harm. And I did! I saw nothing there to give me pause."

"Then *why* were they here?" Randide demanded. "Why would two lone Soldatians hazard traveling this far into Barraid? And don't tell me they were crossing Barraid to bring the woman back to her people! That doesn't add up. The risk would be too high."

"Perhaps she is important. Perhaps she is of Mirren nobility. Perhaps…"

"Maybe so," Randide interrupted thoughtfully. He hadn't considered that. "With an entire contingent of Mirren soldiers crossing our border, moving south, coming *here*," he added, "and then returning before Barraid could react… Estalla. Maybe you have the right of it. Maybe she *is* important to them."

"You see!" Estalla said triumphantly. "Let's see if we can find something of interest." She continued, wading through the tall grass unconcernedly. "Look sharp, now!" she instructed.

Behind her Randide rolled his eyes and smiled at his wife's back. She was a fine woman, he thought. She'd had quite a fright that day at the headland, though. She and their two daughters had been trembling with excitement when they'd returned. Their tales of meeting the two Soldatians and the Mirren woman were told animatedly and all at once as though the news couldn't be contained for a second longer.

Truth be told, his blood had iced at the mention of the men and he'd feared for the lives of his wife and children. He'd feared for his own. He never imagined he'd live to hear that *Soldatians* had penetrated so far into Barraid. Unseen.

He shook his head in disbelief. And now, here he was, where he knew, *knew*, they'd been. He was alone with only his wife at his side! What was he thinking?

Nothing moved in the landscape now, though there was evidence that a great many men and horses had been there. The long grass was largely flattened and torn up, and even the scrub at its edges looked abused. And what was that ahead?

Randide squinted at a dark hump in the trampled grass. What *was* that? Crows, nearly a dozen of them, rose off the mound in noisy unison as they approached.

"Hold up!" Randide told his wife, his voice harsher than he'd intended. He placed a restraining hand on her shoulder and took her place on the path, in the lead now. His stride slowed and then stopped altogether as he finally understood what he was seeing.

A human corpse lay on its side, folded in on itself, one bare arm outstretched. Blood, black and grisly, had congealed on the limb. The familiar rope- like tattoo of a Barraidi hunter was imprinted over the bicep. An arrow protruded from the cadaver's back.

His back! Had the hunter been murdered?

Randide slid his eyes over the terrain once more. "What went on here?" he murmured to himself. He approached the corpse hesitantly and nudged it with his boot, rolling it over. He straightened as he recognized the face.

"Frenel," Randide told Estalla quietly. "What did that greasy bastard do this time?"

Estalla had a hand to her mouth in shock. She was looking over the headland in dismay. "I think I see another!" Estalla cried. "Randide! Let's leave this place. Let's go back. I've made a mistake, a terrible mistake. We should never have come here!"

But Randide had withdrawn the long knife from its sheath and was approaching the second body cautiously. This, too, had been a hunter. An arrow jutted from the abdomen. A wicked-looking knife was still clasped in a bloodied fist.

"Randide!" Estalla begged, an edge of panic in her voice. "Come away with me!"

Randide raised a hand and continued forward, toward the trees. Something scuttled away at his approach and crows, dozens more, lifted out of the grass, their raucous cries a protest at being disturbed at a grisly feast.

Two more bodies lay there, not six feet from one another. One had had its throat slashed, and blood, black and thick now, had soaked into the ground and discoloured the grass. Birds and small animals had ravaged both faces but Randide would swear the larger of the two corpses had been Trand.

Trand had been a dangerous man in life, one he'd not have wanted Estalla to encounter alone at any point in time. Like Frenel, his death would not be grieved.

Randide shuddered and bent over abruptly in a bid not to lose his breakfast. *Fine warrior you are, Randide,* he chastised himself. *Feeling faint and nauseated. Steel yourself!*

After all, he'd seen worse in the war with Soldat. Much worse.

He turned to warn Estalla away but found her right behind him, her face chalk white and her eyes slightly glassy.

"It was there," she told Randide with a vague wave of her arm, "that one of the Soldatians walked out of the forest. We should…" She swallowed audibly. "We should see if…" She closed her eyes briefly to compose herself. "We should look near the woods," she finally finished weakly. She kept her eyes averted from the bodies in the grass.

Randide scanned the headland once more, then nodded slowly. "All right," he said quietly. "If you've the stomach for it, if we both do, we may as well see this through."

He grasped his wife's hand and together they traversed the long, trodden grass, Randide alert to any sound or movement that might signal the presence of men, and Estalla trying to shut herself off from what they had seen and what they *might* see as they neared the woods.

"There," Estalla whispered, pointing towards the ill-defined entrance to a deer path among the trees. "There, Randide."

Just off the path lay another body, this one considerably larger than the rest. The knee-length boots over loose-fitting trousers and the long coat open to reveal the bloodstained, white tunic beneath, marked it as Soldatian.

"Oh, no," Estalla breathed.

Randide sheathed his knife and pushed the scrub bush aside to squat beside the body. The colour in the bronzed skin hadn't faded entirely and the corpse almost looked alive.

The arrow in the Soldatian's chest belied the possibility.

The black hair was, strangely, streaked with white and the brows and the fringe of lashes beneath the closed eyes were jet.

So were the eyes that opened suddenly into his.

Randide jumped to his feet in astonishment, pushing Estalla behind him. He began to draw his knife once again but realized how ridiculous his reaction was. The Soldatian had an arrow through his chest. He was hardly in a position to attack.

He lowered himself to a squat once again and looked into those jet-black eyes. They looked back at him, blinking heavily, the expression unreadable. Was he hoping Randide would help him? Likely he was waiting for Randide to kill him.

He thought about it.

It wouldn't do to have a live Soldatian in the area. Others might come searching.

He looked over his shoulder at his wife. "It would be a mercy," he told her.

But Estalla shook her head adamantly as she realized the direction of her husband's thoughts. "No, husband!" she told him as forcibly as she could. "We must help him. I told you, these two were different." She looked down at the wounded man.

"I… I didn't want to tell you this," she began. "You were already upset, and I was ashamed." She hesitated.

"Tell me what?" Randide asked frowning. *Ashamed?* A little knot of fear unfurled in his stomach.

"Well, when I first saw them, I panicked. I fell backwards into the flooded creek. Our son was strapped into the baby sling! The current… He could have drowned, Randide! But," and now she looked down at Provos again, "*this* one pulled me out of the water. He could have left me, but he didn't!

We will help him," she said again.

Randide let his breath out in relief. For a moment he thought Estalla had been loath to tell him something more sinister. For a moment he thought the Soldatians had hurt her.

So. He eyed his wife. He'd known Estalla all of his life and had been married to her for what seemed like most of it. He'd learned which battles to fight and which to concede. There was always room for negotiation, though. He'd have his terms.

She was kneeling at the Soldatian's side now. His dark eyes slid towards her. His lips moved but no sound came out. Tears leaked from the corners of his eyes. She placed her hand gently on his uninjured shoulder and spoke to him softly.

Provos heard the Barraidi mother's words but couldn't understand them. The tone was kind, though, and he gratefully absorbed the comfort offered.

He'd woken alone in the night at the edge of the woods where he'd fallen after being arrow-struck. He'd been too weak to move, too weak to ward off the relentless small predators that approached. Only his voice kept them at bay. By morning he was weaker yet and they were growing braver. Tonight they'd have him, sure.

Sheftu hadn't come for him. Provos knew his cousin must be dead or dying somewhere else in the Barraidi forest.

"Water," he finally rasped.

Estalla did not need to understand the man's language to know what he asked for. She reached for the flask tucked against her waistband and carefully wet Provos' mouth. He choked but wanted more, and Estalla poured a few small swallows into the side of his mouth.

It seemed to revive him. He looked up at Randide.

"Kill me." His voice was strained, halting. "Do not leave me… here to die."

Randide frowned, torn between wanting to grant the Soldatian's wish, which would in turn grant his own, and wanting to appease his wife. He dragged his hands through his dark hair and summoned up as much of the Soldatian language as he could remember from his time in the war.

"We," he said indicating Estalla and himself, "will you help. Not only you now."

Provos nodded weakly and for the first time those pitch-black eyes lit.

Randide cursed silently to see that first flicker of hope in the Soldatian's dark eyes. He knew he couldn't outright kill the man, but he'd considered merely making a *show* of helping him, ultimately leaving him to die, perhaps even helping him along a little.

It'd be a colder man than he who could do that *now*.

"We won't be bringing him home, Estalla," Randide told his wife. He held up his hand to forestall her protests. "If the people of our village, of the town, found out we were harbouring a Soldatian, they'd fire our house. We can't, *I* can't, let that happen."

"Randide, he will die out here. We can't just leave him, checking on him occasionally. That arrow won't take itself out. And he's too weak to…"

"I'll build a shelter against the weather," Randide told her. "We'll bring blankets, extra water, whatever we need from home. *You'll* have to remove the arrow. I'll stay with him tonight, build a fire, chase predators away. See if he lives to morning." He looked down at Provos.

"If anyone else sees him, though, he's a dead man anyway," Randide added.

Estalla nodded slowly. She hadn't relished the idea of having the Soldatian in her home, near her children. It was true he'd helped her. It was true he'd seemed different. But what if he was *not*? They didn't know him, after all. And Randide was right. They'd lose their home, maybe even their lives, if anyone found out he was among them.

It would be better this way. Not easy. But better.

CHAPTER THIRTY-SIX

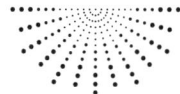

S HEFTU WINCED AT a particularly painful jolt of the cart. Its wooden wheels had banged into a narrow rut and smashed against a rock. The conveyance lurched to a tilted stop, one wheel shattered. Sheftu slid down the slanted bed, his hands still tied to the opposite side.

Several Mirren soldiers swung their legs over their horses and dropped to the ground for a closer look at the damaged cart, then turned their heads in unison to look at Sheftu.

From his awkward position in the tilted cart, Sheftu watched Tishane dismount and approach. The Mirren captain withdrew a long, wicked-looking knife from the leather sheath strapped to his chest. He glared menacingly but his Soldatian prisoner met his eyes squarely and did not cower.

Tishane severed the bonds that tied his captive to the cart and watched impassively as the bigger man slipped the remaining few inches to the ground. He observed Sheftu push away from the damaged cart and attempt to rise. The prisoner's efforts were slow and obviously painful, but Tishane felt no sympathy. The young Soldatian lord was a murderer, an abuser of women, and a rapist.

If he suffered, so be it.

The captain jerked his head in Sheftu's direction, an unspoken order to the three soldiers who stood watching. All three moved immediately to surround the bigger man. Bound as he was with his arms behind him, there was little danger he could mount an escape. Still, Tishane had learned not to take chances.

Shoved roughly from behind, Sheftu stumbled and would have fallen but his drop was arrested by a collision with one of the enormous boulders scattered across this part of the landscape. Using its height and weight, he levered himself upright again and tried to ignore the throbbing ache in his shoulder where he'd struck the rock.

He turned his back to the Mirren soldiers and their efforts to repair the damaged cart, and for the first time he allowed himself to see, really *see*, the terrain before him. His dark eyes swept the ridge they stood on, its pale, barren ground, mammoth boulders and occasional pinnacle—a strange and beautiful combination.

Far, far below him lay the thread of a glistening river and to the northwest a lake so strikingly blue it looked surreal. The majority of the Mirren contingent had set up camp near its cerulean shores, and Sheftu could just make out three riders, presumably scouting ahead or perhaps bearing a message, skirting the body of water on their way north and up, out of the valley to the mountains above.

When he raised his eyes skyward, those precipitous peaks arrested his vision. The snowy crests were jagged and softly tinted with orange in the retreating light. The topography looked impossible to traverse, so rough and wild was it, but a route appeared carved through the mountains to the north. It was a narrow corridor of snow-covered rock and high mountain passage, which was barely visible now in the final glow of the pre-dusk. It must be all but invisible in the brighter light of day.

Mirren-Bar was encased within that precipitous embrace. That meant the border between Barraid and Mirren was nearby, probably in the deep valley below. Perhaps the river marked it.

He glanced again at the mountains in front of him. If Mirren-Bar lay within, then beyond it, through the range to the far side, lay the ocean.

Laran. He should be sharing this moment with Laran.

182

A deep sense of longing and a deeper sense of grief threatened to overwhelm him.

She would have been overjoyed. Her home was within reach and her family was close by now. Her family's reaction to her love for the second son of a powerful Soldatian lord should have been their main concern. That they'd worried at all seemed ridiculous now.

The softly tinted snow on the lofty crags deepened to blood-orange and blood-orange stained the crevices and avalanche paths on their slopes. Colour crawled down the mountain in undulating waves and folds and then slowly faded away.

Another long night had arrived. Lights began to wink into existence in the Mirren camp below as cooking fires were lit.

Had they taken Laran's body? Was it there? Were the soldiers below transporting it home? Or was it strapped into one of the supply wagons he rode with now?

Behind him, Sheftu could hear the grunts of men as the cart was lifted out of the rut it had crashed into. Soon camp would be set up and fires would be lit here on the ridge as well. If he were lucky, he'd be permitted to sleep where he stood.

Though the ground was hard and pitted with rock, he'd welcome that.

CHAPTER THIRTY-SEVEN

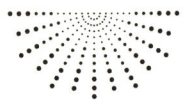

"WAKE, LARAN," THE Tania said softly.

His hand, resting on his daughter's forehead, was cool and soothing, and Laran swam up through the blurry eddy of consciousness toward the sound of her father's voice.

Her eyes opened and she saw him gazing down at her, his love and concern for her clear on his handsome face. His light brown hair curled about his face and was threaded with silver in places it hadn't been before she'd been abducted.

She was suddenly completely awake and finally present in her own body. "Father!" she cried. "You are here? You…"

Sheftu!

"Where is Sheftu? Is he all right? Is he…?" Her memories of past days were hazy, but one, darker and more frightening than the rest swelled to the surface. Laran sat up abruptly.

Dead.

Pain rent her skull and she put her hands to the sides of her head.

Had she been told he was *dead? But that can't be!* Something constricted in her chest.

"Not…not dead, Father! That can't be right."

"It is so, my daughter. You need never fear the man again."

Fear him? She tried to fathom what that meant but found she could no longer think. Laran stared at her father. *It is so, he'd said.* A curious numbness was overtaking her once more.

"Then it's true," she finally whispered. Her head dropped forward to rest against her father's shoulder. *No. Oh, no.* She began to cry great heart-rending sobs.

Dead.

The Smiling Man was dead. She felt her hopes for the future splinter into brittle fragments. The joy she'd known shattered around her like ice. Her love… Her love was gone.

Dead and gone.

"We are here, Laran," the Tania said gently, "in Mirren-Bar. Your mother awaits. So does Shell. Come," he prompted. "Let your family heal your heart and dry your tears."

He drew back the curtains on the litter she rode in to reveal the white stone steps of her home. Almost luminous in the sunlight, that wide stairway was lined with the small, green pyramid trees she remembered. Tiny brown birds lit here and there on the expanse, drawn by the seed left for them there each morning. Red flickered under their wings like a gift. Their song was a three-note crescendo. She'd heard it in her memories of home a thousand times.

Laran stared at them through her tears from the confines of the litter.

She was *home*, where she'd yearned to be. Home. And yet, without Sheftu at her side, there was no magic in the moment.

She took a deep shuddering breath and moved away from her father's embrace, hoping to catch sight of her mother and her sister. Would they be there to greet her?

"Shell!" Laran whispered brokenly. Her sister was racing down the steps towards her, her filmy white gown billowing out behind her. Her feet, shod in delicate white sandals, slapped against the stone as she ran. Her light brown curls, waist-length and shining in the light, had been pinned up but were escaping their constraints to bounce about her shoulders. They framed her lovely face as she ran.

Scarlet flashed behind carved white stone pillars as uniformed palace guards kept a watchful eye from a respectful distance.

Laran jumped off the litter before it had been completely lowered to the ground by its bearers and, pushing dizziness aside for the moment, collided with her sister, wrapping her arms around her. Her sister's embrace was just as fierce. The two sank to the wide stone steps, still wrapped in each other's arms.

"Laran," Shell nearly moaned. "You're home. You're home with us again." She pulled away to look into her sister's tear-ravaged face. Shell squeezed her eyes shut a moment then looked into Laran's golden eyes once more. She swallowed her horror at what must have happened and spoke quietly.

"Without you," Shell told her, "I've been half of who I was—half of a whole. Thank the Holy Ones for your return. Thank you, thank you," she murmured.

But Laran was shaking her head. "Not the Holy Ones. It was Sheftu," she told her sister. "Sheftu brought me back." Her breath hitched in her chest. *It was Sheftu.*

"Laran!" Emeldra Tania nearly shouted the name. She too ran down the wide steps. Both hands and the soft green gown she wore were stained with colour. A splotch of blue stood out on one elegant cheekbone and a drop of the same colour decorated her soft brown hair. Her mother had been painting; to Laran she'd never looked more beautiful.

"My daughter!" Emeldra cried. She threw herself down on the stair beside the two sisters and drew them both into her arms. "You are back, back with us! Oh, Laran, how I prayed for your return!"

"Mother," Laran cried. "I love you," she told her through her tears. "I've loved you every moment I've been gone. Every moment. I… I…" She was silent a moment as grief rose up to choke her.

She'd loved Sheftu, too, but he was gone forever.

Emeldra, too, saw the torment in her daughter's eyes, but put the pain in her mother's heart aside for a time. Nothing must ruin this one pure moment of happiness for her family.

"We never gave up on you, my daughter, not ever! And never did we stop loving you either. Not for one instant, not any of us." Emeldra pulled away slightly to place a warm hand on Laran's cheek.

"Mama, he was supposed to come with me but he… He is dead." Impossibly large tears squeezed out of Laran's golden eyes to slide down her cheeks and over her mother's hand.

"What do you mean, my daughter?" "The Smiling Man."

"Who is this Smiling Man?"

"Sheftu," she told them. She shrugged out of their arms and rose slowly to her feet. She turned and stared out at the mountains in the direction of the pass through which she knew they must have traveled.

"His name was Sheftu."

Emeldra glanced up in bemusement at her husband who stood watching the reunion with a troubled frown. He'd been heartsick at the loss of his first- born daughter but now, at the moment of her return, his expression did not reflect the elation she expected to see. Why not? What *had* happened?

Laran remained standing, silently staring out into the mountains and away from her family.

"Who is this Sheftu?" Emeldra asked the Tania.

Her eyes widened when she saw her husband's narrow and grow icy cold.

Sheftu was a name he obviously despised.

187

Distressed, she rose to stand beside Laran. She put one arm around her daughter's shoulders. Shell rose to take her sister's hand on the other side.

Emeldra allowed her question to remain unanswered. There would be time now, and in time she would hear it all.

"Come, daughter," Emeldra said. "Little Dog has been disconsolate without you. Let's get you settled in your rooms. I'll bring her to you if you wish."

Laran turned her head to look into her mother's eyes. Gold dust seemed to dance in their depths. She looked down at her hand held so tightly in Shell's and then up into her sister's eyes. Gold dust there, too, just like their mother's.

Laran nodded, grateful for the support and comfort of family and by the thought of the exuberant greeting awaiting her. Little Dog would be overjoyed. She glanced back at her father. He was wearing the same expression she'd seen on the litter: love and concern for her, but now there was something else there as well. *Anger.*

It was anger!

Laran was too numb to try to understand. She pushed the troubling thought aside and turned to walk up the steps with her mother and her sister.

Around them the scarlet-clad guards retreated from sight altogether to allow the Tania and his family safe, but private, passage.

CHAPTER THIRTY-EIGHT

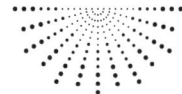

SHEFTU STAGGERED TO his feet, his hands still bound behind him. He'd spent a sleepless night on the rocky ground within sight of the Mirren camp in the valley below. The flickering light from their cooking fires had winked out sometime before dawn and by first light the camp had already been packed up. The long column of men and two horse-drawn wagons had begun the steep climb out of the verdant valley and up into the mountains above. They'd be in Mirren-Bar by nightfall, he imagined.

And so would the supply camp he was part of now. He looked behind him at the wagons and the horses that would haul this smaller contingent of Mirren soldiers down into the valley and up into the mountains beyond. He glanced at the guards who, even now, watched him as though he might launch an attack and murder them all as they were readying to leave.

Sheftu turned back to study the peaks he would soon be immersed in.

He was going to die there. He knew that. He felt a faint twist of fear in his guts. Strange that it elicited no more reaction than that. Perhaps terror would come. Perhaps it would not.

Laran was gone. Provos was dead.

As for him, he was not one to give up. He'd try to escape the moment an opportunity presented itself and he'd fight for his life if it did not, but in truth, if that life held a promise, he couldn't see it now.

Vengeance would be his only motivation.

The sun rose higher, casting pearly hues over the snowcaps. It was a magnificent sight.

He yearned for the golden plains of Soldat.

He yearned for his stoic, undemonstrative father. He yearned for his unrelentingly serious brother.

He yearned for simpler times when the future was merely an adventure and his love for the little Mirren slave girl was still fledgling.

"Soldatian!" a thickly accented voice called. "I'm talking to you." The owner of that voice thrust something hard into Sheftu's back to claim his attention. Sheftu turned the full fury of his pitch-black eyes on the man and the Mirren soldier flinched slightly but did not move away. He carried a long staff and a leather water canteen.

"No trouble, Soldatian," he ordered. He stood on his toes to reach Sheftu's mouth with the canteen and managed to slosh some inside. He capped the container, staring at Sheftu as he did so but only meeting his eyes in stops and starts.

"You may be big, Soldatian, but you are no kind of man," the guard said contemptuously. "Only a coward abuses those who are weaker. Only a coward would beat a woman." He spat into Sheftu's face and watched as spittle slid down the captive's face.

Sheftu grit his teeth in rage but said nothing. *Honour!* Honour had been important to Laran.

Well, by the Seven Gods, it was important to him, too!

He shifted his balance and swung his injured leg high, his boot catching the guard squarely in the jaw. Pain shot through Sheftu's thigh at the impact, but the guard went down, yelling something furious in Mirren. The other two guards prepared to tackle Sheftu. With his arms bound, his only recourse was to lower his head and charge the closer of the two. He hit him in the chest, driving the air from his lungs.

When he turned to the third guard, he was confronted by a fully drawn bow, the tip of the arrow at its core shining dully in the early light. The look on the bowman's face gave testament to his desire to release it.

Sheftu stood quietly now, his injured thigh throbbing with pain, his chest heaving with exertion. His eyes narrowed in rage, but he kept his protests as to his own innocence internalized.

He was not abusive. He did *not* beat women. *I did not hurt Laran!*

The fight went out of him all at once.

I didn't kill her.

He turned his back on the quivering arrow. As close as the guard was, if it was discharged, it would penetrate right through him. He concentrated on standing unwaveringly tall.

He let his gaze rest on the soaring peaks across the valley once more.

CHAPTER THIRTY-NINE

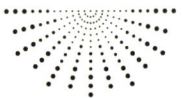

EMELDRA PACED THE wide room, her feet bare against the cool, white stone. Her floor-length sapphire gown brushed against her bare toes as she turned to face her husband.

"Mikale," she said, "I am worried for her, terribly worried." She bit her full lower lip, as was her habit in times of distress.

"I know, Emeldra," the Tania said gently. "We must be patient. It's only been a few days and Laran has been gone a long time. She has seen and experienced things we can only imagine."

Mikale turned away lest his wife see his sudden anger. He did not really need to *imagine* what his daughter had experienced at the hands of the Soldatians. He'd seen what the young lord had done to her, what he and his kinsman were *going* to do to her.

The Tania was a man who prided himself on self-control, but his anger over what had happened to his daughter was beginning to own him. He took a deep breath to regain his composure.

He'd mentioned neither the Soldatian's capture nor the circumstances to Emeldra. That their beloved Laran had been ill-treated was obvious. She'd been battered and abused and was emotionally spent. Mikale saw no reason to add to his wife's concern by explaining the sordid details of the

Soldatian's behavior. That he was not only still alive but likely to arrive in Mirren-Bar that very night could only fuel her upset.

No. He'd deal with the prisoner himself and in due course. In the meantime, let him rot in the cells.

"It is as though she were grieving," Emeldra continued, frowning. She looked toward her daughters' rooms, invisible behind the pale stone walls of the palace.

"Do you know why, Mikale?" she asked looking back at him. "Do you understand it?"

The Tania shook his head slowly. "She has always been a gentle soul, Emeldra. You know that. Shell is the same." *As are you, my wife,* he thought tenderly.

"Perhaps," he said now, his voice heavy with sorrow, "what she experienced at the hands of the Soldatians was too much for her."

Emeldra stopped pacing to stare, anguished, at her husband. Tears formed in her gold dust eyes and spilled down over her cheeks.

"We must be patient," the Tania repeated. He rose to wrap his strong arms around his wife. "We must give her time." He felt Emeldra nod silently against his shoulder, felt the hitch in her breath as she fought the urge to sob. Unseen, he blinked his own tears away.

He felt as though his heart had been broken in two.

Laran had been fortunate, they all had been, that the Mirren sailor, Santago, had seen her on the ship and had recognized her. Thank the Holy Ones that Santago had taken it upon himself to try to protect her. If it hadn't been for him, they might not have found her in time.

"Time," Emeldra murmured. Elation at being reunited with her first born had transformed into a kind of despair. It was clear her beloved Laran had endured more than she could bear.

Her people were skilled healers, but a wounded heart was outside the realms of Mirren ability. She fervently hoped the curative flame in Laran's heart would soon be ignited once again.

And if her daughter were grieving, it was small wonder. She'd lost a great deal. But she had much to gain and a loving family to help her. Yes, she would give her first daughter time.

And all the considerable love she possessed.

The Tania tightened his embrace and glanced over his wife's head.

He admired the span of indigo sky visible through the long narrow windows. A thin slice of the flaxen moon watched over Mirren-Bar, its beauty reflected in a thousand pools below.

He sighed heavily. His life had not always been easy, but he'd been blessed with the respect of his people and with the love of his family. Sometimes it amazed him how something as simple and pure as moonlight could exist for a world where complexity and ugliness often reigned supreme.

He kissed Emeldra's hair absently and swore to himself that he would make things right for his daughter. The wrongs she had endured would be avenged.

CHAPTER FORTY

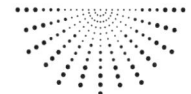

S HEFTU SLID AWKWARDLY out of the wagon bed and stumbled to his feet. He was lightheaded with hunger and thirst and felt sick to his stomach, the sensation having been exacerbated by the jarring movement of the cart and the mounting pain in his wounded thigh. He tried to swallow the urge to gag.

He straightened his back, raised his chin defiantly and glanced over the heads of his captors to the gates beyond.

The entourage had reached the walls of Mirren-Bar well behind the main body of Mirren soldiers.

The gate looming so ominously ahead was faintly illuminated by a glowing slice of new moon hanging suspended in the cobalt sky. Constructed of pale stone threaded with white, the immense structure looked almost luminous in the faint light of the splintered moon.

The massive gate opened gradually to receive them and Sheftu gaped in wonder as Mirren-Bar, that mythical city from the tales of his childhood, was revealed, inch by glorious inch.

He saw the turrets first. Conical, slender and graceful, the tall edifices appeared carved from ice in the moonlight, so white was the stone they were made of. Flags, their colour erased by the moon's pallor, flew from the spires of each one. From the highest reaches of the city to the sides of the gates they stood behind now, the stone turrets stood, mirroring crest after snowy crest of the mountain peaks around them.

The city itself appeared to be engraved into the sides of those magnificent peaks, the upper reaches terraced and bridged in flawless white stone. Wide stone steps descended from the heights to the level of the entrances to the city below.

Sheftu was prodded roughly from behind. He stumbled forward through the gate, limping heavily and wincing at each step, though he barely noticed, so mesmerized was he with the beauty of Mirren-Bar.

The concourse they had embarked upon led to the city entrances. It was broad and lined with tall, conical trees that echoed the turrets and mountain backdrop. The concourse was paved in white rock that gave the lustre of daylight to the boulevard though the sky was darkening to indigo.

Sheftu looked up. Here, above the snow-capped peaks, the roof of the world was a diamond sky. Tiny pinpoints of light seemed to condense to form swirls of light on a black velvet background. It was spectacular. And absolutely foreign.

The twist of fear in Sheftu's guts intensified. He turned suddenly, startling his guards.

"I wish to see Tishane," he told them. When they only stared, Sheftu repeated, "Tishane. I need to speak with him."

One of the guards snorted derisively. "What makes you think he will want to speak with *you*, Soldatian?"

"Find him," Sheftu demanded. "Tell him I have something to tell him."

The captain of these men would not likely have any interest in what Sheftu had to say, and he'd said it all before, but he needed to try. He *needed* to have the man listen to him.

One of his guards was nodding grudgingly. Good. Sheftu hadn't expected a response.

"I will tell him, Soldatian," the guard acknowledged. "Perhaps he will come to you. Perhaps he will not." The guard shrugged his indifference and then set off through the gate for the front of the supply line, presumably in search of his captain. That left the remaining two guards to watch their prisoner. Both drew long, ugly knives, ready to respond to any move on Sheftu's part.

But this was not the time to try an escape. Bound and lame, he wouldn't get far and he had no wish to die here, now, before he'd had a chance to redeem himself.

He wanted to get word to Laran's family.

Tishane rode toward Sheftu grudgingly from the front of the line. He likely resented not arriving in Mirren-Bar at the head of his men and his expression showed no pleasure in being asked to backtrack to his Soldatian prisoner now. The captain's black stallion showed him the whites of its eyes and drew equine lips back aggressively.

"What is it, Soldat?" Tishane demanded in his heavily accented Soldatian. He'd turned his horse upon reaching Sheftu but had not only remained mounted, he'd commenced forward motion once again.

Sheftu had to force his injured limb to a quicker pace to keep up. The pain in his thigh was excruciating. It was getting harder and harder to think.

"Captain," he began. The word was ground out through gritted teeth. "I did not..."

"You are trying my patience, Soldatian," Tishane interrupted fiercely. He touched his foot to the stallion's side and swiftly outdistanced his limping captive.

"My shirt!" Sheftu called out. He was desperately aware of time running out. "My tunic shirt was beneath Laran's head!" Sheftu shouted at the man's back. "If I had intended to rape her, would I have made her comfortable first?"

Tishane was some distance ahead now, halfway up the supply line, and Sheftu wondered if he'd heard.

By the Seven Gods, listen to me!

"Captain!" Sheftu shouted once again, his outburst earning him a Mirren obscenity and a vicious prod in the back by one of his guards.

But Tishane was bringing his horse to a standstill ahead. He turned slowly to look at his bare-chested prisoner. *Had* he heard?

"Search your memory, Captain," Sheftu called out. "Remember the tunic!"

A violent shove sent him sprawling. Unable to break his fall with his hands bound, his face collided with the rocky ground. He tasted dirt in his mouth, grainy and unpleasant, and tried to spit it out from a mouth gone dry as the soil beneath him.

He struggled to his knees, the wound in his thigh making him sick to his stomach once again. "It was the Barraidi!" he gasped. "The Barraidi." He tried to shake the dirt from his hair and felt instead the sting of blood as it ran into one eye from a fresh scrape on his forehead.

Tishane watched as the young lord's guards hauled him roughly to his feet. He noted the dark splotch of blood high on the leg of his trousers, noted, too, that it appeared to be wet once more. Perhaps it was time to allow a Healer to see him for the wound on his thigh.

After all, the Soldatian lord could not be allowed to die before the Tania had decided his fate. Not, Tishane thought grimly, that there was any question of what that would be.

He allowed Sheftu to catch up to him. He saw the faint glimmer of hope in his captive's eyes. It sickened him.

"Suffer, Soldatian," Tishane hurled ruthlessly. "Suffer as our Saharani suffered at your hands." He shifted in his saddle, touched his mount's ribs with his heels and rode away at a gallop.

Behind him, Sheftu watched in despair, his last hopes draining away. Death was waiting.

He could feel its jaws tightening.

CHAPTER FORTY-ONE

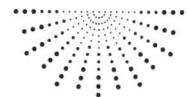

JODPUL SMILED, HIS golden cat's eyes crinkled at the corners. Dimples appeared at the sides of his generous mouth. His hair, unfashionably long for a man, was tied back from his face with a leather thong, but curling strands softened his handsome face, giving him an even more appealing aspect.

"Saharani," he said softly. His smile widened, and then broadened to a grin. Straight white teeth flashed briefly. He bowed courteously then winked at her as he straightened. He opened his muscular arms wide to receive her.

Laran grinned back in spite of her melancholy. Her childhood friend had never looked so handsome! And that smile! It would seem his good nature had not abandoned him. How wonderful it was to see him again!

Warmed by his welcome, she walked into his embrace but drew away quickly. Her answering grin faded away. The shadow of sorrow she had been living under since Sheftu's death reasserted itself.

Besides, she reasoned, Jodpul was aware that she'd been abducted. He would know that she'd been sold and enslaved in Soldat. What must he think of her now? She was no longer the innocent she had been.

Perhaps he is appalled.

But Jodpul had never been one for artifice and his smile seemed genuine.

He reached out to touch her cap of soft brown curls. The expression in his eyes was affectionate and his beautiful smile deepened.

"Short hair," he said softly. "It becomes you."

Laran felt tears well up into her eyes at the kindness of his words. She tried to blink them away, but failed.

Jodpul bent to kiss them from her face and Laran stiffened in surprise.

"Forgive me, Saharani," he said tenderly. He was looking into her eyes. "We have been friends all our lives. I do not like to see you unhappy." He raised one finger to her cheek to trace the path of her tears. "You know," he murmured, "I don't believe I've ever seen you cry. Not even when you fell from the pear tree and broke your arm. Do you remember, Laran?"

Laran nodded. "I remember," she said quietly. Those long-ago days were so far removed from her present existence that her memory of them seemed to have belonged to someone else's life.

Clearly, Jodpul still felt the connection between them, even if she did not.

But perhaps she would feel that connection again in time. She wanted to. Jodpul loved her in his way. She wanted to be loved.

"I..." How could she explain herself to her old friend? "Things have... happened. I am not the same person I was." *Did that make sense? Could he accept that?*

Jodpul remained silent for a moment.

"I have waited for you, Laran," he finally said. "My heart was filled when I heard that you still lived, that you would be returning to Mirren-Bar. I have waited a long time. For you, I would wait forever."

Laran looked up into his face. He meant it.

"But, my Saharani," Jodpul continued softly, "I do not *wish* to wait any longer. Marry me. Now. Tomorrow. I will help you heal. I will love you unconditionally. You know I will be a good husband and I will bring you happiness. We will have children, *ashaii?* Three children, just as we always planned. There will be joy.

And," he continued, "all that has happened will be erased."

Erased. *Sheftu erased? The memory of The Smiling Man wiped away?* Never. Not ever.

"I need time to think, Jodpul. Time to just... be."

Jodpul bowed once again. He picked up her hand and pressed his lips to the back of it. "As you wish, my Saharani. I am your friend. I always will be. I have loved you. I always will. Do not forget that." He smiled into her eyes once more, and then turned to stride away.

Laran watched him go. She wanted to call him back but the hurt she felt was too fresh, too deep. Perhaps marrying Jodpul *would* help her heal. But she was not in love with him! She never would be.

Sheftu would always be a shadow between them.

She turned and entered the deeper shade at the centre of the garden they'd met in. She sat on the edge of its reflecting pool and gazed at the clear water. Something stirred in its depths, a fish perhaps. When the leaves above began to rustle in the breeze, she could have sworn she heard Sheftu's laughter.

How long would she hear it? How long before she stopped hearing his voice in every conversation? How long before she stopped comparing every man she met unfavourably?

How long would he haunt her dreams, her every waking moment?

Forever.

She knelt on the ground, put her forehead to the soft earth of the garden, and wept.

* * *

LARAN! SHEFTU SAT up abruptly and shook the cobwebs of sleep from his mind. Laran. She filled his dreams. She'd been calling out to him in this one, sobbing, her heart broken. She hadn't been battered; she hadn't looked as he'd last seen her. She'd been whole and beautiful and alive. And full of sorrow.

Sheftu shifted on the cold stone, trying to ease the burden of pain in his thigh. It was definitely growing worse. He glanced about at the grey stone walls, at the ceiling barely high enough to stand in, at the bars on the door to the tiny cell. He could see no hint of the sky and wondered if night had fallen once again.

He'd been sleeping fitfully the past few days and nights. At least he *thought* it was two days and nights. Guards had appeared and re-appeared, food, such as it was, had been thrust at him, but water had been scarce. He was desperately thirsty.

He wondered how long it would be before Tishane came for him, how long it would be before they killed him.

No! He'd sworn on the Seven Layers of Darkness that he would *not* find death before he found Santago. He'd hold him accountable for his betrayal.

The little sailor was going to die.

But none of that would bring Laran back to life. Unbidden, he saw once again the image of the Barraidi hunter across the tall grass of the headland. He'd been strong and powerful. He'd held Laran with one hand while she struggled, his other raised to strike her down.

If only, Sheftu thought, he hadn't hesitated over the body of his cousin on his run to the headland. The brief moment of grief he'd allowed himself had meant Laran's death. If he'd released the arrow from his bow a split second earlier, that Barraidi bastard would have been impaled before delivering the blow that killed her.

By the Seven Gods, how he'd loved her! In the days that remained to him, and even if a miracle happened and he lived to old age, that would never change.

He scooped up the only modicum of comfort he'd been allowed, a single threadbare blanket. He wrapped it as tightly around his bare torso as he could. He leaned back against the cold stone and closed his eyes.

He tried to imagine the golden plains of Soldat. He tried to picture himself riding across them, the mountains so far in the distance they were invisible.

"Get up, Soldatian."

Sheftu ignored the intrusion and kept his eyes shut. He could almost feel the wind in his hair, the power of his stallion between his knees. He imagined himself holding onto the blowing mane and bending low over the arching neck.

"Get up, Soldatian," the rough voice repeated, insinuating itself into his vision. Sheftu heard the grating sound of metal as his barred door opened. His eyes remained closed.

Faster! He imagined himself outdistancing his hurt and his thirst and his fear. He tried to outdistance what he knew must be coming next.

Pain burst across his neck and lower face and now Sheftu's eyes flew open. The lash tore into him again, this time across his upper shoulders, leaving a swath of pure fire in its wake. The man wielding it had stepped inside the cell. He laughed cruelly.

Sheftu shuffled awkwardly to his feet. His face did not betray his anger as he slid his black-eyed gaze to his tormentor. The man was still grinning sadistically. Two more stood outside the cell looking in, cheering their comrade on, and obviously eager to watch the entertainment.

When the lash slit the air a third time, Sheftu reached out and grabbed it. The leather strip bit deeply into his hand, but he closed his fist around it and yanked, hard. The man wielding it was too surprised to let go and was dragged abruptly into arm's reach.

Sheftu balanced on his good leg and kneed the man in the groin with his injured leg. Before the guard could scream out his agony, before Sheftu could react to his own, he took hold of his tormentor's head with both hands and twisted, the sound of his breaking neck sickening in the sudden silence.

Eyes wide open in shock, the guard crumbled to the floor of the cell, dead.

Sheftu leapt over the man and plunged through the open cell door. He barreled into the remaining two guards, who stood momentarily stunned by how swiftly their plans had gone awry.

One went down hard, striking his head against the bars. The other began to yell, presumably for more guards.

Sheftu sprinted, limping, down the long corridor as fast as his injured leg would allow. He had tried to memorize the twists and turns of the prison labyrinth as he was brought in. His guards hadn't thought to hide it from him. They'd been certain that their captive would never again see the light of day.

Only a set of carved stone stairs and then two more turns to round, he thought. But he skidded to a stop as he entered the stairway. Two guards blocked his passage, both armed with drawn swords.

Sheftu half spun to retrace his steps to his last turn, but found his way back choked as well. Two more guards stood in his path, both panting heavily, both with bows drawn and arrows notched.

There were no other avenues of escape.

If he attacked the swordsmen, the bowman would launch their arrows at his back. If he backtracked toward the bowmen, he'd likely be skewered by both sets of arrows before he reached them and the swordsmen behind him would run him through regardless.

Sheftu turned slowly toward the swordsmen. One was smirking. Fury began to thrum in Sheftu's chest once more. By the Seven Layers, he'd wipe the smirk off that one's face!

He charged them, dodging the arc of the first sword and knocking the smirking son of a bitch onto his back on the steps.

He felt the first of two arrows pierce his back. He wasn't aware of the second at all.

Ahead, up the stairs, he caught a glimpse of daylight. Not night yet, then. Not yet.

But blackness descended just the same.

CHAPTER FORTY-TWO

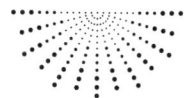

JODPUL ADJUSTED THE scarlet sash of his noble house nervously. He made a conscious effort to straighten his already erect posture, took a deep breath, and then strode into the Tania's antechamber, feigning confidence.

He bowed deeply.

Mikale inclined his head and smiled warmly at the young man.

"Forgive the intrusion, High Lord," Jodpul began, but the older man raised his hand to quiet him.

"You do not intrude," the Tania said generously. "It is a pleasure to see you."

Jodpul smiled in relief, his apprehension suddenly forgotten. After all, he'd known the Tania and his family all of his life. He bowed to Emeldra as she, too, entered the antechamber.

"Jodpul," she said holding her hands out to him, her smile genuine and warm.

He took them in his own and smiled down on her.

"Tania, Lady Tania," he began again, addressing them both. "I have come to speak with you about Saharani Laran." He hesitated a moment.

The Tania raised a brow. Emeldra smiled serenely. "What is it, Jodpul?" she asked kindly.

"I wish to marry her. I will be an admirable husband. You will never have a moment's regret…"

"Jodpul," the Tania interrupted quietly, "you know you have our blessing. This marriage has been planned since your childhoods. Both families have agreed. As long as you are both still willing…"

"But that's just it," Jodpul interrupted in turn. "Laran is confused now. She says she needs time, but I feel her slipping farther and farther away from me."

"What is it you thought we might do?" Emeldra asked him.

"Perhaps you would speak to her on my behalf ? Remind her of our lifelong friendship and of our love for one another. Reiterate what I have been telling her—that our union will bring her both happiness and healing. I *know* I can help her." He paused, thinking about his family.

They were counting on this marriage to further their own aspirations. An alliance with the Tania family would impact the futures of the Degere family for generations to come.

He *had* to make it happen for their sake as well as his own.

And if Laran no longer felt the bond they once shared? The marriage would still be a good one, a happy one, and a beneficial one for both of them. He believed that.

She must be made to believe it, too.

"Perhaps she feels she is… damaged now." Jodpul glanced at the Tania, saw him frown, and heard Lady Tania's sudden intake of breath. *Careful,* he told himself. *Do not risk angering them.* He took a deep breath.

"I do not know what wrongs were committed against her," Jodpul continued. "But whatever they were, whatever scars they have left behind, I want to assure you, to assure *her,* that I could never judge her for them. What I mean is…" He rubbed his hand over his jaw in exasperation. *By all that was sacred, this was hard to voice.*

"What I mean is, society may frown upon… I mean, if certain things…"

What is the matter with you, Jodpul?

He bowed once again to show his respect and to give himself time to regain his composure.

"Forgive me. The matter is disturbing and I mean no offence. I assure you as I have assured the Saharani that no matter what may have befallen her at the hands of others, I would be deeply honoured to accept her to my marriage bed. Honoured," he repeated emphatically.

The Tania and his wife glanced at one another, their faces expressionless. Jodpul held his breath. *Have I been a fool to speak of this?*

Emeldra took his hands once more. "I will speak with my daughter, Jodpul. I will explain what you have said." Her voice was still warm.

Thank the Holy Ones.

Mikale rose, frowning, but said nothing for a moment. He glanced over Jodpul's shoulder and raised his hand once more, this time to put an end to their conversation. "We will speak of this another time."

Jodpul bowed once again. Shaken by his unexpected inability to articulate the importance of the marriage, he turned to retrace his steps to the door of the antechamber, nearly failing to see the Captain of the Guards who awaited audience there.

Though it was a distinct breach of court etiquette, Jodpul looked back at the Tania. The older man was waving his Captain in. His frown had deepened. That the Captain had sought out the High Lord in his private rooms could only mean something urgent had occurred.

Tishane stepped inside. He dropped to one knee and then rose again. He waited for Jodpul to leave the antechamber.

Jodpul dipped his head slightly at the Captain of the Guards as he passed him and Tishane bowed in return.

"Tania," Tishane said respectfully when Jodpul had passed through the entryway. "I have news of the Solda…" He seemed to see Emeldra there for the first time. "I have news of the prisoner you were interested in," he amended, his face reddening.

Outside the antechamber, Jodpul stopped suddenly, turning to stare at the closing door. *Soldatian prisoner?* Was that what the captain was going to say? Had he heard that right? Was the man responsible for harming Laran imprisoned below? He felt a surge of anger that it might be so and walked away from the antechamber pondering what he should do with the knowledge inadvertently thrust upon him.

CHAPTER FORTY-THREE

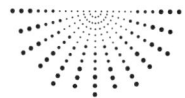

T HE TANIA STOOD over the bloodied body of the Soldatian.

Clearly, he lay as he was thrown, face down on the stone floor of his cell. Two arrows still protruded from his naked back. He appeared bathed in red from neck to waist and a single narrow rivulet of blood ran down his ribs to stain the floor beneath him. He looked impossibly large sprawled as he was in the small cell. He was well muscled and despite his wounds, he looked powerful.

His daughter was small and slender. Rage surged through the Tania once again as he imagined her subjugated beneath this man.

He nudged his prisoner half over with his foot. The Soldatian's face was swollen and bruised, apparently from a previous beating, and angry red welts, crusted with blood in spots, striped his lower jaw, neck and upper chest. One arm was beneath him, but the exposed arm was bruised and scraped. Raw, purpled restraint marks marred the skin of his wrist and blood leaked from a cut across his palm.

The Soldatian had been abused, that much was clear. Possibly tortured. The Tania turned away a moment, disturbed. After all, for all the prisoner had done to his daughter, it was by his own decree that no quarter had been given the man.

He glanced at Tishane, whose face reflected his own unease over the abuse so clearly meted out. He looked down at the young lord once again.

Did he breathe? Yes. The rise and fall of his chest was faint but steady. Wouldn't be for long. Blood loss alone would soon kill him even if his injuries didn't.

"I have much to ask this one," the Tania told Tishane softly. "I will need to know who it was that abducted Laran, how she was transported across both borders, and exactly what befell her. And then," he promised grimly, "retribution will be made."

His previously spirited daughter was distant now, immeasurably sad. She spent her days in the garden near her chambers. She seldom spoke, and never about what had transpired.

The Tania turned back to stare at the bloodied Soldatian at his feet.

"Send for a Healer," he instructed his captain. "Restore him to health. Make sure he is restrained. There must be no more death attributed to this one but his own."

Tishane, still uneasy, bowed his assent. He turned swiftly to do the Tania's bidding. Time, it would seem, was of the essence. The Soldatian would not last much longer.

And, he decided, he would guard the prisoner himself while the Healer worked on him. No more death? Perhaps the man had been desperate.

He tried not to remember the tunic beneath Laran Tania's head on the stony ground of the Barraidi headland.

* * *

THE HEALER STUMBLED nervously into the prison corridor outside of Sheftu's cell. Here, in the presence of the Tania, and surrounded by guards including their captain, she was expected to perform her duty, however unsavoury. She was to restore health to a wounded prisoner, a prisoner, she'd heard, who had killed a guard and had done who knew what else.

I cannot falter, she thought. Along with the Lady Tania herself, she was one of the strongest Healers in all of Mirren-Bar. But ahead stood the Tania.

He was simply dressed but still managed to look elegant in this terrible place. Of middle years, with silvered hair and standing a head taller than most Mirren men, he exuded authority and grace.

He was looking in her direction impatiently.

"High Lord," she murmured. She dropped clumsily to her knees and pressed her head to the floor.

She felt a hand upon her shoulders. Was it *his*?

"Do not fear me, Healer," the Tania said. "I am here to see that life is returned to this man. I am not here to judge your skill or your devotion to your art. Understand?"

The Healer nodded, her head still pressed against the stone. "Rise. The man is dying."

The Healer rose unsteadily, averting her gaze from the Tania who stood unnervingly close. She approached the wounded prisoner. Her eyes widened in dismay. He was huge! And Soldatian! They were a warrior society, she'd heard, and…

"Healer! You will be well guarded. Do not fear this one either."

She gulped down her panic. A guard yanked the two arrows from the Soldatian's back and the Healer bent to her work.

The Tania stood back in the cell and watched while gradually, gradually, life returned to the wounded Soldatian lord. As the Healer absorbed the last of the injury done to the man's back, he began to moan, mumbling unintelligibly in his own language.

The Healer signalled two guards to roll the man over onto his now mended back. She sat back on her heels to compose herself. She was tired, the Tania could see that, but she was as powerful a Healer as he had seen, and not yet exhausted.

When she placed her hand against the Soldatian's thigh, his eyes fluttered opened. Jet black, and oddly shaped without the slant characteristic of the Mirren, those dark eyes looked up into hers.

Disconcerted, the Healer jerked her hand away and tensed to jump back, but he was saying something to her, his words soft and gentle to her ears.

"Thank you," he murmured. She didn't need to understand Soldatian to know what he'd said. He was trying to frown her into focus and blinked heavily, evidently in an effort to remain conscious. Sweat shone on his brow and soaked his hair, which stuck to his neck. It was as straight as a spear, and strangely white streaked with jet black of the same dark intensity as his stygian eyes.

She placed her hand on his thigh once more. The wound there was not a new one and had become infected. Another day, perhaps two, and it would have spread into his blood stream, killing him. It must have been excruciatingly painful, and clearly it was painful to the touch now.

"Laran," he gasped. One large hand rose to cover the Healer's and she knew he was confusing her with someone else. "Laran," he mumbled again.

She turned behind her to see if the Tania would allow her to respond, but he was no longer there. The Captain of the Guards was, though, and his expression reflected surprise at the Soldatian's words.

By the Holy Ones, Tishane thought. The Soldatian had suffered and nearly died and *still* the Saharani's name was the first he uttered upon regaining consciousness.

Was there something to the man's claim that it was not he who'd hurt her? *Had* it truly been the Barraidi whose corpses littered the headland? Had this man actually killed them in *retribution* for hurting the Saharani? Or in an effort to *protect* her? The thought horrified him.

The Tania harboured no doubts. Tishane's duty was therefore clear.

But if it *were* true, then the Soldatian was innocent. And if not... He narrowed his eyes at the man. If not, the bastard could rot here in these lightless cells.

Sheftu could feel his life returning to him. The pain in his thigh was beginning to recede. The woman bending over him was taking it away. She wasn't Laran. He didn't know her. Slowly, the pain began to diminish and fade away, and slowly his mind began to clear.

He was in Mirren-Bar, trapped and alone in the Mirren prison. His surroundings became distinct. He lay on the hard stone floor. There were men standing outside the cell holding him in and two men stood above him. One of them looked familiar. His brawny arms were folded across his wide chest and a deep frown stood between his golden eyes. A small scar rent his bottom lip, giving him a pitiless aspect.

Tishane! By the Seven Gods, it was Tishane!

Sheftu sat up abruptly, his eyes fastened on the Mirren captain. The Healer fell back in surprise, and Sheftu jumped to his feet, the remaining pain in his limb suddenly inconsequential.

"What are you…?" he began, but Tishane was signaling his men to take hold of his arms and legs.

No! Sheftu smashed his fist into the face of the guard who reached for him first, sending the man reeling against the stone wall. As he tensed to continue to fight, Tishane raised both hands, palms up; one to stop Sheftu's forward motion, the other to halt his men.

"*Cept!*" he shouted in Mirren. "Stop." He stared at the Soldatian captive. "Yield," he told him, "and I will hear what you have to say."

Tishane glanced at the Healer and jerked his head towards the corridor. She backed out of the cell, then turned and ran.

"You will listen?" Sheftu asked dubiously. He was still poised to do battle.

Tishane nodded. "*Ashaii.* So I will. Yield, Soldatian. I have orders to restrain you."

"You will *hear* me?"

Tishane nodded again and Sheftu slowly straightened. He dropped his arms and allowed two of Tishane's men to bind them behind him once again.

"Speak," Tishane said solemnly.

"Santago," Sheftu began. "He must have hired the Barraidi hunters to kill my kinsman and me. It must have been his intention to bring Laran Tania here himself. He must have had something to gain. A reward perhaps? Was there a reward?"

Tishane said nothing.

"The Barraidi killed Provos, my kinsman. Tried to kill me. Perhaps they would have allowed Santago to take Laran, perhaps not. They brutalized her, intended to rape her."

Sheftu locked eyes with Tishane.

"I killed them."

The older man remained silent.

He doesn't believe me.

"One man escaped," Sheftu continued. "Ran. I only had eyes for Laran then and didn't pursue him. Find him, Captain! If he can be made to speak the truth, you will have it. You will know the truth of my words."

"Why should I believe this story?" Tishane snapped.

"Find him, Captain. If you cannot believe me, then find the man that ran." Sheftu licked his lips. By the Seven Gods but he was thirsty.

"I need water," he began, but Tishane was already turning away. He silently indicated a retreat from the cells to his men and strode out of sight.

The captain hadn't commented at all.

"Tishane!" Sheftu yelled. *Don't leave me bound, you son of a bitch. I cannot defend myself bound!*

One of the prison guards sauntered by. He grinned maliciously. "All tied up, Soldatian?" the man asked softly.

CHAPTER FORTY-FOUR

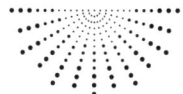

I N THE BARRAIDI woods, rain pattered softly on the makeshift roof of the tiny shelter.

Provos lay within. He stared blearily at the crisscrossed cedar boughs above his head. Squinting, he thought he saw finer boughs beyond the first layer of branches. Had those finer boughs been woven tightly and interlaced to form the watertight layer above? The shelter was dry. He tried to visualize how it had been done but found he didn't have the strength to fathom it out.

He turned his head to one side, a movement that seemed to take enormous energy. Larger branches, mostly cedar, some fir, had been woven together there to form a windscreen. It must render the shelter nearly invisible from the headland.

And that must be where he was. He must be lying now close to where he'd fallen near the wooded entrance to the headland.

He was alone.

Fear churned in his stomach and he squeezed his eyes shut in misery and dread. Wracked with pain, the minutest movement intensifying it to unbearable levels, he was completely vulnerable.

Someone had brought him here. Someone had constructed this shelter and laid him within. Perhaps that someone would return.

He had a vague recollection of the Barraidi mother they'd met on the headland, of tender words and the warmth of kindness. But surely it could not have been her. The sight of the two Soldatians, Sheftu and himself, had terrified her.

Where *was* his cousin? Was he lying injured in the Barraidi woods or dead in the tall grass of the headland? And Laran? Had the Barraidi hunters taken her? Had they killed her? What had they *done* to her?

Santago! He remembered now. Santago had betrayed them. Anger and grief surged through him.

"Sheftu!" he gasped, trying to elevate his head. Pain shot through his shoulder and chest and he dropped his head back to the moss padding on which he lay, moaning. His fingers clenched and squeezed the soft moss in his fists into coarse mounds.

When the pain subsided, his searching fingers felt the pliable surface of branches beneath him and the harder wood beneath that.

The thin trunks of smaller trees from the woods' edge must form the platform under him, keeping him off the damp ground. Overlain with branches, it had been cushioned with thick moss. A blanket covered him to his bandaged chest. His shoulder, which had been pinned to the tree, had been cleansed and dressed.

Someone had taken care to help him mend, to make him comfortable, to protect him from the elements. *Please, by all that is sacred, please let them make an appearance soon.*

Provos drifted into uneasy sleep once again, the sound of the rain a soothing refrain.

* * *

"RANDIDE," ESTALLA CALLED softly. "I think he awakens." She placed a cool hand gently against Provos' fevered brow. When his eyes fluttered open, she smiled into his eyes.

It was she! The Barraidi mother. She didn't look frightened now.

"Hello," he whispered. Weak as he was, he forced a half-smile in return. He became aware of another presence and slowly turned his head in that direction.

A man stood there, his hair a wild tumble of dark brown, and a frown between his eyes. He looked as though he was debating whether or not to let him live. Finally, the man nodded once, a brief, efficient gesture. If the man wanted to end his life, he could. Provos would have no recourse. He nodded back carefully, trying not to disturb his shoulder with the movement.

"You did this?" Provos asked. His voice had elevated from whisper to softly hoarse. He indicated the structure with his chin.

"*Aey*, we build," the Barraidi answered in stilted Soldatian. He looked at the injured man pointedly. "*Should* we have?"

"Randide!" Estalla scolded her husband. Her own understanding of the Soldatian language was rudimentary, but Randide's tone had been abundantly clear.

Randide sighed.

"How...do you know...my language?" Provos asked. Speaking was tiring him and he had to blink heavily to remain awake.

"War," Randide answered succinctly.

Provos' heart fell. "Oh," he murmured. He tried to focus on Randide's face. "Do you plan... to kill me?"

Randide looked down at his wife, then back at Provos. "No," he finally said. "Not if I do not have to."

Provos nodded again, his eyes losing their battle to remain open.

"Will you leave me to die, then?" he mumbled. He could barely see Randide through his lowering lashes.

Again Randide indicated that he would not, but his frown deepened.

"You are danger for us, Soldatian. For family." The Barraidi relented, his voice softening. "But we here for you now. When we can."

What was it I needed to ask? Provos fought his way back to semi-alertness.

Sheftu. Something about Sheftu.

"My cousin," Provos mumbled. Sleep was stealing his ability to think. "Do you know...where he is?"

Randide only stared in bemusement.

Provos tried again. It seemed to take Herculean effort. "The other Soldatian. Does he live?"

"We do not see. Mirren take."

"What?" Provos' eyes re-opened now as he struggled to understand. "What do you mean?"

Randide grew impatient. "Mirren take! Village see Soldatian...prison. Prisoner. Mirren take," he repeated. "Soldatian...tie." He held his wrists together to illustrate being bound.

"Why?" Provos muttered, horrified. "Why would they do that? He was trying to help one of their own. We both were."

Randide shrugged indifferently. He spoke to his wife in their own language and she looked at Provos in surprise.

"It is true, husband," she told Randide. "The little Mirren girl told me they were returning her to her homeland."

Randide looked at Provos thoughtfully, then back at Estalla.

"Then perhaps," he told his wife, "we are in possession of information that might be useful to the Mirren. Perhaps we can help this man, as *you* wish to do, and perhaps we can help ourselves as well. Perhaps this information is worth something to our Mirren neighbours." He looked down at Provos as he considered the possibilities.

"But Randide," Estalla began, "it would only be of use to the Mirren if the little Mirren girl is dead. Otherwise, they would *know* these men were only trying to help. The Barraidi hunters whose bodies we found must have killed her!"

She rose suddenly to her feet, her eyes wide. "And the Mirren must think the other Soldatian is responsible! Randide!" she exclaimed. "They must be told the truth! The little Mirren told me they had no wish to harm us. I could see that they did not. They are good men!"

Randide grunted. The wounded Soldatian at their feet had succumbed to healing sleep once again, though he wore a troubled frown to his slumber.

CHAPTER FORTY-FIVE

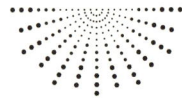

TISHANE BOWED, DISCOMFITED in the presence of the Saharani Shell. He looked down upon her, his unease clear in his golden eyes.

"I would speak with you, Saharani," he told her respectfully.

Shell smiled at the captain. Among her people, he was considered a big man, and formidable. The scar on his lower lip made him look as though he was perpetually displeased, but she knew better. His gentle heart was well hidden beneath a rough exterior. He could be ruthless though. She knew that. She'd seen it first-hand.

He'd taught both sisters to ride and had instructed them in the art of self-defence. Tishane was both a masterful horseman and a master swordsman. He was also adept with bow and staff, and these skills he'd patiently passed on. As they'd learned, as their own skills began to unfold and improve, Shell had seen that craggy face soften with pride and affection for the little girls they'd been.

Shell knew the captain and his wife had been unable to have children of their own and she had long been aware that the seasoned warrior, so intimidating to others, looked upon the two girls of the Tania family with love.

To Shell and Laran, Tishane had been more than their father's Captain of Guards. He was like a trusted uncle, perhaps—a man to rely upon. Shell knew Laran had confided in him many times. So, for that matter, had she.

That he had sought her out here was unusual, though, and so was the expression on his face.

"Is something wrong, Captain?" she asked him worriedly.

Tishane looked behind him at the gardens. He had just returned from a field exercise and still held his great black warhorse on a lead. He signalled a stableman to take the beast from him. He took Shell's elbow in his hand and steered her gently toward the gardens and away from prying eyes.

"Perhaps," he told her. He was frowning, trying to decide how best to approach a delicate subject. "I wish to speak with you about what happened to the Saharani Laran."

"Oh," Shell said in small voice. Laran had barely spoken in the two weeks she'd been back. She was distant and dispirited. Whatever had happened to her had changed her. It was breaking Shell's heart to see her so.

"Do you *know* what happened to her?" Shell asked. It shamed her that she feared the answer. Laran was her sister and Shell had admired her all her life. Before she'd been abducted, Laran had been brimming with life and happiness.

But the light had gone out of her eyes.

"I *thought* I did," Tishane said slowly. "I am no longer certain." He hesitated.

Am I doing the right thing? If I burden this innocent with the knowledge of what happened to Laran, will I damage her? Will I damage how she feels about her sister?

He didn't really believe the latter. Shell looked fragile and he knew her heart to be tender, but like the other women in her family, she had strength beneath that delicate façade.

She'd need all of it to endure what he had to ask of her.

Tishane knew that the Tania had kept the presence of the Soldatian prisoner a secret and that he intended to interrogate him himself. He understood his reasons for doing so. He also understood that the Tania had no doubt as to the man's guilt based on what he'd witnessed him doing to his daughter when they arrived.

But Tishane had doubts.

Small though they were, he could not in good conscience let them remain unexplored. If he found the man was innocent, he *had* to bring it to the Tania's attention.

"Find the man that ran," the Soldatian had said. *"If he can be made to speak the truth, you will have it."* But the Soldatian thought Laran Tania was dead.

She knew the truth, *all* of it.

"When we found your sister," Tishane began, "there was a man bending over her. He was Soldatian. He was naked from the waist up and bloodied. It appeared that he was in the process of... That he intended to..." Tishane swallowed his horror and tried not to see Shell's.

"The bodies of five Barraidi hunters littered the grass around him." He took a deep breath.

"The Saharani was unconscious. Her clothing had been ripped from her body and lay nearby. She'd been badly beaten."

Tishane was silent a moment as he watched Shell. Her face had gone as white as the stone beneath their feet and one hand rested against her throat in distress.

"Go on," she whispered.

That Tishane was upsetting her was certain. She was trembling and bravely trying not to show it.

He squeezed his eyes shut, then opened them again, resolved to continue. The Soldatian down in the cells had suffered greatly. He would continue to suffer. The truth *had* to be heard.

"The day before," he continued, "we had been approached by a sailor, a Mirren named Santago. He told us where she was, how to find her. He told us..." *By the Holy Ones! How can I say more?*

"Please, Captain," Shell implored. "Tell me what you must!"

Tishane shifted uncomfortably. The Tania had trusted him with this knowledge. He would be furious that his captain had betrayed his confidence. And to his youngest daughter, no less! He took a deep breath and spoke on.

"The sailor told us that a Soldatian lord and his kinsman had taken Laran out of Soldat, that they were returning her to Mirren-Bar. They expected money, a reward for doing so. He told us that the two men had... ah... abused her on the trip, that they'd..."

The look on Shell's face arrested his tongue.

"Raped her?" she whispered. "Tishane, is that what happened?" Shell began to cry, great heartfelt sobs. "They *raped* her?"

She dropped her gaze to the pale stones at her feet. Tishane raised his hands to her shoulders. His heart ached for her.

"Shell. Little Saharani. Can you forgive me? I was a fool! I should never have..."

But Shell looked up into his eyes, interrupting. Hers were shining with tears. They spilled down her cheeks to drop on the diaphanous sheer she wore over her floor-length saffron sheath.

"Why did you tell me this?" she asked unsteadily. "What was your purpose?"

Tishane steeled himself.

"The Soldatian lord, Saharani. He is here. Imprisoned. His presence has been kept quiet. Only a few soldiers and a few guards know, and they have been instructed to remain silent."

"Why?" Shell asked, though she had the answer before the word left her lips. It was in her father's makeup to want to protect his wife and his daughters from further distress.

She whole-heartedly wished it had remained a secret.

What am I to do with this information?

But Tishane was not through. "Your father saw the scene I described with his own eyes. He *knows* the Soldatian is guilty. And yet..."

223

His big hands on Shell's shoulders contracted and squeezed unknowingly.

"And yet, you have doubts?" Shell asked, astonished. She began to weep softly. "Did…did you not see what my father saw?"

"I did. Many of us did." Shell's upset and horror caused a tremor in Tishane's voice. "But it's possible that what we saw may not have been what it looked like." He swallowed his distaste. "The *truth* may be something else entirely. It *may* be that the Soldatian was doing just as he claims."

"What does he claim, Captain?" Shell asked him, a hitch in her voice.

"He claims he did *not* hurt her. He claims he was helping her. He *claims* that this Santago hired the now dead Barraidi to kill him and his kinsman. He *claims* it was the Barraidi who harmed her, that he killed them all in self-defense and in defense of the Saharani Laran. He *claims* he is innocent."

Shell and Tishane regarded each other intently.

"Could…could that be true?" Shell asked him.

Tishane nodded solemnly. "Perhaps," he said simply.

"Will you help me find justice, Saharani? Will you ask your sister for the truth?"

Shell wiped the tears from her face with the back of her hand. Dread climbed into her chest.

"*Ashaii*," she whispered.

She turned and ran from the courtyard to seek the solace of her chambers, the terrible images Tishane had planted in her mind replaying over and over again.

Laran distant? Dispirited? By the Holy Ones, it was a miracle she was even alive. And what other terrors had she borne in her many months as a Soldatian slave? She'd spoken of none of it.

I saw that what she had endured had changed her. How could it not have?

And the imprisoned Soldatian lord? Was it *he* who had enslaved her in Soldat? Had he been cruel to her? What *had* he done?

No! This train of thought was not helping Laran and it would not help the Soldatian if he were, indeed, innocent.

Tishane was right, Shell thought. The truth must be discovered.

But how will I begin? By all that is sacred, I do not want to stir all the hurt and the horror of that unspeakable time to the surface once again.

She stood still a moment in the wide corridors of her home and gathered her courage. The Lady Tania would know what to do. She always did.

Shell set her feet in the direction of her mother's studio instead.

CHAPTER FORTY-SIX

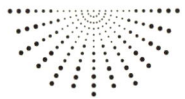

JODPUL STOOD SILENTLY in the corridor outside the prisoner's cell. The man hadn't noticed him yet. He was seated on the stone floor, his back to the wall, and his arms behind him. His eyes were closed, though one was purple and swollen and unlikely to open regardless. Twin tracks of dried blood trailed from his nose. Both upper and lower lips were split. There was an angry, purpled abrasion across his bare ribs and Jodpul wondered if at least one rib might be broken.

"Soldatian," he called quietly.

Sheftu came awake with a start, pulling in a sudden deep breath. He tensed for a blow.

But there was no one inside the cell with him this time. He would remain unmolested for the moment. He narrowed his one blurring eye to bring the man who stood outside the barred door into focus.

He was tall for a Mirren, and well dressed in sleeveless snow-white linen with a scarlet sash. His legs were bare under some sort of wrapped fabric. His hair was longer than most of his countrymen and appeared to have been tied back against his neck. He was well muscled and erect of posture. His golden eyes were gentle.

He looked as though he would prefer to be anywhere else at all.

So would I, Sheftu thought sardonically. "Who are you?" Sheftu growled.

Jodpul watched as the Soldatian climbed to his feet unsteadily using the wall at his back for support. His arms remained behind him, probably bound.

He raised his brows as the prisoner gained his full height. The man was nearly a head taller than he was himself, and well formed: wide in the chest and shoulders and narrow in the hips.

His one visible eye was raven black, framed by brows and lashes of the same hue. His hair, curiously, was streaked with white.

He was bare-chested. The trousers he wore were filthy, loose and tucked into knee-high leather boots of good quality. He was probably a good-looking man under all the dirt and the bruising.

"I would ask you the same," Jodpul said. His voice was calm, but serious. "Who are you?"

Sheftu tried to swallow but was unable. His throat was sore and dry. The pain in his body was nearly incidental to his thirst.

"Water," Sheftu said. "I need water."

Jodpul glanced down at his feet. A flagon of water had been set outside the cell, just out of arm's reach. Not that he could have reached for it with his arms bound behind him as they were. He looked up at the prisoner in surprise. *Not merely beaten but tortured as well.*

"Come closer," Jodpul instructed. He picked up the flagon and held it out when Sheftu hesitated.

"My arms are bound," the prisoner told him.

Jodpul grunted, tipped the flagon forward, and Sheftu leaned in to drink greedily of the stream, consuming it all.

He nodded his gratitude.

Jodpul nodded. "Who are you?" he repeated.

Sheftu took a step back and concentrated on standing unwaveringly straight. "I am Lord Sheftu Morrow, second son to the Morrow Lord of the Noble House of Morrow. I am from Soldat."

"Why are you imprisoned, Lord Sheftu?"

"I have been accused of… I don't know what I am accused of," he realized. "Abuse perhaps. Murder most likely. Maybe kidnapping." Sheftu shrugged, then shuddered visibly at the pain the movement wrought.

Murder, was it? "And who is it you might be accused of murdering? Or perhaps merely abusing?" Jodpul stood very still, his eyes boring into Sheftu's.

"A young Mirren woman, Laran Tania." Sheftu shook his head in disbelief. *How in the Seven Layers of Darkness had this happened? I wanted to help her. Just to help her!* Instead, he'd lost her, lost Provos. He'd lost everything.

"Why would you harm her, Lord Sheftu?" Jodpul asked softly. He was careful to keep any inflection from his voice, but Sheftu looked at him curiously.

"Why? Why do you care?" Sheftu asked. Standing was becoming more and more difficult. He shifted, spreading his feet further apart to keep his balance. "Who are you?"

"I am Viscount Jodpul Degere. I know well the woman you are accused of harming."

Sheftu's one open eye widened. "Jodpul!" *The non-dazzling Jodpul. Well, he looked dazzling enough now.*

Jodpul frowned. "You know of me?"

"*Aey*. Laran spoke of you. She told me you had been friends since childhood, and that you were expected to marry."

Jodpul looked surprised. "She told you that?"

"She loved you," Sheftu told him softly. "She told me that as well." *It could do no harm now. They were hardly in competition. Laran was dead.*

Jodpul was taken aback. "What else did she tell you, Lord Sheftu?"

"That you'd played at marriage as children." Sheftu felt the shattered remnants of his heart crumble away. "She wondered if you had waited for her."

"Why would she tell you this?" *Why would she tell her abuser her heart?*

"I did not hurt her, Viscount Jodpul. I was trying to help her. Others did what I am, or will be, accused of."

"Can you prove this?"

Sheftu shook his head. "The man who betrayed me, Santago—he knows the truth of my words though it will not be in his best interests to say so. There was another man, a Barraidi, one of the men responsible for hurting Laran; he, too, knows the truth."

"Why have your accusers not asked Laran herself? Surely she knows who it was that harmed her?"

Sheftu looked at Jodpul in bemusement. Was he not aware that Laran died on the Barraidi headland that day?

"She is dead, Viscount," Sheftu told him softly.

Jodpul was silent a moment, considering. Did the man really not *know*?

"She lives," he told Sheftu.

Sheftu stared at Jodpul in disbelief. He moved back until his back touched the cell wall once again. "What is this?" he demanded, his voice suddenly husky with emotion. Rage surged through him. "What game are you playing?"

Jodpul gazed at the Soldatian prisoner thoughtfully. He watched his changing expression carefully. The big man's amazement had transformed almost instantly into anger. Clearly, he did not believe that the Saharani was alive.

"She lives," Jodpul repeated quietly.

When the one black eye met his own, Jodpul saw the first spark of hope ignite in the stygian depths.

"Why has she not come to me, then?" Sheftu demanded.

Jodpul was silent.

Let it be true, Sheftu thought fervently. *Please, by the Seven Gods, let it be true!*

"If she were alive, she would have spoken for me."

Sheftu's one eye widened again, this time in alarm. "She is unable? She is hurt!"

Jodpul finally relented. "She believes you dead, my lord, and does not know you are here. Few do. It is apparently the Tania's wish that knowledge of your presence be limited."

Sheftu pushed his bound hands against the wall. His strength was waning and he would not remain on his feet for much longer.

"Why?" he whispered despairingly, but he already knew the answer. Laran's people believed he was the one who'd harmed her. They wished to spare her further upset.

I cannot die here, not here so close to Laran. She'd never know.

"The Tania," Sheftu murmured, turning the words over on his tongue. *Laran Tania.* That Tishane was not her father had been clear from the outset. "Laran's father." He locked eyes with Jodpul. "Tell him he has made a mistake! Demand that he hear the truth! Tell him…"

"Tell the Tania he has made a mistake?" Jodpul laughed humourlessly. "It would be a braver man than I to *demand* him do anything, Lord Sheftu."

"Why?" Sheftu demanded. "Why do you fear him?"

"You do not know?" Jodpul cocked his head in disbelief. "Just who do you think the Tania is, Lord Sheftu?"

"A religious leader, perhaps? A man of influence, certainly."

"He is," Jodpul instructed solemnly, "the High Lord of Mirren."

"High Lord?"

"In Soldat," Jodpul said, "he would be called *King.*"

Sheftu slid down the wall to the floor.

King. That was the "truth" Laran worried over, the "truth" he hadn't let her tell him.

Laran was alive.

And her father was the Mirren ruler.

Her father, the *king,* believed him to be a murderer and a rapist.

Sheftu began to laugh. His ribs caught fire but still he laughed. He was still laughing when Jodpul strode away in bemusement.

CHAPTER FORTY-SEVEN

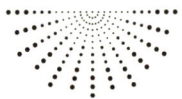

"LITTLE ELF," SHEFTU *called softly.*

Laran swam slowly toward the beckoning surface of wakefulness. Her eyes were still closed, and sleep still claimed her mind, but she felt the warmth of the smile in Sheftu's deep voice.

She murmured her greeting. "Tulah," she said sleepily in her own language. She was closer to the surface now. Sunlight shone in hazy stripes across her face and played against her eyelids.

From somewhere outside of herself, she realized that Sheftu would not have understood her greeting. He did not know the Mirren language.

The surface sparkled directly above her now and through her lashes she could see the wavering image of The Smiling Man bending over her, his raven eyes crinkled at the corners in amusement. He touched his lips to her forehead gently.

"Wake," he said.

Laran opened her eyes just as her head broke the glittering surface of sleep. Her vision sharpened suddenly.

Du-kar! It was Du-kar bending over her, not Sheftu! Du-kar, whose tomb-black eyes had been as cold as death itself. He was grinning at her evilly.

"Found you, didn't I?" he intoned. His terrible grin grew wider.

"No!" Laran screamed. She bolted out of bed. Her feet tangled on something large lying on the floor of her chamber and she fell headlong to the white stone beside it.

Sheftu! It was Sheftu! He was lying on his back, still and silent, his bronzed skin pale and his dark eyes open and glazing. An arrow protruded from his neck. Blood ran in a steady stream down the shaft to drip on the stone beneath.

"No!" she sobbed. "Oh no!"

"Laran! Wake up, Sister!"

She looked up at Du-kar but he was no longer there. Confused, she glanced down at her arm. A small hand rested there, and another caressed her cheek.

Shell.

"Run!" Laran urged her desperately. "Run, Shell!"

"It's another nightmare, Laran. Just a dream. Wake, now. Wake."

Laran jerked upright in her bed and looked around frantically. The furnishings, the sapphire covering on her bed, her white gown draped over an exquisitely carved chair—these were all familiar. Outside her open window the stars hung sparkling against the velvet sky. It was still night. She was in Mirren-Bar.

Sheftu was not lying dead upon her floor. Du-kar was not there.

"I... I am sorry, Shell," she whispered to her sister, her cheeks wet with tears.

Shell tucked her legs into the bed beside Laran and pulled the sapphire linens around them both. She placed her arms around her sister and pulled her close. Laran resisted the comfort offered for a moment, then settled against her younger sibling gratefully.

"I miss him, Shell," Laran said. Her voice was filled with sorrow. Shell tightened her embrace.

"Who, Laran? Who do you miss?"

"The Smiling Man. I loved him," she said, her voice breaking. "I will always love him."

Laran had been in love! On top of everything else, her heart had been broken! Shell's felt heavy in her chest. A fleeting thought of her own heartbreak over the man she loved was stifled and pushed aside.

"Who was he, Sister?" Shell asked quietly.

Laran had spoken of him before, on the day she returned to them. "Who was this Smiling Man?"

"He was the reason I survived enslavement in Soldat, the reason I am here with you now. He became my reason for... for everything."

Shell remained absolutely still. This was the first Laran had spoken of her ordeal, the first tentative glimpse she had allowed any of them to see into what had happened to her. *Can I keep her talking?* She didn't want her sister to withdraw into that dark space within again. *I want her back,* Shell thought. *Please come back to us, Laran.* How can I keep her talking?

"His name was Sheftu," Shell said, remembering her sister's words.

"*Ashaii,*" Laran answered. *Sheftu.* "He was Lord Sheftu Morrow."

She didn't notice when her sister stiffened beside her.

The Smiling Man, this Sheftu *was a lord! Could he be the man imprisoned? Tishane hadn't given her a name; he'd only referred to the prisoner as a Soldatian lord!* But Laran had spoken in past tense. She believed him dead.

And she loved him!

This was unexpected. She had to ask her about him. She had to know!

"Laran, is Lord Sheftu the man that hurt you?"

"Hurt...? No!" Laran squirmed out of her sister's embrace to look into her gold-flecked eyes. "Never. He saved my life, Shell. Took me away from Dukar, the man I was sold to in Soldat. He protected me, helped me. He made me happy. He..."

Laran's voice dropped to a whisper again. "He loved me, too."

"But..." *How can I ask what I need to hear? How can I dredge up the horror she endured? I don't want her to have to relive any of it. Not a single moment!* "But when our father found you," Shell continued, "you were terribly hurt and... and Tishane thought you might have been... ah..."

Laran said nothing, but she squeezed her eyes shut in misery.

"Barraidi hunters," she finally said. "They were the ones. Santago set them on us. They must have killed Sheftu. They even killed Provos. Oh, Shell, even Provos!"

"Provos?" Shell was bemused.

"Sheftu's cousin. He loved him like a brother. They'd been friends since childhood and did everything together."

"Just like you and me," Shell said softly.

Laran nodded tearfully. "And now they are gone." Laran grew quiet in Shell's arms. "And I will never see Sheftu again."

"Laran," Shell said. "It appears this Sheftu you speak of is the man our father believes responsible for your injuries. Tishane told me as much. Are you telling me this is not true? Are you saying he *never* hurt you?"

Laran looked into Shell's eyes once more. "Never, Sister. It was not in his heart to hurt *anyone,* though he could protect himself when he had to.

And he protected me when he could." She nestled back down in her bed, eyes wide and sorrowful.

"I was going to show him the sea," she whispered to Shell. "He'd never seen it." Tears leaked from the corners of her eyes and slid down the sides of her face to wet the soft brown curls of her hair.

Shell slid off the bed, placed her bare feet on the floor, and then turned to pull the linens up to Laran's shoulders.

"I must go," she told her. She felt a sudden sense of urgency. *Hurry! I must hurry!* "Will you be all right?"

Laran looked over at her sister and nodded. "Shell?" Shell turned at the door and glanced back.

"Jodpul wants to marry me," Laran told her. "I... I have been thinking about it. You see, I..." Laran swallowed, but the sorrow in her eyes had turned to something else. It looked a little like fear.

"You... what?" Shell asked, alarmed.

A Promise between Laran and Jodpul had been expected since childhood. It was based on more than love alone. If Laran refused him now?

No. She couldn't let herself think, even for a moment, what that could mean. "I've been thinking about it," Laran finished lamely.

Shell looked at Laran a few moments trying to decipher the change in her sister's expression, but her sense of urgency was escalating.

This "Sheftu" was likely the man imprisoned below. He hadn't harmed Laran. He was innocent. Tishane's instincts had been right! What the men thought they'd seen on the Barraidi headland that day was not as it had appeared.

She turned her feet in the direction of their mother's studio once more. The Lady Tania would likely still be at work there. She often painted through the night and she'd been completely immersed when Shell sought her out earlier.

* * *

IN HER CHAMBERS, Laran dragged the sapphire covering from the bed, enveloped herself in it, and padded on bare feet to the open window. Stars were still suspended in the velvet sky. The air was cool on her face and stirred her softly curling hair. Grief weighed heavily upon her.

One hand crept, seemingly of its own accord, to rest upon her flat belly. She was carrying Sheftu's child. She was certain of it now.

If she married Jodpul, her child would have a father. He knew she'd suspected she was pregnant. Jodpul had already agreed to raise the child as his own.

And if the child looked like Sheftu? If the oval of his eyes was not slanted as Mirren eyes were—if those eyes were black, not golden; if the hair was straight and dark, not light and curling; if his stature was larger, taller than her people normally were? All of Mirren would know the child was not Jodpul's. All of Mirren would know he was half Soldatian.

Their Saharani had been enslaved in Soldat. It would not be difficult to put the pieces together. The child would be ostracized.

Her other hand rose protectively to cover the first.

But this was *Sheftu's* child. She would die to protect their baby just as she would have died to protect his father. She would *not* end the pregnancy.

Holy Ones, she implored silently, *protect me. Help me shield the life I carry from harm and from the contempt of others. Grant our child the lasting happiness his father and I were denied.*

She would give Jodpul the answer he sought today. She'd marry him. She had to.

They were friends. He knew the child's father had been Soldatian. He understood the risks for her child's future. It would be as good a union as it could be under the circumstances and the child would have a loving father.

The love she felt for The Smiling Man could not be duplicated, but, with Jodpul, perhaps contentment would come in time.

CHAPTER FORTY-EIGHT

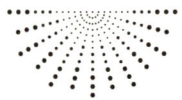

EMELDRA STEPPED BACK a pace to scrutinize her finished work. Innumerable candles lit the garret in which she painted. Her latest piece was done and though the subject matter was sombre, she was well satisfied with the result. She rubbed the tip of her nose with a paint-wet hand and unknowingly left a dash of orange there.

She would seek out her husband. She straightened, cheered by the prospect. It had been nearly two days since she'd seen him, two days! She smiled in anticipation. The Tania was a patient man. He kindly endured her absences. He seemed to understand that *not* painting was not an option. She *had* to paint.

Yes. She'd seek out his bed and make him happy she had returned to it.

She looked around at the portraits and studies of her eldest daughter. Sorrow hung on each of them and was evident in every nuance of posture in the subject. Though it broke her mother's heart to see and portray Laran like this, it helped Emeldra come to terms with the anguish Laran's situation had wrought.

And now another torment was to be visited upon them.

Shell's visit earlier that evening had left no doubt—they could no longer wait for Laran to confront her demons in her own time. She must be drawn into a conversation about her ordeal, a conversation that could set her back, lengthening the path to healing. Emeldra had little heart for such a venture.

But if Tishane was correct, it was *possible* that an innocent man had been imprisoned. And not *just* an innocent man, Emeldra mused, but a man who had been instrumental in helping Laran return to them.

If he was the villain her husband believed, their visit to the cells below would be even grimmer than expected. Shell would be dismayed regardless.

She'd never before visited those bleak and desolate rooms guarded by men who seemed little better than the denizens within them.

Emeldra glanced out one of the many windows in the garret. It would be dawn in a few hours. Best hurry to Mikale's bed while she still could.

After all, first light would see her slipping from the warmth of her husband's presence once again. At dawn, she and their youngest daughter would be embarking on a dismal quest for the truth, *if* it could be fathomed from a man who might desperately say *anything* to escape his confines.

She gathered her cloak, took a final look at her finished painting, and stepped over the threshold. A sleepy servant without rose from a prone position immediately.

"My lady?" she said, trying and failing to feign alertness.

Emeldra smiled. "Go back to your dreams, Lottie. I can find my way through my own home without assistance and have no need of anything else for now."

Lottie bowed deeply and gratefully turned away to seek her own bed. "Mother!" Shell cried from the hallway.

Emeldra frowned. Her daughter was running, *running,* toward her. In the middle of the night?

"What is it?" Emeldra called anxiously. "Has something happened? Are you all right? Is Laran…?"

When Shell reached her, she grabbed hold of both of the Lady Tania's arms to emphasize the exigency of her next words.

"I've spoken with her, Mother, with Laran. She told me all we needed to know. If the Soldatian lord is Sheftu Morrow, he is innocent! He didn't hurt her. He's *never* hurt her. He was just trying to bring her home."

"Slow down, my daughter," Emeldra said. "Come, away from curious ears. Come into the garret to speak."

When the door closed behind them, Shell's words bubbled out all at once.

"The anguish she's endured since she returned to us has been *grief* ! Grief over what happened to *him,* not upset over what happened to *her,* though that must have been a part of it." Shell looked deeply into her mother's eyes.

"She's in love with him, Mother! And she says he loves her, too. She believes him dead. I didn't tell her otherwise. I thought… Well, I thought you and I would ascertain who he is; that we'd judge the man and his motives ourselves."

Emeldra nodded thoughtfully. "That was wise, my daughter."

Lady Tania was silent a moment as she absorbed what Shell had just revealed.

"We should go," Shell told her. "We should go to him now!"

"Your father…" Emeldra began.

"Believes him to be guilty of doing terrible things! But if he knew the truth, if he knew he'd made a mistake, he would make it right! You know he would!"

"*Ashaii,* so he would," Emeldra agreed. She also knew that once her husband was set on a course of action, it would take a greater force than the mere supposition of truth to sway him. It must be proved.

And Laran must be the one to tell him. If the prisoner was indeed Lord Sheftu, she would soon know about the Soldatian's presence there in Mirren-Bar.

"Gather your courage, daughter," Emeldra said to Shell. "The prison is a dreadful place, a place of nightmares."

"Then we must make even greater haste, Mother," Shell said. "I have a feeling we must hurry!"

Emeldra nodded soberly. Shell's "feelings" were legendary. "Let us call for Tishane and be on our way."

CHAPTER FORTY-NINE

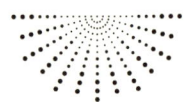

MIKALE REGARDED THE bowing messenger with distaste. His hair was jet black and so were his eyes. He was a head taller than the Tania was himself. He was Soldatian.

"Soldat," the Tania repeated, the word grating to his ears. "Why have you been sent from Soldat?"

"High Lord Tania," the messenger said, bowing low once again. Clearly, he was intimidated by the presence of the many Mirren guards in the great hall and by the power wielded by the Tania himself.

As he should be, the Tania thought uncharitably.

The messenger was beginning to shake. Mikale could see his knees knocking together.

"Speak." He was growing annoyed.

The messenger visibly gathered his waning courage.

"The Morrow Lord asked that I deliver this packet into the hands of your Captain of Guards. Your captain re-directed me here. I would be most grateful if you will agree to take it from me."

The Tania rose and beckoned the messenger forward impatiently. He had no interest at all in *anything* the Morrow Lord had to say. Doubtless it was a treatise for his son, now rotting in the cells below. Perhaps the Morrow Lord believed his elevated position in the Soldat court held weight with the High Lord of Mirren.

It did not.

Still, Mikale could admit curiosity, at least to himself. If the message had been addressed to Tishane, whom the young Soldatian lord had mistakenly assumed was Laran's father, then it was probable that *his* father, the Morrow Lord, had unknowingly meant the message for the Tania himself.

He held out his hand for the packet, then signalled his guards.

"See that this man is fed and rested," he instructed. "But do not release him. I may have use of him later."

His guards bowed and stood on either side of the Soldatian messenger. The man's eyes widened in apprehension, but he meekly followed the Tania's guards out of the meeting room regardless.

The Tania broke the wax seal and extracted a sheet of fine parchment paper from the packet. It was addressed to Tishane, Captain of the Guards in Mirren-Bar from the Morrow Lord in Soldat. An elaborate golden crest, that of the Morrow House, the Tania supposed, decorated the corner of the parchment. There was the usual flowery language of greeting, followed by the meat of the matter.

Captain, I inquire as to the health and whereabouts of Lord Sheftu Morrow, my son. I understand he was in contact with you prior to embarking on a journey to your land to return your daughter to you. He was last seen near the Soldat border with Barraid after taking ship from Soldat. The messenger I have dispatched has been instructed to return with your response to this discourse.

Mikale sat back in his chair and frowned at the parchment. The prisoner's father was an influential Soldatian lord. As High Lord, what Mikale did next could have political, even military, consequences. Perhaps he should think about his response.

Then again, he thought grimly, perhaps not.

He rose abruptly and called for the immediate return of the Soldatian messenger.

A *"response to the discourse"*? *Ashaii*! He had one. He doubted the Morrow Lord would be well pleased to receive it.

* * *

PROVOS MOVED HIS legs, inch by tortuous inch, off the sleeping platform. When his feet touched the ground he paused for a moment, gathering his remaining strength. He reached up for an overhanging branch with his good arm, clenching his teeth in pain as he did so, then drew himself to his feet.

He was standing!

He straightened to his full height slowly, fighting off waves of dizziness and nausea.

Standing! He let go of the branch and took a tentative first step, but the ground seemed to tilt beneath him and he suddenly found himself sprawled out upon it.

He lay on the forest floor waiting for the crests of pain to subside from his shoulder and chest before maneuvering to his knees. He crawled onto the platform once again. He remained sitting this time.

Progress. I've made progress.

Exhaustion crashed over him and he looked longingly down at the mossy mattress of his bed and at the warm blanket that awaited him there. They looked a long way away.

He needed his strength back. He *needed* to continue his journey to Mirren-Bar, although the prospect of traveling alone and injured was not appealing. If Sheftu was still alive, Provos knew he would find him there.

And if his cousin still lived, it was clear he needed help. If he didn't, he would have returned for Provos. Even if Sheftu thought him dead, he would have returned for his body.

Provos was as certain of that as he was that he must continue to Mirren-Bar, no matter the consequences.

Voices!

He turned toward the headland, invisible behind the branch screen. The owners of those voices were still some distance away, but apparently coming closer. He wanted to believe it was Randide and Estalla crossing through the long grass toward him, but it didn't sound like them. He heard raucous male laughter and a good-natured shout. The owners of *these* voices were proceeding without discretion.

Not Randide and Estalla, then.

Provos looked out at the forest longingly. He couldn't defend himself. He wanted to *run*! But the approaching men were unlikely to traverse the narrow deer path and were therefore unlikely to see the structure of his shelter. They would not likely find him.

If they *did*, they'd kill him sure.

The voices were coming closer, the laughter louder.

Provos reached up to grasp the overhanging branch once again. He pulled himself to his feet and took one step into the woods, followed by another, and then another.

The voices seemed to pause at the very entrance to the deer trail. The owners wouldn't take the path. Why would they? Unless they were hunters, of course.

As likely they were.

By the Seven Gods! I can't have come this far from this side of death to die here, now. *Damn this weakness!*

He took another faltering step, which placed him on the far side of a wide fir. He leaned his back against it and tried to will away the dizzying fatigue that threatened to send him to the forest floor once again.

A nearby burst of laughter sent dread thrumming through his wounded chest. He heard the crunching footballs of Barraidi boots against the dried twigs littering the deer path and then their sudden cessation. Silence followed.

Provos concentrated what little strength remained to him. He had to remain standing. He could not fall! If he remained out of sight behind the fir, perhaps the men would pass his shelter by.

He heard the sounds of their language, murmured now, and the softer sound of metal against leather as he imagined knives or swords were drawn from sheaths.

Men were moving cautiously around the shelter to peer within. Undoubtedly, they would see the discarded blanket. They would know someone had been there only moments earlier.

Provos felt the earth beginning to tilt beneath him once again. A low roar sounded in his ears and his back slid down the fir until he was sitting upon the ground.

Two Barraidi hunters appeared in the woods on either side of him, and a third moved to stand directly in front of him. Their short swords were drawn, and one had also palmed a wicked-looking skinning knife.

All three stared at Provos, incredulous. The sight of the wounded Soldatian in their midst had rendered them immobile. None made a move against him.

"*Ce-tal La,*" Provos said lamely. These were the only Barraidi words he knew. Estalla said them every time she came. They appeared to be a greeting.

The Barraidi looked even more incredulous, but one by one they slowly lowered their swords, though the weapons remained unsheathed. The men spoke quietly to one another and a short argument ensued.

They debate my death.

Provos struggled to put his feet under him. He pushed himself upward on shaking legs, using the fir at his back for support. When he finally stood, when he could focus once again, the three hunters were backing away and moving toward the deer path once again. The woods swallowed them up as they retraced their steps to the headland.

Only one had looked back at him.

Provos staggered back to the shelter. He dropped carefully to a seated position on the moss, breathing heavily. He could feel the sweat of exertion on his brow and prickling between his shoulder blades.

The Barraidi would be back. There would be more of them. The debate over his death would be short, the results swift. He had to leave.

How in the Seven Layers of Darkness was he going to accomplish that?

He tried to swallow his exhaustion. The crunch of at least three pairs of running feet sounded on the deer path.

The hunters had returned!

Provos glanced about for a weapon to use, a stick to wield, even a rock to cast, but the forest did not provide and he hadn't the energy, or the time, to improvise. The runners were upon him.

Now, Provos thought, *I die.*

But it was Randide tearing around the corner of the shelter and grabbing up the discarded blanket.

"Come!" he demanded. "Come now!"

Estalla appeared on the trail now, the babe Notel strapped to her chest, and both daughters in tow. She wore a worried frown on her pretty face. Though she prompted the wounded man to speed in her own language, Provos understood her tone and needed no urging regardless.

He rose shakily once more, this time without the support of the overhanging branch. Sweat bathed his face now. His legs shook with effort but did not collapse.

Randide pushed his shoulder under one of Provos' arms and half supported his weight as the group moved down the deer path. In the tall grass stood a cart piled with straw, an ancient horse tied to its back and another harnessed to pull it.

Estalla and the girls pulled straw from the cart and heaped it on the ground.

"In!" Randide demanded and Provos clumsily complied. He could feel sweat under his arms now and wet across his back. Fatigue was claiming him, and he was losing his battle against it. He lay back in the cart. Estalla covered his head and face with the blanket, then loaded the straw on top of him, presumably to conceal his presence within.

He felt the cart vibrate as the little Barraidi family climbed aboard, and then a painful jerk as the ancient horse began his trek. To where, Provos had no idea and no longer cared.

He sank into exhausted sleep once again.

CHAPTER FIFTY

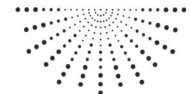

"ARE YOU *CERTAIN* you wish to do this?" Tishane asked for the second time.

He'd already far overstepped himself by involving the Saharani, and now her mother, in his quest for the truth regarding their Soldatian prisoner.

And now *this*?

He felt as though he'd been strapped blindfolded to the back of a galloping horse.

"We must," Emeldra said. The Holy Ones alone knew she had no *wish* to descend into the hell of the cells below. *No choice!* Especially not now that Tishane had confirmed the identity of the prisoner they sought.

The captain knew that if he agreed to accompany Lady Tania and the youngest Saharani through the cells, the Tania would never forgive him.

On the other hand, Tishane thought, the Tania knew well the sheer force of his wife's will. Her mind was set on this path. There would be no stopping her. Perhaps he would be *grateful* Tishane had been there with them, to protect them and keep them safe from harm.

He waited until the two women had turned the corner ahead of him before swearing mightily under his breath. Try as he might, there was *no* rationale for introducing the youngest Saharani to the filth and degradation of the cells! She'd likely have nightmares for months and her mother, determined though she was, would likely be just as disturbed by what they were about to witness.

It was no place for the tenderhearted.

Tishane lengthened his stride and caught up to them in three long paces.

"Follow me, then," he said reluctantly. They were nearing the entrance to the prison below. He spoke with authority to the guards on either side of the heavy wooden door.

One of them unbolted the portal, and both of them stepped aside respectfully, bowing, to allow the trio passage within.

"Stay in the centre of the corridor," Tishane instructed.

Shell felt her stomach clench at the sight of the long staircase ahead. Though constructed of the same white stone as the rest of the city, little light was reflected back from its surface from the dim light of the torches above.

She glanced at her mother but found little reassurance there. The Lady Tania's eyes looked intense and not a little afraid.

A quick look at Tishane showed a similar expression.

Tishane *afraid*? But that couldn't be. Tishane was as solid as the stone walls around them.

But perhaps it was not the prison itself that worried him. Perhaps what concerned him were the possible repercussions of what he was doing without her father's consent. Why hadn't she realized that before? She'd been too tied up in the drama to see the position Tishane had been put in simply by being there with them!

She reached for his hand and held it as they walked. Tishane looked down at her in surprise.

Shell knew the gesture was as much for her own comfort as to reassure the captain. Lady Tania walked behind them, her head high, her back erect, looking every inch the queen she was despite the dash of orange paint on the tip of her nose.

Shell's step faltered as they rounded the third of three corners to see the vast prison set out before them. Here the light was dimmer yet and the stench of unwashed humanity and sewage was nearly overwhelming. Tiny cells lined the corridors. Many were empty but sounds of insanity and misery emanated from those that were not. A long pair of filthy, emaciated arms reached out for them, and when Shell released Tishane's hand and backed away in horror, another pair successfully grabbed hold of her from behind, pulling her against the barred door of a cell. Its occupant whispered something foul into her ears.

She cried out and Tishane whirled, his fist snaking out between the bars to strike the man holding her square in the jaw. He dropped to the stones unconscious. Or dead.

"You all right, Saharani?" Tishane asked Shell.

She nodded shakily, her face pale and her eyes shiny with tears that she would not let fall.

Emeldra stood in the centre of the corridor away from grasping hands, one of her own pressed to her lips as though to stifle a scream. She wrapped one arm around her daughter and held her close.

By the Holy Ones, Shell thought. *What hell is this? I want to go back to the light! I want to go back!* She looked behind her in the direction of the now invisible staircase, then ahead to the long row of cells before them. Lewd and hateful comments swelled from within as the occupants caught sight of the women in their midst.

She swallowed her panic and tried to imagine herself imprisoned there for doing violence that she hadn't done and never would. She'd never survive!

She glanced up at Tishane, who regarded her carefully.

"Hurry," she said, though her voice lacked the conviction she felt.

He nodded briskly. He pressed his lips together to restrain himself from snapping out his original instruction to stay in the *centre*. Clearly, though, the warning was no longer necessary.

"Ahead," he said succinctly. Three cells stood alone and removed from the rest. The first two were empty. Tishane moved toward the third one cautiously and looked within.

He turned and signalled to the two women to wait, forgetting just this once who his two companions were. He glanced back but saw they had taken no offence and were content to do as he'd said.

The prisoner, he saw, was lying on his back on the stone floor, unbound now, one arm over his eyes, the other resting across his bare stomach. One of his legs was bent, the other stretched out full length.

"Soldatian," Tishane said quietly.

Sheftu opened his eyes slowly and blinked Tishane into focus. The captain appeared to be alone this time. Good. Little strength remained to him, and he had no wish to use up the balance defending himself from the brutal guards that peopled this place.

Sheftu spared himself the excruciating pain that movement wrought on his broken ribs. He remained prone.

"Have you come to release me, Captain?" Sheftu spoke through parched lips. "Have you finally decided you cannot live with the knowledge that an innocent man is to die tomorrow?"

"Tomorrow? What do you mean?" Tishane growled.

"Interrogation," Sheftu supplied. "I will not survive another."

Interrogation! Tishane bit off his retort as the impact of the Soldatian's words hit. *Another?* By the Holy Ones, this man was being made to suffer!

He is not guilty. He is not the one. This is not right!

"There is someone here to see you, Soldatian," Tishane said. His voice had been gentler than he'd intended.

Two small figures stepped into the weak light of the nearest torch. A head shorter than Tishane, and slender, their clothing was vibrantly coloured and seemed to flow to the stones upon which they stood. Sheftu had the impression of long, curling hair and large slanted eyes. The figures were distinctly feminine.

Emeldra and Shell watched the man struggle to a seated position. His teeth were clenched in an obvious effort not to cry out. Clearly, he was in considerable pain. When he finally reached his goal, he leaned back against the stone wall a moment, breathing hard, and then he gathered his feet beneath him and rose.

He was large! Certainly the biggest man Emeldra had ever seen. She glanced at her youngest daughter. Shell's eyes were huge in her now pallid face. Her lips parted slightly in astonishment as she stared up at the man in the cell. He was standing in the shadow and his features were hidden, but it was apparent that he was naked from the waist up.

He stepped into the light, his jet-black eyes fastened on Shell. "Laran?" he breathed in amazement.

"N...no," Shell whispered. The man looked strong, but she could see that his bronzed skin was pale. Perspiration stood on his brow though the air was cool, and she wondered if he was fevered. His face was battered and cut, and a terrible purpled abrasion covered much of his bruised ribs. His hair was tangled and matted, and he was dirty. The scent of his sweat was strong.

"Laran is my sister."

"Shell," he said. He sounded incredulous. Shell was shocked silent. *He knows of me!*

"Laran knows now that I live?" Sheftu asked. "She knows I am here?" Tishane winced at the sudden lift in the Soldatian's deep voice.

"She does not know," he answered for Shell.

Sheftu's gaze swung from Tishane to the two women. The light went out of his face. His black, black eyes were growing cold. "Then why are you here?" he asked them softly. Ice had crept into his tone.

"Captain Tishane thought..." Emeldra began.

"Thought *what*?" Sheftu suddenly roared. He was glaring now at Tishane. "Thought to torture me once again? Like *this*?" he asked with a significant glance at the women. "Does it *never* stop?"

Tishane put his arm out to push the two women farther from Sheftu's cell door. He was shaking his head.

"You are mistaken," Tishane told him.

"Mistaken?" Sheftu snarled. "You son of a bitch! The beatings, the starvation! *This.*" He gestured at Emeldra and Shell.

"The interrogation..." he continued. "But no. I take it all back, Captain. It *does* stop, doesn't it." It wasn't a question. "Tomorrow."

"*This,*" Sheftu continued, obviously referring to the women, "is something new. I'll say one thing for you Mirren," Sheftu hurled. "You're an inventive lot!"

He stepped back into the shadows of his cell until he could feel the stone at his back once again. His ribs were on fire and despair enveloped him like a shroud. Tears leaked from his eyes and ran down his cheeks. It shamed him that it was so, and he'd be *damned* if he'd let these people see it! He raised his chin defiantly and tried to drown out the sound of murmured conversation, though one voice was more adamant than the others. Shell. It must have been Shell's voice.

By the Seven Gods, but she looked like Laran.

She was clean and beautiful and soft. He drank in the sight of her hungrily as she stepped close to the barred door of the cell. He remained in the shadows.

"Lord Sheftu," she said. Her voice was hushed and anxious. She said his name with a musical lilt. *Like Laran.*

He didn't reply. He wouldn't have his feet for much longer and he couldn't bear any more of *this*!

"Sheftu," she tried again. "It is true that my sister is not aware that you are here. My mother and I learned of your presence only yesterday. And it was only last night that I learned from my sister that it was not *you* who'd hurt her."

Sheftu remained silent. His own injuries suddenly seemed insignificant.

They knew!

"We didn't tell her you were here because... well, because she has been plagued with nightmares and overwhelmed with sorrow since she came home to us. We wanted to..." Shell hesitated. That they'd meant to judge him for themselves sounded cold.

"To see the big, bad Soldatian for yourselves?" he asked quietly.

Shell looked up, trying to see into his raven eyes.

"Yes," she admitted.

"Well, it's a fine figure I make now, isn't it? I imagine I look completely upstanding and trustworthy."

Shell ignored the sarcasm in his voice.

"You look terrible and you smell nearly as bad," she told him.

Sheftu laughed, the sound surprising even himself, but the movement tore at his shattered ribs and he quickly stopped.

"She told me that she loves you," Shell said. Still the Soldatian said nothing, and Shell couldn't see his expression. "She... she believes you love her, too. It is so?"

The big man stepped back into the light and closer to the barred door. He wrapped his fingers around two of those bars directly above Shell's own. She forced herself to remain where she was and not to jump back in alarm. She heard Tishane shift warily.

"I love her," Sheftu said quietly.

Shell saw the tracks of tears on his cheeks and had to blink her own away. She swallowed her trepidation.

"And you did not harm her? Not ever?"

Sheftu shook his head. "No." He felt his knees begin to buckle and he willed himself to remain upright.

"Is she all right?" he asked. "Is she still hurt? Has she been...?"

"Why did you come to Mirren-Bar, Lord Sheftu?" Emeldra interrupted.

255

Sheftu swung his head in her direction. He'd been standing too long. Black was beginning to appear at the edges of his vision and his focus began to blur.

His legs gave way and he collapsed to his knees on the stone floor, one hand outstretched for support.

"She saved my life," he gasped. The fall had jarred his ribs badly. "I wanted…to… help her." He lowered himself the rest of the way to the floor and rolled painfully to his back.

"Let me in," Emeldra said to Tishane.

"Lady Tania," Tishane protested, "I do not believe it wise. I think…"

"Now," she told Tishane imperiously.

"*Ashaii*," he said, bowing. The Soldatian did not appear capable of being a threat at the moment. Tishane selected a long key from several others hanging around his neck under his shirt and unlocked the door. Emeldra stepped inside fearlessly.

She knelt at the injured man's side, oblivious to the filth coating the floor and soiling her gown. The sight of a dead rat near Sheftu's outstretched arm arrested her a moment, but she could not allow herself to be distracted.

She placed a small hand over the prisoner's wounded side, her fingers brushing the broken ribs. He tensed in agony but settled again as Emeldra began the healing.

Sheftu felt the first layer of pain dissolve away as the bone within began to knit and the tissues around them became whole once again. As another layer released and then another, as the pain receded entirely, he began to relax his body, which had been rigid with discomfort. He watched the woman leaning over him.

Laran's mother was of middle years and still beautiful. She was small and slender like Laran and Shell. Her eyes were clear and bright and focused on the task at hand. They weren't golden like Laran's were, though, but were instead a tawny brown with flecks of gold throughout. They were mesmerizing.

Lying injured on the filthy floor of a prison cell, unwashed, beaten and starving, *this* was not how he'd pictured meeting Laran's mother.

He told her so.

Emeldra lifted her hand from his once damaged ribs and looked down into his eyes. She had been aware that as the pain left him, he had begun to study her. "What did you picture, Lord Sheftu?" she asked him curiously.

"Not this," he repeated grimly. He'd imagined courtesy, possibly even gratitude for helping Laran escape enslavement in Soldat. He hadn't expected to be liked. He was Soldatian, after all. But, by the Seven Gods, he'd *never* expected to be imprisoned and abused.

"First light will break soon," Tishane told them. He was standing inside the little cell just behind Emeldra, positioned to protect her from attack as the prisoner revived.

First light. Last day. Sheftu elevated himself to a seated position on the stone floor, his head now even with Lady Tania's. "Thank you," he murmured.

"It is *we* who are grateful, young lord," she replied.

"The Soldatian here believes he is to die today," Tishane said. "If we are to change his fate, we had better go now."

"He comes with us," Emeldra said. She rose gracefully from the prison floor.

"What?" Tishane was alarmed. "No!" The Tania would have his very *life* for *that* transgression. His *life*.

"Fear not, Captain," Shell told him softly. "We will protect you."

Tishane looked down at the youngest Saharani with affection. He put a finger out to brush a wayward curl from her brow, then turned decisively. He was committed now regardless of the consequences.

He reached a hand out to Sheftu and noted the Soldatian's hesitation to take it.

"Put aside your distrust, Lord Sheftu," Tishane said. "I am here to help you now."

Sheftu grasped the hand strongly and used it to leverage himself off the stones. When he reached his full height, Tishane insinuated his shoulder under Sheftu's arm and Sheftu gladly took the support offered.

Leaving! He was leaving the cells. *Could it be so?* Would they be stopped before they crossed the prison threshold? This was his last chance at life. *The last!* Before this unimagined moment, only interrogation and death had lain ahead.

Despite his other injuries, despite his weakness, Sheftu suddenly felt euphoric. He would live! He would see Laran again! He would travel to the Barraidi headland to bury his cousin's body, what remained of it.

And he would find Santago, the root of all of it.

* * *

HIS STEP FALTERED and he felt Shell move against him. She wrapped one arm around his waist, then took *his* arm and placed it over her shoulder. As tired as he was, he was careful not to rest his weight against her small form, though he took comfort in her invitation to do so. Tishane glanced at him and nodded approvingly.

* * *

THEY WERE IN the palace now. Sheftu could see dawn breaking through the open windows. He was growing weaker and knew he was leaning too heavily against Tishane, but he was powerless to stop. He concentrated on placing one foot in front of the other. The alternative was to fall, here, and risk being seen as the people of Mirren-Bar began their day. Already he could hear the bustle of activity, but so far all had remained out of sight.

"Hold," Emeldra said, lifting her hand. She turned to Sheftu who seemed to be growing paler with each step. "If you can remain upright, young lord, if you can remain silent, there is something you might wish to see. Come," she said.

Unaware of his surroundings, he hadn't realized they'd climbed to a second floor. Now he looked out over an open stone balustrade to gardens spread out below. They were small, private perhaps, surrounded on all sides by

258

open corridors such as the one they had stopped in. Several ponds rested peacefully amid a riotous display of spring flowers and delicate, overhanging trees.

An impossibly large brown dog tore out into the garden from an unseen entrance, then skidded to an abrupt stop to bark, loudly, at a squirrel scolding from a tree.

A young woman followed from that same entrance. She was small, as Mirren women were, and slender like the two women at his side. She wore a hooded, ankle-length indigo sheath covered with some diaphanous material, which looked so fragile as to be insubstantial. Her feet beneath the gown were bare. Her head was covered and her face turned away.

She spoke, apparently to the dog, in her own language and though Sheftu could not comprehend the words, he knew the voice. He'd carried the sound of it in his heart through all his time in the cells. He'd thought never to hear it again. Not in this life.

Laran!

She tilted her head toward the sun, which was just now making an appearance, and closed her eyes to savour the earliest warmth of the new day. When she pushed back her hood, the first slanted rays of morning shone directly into her short cap of light curls.

"Laran," Sheftu whispered. He jerked his arm from Tishane's shoulder and broke Shell's grasp on his waist. He took hold of the balcony railing for support and started forward. He looked frantically for a staircase, anything, to access the garden. He began to contemplate leaping over the railing.

Laran!

Tishane grabbed him around the waist and pulled him behind a large stone pillar.

"Think what you are doing, Soldatian," Tishane hissed.

When Sheftu broke away again, Tishane took hold of his arm.

"She doesn't know you are here. Doesn't know you are *alive*. Do you really want to *surprise* her like this, to have her see you this way?"

Sheftu stopped moving and looked down at himself in dismay. Half naked and dirty, dried blood coated his skin in places and bruising marred most of his arms and torso. He was weak with hunger and thirst. He put a hand to his unshaven face and winced at the reminder of his split lips.

"No," he said slowly. He looked at Tishane. "Water. I need water. Something to eat." *Anything.* "And then I will want a bath, clean clothes."

"You will have those things, young Lord Sheftu," Emeldra said. "Come away now. We are nearing our private chambers."

"Bring him to mine," Shell said.

Tishane looked scandalized but reluctantly acquiesced when he saw Lady Tania's nod.

"My father seldom enters them," Shell said. "It will give us time to decide how next to proceed."

Tishane sighed heavily. *Now I am delivering a half-naked Soldatian male to the youngest Saharani's private chambers.* An overwhelming urge to laugh bubbled up in his chest. He choked it down, but a wide grin appeared on his rugged face.

"What is it, Captain?" Emeldra asked, a frown between her eyes. "What is it you find amusing?"

"Amusing," Tishane said, still choking down his laughter. "By the Holy Ones, Lady Tania, I find *nothing* amusing in this scenario. I was merely smiling at the unexpected turn my, as of now, very short future has taken." His grin disappeared altogether as he contemplated what his wife would say.

She'd mourn him, he knew that, but she would also be furious and would be unlikely to forgive him. That distressed him more than he thought it should.

"Come, you great hulking Soldatian," Tishane said resignedly. He grunted as he once again took Sheftu's weight upon his shoulder. It had occurred to him back in the prison that he should begin addressing the young man more respectfully than simply "Soldatian", but he found now that he no longer cared.

After all, it would make no difference to the life, or rather, lack of one, that he looked forward to now.

In the gardens below, Laran swiveled her head to stare up at the balustrade. Had she seen movement there? *Sheftu!* But no. That was impossible. She'd been seeing The Smiling Man in every crowd, hearing his voice and his laughter in every gathering. This was but one of those moments.

Grief played tricks on the mind. She'd long heard that it was so, and she had every reason to believe it now.

Laran reached down to stroke Little Dog's big head, then knelt to hug her shaggy neck. The faithful animal sat patiently and still, attuned to her upset.

Jodpul would soon be there.

She needed to keep her feet on the ground! She'd heard the old saying from her father countless times since childhood. *Let your dreams lift you up, but keep your feet on the ground.* She pondered the incongruity of the saying a moment before dismissing it entirely.

Her dreams were dead and no longer buoyed her. She'd *have* to keep her feet on the ground if she was to protect the life growing inside her.

She willed Jodpul to make his appearance. She wanted to be done with it all. She would accept his proposal and try not to fear for the future of her child, or for her own.

After all, her fears would neither help nor hinder.

CHAPTER FIFTY-ONE

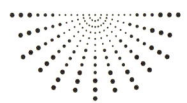

"LOOK, SOLDATIAN!" RANDIDE said.

"Provos," Provos grumbled. "My name is Provos, Barraidi!"

"Aey," Randide said absently in Soldatian. "Look there!"

Provos swiveled slowly to spare his shoulder and chest unnecessary movement. Despite his days in the back of the cart and his nights on the hard ground, he was definitely growing stronger.

He fixed his eyes on the view ahead and gaped in astonishment. "Mirren-Bar," Randide said.

It was beautiful. A multi-leveled, fairy-tale city of long avenues and white spires, it appeared to have grown from the sides of the mountains surrounding it.

"That is no myth," Provos murmured. He wondered if his cousin had seen this view on his journey.

"Myth?" The word was not in Randide's limited Soldatian vocabulary.

"A tale," Provos began. Communicating with Randide was frustrating but he had to give the Barraidi credit. At least he *attempted* to converse. "Like a... a children's story." Best he could do.

"Ah," Randide said. He looked at Provos curiously. Soldatians had strange notions, he thought.

"You cousin there, perhaps."

Provos nodded. Did he live? Was it even possible after all this time?

And Laran? He looked over the incredible sight that was Mirren-Bar. All she'd wanted was to return to her family and her home. She'd come so close. His chest ached at the thought of what might have befallen her.

Had Sheftu learned the truth about her? Santago had known who she was. He'd *knelt* before her on the ship. That Laran was not the daughter of the Captain of Guards was clear. Rather, she must have been from a prominent family, a noble's perhaps, or a religious leader's. He hoped this *Tishane*, this captain she'd spoken of, knew her parentage. Whether or not he did, Tishane was a logical starting point in Provos' search for Sheftu.

He looked around them at the mountains and the enormous boulders that marked their passage. It seemed strange that there had been no Mirren presence to challenge them.

"Sentries," Randide said, indicating the bluffs above them. "Up there. See us. Two days."

Provos glanced at Randide, who appeared to have read his thoughts, then up at the bluffs above.

Watched for two days? He'd been too caught up in his own discomfort to notice! The Mirren had been aware of them, then, since crossing the border. They knew that the Barraidi family traveled with a wounded Soldatian. He hoped that didn't bode ill for them.

He turned away from the view of the city and settled back against the rock on which he'd been resting. Estalla handed him a container of hot liquid. Chicken broth? More likely deer broth. It smelled good. He smiled his thanks and she smiled back, no longer afraid of him. Thank the Seven Gods. Her continuing good nature in the face of adversity was heartening.

Little Seren came to sit at his side. She stared into his container of broth and wrinkled her nose. Provos gulped the liquid noisily, making loud slurping noises for her giggling amusement. He grinned at Estalla in apology, but she was smiling, too. Six-year-old Alam stayed on the other side of the cooking fire, staring at him fearfully. He winked at the girl, but she only widened her eyes in distrust.

This was the little one who'd thrown the rock so efficiently. Did she *still* fear retribution? Provos rubbed the back of his head theatrically. "Good arm," he told her, then glanced at Randide to translate.

Randide did so, looking bemused, and Alam stared at Provos in horror. His grin began to disarm her, though, and she finally attempted a smile when he tensed his bicep and then pointed at hers. "Good arm," he said again.

She grinned, perhaps a little *too* proudly.

Provos relaxed. Despite the circumstances, despite the pain and his weakness, despite his fear for his cousin's life, and despite the unknown reception awaiting them in the city beyond, he was beginning to enjoy himself.

CHAPTER FIFTY-TWO

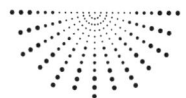

MIKALE TANIA AWOKE with a start, his nightmare still clear in his mind. He sat up in bed abruptly and swiped his hand over his bristled jaw. He looked to Emeldra for comfort, but she was not beside him.

The Soldatian! He'd dreamt that his beautiful daughter, his lovely Laran, was beneath the man as he tore at her clothes. She'd been sobbing in terror, calling for her father to help her. Mikale swore inarticulately and placed his feet on the cool stone floor. Rising, he pulled the linen off the bed and wrapped it around his naked form before striding to the window.

He stared sightlessly at the mountains, a view which filled every window in the room and was often a source of both solace and inspiration. Today it was neither.

It was no wonder he'd dreamt of the Soldatian. The man was to be interrogated this morning, this time by Mikale himself. He'd glean what he could of the trader who'd abducted Laran and of the route taken to sell her into slavery. And then he'd find out exactly what had happened to Laran and what role the young lord and his kinsman had played in it all.

He owed it to his people to put an end to both the slave trade and its traders. That his people would no longer be in danger of abduction and enslavement should be reward enough, but he was man enough to admit that retribution for the wrongs his daughter had suffered would give him a dark sort of pleasure as well.

He pulled the linens around him tightly. He had little stomach for what he was about to do, and the Soldatian in the cells below might have no information to give regarding the slave trade regardless.

Still, it was time he dealt with the man. *His* role in the hurt done his daughter was clear.

The Tania turned to stare at his empty bed. Where *was* Emeldra? His wife had been absent from their chamber for two nights, and though it was not unheard of, it was rare for her to paint through more than one.

He wondered if she'd slept at all. Or if she'd eaten! She had but one master: her art. Mikale knew that well. He smiled at the thought.

He was also man enough to admit that his wife gave him strength. He'd seek her out at the garret in which she painted *before* he descended into the hell of the cells below.

Today he would take the Soldatian's life. He'd taken others in the name of justice. It was never easy. Death had to be warranted. He could feel the *rightness* of this one deep inside.

Unbidden, he saw once again the image of the half-naked Soldatian, bloodied and breathing hard, bending over his unconscious daughter. He saw again her battered face and the terrible bruising on the inside of her outstretched arm. He saw her bare legs and half-covered torso. He saw the shredded remnants of her clothing.

Grief and anger surged through him. *Ashaii!*

The life he would take today felt *right*.

He pivoted on his heel, dropped the linen to the floor, and sought his clothing. He wanted to *move*. He wanted to be away. He *wanted* Emeldra.

* * *

SHEFTU LEANED BACK gingerly in the bath. It was an oval vessel forged of metal roughly half his length. When he sat inside, the water came up to his chest. It felt *good!* The water was warm and lightly scented with some sort of oil. Soap and washcloths lay on a stool nearby.

He allowed himself the luxury of sliding down the back of the vessel until the warm water completely covered his head, drowning out the sounds of the strange world he inhabited now. His time in this world would likely be short, one way or another, but by the Seven Gods, he was enjoying it now at this moment.

He thought of Laran, immersed in his bathing pool in Soldat. She had likely felt the same sense of pleasure in the simple luxury as he did now. Baths would not have been a part of her life as a slave, though she'd obviously been permitted to wash. Even *that* comfort had been denied to him as a prisoner. *"You look terrible and you smell nearly as bad",* Shell had told him. *Aey.* That must have been so.

He broke the surface of the water again and rubbed his eyes dry with his fingertips. When he opened them, he saw that he was no longer alone. Laran's mother stood not six feet away, her arms crossed on her chest. She was staring down at him speculatively.

Sheftu sat up abruptly, spilling water over the side of the vessel. He could hear it splashing against the stone floor. He fought the urge to grab a drying cloth to cover his genitals. *What was this?*

"Have I stumbled upon a Mirren tradition I am ignorant of, Lady Tania?" Sheftu asked. He kept his tone as civil as possible.

"I have questions, Lord Sheftu," she answered. Her voice was cordial, the tone oddly conversational under the circumstances.

"And you wished to ask me when you had me at a disadvantage?"

He was astute. Emeldra took in his great height and the breadth of his shoulders. He was a fine-looking man, to be sure. But was there more to him than the masculine figure he presented? *Who* had Laran allowed herself to fall in love with? What motivated him?

He picked up the soap from the stool and began lathering his arms and neck.

"Be sure to get the dried blood on your chest, young lord," Emeldra said. Sheftu raised a brow. "How did you know?"

"Know what?" Emeldra asked.

"How did you know Laran would come out to the garden at the moment we passed?"

Interesting, Emeldra thought. *His* first real question was for Laran.

"Since she returned to us, it has been her habit to go to the garden every morning at first light. I suspect she is not sleeping well, Lord Sheftu."

Sheftu nodded faintly.

"The reward for bringing the Saharani back to us will have been substantial," she continued. "I believe the sailor, Santago, has claimed it instead." She watched for his reaction and awaited his comment.

"Saharani," he repeated softly. His Little Elf had a title!

Reward?

Sheftu frowned. "I did not wish a reward, Lady Tania. You do me insult to suggest it."

"Do I?" Emeldra cocked her head at him sideways. *As if accusing the man of rape and murder were not enough!* "Are you not a second son? Is it not tradition in Soldat to give all inheritance and holdings to the first-born male? Could you not *use* the comfort the reward would have given you?"

Sheftu stopped lathering. He sank below the surface of the water to rinse, knowing as he did so that he was being rude. Still, it was *she* who had intruded so inappropriately on his bathing.

He rose above the surface once more, swiping soapy water from his face. He looked her in the eyes.

"I want *nothing* from you, Lady Tania; nothing from your family, nothing from your people. *Nothing.* Except, perhaps, to continue this bath without an audience."

Emeldra ignored the jibe. "I don't believe that is entirely true. There *is* more that you want, young lord. Is that not so?"

"*Aey,*" he amended quietly. "So there is." *Laran. He wanted Laran.* He sat up straighter in the bath. "I would see your daughter again. Now. As soon as I am cleansed."

"And perhaps something else?"

"I would have my freedom. I would have justice, Lady Tania."

Emeldra hesitated. "I have caused you discomfort being here, now, as you bathe." She didn't look in the least remorseful. "This minor social impropriety is certainly the least you have had to bear at Mirren hands. And there will be more to bear before we are done. I will do what I can to keep you free, but before justice is done, you must marshal the strength to endure what comes next. Can you do that?"

Sheftu nodded, frowning. "And Laran?" he asked.

"A meeting will be arranged," Emeldra told him.

Her gaze took him in, *all* of him. "I will leave you to your bath. When we are done, I will finish healing you, and then we will consider what must come next."

She signalled for a servant, a young girl whose eyes widened with apprehension when she saw the naked Soldatian stretched out in the bath.

Emeldra spoke a few words in her own language to the girl, who darted a near-panicked glance at Sheftu as she bowed her acquiescence.

"You will need assistance with your hair and your back," Emeldra told Sheftu.

The girl moved cautiously into the room, casting terrified glances at the big man in the bath.

Sheftu sighed in resignation. Truth be known, he *could* use the help. Though his ribs had been healed, the rest of his body was still a mass of bruising. Stretching his muscles to wash caused the ache to run bone deep.

Consider what must come next? Laran. I want to see Laran next. Healing, and everything else, can come later.

269

* * *

"LARAN," JODPUL CALLED softly. He smiled into her eyes as he drew near. "You wanted to see me?"

"*Ashaii*," she told him. She looked up at his handsome face and saw affection warm in his golden eyes. "Will you sit with me?"

"By the pond," he suggested. He held his arm out to her and Laran took it. The gesture set the sensation of butterflies swirling inside of her. He guided her to the largest of the three garden ponds, this one more private than the others and completely shaded by an ancient willow. Redolent with new growth, the lime green and yellows of its foliage cast a dappled pattern upon the jade waters. Long, sinewy fish swam silvered through the lilies at the pond's edge and disappeared into its depths.

This man, Laran thought, *will be my husband and father to my child. He will become my life. He is a good man and both families approve of the union. Marrying him is the right thing to do.*

Then why did it feel so wrong?

Jodpul drew her down to the large, flat stones at the water's edge. He raised his brows in question.

"I…" Laran began. Anxiety rose up in her chest and closed her throat. Tears rose to her eyes but remained unshed.

"I have given much thought to your proposal, Jodpul," she told him softly. Her hand still rested on his arm. Beneath it, she felt him stiffen.

"What have you decided, Saharani?" he asked quietly.

"That you still wish to marry me after all that has happened honours me," she told him. "Your readiness to father the child that I carry means more to me than you can possibly imagine. I have known you all of my life. You are a kind, gentle man, and an honourable one. I have always loved you, Jodpul, as a cherished friend. That love will not diminish." She hesitated, looking down into the dappled water.

"What have you *decided*, Saharani?" he repeated. He was staring at her intently.

She looked up into his face. "I will marry you, Jodpul. Now. Today, if you wish it."

He expelled his breath noisily and grinned hugely.

"I thought…" He shook his head. It no longer mattered what he'd thought. She was going to marry him! His family would be relieved. *He* was relieved!

Wasn't he?

Of course. Of course, he was. This was the path he was destined to walk. He shut his eyes a moment against the brief image of another that his mind, and his heart, had conjured.

"You will not regret it, Laran," he told her, his tone sincere. "Ever. And our wedding will be a wondrous affair! It will be as we dreamed it as children."

But Laran was shaking her head. "No," she said. "My dreams are…" *Dead,* she thought. "Different now," she said. *Everything is different now.* "I wish a small wedding, Jodpul, with my family and yours, maybe a few others who are special to us. No more than that. Does that disappoint you?"

He laughed. "In truth, not at all."

Laran rose, reached out both hands to his, and he took them, rising. "Then let us tell our families. Let us make arrangements to be married now, today," she said.

"*Ashaii,*" he said happily. "All right. I will leave you now to confer with my family. Will you do the same?"

"I will."

He took one of her hands and pressed his lips to the palm. "We will have love, Laran. And great happiness."

He turned and strode away from the ancient willow, away from the silvered fish in the jade depths of the pond, away from the woman who would become his wife.

He leapt over the last row of lavender flowers, then stopped abruptly on the other side as thoughts of the imprisoned Soldatian in the cells below intruded on his thoughts. He wanted to forget the man existed, to forge on with his plans for marriage, but found he could not.

He turned back to the garden, the smile on his handsome face fading.

I can't do this!

Laran had been deceived into believing the Soldatian was dead. If he were the one who'd hurt her, his ultimate death in the cells was warranted. But if he were proven innocent…

Jodpul felt his heart sink. He couldn't begin his marriage without knowing the truth. He owed that truth to Laran and to the child she carried.

No. He needed time to find the Barraidi hunter the Soldatian had spoken of. Time, too, to track down the Mirren sailor, Santago. The search for the truth was already underway.

"Laran," Jodpul called.

She was walking slowly away toward the entrance to her rooms, Little Dog at her heels and nudging the back of her legs with her shaggy face. She turned back toward him. The indigo hood of the sheath she wore once again covered her hair. The diaphanous covering was immaterial in the sunlight, but the hood shaded her face and Jodpul could no longer see her expression.

"Laran," he said, his tone quiet now. He had no heart for the question he needed to ask. "The father of the child you carry…"

"Sheftu," she murmured.

"*Ashaii.* Sheftu." He strained to see her face under the indigo hood. "If he had lived, would you have agreed to marry me?"

"I… I don't know," she stammered. She was silent a moment. *He deserves to hear the truth.* "No," she finally whispered. Beneath the hood, tears streamed down her cheeks at the hurt she felt that it was so, and at the hurt he must feel now at that simple word.

Jodpul looked at her a long moment, then turned on his heel to leave the garden.

"Two weeks," he said over his shoulder. His voice sounded different now. "We will wed in two weeks."

Laran's eyes widened. *Two weeks?* Why did he wish to wait when she was willing to marry him *now?* Her honesty had upset him. Did he wish to reconsider? It seemed unlikely. Perhaps he wished to give *her* additional time to rethink the union? She wouldn't.

She was Promised to him now.

CHAPTER FIFTY-THREE

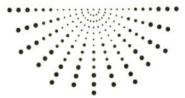

MIKALE TANIA GLANCED down at his clothing. He wore sturdy leather sandals that laced to mid-calf with leather ties. His muscular legs were bare under the knee-length wrap-around *talom*, which hung from his hips. The sleeveless shirt he'd chosen was scarlet, Emeldra's favourite. He ran his hand over his jaw, testing its smoothness. Clean shaven now, as Emeldra preferred him, he stepped over the threshold of the garret, a smile of anticipation on his lips.

It was empty save an impressive collection of both blank and finished canvasses, some draped against the light of day, others exposed. The white stone floor was liberally splattered with multi-coloured paint. Splashes of blue and yellow decorated the windowsills and the walls. Wooden benches lined the perimeter of the garret and a neat array of brushes rested on surfaces coloured in hues a rainbow might envy.

Disappointed not to see his wife there, Mikale spied her new work on an easel by the window and strode over to see it.

Laran. The subject was no surprise. Emeldra painted whatever weighed most heavily upon her mind. It was her way of coming to terms with her upset and she claimed it helped give her perspective. He knew it helped calm her thoughts.

This latest work was poignant. In it, Laran stood in a shaft of light. She was gazing into one of the ponds in the courtyard garden she loved. The big shaggy form of Little Dog lay stretched out on the grass, her adoring eyes on her mistress. Laran was wearing the long indigo gown she seemed to favour, the hood drawn half over her hair. Short, unruly tendrils danced across her brow in an apparent light breeze and the wind pushed the fabric against her lithe form. Both hands were folded gracefully over her flat stomach.

She looked... lost.

He looked again at the position of the hands. Was there meaning there? Surely not! *By the Holy Ones! Was his daughter with child?* Fury built in his chest until it nearly choked him, and he had the irrational desire to smash his fist through the painting. *The Soldatian!*

But perhaps he was mistaken. Perhaps the position of the hands meant nothing. *Emeldra!* He needed to see her *now!* Perhaps she was with their daughters. Yes. He would seek her out there.

* * *

"THE TANIA, SAHARANI Shell!" The serving girl was nearly breathless with the news. She had not been in service for long and the sight of the High Lord striding purposefully toward the Saharani Shell's chambers was cause for both excitement and apprehension.

"Oh no!" Shell whispered, horrified. He *couldn't* be coming now. Not *now!* She cast about helplessly for a diversion, but her mind was suddenly completely blank. She dashed out the chamber door to try to forestall him and crashed headlong into his chest.

"Whoa, daughter," Mikale laughed. "And where are you going in such a hurry?"

"I... I... I..." Shell stared up at him, utterly dismayed. "Father!" she sputtered. "Laran! Let's... ah... go to see her." She grabbed Mikale's hand and tried to tug him away from her chamber door.

"What are you up to, Shell?" he asked softly, but Shell was both speechless and utterly transparent.

Mikale frowned at the sight of the two guardsmen on either side of the portal.

"What's going on here?" he asked.

"Father, we've learned something. Something you must hear!"

Mikale looked at her strangely, then brushed by her to step through her chamber door. "Emeldra?" he called. He walked through the first of two anterooms, then pushed aside the beaded curtain hanging in an inner doorway. He stopped abruptly, astonished.

"Tishane!"

Tishane jumped to his feet, startled, then bowed deeply. When he looked up at the Tania, his face was nearly white with dread and his eyes reflected the same dismay Mikale had seen in Shell's.

The frown between Mikale's eyes deepened. He looked about. His captain appeared to be alone. *In the bedchamber of my youngest daughter?* "What is going on here?" he demanded once more.

"I..." Tishane began. "I have something to tell you, High Lord."

"Speak," Mikale prompted. His voice was cold.

Tishane glanced quickly at the second anteroom, then back at the Tania. "It... it regards the Soldatian." When his glance darted to the anteroom again, the Tania turned and strode toward the curtained door and swept the delicate fabric aside.

By the Holy Ones!

The Soldatian was within! He was lying on his daughter's couch, one long leg bent at the knee, the other stretched out and hanging over the edge. One arm was draped over his eyes. At the sound of the Tania's entry, he dropped the concealing arm and bolted upright, wincing as he did so.

Mikale's left hand flew to the dagger sheathed at his hip. "Mikale!" Emeldra cried.

Unseen until that moment, she quickly moved closer to the couch, her posture defensive. *Of the Soldatian?*

She doesn't know who he is, what he's done! Tishane hasn't told her!

Mikale's stomach lurched in fear for his wife. He grasped her arm, jerking her out of the Soldatian's reach. He pulled her behind him and out of harm's way.

"Tishane!" he snarled, his voice a mixture of disbelief and icy rage.

Emeldra's eyes widened at her husband's tone. She'd noted the drawn dagger. When Tishane appeared, distress etched into every line of his craggy face, she jerked her arm from Mikale's grip and tried to insinuate herself in front of him in order to face him, but he wouldn't allow it.

"Husband," she protested. "I don't need protection! Listen to me!"

But with Emeldra safely behind him, the Tania was dividing his attention between the towering Soldatian and Tishane.

"You released him from the cells? You brought him *here?*" he demanded of his captain. "To my daughter's chamber?"

He stared at Tishane, incredulous.

"You left my wife *alone* with him!"

"High Lord," Tishane began. *I had neither authority nor permission. How can I defend my actions now?* "The Soldatian did not..."

"I want a contingent of guards on him *now!*" Mikale interrupted. His rage seemed to be a physical force in the small room.

"I did not harm your daughter, High Lord," Sheftu said quietly. He concentrated on remaining absolutely still, though he'd straightened visibly and had elevated his chin. He wore a frown of his own between his raven eyes and his lips were set in a grim line.

"Get him out of here!"

Tishane bowed low, took one step out of the anteroom, and called for the guardsmen he'd left outside of Shell's chamber. "Restrain him," he told the guards numbly. He glanced at the Tania.

"High Lord," he tried again. "The Soldatian..."

"No!" Sheftu snarled at the approaching guards. He looked first at Tishane and then to Lady Tania for help. "Tell him!" he implored them. When he looked back at the Tania, he saw his own death reflected in the man's eyes. *No!*

Sheftu lunged at the nearest guard, riding him down to the hard stone. He rolled off him and twisted, kicking out the legs of the second. He leapt to his feet and stared at Laran's father a moment.

"I have no wish to hurt you," Sheftu told him, but Mikale did not move aside, nor did he lower his weapon. Sheftu saw the nearly imperceptible tension in the man's stance and understood that Laran's father was about to launch an attack.

Sheftu cast about for another exit but found none. Both guards had regained their feet and were approaching once again with short swords drawn and ready. Instead of lunging low this time, Sheftu jumped to the back of Shell's couch and dove *over* the first guard's sword arm and directly into the chest of the second. He felt the burning prick of a point in his side and the fiery path of a blade across his back, but his momentum carried him to Tishane's feet.

When he leapt to his own, Tishane had pushed the Tania aside, and stared into Sheftu's eyes in bewildered horror.

Sheftu bolted past him and out the chamber doorway. He ran for the balustrade he'd seen Laran from, placed a hand flat against it, and vaulted over into the garden a full storey below. He grunted in shocked pain when he hit the ground, but he rolled to break his fall, and came out of the roll in a wary crouch.

"Laran!" he yelled. "Laran Tania!" *Where is she? Where?* He could see the guards running for the balustrade and spotted two more in the corridor on the opposite side of the garden. And there, behind him, two more! "Laran!" he yelled again. He sprinted for the area he thought he'd seen her emerge from and cast about for a doorway.

"*Cept!*" he heard Lady Tania shouting. "Lord Sheftu! Stop! Allow them to take you! Please! Give me time to explain!"

Sheftu glanced up at her in despair. All six guards were closing in on him. *I don't want to die! Not now when I am so close! Where are you, Little Elf? By all that is sacred, show yourself now!*

The first two guards were within arm's reach.

Trust. I must trust in Laran's mother.

He allowed one to take hold of his arms from behind, while a second held a sword to his throat.

Trust, Sheftu reminded himself. Don't run. Don't fight. *Trust.*

The remaining four encircled him, weapons drawn, and Sheftu stood still. He tried to glimpse the Lady Tania once again but couldn't see her.

A grey shroud of misery and despair enveloped him once again. Tenacious to the end, Death had found him at last.

* * *

SHELL THRUST HER way into Laran' rooms unannounced. "Sister!" she cried. "Sister!" She was nearly sick with foreboding.

Laran whirled from her place at the window. Surprise quickly turned to alarm at the near panic in Shell's usually quiet voice. "What is it, Shell?" she said. "What's happened?"

"Come, Sister!" she cried, tugging on her hand. "Come with me now!"

Laran slipped into her sandals in one deft move and grasped both of Shell's hands in her own. "What is it?" she begged. Shell's urgency was contagious, and Laran felt her heart accelerate in response.

"It's Sheftu!" Shell told her.

"*What?*" Laran whispered. "What are you talking about?"

"He's alive, Laran! But Father doesn't understand. He means to kill him. You should have seen his face!"

"Is this true?" she asked in amazement. "He is alive?" *Please let it be true!* "Where?" she demanded suddenly, her own sense of urgency accelerating. "Where is he?"

He is in danger!

"The garden," Shell exclaimed. "*Your* garden! He must have jumped over the edge from the corridor above! I heard him calling your name as I entered your chamber!"

Laran dashed from the chamber, past her startled housemaids, and down the short corridor to the arbour entrance of the garden, her dog in close and worried pursuit.

"Sheftu!" she cried. *It wasn't a joke, was it? No! Shell would never be so cruel!* "Sheftu!" She sprinted past the shaded pond and out into the open. She skidded to a stop at the sight before her.

She stood behind five armed guards who held a captive male—a *large* captive male—while a sixth pressed the tip of his sword to the man's throat. He was tall, this man, and his skin was bronzed. Laran couldn't see his face, but as she darted around them, she saw his hair. White, streaked with black.

Was it Provos? She felt guilt stir at her fervent hope that it was not. Please let it be Sheftu! *Please.*

She moved closer.

It was! By the Holy Ones, it was Sheftu!

The Tania saw her with a sinking heart. "Laran," he murmured, and his rage accelerated. Seeing her tormenter again could only do her harm.

"Let him go!" Laran implored.

"Mikale!" Emeldra cried. She was running into the garden, her waist-length curls moving with what seemed to be a life of their own. "There has been a mistake! Listen to me!" she demanded of her husband.

The Tania stared at her. He looked back at his daughter, then over at the Soldatian once more. His eyes narrowed.

"There is no mistake, Emeldra," he told her quietly. "I was there to see…"

"Father," Laran interrupted. "Father, let him go. Please. He saved my life, not once, but many times! Please, Father. He deserves better than this!"

280

"Laran?" Sheftu sounded incredulous. He tried to twist in his captor's grasp but couldn't see her.

As before, though, he recognized the voice he'd carried in his heart.

Laran tried to shoulder her way into the closed circle of guards. *Was he choking? They were hurting him!*

"Husband!" Emeldra was insistent. She looked up into Mikale's face, willing him to see her, to listen to her. "What you saw was *not* as it seemed. This young man was wounded trying to *defend* Laran. If he was bending over her, it was in an attempt to revive her! His were not the hands that hurt her. It was the Barraidi hunters you saw dead in the grassland!"

Mikale stood absolutely still, disbelieving. He looked to his eldest daughter skeptically.

"*Was* I mistaken, Daughter?" he finally asked. He watched Laran's reaction carefully. "*Is* this man innocent of harming you? Despite what I saw?"

"He is innocent, Father."

"And the murdered Barraidi?"

"Killed in defense of our daughter," Emeldra said. He raised his brows, doubt clear on his face.

"By *this* man? He killed *all* of them?" Mikale's dubious gaze slid over to his captain.

Tishane was still white with dread, but he had bravely entered the garden with the rest of them.

"It would seem his intentions were honourable, High Lord," Tishane said respectfully. "And his skill considerable," he added quietly.

Mikale impaled Laran with his eyes. "And you can swear to me that he has *never* hurt you? Never forced you... in any way?"

Laran shook her head and looked deeply into her father's golden eyes. "I swear it! Release him, Father."

Mikale moved slowly to stand in front of his captive. His guards moved to the sides. The sword still pressed against the man's throat. He hadn't begged, hadn't tried to bargain his way out of his predicament. He'd shown considerable courage, in fact. Mikale locked eyes with his prisoner.

Night black, they were shining with anger and something else, something indefinable.

Anger he understood. The Tania felt as though he'd been struck. His own fury, carefully nurtured since his return with his daughter from Barraid, had been disarmed. He was having difficulty letting it go. He placed his hand upon the guard's sword arm and gently moved the blade down to the Soldatian's chest, and then away entirely.

"Let the Soldatian go," he instructed. To Tishane he said, "Keep your men here, Captain, until I indicate otherwise."

Tishane bowed low, still waiting for the repercussions of his transgression, to which he could now add pushing the Tania out of the way. *Pushing him!*

So steadily was Sheftu watching Mirren's High Lord, that he felt, rather than saw, the sword being withdrawn from his throat. He slid his gaze to Laran, who was visible now behind her father. She was pale but seemed well. Her lovely eyes were apprehensive, but when she met his gaze, a smile began to form upon her lips. It drove the chill from his heart.

The pressure of restraining arms lessened and fell away, and Tishane's guardsmen vanished from his consciousness.

Sheftu stood alone and unrestricted now. The sight of Laran there in the garden made him feel like a man who, dying of cold, had been abruptly propelled out into the sun. Warmth stole over him like a blanket, and he thrilled to the sensation.

Laran. He felt the faint echo of her smile curve his own lips and all others in the garden with them faded from thought and awareness.

"Sheftu," Laran said softly. One hand rested over her heart. Tears stood in her golden eyes.

Sheftu felt rooted to the spot, unable to move. Tears leaked from his raven eyes and rolled down his face unchecked. He slowly raised his arms and she stepped into his embrace, her arms around his lower back and hugging hard. He placed his hands on her shoulders gently, then dropped them to caress her back. He finally wrapped his arms around her firmly and dipped his head into her hair, murmuring inarticulately. His tears continued to fall, dampening her hair and wetting her forehead, and when he tightened his embrace, she felt his broad shoulders begin to shake.

"I thought you were dead," he whispered brokenly.

Laran hugged him even harder, trying to return the comfort he was lending her. "Don't let go," she whispered back. "Don't let go!"

Sheftu shook his head silently but loosened his hold slightly, suddenly aware of the strength of his embrace. He kept his face buried in her hair.

"I love you," he murmured into the soft curls.

Laran pushed away from his chest to look up into his face. She noted the purpled eye and split upper and lower lips. His face was paler than it should have been and there were dark smudges beneath his eyes as though he hadn't slept in a long time. He was thinner, too. There was a half-healed scar across his jaw that looked like it had been made with a lash, and another disappeared beneath the shirt he wore.

She pushed away further to take in all of him. Fresh blood stained his side, though it seemed not to bother him. His muscular arms, exposed in the sleeveless Mirren shirt, were covered in bruises and abrasions. She knew he had a cut across his back; she could feel the wet warmth of his blood on her hands.

"What's happened to you?" she asked him, dismayed. "You're hurt! And how is it you are still alive? I thought... Oh, Sheftu, I thought *you* were dead! I thought..." Her breath hitched and she pressed her face into his shirt.

Sheftu looked over her head to meet her father's eyes, but said nothing. His hand rose seemingly of its own accord to stroke the back of Laran's head consolingly. He looked around him at the assemblage. He noted the shocked expressions on every face but three. The Lady Tania's expression was serene. Shell was wide-eyed with wonder. The two women stood apart from the rest, arms around each other, evidently relieved. Tishane looked anything but. He nodded solemnly at Sheftu just the same.

Sheftu inclined his head to the captain in gratitude, and then turned away from all of them once more.

"Laran," he said quietly. "There is something we must do now, *aey?*"

Laran nodded against his shirt, wet now with her tears. She moved in his arms to face her father, but did not relinquish her hold on Sheftu's waist. If anything, it tightened. He kept one arm around her and held her close.

The Tania was tall for a Mirren and he stood erect now, his arms folded across his chest. His head was raised but rested at a slight interrogatory angle. His features were not contrite, but were no longer twisted in rage either. He was staring at Sheftu as a cat might stare down a mouse.

This Soldatian was no mouse, though, Mikale thought. *And this was an unexpected turn of events.* The twin trails of the Soldatian's tears still shone on his battered face but he was not ashamed, and they did not unman him. Surrounded as he was by Mirren guards, he continued to show courage and did not flinch under the Tania's scrutiny, though more important men than he had been known to cower beneath it.

Mikale nodded at Sheftu and once again Sheftu inclined his head. Briefly, Mikale noted, though others around him were bowing low. He decided not to react to that indiscretion in either thought or action under the circumstances.

But by the Holy Ones, the young lord's continued hold on his eldest daughter was beginning to rankle!

Emeldra moved to her husband's side, intuitively having guessed the direction of his thoughts. She placed her arm around his waist in a public display of affection and support not usually seen outside of their private quarters. Mikale sighed mightily and draped a strong arm around his wife's shoulders and pulled her against him briefly. And then he released her.

"Enough," he growled to Sheftu and Laran. He tried not to notice the almost imperceptible motion of his wife's head, her signal to her daughter to move away from the Soldatian. They separated but remained close.

Laran clasped the young man's hand in a show of solidarity and Mikale frowned.

He glanced at Tishane wondering what to do with his captain. *Later. He would think on Tishane later.* Now he must see to the Soldatian's wounds, though he imagined Emeldra had already begun to heal him.

He wouldn't apologize. The Tania believed he'd done what any leader, what any *father,* would have done in the circumstances. And in the end, he'd listened.

Justice would prevail now.

Though he did not have Emeldra's strength in healing, he would personally oversee the repair of the damage suffered by the Soldatian as an act of contrition.

There would be no other.

CHAPTER FIFTY-FOUR

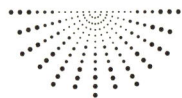

THE GREAT HALL was a massive chamber two stories high. Long, narrow windows let in the light and the magnificent view of the mountains into which Mirren-Bar had been carved. Unadorned, those windows painted stripes of the orange-tinted sunset across the white, nearly translucent stone of the floor. The hall was sparsely furnished in light woods and lighter fabrics and reflected a sense of elegant simplicity.

A long wooden table, empty of diners and no more elaborate than the others, stood against the only windowless wall, which was hung with an opaque material imprinted with shades of sapphire, crimson and yellow in elongated, three-foot strips. The effect, Sheftu thought, was beautiful.

Round tables covered half the remaining floor space around which stood or were seated 75 or 80 Mirren, nobles perhaps, though Sheftu spotted Tishane at one of them. They were dressed predominantly in white though it was clear that jewel tones were favoured among the Mirren as well. Splashes of crimson, sapphire and yellow, the same colours as the wall hangings, stood out here and there, and with them emerald and amethyst.

The Tania stood among them, head bowed, listening intently to an animated treatise of some sort from an older man with a crimson sash across his chest.

Sheftu frowned. Hadn't Viscount Jodpul worn a crimson sash when he'd come to the cells? Perhaps this was a kinsman of his.

Jodpul. Conjuring up an image of the handsome viscount gave Sheftu pause. This was Laran's life-long friend, the man who had intended to marry her. He'd never returned to the cells. He'd left Sheftu there to die.

Had he seen him as a rival?

Sheftu shook his head mentally. *A rival!* When he'd met Laran, she'd been a slave. As a Soldatian noble of the high-ranking Morrow House, a union between them would not have been taken seriously or, at the very least, would have been deemed absolutely unsuitable.

The roles were reversed now. Laran was the eldest daughter of the ruler of her country and Sheftu was merely the lowly second son of a foreign noble. As wrought with social discord as the first scenario would have been for *his* family, *this* one might well prove impossible for hers.

He'd not give up. Though he had no interest in the Mirren throne, he definitely had an interest in Laran.

Leaning seemingly casually against a white stone pillar near the entrance but to the side of the Great Hall, Sheftu's gaze became more intent as he spotted Laran walking hand in hand with her sister, Shell.

The two young women were dressed similarly, Laran in sapphire blue and Shell in saffron yellow. Both wore what Sheftu now recognized as traditional Mirren garb, at least among the noble women: a simple sheath beneath a layer of diaphanous material. It was very feminine. And very flattering. Lady Tania preceded them, her own gown emerald green. The trio presented a stunningly lovely sight.

Lady Tania was smiling and speaking briefly with her people as she passed. She glanced over and locked eyes with Sheftu for a moment, then continued on, her demeanor relaxed and her manner gracious.

Laran's eyes, Sheftu saw, were scanning the crowd before her. When she finally saw him standing at the side of the hall, her face lit with a welcoming smile. She stopped walking a moment and Sheftu straightened in anticipation. She'd seemed about to come to him, but Shell stopped her with a whispered word. Laran apparently thought better of her first notion, and continued through the hall toward the long table, which, Sheftu imagined, would seat the Tania and his family. She threw a single swift glance at him over her shoulder as he watched her.

He hadn't spoken with her since their reunion in the garden.

The golden-eyed gaze of more and more of the Mirren nobility in the Great Hall turned toward him, but he'd adopted his casual stance against the pillar once more and seemed unmoved by the attention. Inside, his stomach roiled as had the wide river they'd taken ship on. He hoped this particular journey would not be as ill fated.

Tishane appeared at his elbow.

"Come, Soldatian," he muttered. His expression implied that merely being in Sheftu's company was an onerous task. *It probably was.* Being seen with a Soldatian, and one so recently freed from the cells, would probably bring the captain no end of grief.

Then again, the majority of these people would not realize he'd been imprisoned. After all, the Tania had thought to keep his presence there secret, for his family's sake.

Sheftu sighed and moved to follow Tishane to whatever social disaster awaited him now.

"You are to sit at the head table with the Tania and his family," Tishane told him. "In appreciation for your efforts in returning the Saharani Laran to Mirren-Bar."

Sheftu raised his brows and Tishane forged on. "There. At the place on the end."

Sheftu looked at the empty place with dismay. Surely seating himself before his hosts would be considered a breach of etiquette? He sought succour from Laran, but she was engaged in conversation with a matronly woman of indeterminate age who seemed bent on keeping her within close speaking distance.

Besides, Laran had rethought her initial response to the sight of him. Perhaps conversing with her here, in this public place, would also constitute a breach of etiquette. He fervently wished Tishane had not walked away leaving him there alone.

He turned to face the gathering and spotted Viscount Jodpul Degere striding up the aisle toward him. His posture was straight and proud. Like Sheftu, Jodpul wore a *talom*, a white knee-length section of fine cloth that hung low on his waist. It wrapped around his hips, leaving his muscular legs bared. It was an unusual garment to Sheftu's eyes and appeared to be favoured by at least half of the men present. The crimson sash of Jodpul's station or his House crossed his embroidered white shirt.

"Lord Sheftu," Jodpul said. He inclined his head slightly in greeting.

Sheftu narrowed his eyes. "Viscount," he said. His voice was icy, his raven eyes cold. "Come to see me cleaned up, have you?"

"And healed," Jodpul observed.

"No thanks to you," Sheftu all but growled.

Jodpul raised his brows at the tone. "Did I owe you something, Lord Sheftu?"

"Decency, Viscount. I expected no less and would have given no less."

"Is that so?"

"It is. Your affiliation with the Tania family, to Laran in particular, should have given you reason to seek justice. You did not."

"You know that for a fact, do you?" Jodpul asked conversationally.

Sheftu reached out, fisted Jodpul's shirt front and twisted, drawing the man closer. "You left me there to die," Sheftu snarled.

"I see you two are acquainted," the Tania said dryly.

Sheftu released Jodpul's shirtfront and Jodpul smoothed it, staring all the while into the black of Sheftu's eyes, his expression unreadable.

"*Ashaii,*" Jodpul finally said. He bowed respectfully. "So we are."

The viscount wondered if the Tania had heard the edge in his voice. He hadn't meant to display it. He'd heard of the Soldatian's release from the cells that morning; heard, too, of the man's innocence, proved now by Laran herself. He'd also heard of the embrace in the garden in front of her family, the guardsmen, and the many servants who had gathered on the balustrade above.

He'd heard it *all* while he was making their wedding arrangements! Jodpul shifted his gaze to the High Lord and then bowed low.

"Forgive me, Tania," he said in his own tongue. "I did not mean to give offence." He slid his glance back to Sheftu but did not defer to his language. "To either of you," he said in Mirren.

Mikale stared hard at both men, then looked significantly at his wife before seating himself at the centre of the table. Sheftu noted that those already seated at the round tables hastily stood and remained standing while the Tania took his place. The Lady Tania excused herself from conversation with a tall, distinguished looking gentleman to join her husband.

"You will wish to remain standing until the entire family is seated, Lord Sheftu," Jodpul informed him.

Sheftu shot him a venomous glare and Jodpul smiled with exaggerated innocence.

Sheftu watched him move to the other end of the long table where, apparently, he, too, was honoured with a position.

Why? Why would he be? Was it by virtue of his friendship with Laran?

Laran and Shell were once again hand in hand as they walked to the dining table, the delicate fabric of their gowns flowing around their sandaled feet like liquid. Laran flashed Sheftu a brilliant smile, but her eyes were troubled and both young women moved toward the opposite end of the table and away from him.

Jodpul stood there waiting, his legs braced as though readying for a storm. He had observed Laran's smile, which had been for Lord Sheftu alone, and now, her quick glance in the Soldatian's direction as she approached.

Laran bit her lip and focused on her life-long friend and, now, soon-to-be husband.

"Jodpul," she said as she reached him.

"Saharani," he replied. He bowed politely. He took her hand, raised it to his lips and kissed the palm. He looked into her troubled eyes.

"There has been talk," Jodpul began softly. He glanced at Shell, who nodded at him in a friendly fashion before continuing on to her seat at the dining table, and then at his father, Count Degere, who stood not ten feet away watching his interaction with Laran carefully, his countenance stern. Beside him, Jodpul's mother looked equally severe. He tore his eyes away from them.

Laran had paled. "May we speak of it later, Jodpul?" she asked. "After we dine? When we are alone?"

He looked deeply into her golden eyes and saw his own heartbreak within. "*Ashaii*," he said, bowing once again. "As you wish." He concentrated on *not* looking at his parents again. He shot a swift glance down the table at the Soldatian.

The place to the left of Sheftu was taken by Shell. The Lady Tania was positioned between her youngest daughter and her husband. Laran was seated between her father and Jodpul at the other end.

When she finally took her seat, Sheftu noted Jodpul and the rest of the assemblage doing the same. He sat.

Servants, laden with wine, meat and fruit, suddenly appeared in the aisles. Some carried vegetables that Sheftu did not recognize; others bore platters of rice upon which rested strange pallid creatures that must have come from the sea. Sheftu watched the progression of dishes with interest.

Laran was acutely aware of his presence and leaned forward, seemingly casually, to catch a glimpse of him. Her mother shook her head almost imperceptibly and Laran moved back, but not before Sheftu caught her eye. His quick glance poured through her like spiced wine.

At the end of the table, Sheftu lost interest in the food. Laran was once again foremost in his mind. He wanted to touch her. He wanted to lose himself in her beautiful golden eyes. He wanted to kiss her. He *wanted* to claim her as his own.

Her presence there at the same dining table, separated only by family members and by the prying eyes of the Mirren assemblage, was nearly as difficult to bear as had been her absence.

"You do not find the food to your liking, Lord Sheftu?" Emeldra was asking.

Sheftu glanced up, aware that he'd been distractedly poking at his dinner. He smiled at Laran's mother.

"To the contrary, Lady Tania," he said courteously. "It is, in fact, delicious. Especially this…" He poked at one of the pallid creatures on his plate.

"Squid," Emeldra told him. "Baked with lemon and spices. It comes from the sea. Its taste and texture is unusual to your palate?"

"*Aey*, so it is," Sheftu answered. He looked down the table, trying and failing to catch another glimpse of Laran. *She'd* spoken of the sea. He'd implied he'd wanted to see it. It had been a ploy, albeit a truthful one, to find a reason to stay close to her in Mirren-Bar.

"It's an ocean creature from the other side of the mountains, Lord Sheftu. Packed first in icy cold salt water, and then in snow, its journey to our dinner table tonight had to be swift and must not have been without hardship. We are in debt to our Mirren fishers and their bearers."

Sheftu looked down at Laran's mother in surprise.

"In my experience, Lady Tania, those with both privilege and power seldom express gratitude for, or even notice, the efforts of those in service to them. That you do so does you credit," Sheftu told her quietly.

"We are not far separated from those in service to us," Emeldra said smiling. "Would you not agree, Lord Sheftu?"

"I do." He smiled back at her, genuine and warm.

Oh my, Emeldra thought. His eyes, night black as they were, had crinkled deeply at the corners as though smiling came both naturally and often to the young man. She had seen only distress, pain and a seriousness of expression that until now she'd thought intrinsic to his nature. The young Soldatian's smile had transformed him. It was fading now, she noted, and a slight frown appeared between his eyes at her scrutiny.

She turned away to address her husband in her own language, leaving Sheftu bemused and wondering what had just happened.

The noise of laughter, discussion and the clink of glass and eating utensils died away abruptly as the Tania rose from his seat to address those dining with them in the Great Hall.

Sheftu heard the word "Soldat" mentioned a few times and was uncomfortably aware that every face in the massive chamber had turned toward him. Some were openly hostile, but most were merely curious. A few were lit by smiles, which appeared aimed in his direction. He felt cornered. He straightened and hoped to the Seven Gods that someone would enlighten him.

Shell leaned over to address him.

"Lord Sheftu," she began, "our father is speaking of the role you played in bringing my sister back to us. He is telling them that he made a grave mistake when you first came to us, that he distrusted you. He is telling them that he has now heard the truth and that you are an honourable man. He is telling our people that we owe you our gratitude."

Gratitude. He could keep his... *He has admitted his mistake?* Sheftu's astonished glance darted from Shell to the Tania, who was still speaking. *Admitted it in front of his nobles!* He looked back at Shell to hear the rest.

"He is telling them that another man falsely claimed the reward offered for the Saharani Laran's return, but that you will be rewarded handsomely just the same."

Sheftu froze. His amazement faded and his temper spiked. He darted a dark look at the Tania then rose slowly despite the fact that the Tania was still speaking.

Mikale glanced up at Sheftu with one brow raised.

"Because you are unfamiliar with our customs, Lord Sheftu, I will grant you an opportunity to speak if you so wish." He spoke quietly, certain that his voice carried regardless and confident that enough of his Mirren nobles understood Soldatian to translate for the rest.

"Mirren has been generous to me since my arrival," Sheftu said, his deep voice heavy with irony. "No further reward is necessary. Or *desired*." He emphasized the last word with a raised brow of his own.

"Perhaps you will change your mind in time, Lord Sheftu," the Tania said. "No," Sheftu replied, his tone certain. "I will not."

Still standing, Sheftu took the opportunity to look over at Laran and missed the glance exchanged between the Tania and Lady Tania. Laran was staring at her father in appalled silence, apparently embarrassed by his words. Doubtless she understood the insult Sheftu felt.

When she returned Sheftu's gaze their eyes locked intensely, their awareness of each other almost palpable and inadvertently on display for all to see.

"Laran!" Shell whispered.

Laran dragged her gaze from Sheftu and concentrated instead on the untouched plate in front of her as though its contents fascinated her.

The spell broken, Sheftu looked once again at the Tania, saw the displeasure in his face, saw, too, the unease in Lady Tania's. He looked down the table toward Jodpul. The viscount was staring at him, his expression once again unreadable.

Sheftu sat down abruptly and tried not to look out at the assemblage. Doubtless he had the golden eye of every Mirren there.

He'd obviously been indiscreet.

He sat back and folded his arms across his wide chest, frowning. *May the Seven Layers of Darkness take them all!*

He just wanted Laran.

How can I arrange to see him? Laran was wondering. *I want to tell him my heart. I need to tell him about Jodpul. I need to tell him about the child I carry. Our child.*

Sheftu, she thought, looked magnificent in the white *talom* he wore. His clothing must have been made for him that very day. A *talom* borrowed from one of her people would have been too short, the sleeveless shirt

294

typically worn over it, too small. Even in Soldat, Sheftu had stature; here in Mirren he towered over other men. Though he'd lost weight in the cells, his long, bare legs were still powerful, his chest wide and strong. His bare, bronzed arms still swelled with muscle.

She longed to trace the hard, rounded lines of his biceps. She imagined herself on tiptoe stretching to kiss him. She imagined the dip of his head, the brush of his lips against hers. She imagined his hands, warm and gentle against her back and sliding down, down to…

She took a breath in sharply. *What are you doing? Keep your wits about you, Laran. There must be a way to see him, to talk to him, to touch him...*

Dinner was being cleared away and requests for audience were being heard. Laran heard her mother's quiet sigh as Count and Countess Degere stepped forward.

Jodpul was looking at his parents, decidedly ill at ease.

Oh no! Laran thought. She looked furtively at Sheftu, and then away. *Not now. Please, not now!*

Jodpul rose from his seat reluctantly to join his father and mother who were already standing before the Tania and Lady Tania, their expressions carefully schooled. They appeared to be waiting for their son to speak, and his mother prodded him silently with her eyes to do so now.

Sheftu's eyes were intense as he tried to understand what was happening.

"Jodpul," Lady Tania said quietly in Mirren. "Your family wishes to speak to us on your behalf. Have you something to say before they do?"

"*Ashaii*," he told them. "I do." *Though by all that was sacred, these were not the circumstances I would have chosen to do so!* He looked over at Laran still seated behind the table, her eyes wide and begging him not to speak. *No choice, now.*

Jodpul braced himself to address the High Lord and Lady Tania directly.

"Laran and I Promised to one another yesterday. Our marriage vows will be spoken two weeks hence. Arrangements are underway. We are grateful for your blessing to the union," Jodpul hurried on. He avoided looking at

Laran now. He avoided seeing his parents. He tried to avoid seeing anything at all.

Sheftu looked to Shell to translate, but her eyes were wide, her mouth a tiny "o". She glanced at Sheftu once and then away. She clearly did not want to relay Jodpul's words.

Why? By the Seven Gods, why? What was he saying?

The Tania raised a brow at his daughter, then shot a quick glance at the young Soldatian lord who stared at them so intently from the end of the table. Did Lord Sheftu also have designs on his daughter's hand? Had *he* imagined marriage?

He was hardly a suitable match.

Emeldra masked her astonishment and spoke for both of them.

"You *do* have our blessing, Jodpul, if a union between you is what you both want. And if it *is* what you both want, we are delighted to hear that the Promise has been made. We were unaware. Much has happened over the past few days."

"As to that…" Jodpul began.

Count Degere stepped forward impatiently and bowed to the High Lord. "The marriage between my son and your daughter is now imminent," he said unnecessarily. He turned and looked straight at Sheftu.

"There has been talk about the… foreigner," he continued. He directed his gaze at the Tania once again. "Talk of an unsettling nature."

Unsettling? Mikale stifled an outburst of laughter at the massive understatement. He looked over at his wife. Her front teeth pressed into her bottom lip and her eyes were fixed on the floor as though captivated by the patterns in the stone. *Unsettling.* He sighed. *Ashaii!*

"What is it you wish to say, Count Degere?"

The Count drew himself up to his full height, a full head shorter than Jodpul and the Tania, and two shorter than Sheftu.

"A Promise is a contract. Do you not agree?"

"I do," Mikale answered uneasily. He looked at his daughter, who had paled.

"Laran," her father said. "Come to me."

Laran was aghast. She *had* Promised to Jodpul. Had it only been yesterday? But she hadn't known that Sheftu still lived then! She glanced over her shoulder at Jodpul as she rose from her place at the long table. The friend she'd loved all her life looked decidedly unhappy.

"Laran," Mikale said. He took both of her hands in his and drew her close. He lowered his voice so that none could hear but those intended. "You are Promised?"

"*Ashaii*," she murmured miserably. "But Father, I didn't know..."

"And would you break your Promise to your life-long friend? Would you break *our* promise to unite the families Degere and Tania?"

He leaned closer to her yet, his voice almost inaudible. "There is more at stake than your misguided feelings of affection for the man who delivered you here."

Laran grew paler still. *Misguided?*

"Father, I cannot..." But she didn't finish her sentence. Laran slipped her hands out of her father's grasp and turned back to Jodpul, her eyes wide with upset. And sudden insight.

"You *knew*! Jodpul, you knew he was alive! Is that not so?" She felt a nearly overwhelming urge to weep. "You *knew*!" she accused him, dazed by the revelation.

She glanced at Sheftu who watched, uncomprehending and clearly disquieted.

Jodpul swallowed and raised his chin. He frowned at her. "I did. I had to..."

"You didn't tell me," she interrupted, speaking the damning words quietly. Her sense of his betrayal was written in her face.

Jodpul had the look of a drowning man. He pressed his lips together and remained silent.

297

Jodpul! Laran stared at him in silence for a moment. "You knew what Sheftu meant to me! You knew I was carryin…" She stopped abruptly, aware of the weight of her words. "You knew what was at stake!"

"And I still do," he said gravely. "I know *exactly* what is at stake!" He looked pointedly at her mother, then directed a fleeting glance at her father. He looked over at his own parents.

"I confided in you," she whispered. "You would hold that against me?"

Jodpul shifted. He was on edge now, and uncomfortable in his own skin.

"No! Laran, I…"

But Laran turned away from him. She looked up at her father. "I have no wish to continue this interview," she told him flatly.

Mikale nodded his acquiescence and Laran ran for the entrance of the Great Hall, pausing only once to gaze, distraught, at Sheftu. He had risen and was staring at her in confusion. She pulled her gaze away and fled the Hall.

Sheftu frowned. He reluctantly reigned in the impulse to follow Laran. He looked to Shell to explain, but no explanation was forthcoming. Lady Tania looked troubled. The High Lord looked angry.

What just happened?

As the three Degeres prepared to leave, Sheftu strode after them. "Viscount Jodpul," Sheftu called.

Jodpul hesitated, then paced off without turning around.

Sheftu maneuvered in front of the trio. His hand shot out. He placed it flat against Jodpul's chest, effectively putting an end to his passage.

Jodpul looked down at Sheftu's hand in annoyance and then up into the Soldatian's raven eyes. An unaccustomed urge to do violence flared in his gut. When he met Sheftu's gaze, though, he saw the confusion there.

So, Lord Sheftu had questions. Jodpul had taken steps to prepare for his audience with both families, but it had been too soon to address them! He hadn't been ready! Frustrated, he plucked Sheftu's hand off his chest, and continued on his way.

The Soldatian could get his answers somewhere else.

"You left me there to die," Sheftu accused his back. Though he'd spoken quietly, his words carried in the sudden silence in the Great Hall.

Jodpul stopped on the threshold of the Hall and turned to look at Sheftu. "No," was all he said.

And if his apparent lack of action gave evidence to the contrary, Jodpul didn't give a damn.

Besides, *now* the idea of leaving the Soldatian to die had appeal.

Jodpul turned on his heel and walked away. Sheftu saw him shake off his mother's arm and heard the angry murmur of his father's voice as the viscount outdistanced his parents and disappeared down a long corridor.

Sheftu turned and registered shocked disapproval at his conduct in a number of Mirren faces. He stalked off through the entrance arch of the Great Hall in search of the garden he'd seen Laran in. He hoped he wouldn't lose his way.

He hoped she'd be there.

CHAPTER FIFTY-FIVE

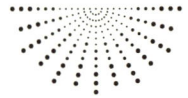

TISHANE BOWED TO the High Lord.

"Tania," he said respectfully. "I have received word of a Barraidi family waiting at the gates of Mirren-Bar. They've asked to speak with me, but I thought you might have an interest yourself."

"And what would make you think that?" Mikale asked impatiently.

He had yet to deal with Tishane's transgressions. He looked at his captain, wondering for what seemed like the hundredth time what he should do with him.

Tishane saw the direction of the Tania's thoughts. He swallowed apprehensively and once again thought of his wife who awaited him at home.

But Mikale only sighed. The unwanted task of determining a fitting punishment for Tishane, a man he greatly admired, hung like a weight over his head.

He shook that head in frustration. He had a country to run and had no wish to be embroiled in the vagaries of everyday life! Lord Sheftu, Jodpul and the Count and Countess Degere had just left the Great Hall, trailing a wake of emotional turbulence and whispered conjecture.

Laran was obviously troubled by her Promise to Jodpul, and Jodpul, a young man the Tania was extremely fond of, appeared ill at ease with the whole situation. The Degeres, on the other hand, were pushing hard and were openly agitated by recent events especially, it would seem, his daughter's reaction to the seemingly sudden appearance of Lord Sheftu.

The Soldatian was the catalyst for it all.

Mikale was beginning to yearn for an hour, just an *hour*, in the peace and quiet of his chambers in the soothing company of his wife, and *only* his wife.

"The Barraidi have an injured Soldatian with them," Tishane said, jerking Mikale back to the present.

Another Soldatian! Mikale could count on one hand the number of Soldatians who had appeared at the gates of Mirren-Bar over the last three decades! He glanced at the entrance of the Great Hall, but the young Lord Sheftu was already out of sight.

He nodded wearily. "Bring them to me here, in the Great Hall," Mikale said. "Call for me when they have arrived. I will be in my chambers at rest."

He looked for Emeldra and spotted her watching him from across the room. When she understood his intention to leave, she moved to his side and smiled into his eyes. She was like balm to a burn, Mikale thought.

"Will you join me, Wife?" he asked softly.

"With pleasure, Husband," Emeldra agreed. She laced her arm through his, a less than subtle indicator to passers-by that the Tania and his lady were desirous of privacy, at least for the short term.

PROVOS GRIT HIS strong white teeth and concentrated on standing tall. His chest and shoulder still burned with pain, but he'd won a small measure of vigour back. He'd known it would be short-lived and could already feel it unraveling.

The Captain of Guards for Mirren-Bar stood before him, a rugged-looking individual of middle years, straight, muscular and well-armed. He was clearly taking Provos' measure.

Tishane could see the pain this second Soldatian was trying to hide, could see, too, the weakness he endured. He wondered if this one was as courageous as his countryman. Unlikely. Few were.

His gaze rested now on the Barraidi family who had accompanied him. In bringing the Soldatian here to Mirren-Bar, *they'd* shown either great courage or foolhardy naivety.

"Come," he instructed the group in Barraidi. He raised a brow at Provos and changed languages. "If you can walk?" he asked.

Provos noted the courtesy shown. He nodded confidently but felt anything but. He eyed the long stone staircase ahead with dismay.

Tishane turned on his heel, signalled four guards to accompany them, two on either side, and began the climb.

Behind him Estalla and Randide were gawking at the palace ahead, the long avenues behind, and the view of the city below and all around them carved into the white stone flanks of the mountains. They stared, openly curious, at the Mirren people, at their unusual and beautiful clothing, and at the elegance and strangeness of it all.

Five-year-old Seren ran up the steps past Provos to climb beside Tishane. She attempted to take the wide stone steps two at a time until her nearly boundless energy began to flag.

"Seren!" Randide called, alarmed. His little girl had slipped her hand into Tishane's and the Captain had reacted. He stopped, and looked down at the child. With a quick glance at her parents, he bent, picked Seren up and hoisted her onto one hip.

Provos shot a glance at Randide and Estalla and shook his head at what he imagined their frightened response would be.

"He means her no harm," Provos said, sure, and Estalla began to relax. Randide remained tensed, watching Tishane carefully from behind for any indication that he meant otherwise.

Tishane swung Seren down at the top step. He turned to watch Provos struggle the final few feet. The injured Soldatian had broken into a sweat, Tishane noted, and he had paled considerably though his pace was still measured. When he reached the top, he was breathing hard. His efforts to stand erect were obvious.

Tishane raised a brow and re-evaluated this second Soldatian. Like the first, he was tough and proud. Perhaps these two Soldatians, the only two he'd ever met, were not an anomaly in Soldat. Perhaps these two, though clearly born to nobility, exemplified the seemingly indomitable Soldatian armies.

An interesting notion—he would file that thought away to be examined later.

Tishane signalled two of the four accompanying guards to move to either side of Provos. He issued a quiet command and the two guards closed in on the Soldatian. Provos stiffened, but quickly understood their intention to help. Though his first instinct was to refuse, common sense prevailed and he gratefully draped an arm over each, taking the support offered. Behind him he heard Randide and Estalla gathering both girls to their sides, doubtless still gaping in wonder.

A part of him was as astonished at Mirren-Bar as they seemed to be, but remaining upright and alert was taking all of his attention now.

Provos was vaguely aware of a long, white stone corridor, which passed through several small gardens overhanging with vines and fragrant with spring blossoms, and then finally through an enormous entrance arch. Stone columns, vast and strikingly white, supported the massive Great Hall beyond. The furniture within was simple and did not detract from the architecture nor from the magnificent view visible through the many long, narrow windows seemingly carved into the stone walls. Strips of jewel- coloured cloth were the room's only adornment.

Tishane indicated a chair near the entrance and the guards deposited Provos into it rather unceremoniously. He flinched openly at the rough handling but sat back in exhausted relief. Estalla and Randide did the same, drawing Alam and Seren into their laps. The eyes of four of the five

Barraidi were wide with amazement. The babe Notel slept soundly in his carrier on Randide's chest.

"You will wait here," Tishane told them in Barraidi. Provos understood the gist.

"Captain!" he said to Tishane's departing back. "It is *you* we wish to speak to, *you* we have come to see."

"And so you have," Tishane answered in heavily accented Soldatian. "Now you will see the High Lord. He will have questions and will determine what happens next." He turned once again and strode away.

Provos sat back once more, trepidation rolling through his guts.

By the Seven Gods, he thought. *What now?*

* * *

SHEFTU LOPED THROUGH the open corridors. He'd outdistanced and outfoxed the servant obviously assigned to watch him and now, at last, he recognized his surroundings and knew the garden he sought lay ahead. He fervently hoped Laran would be there.

She'd been at his side as he was healed. She'd watched as his clothing was removed, she'd seen at least some of the damage that had been done; she'd watched as the cuts and bruises faded away and as the lingering pain of his wounds receded. She'd watched his raven eyes and he'd stared into hers. There had been comfort there, and peace.

They had not exchanged words and he hadn't seen her again until she walked into the Great Hall with her sister.

He wanted time with her. He wanted to stay with her, to make a life with her here. He needed to sort out what they must do next to allow that to happen.

But it was Jodpul who stood in his path now. Had he had the same idea, to seek Laran out? Perhaps he'd…

Laran stepped out from behind the viscount, her eyes wide with surprise. She looked slightly desperate at seeing Sheftu there.

Sheftu looked from one to another. "Laran?" he asked quietly.

"Sheftu," she said. "I... I am..." she stammered. When Sheftu frowned, she added, "I am glad to see you." She didn't look it.

"What are...?" Sheftu began, frowning.

"The Saharani and I were Promised yesterday, Lord Sheftu," Jodpul interrupted. *Best get this over with.*

Promised! Sheftu stared at Laran in shock. *Yesterday. The day Laran learned I still lived?*

Jodpul was watching Sheftu carefully for his reaction. "The wedding will take place in just under two weeks," Jodpul continued. "We would be honoured to have you attend."

Sheftu felt as though he'd been struck. He moved back a step, straightened and elevated his chin. He directed his gaze to Laran.

"You are to be wed," he said, voice flat.

"*Ashaii*," Laran answered miserably.

Sheftu continued staring at Laran in silence.

"Congratulations," he finally said trying, and failing, to hide the enormity of his hurt.

"Sheftu," Laran whispered tearfully, but he was walking away.

Away from the garden he'd sought, away from Laran and Jodpul, and away from his heart's desire.

Away.

He began to run. He couldn't outdistance the hurt, he knew that, but still he ran, his strong legs pumping harder and faster. When he reached an area of the palace he no longer recognized, he slowed but did not stop. He began to climb staircase after staircase, loped down corridor after corridor, and still he ran on.

Few residents or servants seemed to linger here, so far from the Great Hall, and only a few jumped back in sudden fright at the sight of the lone Soldatian running the passageways.

When he reached an apparent dead-end, high above the Great Hall and the gardens, he finally stopped altogether. He rested his back against the cool strength of a stone pillar, bent his knees, and allowed himself to slide down to sit upon the hard, white floor. He placed his head in his hands in despair.

He'd wanted Laran. Nothing else. Only Laran. That would never change.

Night had already fallen, and now darkness enveloped him utterly. After a time, his hands fell away from his face and he lifted his head to look incuriously at what little he could see of his surroundings. The white stone seemed to glow faintly, though he could see no obvious light source. But there, to his right, he could make out the open corridor he'd entered from, and across from it, to his left, a stone balustrade. He rose to stand against the cold, waist-high structure, and his stomach lurched at the sight of the abyss below.

In his despair, he'd climbed higher than he'd realized. He'd known the palace had multiple levels—he'd seen the buildings scaling the mountainside as he'd been brought in. He hadn't recognized, though, just how high into the mountains the upper reaches were.

Here, he could see all of Mirren-Bar spread out below. The city seemed to amble up and down around the rises and falls of its precipitous terrain, its homes, narrow lanes and wide avenues all carved into the white stone of the mountains, all glowing faintly under the night sky.

His eyes rose to the firmament. No hanging moon cast a spell, but the starry landscape wove magic of its own. The celestial light cast should have been inconsequential, but the result was devastatingly beautiful, reflected as it was on the white stone city. Behind it and on all sides the Mirren Mountains soared, utterly black against the smoldering stars and the white stone below.

People gave birth and raised children in those seemingly tiny homes. They loved and grieved, laughed and grew old. Did their daily struggles, their happiness and their misery seem insignificant to the gods? And if so, how much less significant would they seem from the stars above?

Sheftu felt an almost overwhelming sense of weight emanating from the glittering skies and pressing him firmly to the earth. He knew, *knew* that his life was not momentous; that his most important deed could only be relevant to the world he lived in now. He would have no mastery over that world's place in the heavens above.

And if he was inconsequential, if his love for Laran *meant* nothing, if all that he had suffered and endured meant *nothing*, why was he so desolate?

Because it meant something to *him*! How many of the Seven Layers of Darkness had he descended? How *many?*

By all that was sacred, if he meant *nothing* to *anyone*, he *was* nothing! Provos was dead, his mother, who had loved him fiercely, was dead, his father and his brother cared not, and the woman he loved had Promised herself to another on the very day she'd learned that he still drew breath!

His chest hurt.

Nothing.

Laran had been troubled. Upset. Well, by the Seven Gods, so was he! But he could have sworn that she still loved him. He could have sworn…

She did.

Sheftu moved away from the balustrade and stared down into the black recesses of the palace. *She still loved him.* He'd seen it in her eyes. *Hadn't he?*

Laran was Promised to Jodpul. Ever since she was a child, the marriage had been expected. She was the daughter of the ruler of the country; Jodpul was a viscount, and obviously in high favour indeed to be included as a matter of course at the Tania's table.

Likely both families considered the marriage beneficial. Perhaps the audience with the Tania that had so agitated Jodpul and his family was because of *him*, because of Sheftu's reaction to Laran.

And because of *her* reaction to the sight of Sheftu!

Many saw the embrace in the garden. With a wedding to Jodpul imminent, the embrace between the Saharani and a Soldatian lord, a stranger in every sense of the word, must have been considered unseemly at best, a threat to the promised union of Laran and Jodpul at worst.

It was! By the Seven Gods, he *was* a threat!

307

Damned if he would stand about here admiring the view and wallowing in self-pity while another man had his sights set on Laran.

And perhaps more.

He didn't want to contemplate that, though it crept into his consciousness unbidden. *Had* Jodpul touched her? Had he *kissed* her? Had she let him? Had she given Jodpul the gift of her body in his absence?

That it might be so made him feel murderous.

Had she Promised to Jodpul knowing Sheftu still lived? If she had, had she felt she'd had no choice?

He was going after her. If his life was so inconsequential then what did it matter if he made enemies of certain of the Mirren nobility? What in the Seven Layers did he *care* if his actions had been, and would be, considered *unseemly*?

Once Laran explained herself, he would either claim her as his own and fight for her, or move on. The pain in his chest intensified and he closed his eyes a moment to shut out the thought of leaving Mirren-Bar without her.

If she wanted him to, he would.

Though where he'd go was uncertain. He felt as though he were drifting, unanchored. He looked down at the city below and out at the mountains beyond once again. He tried to imagine a life *here* among the Mirren.

He could.

There was nothing for him in Soldat anymore. If she still wanted him, he'd start by trying to convince the Tania and his family that he could bring more to a union between them than merely his modest status as the second son of a foreign noble. Though what that could be, he couldn't imagine at the moment.

CHAPTER FIFTY-SIX

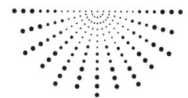

M IKALE STOOD A moment at the entrance to the Great Hall watching the Barraidi family and the clearly exhausted Soldatian. Surely, the presence of yet another of Lord Sheftu's countrymen was not mere coincidence.

He waved his guards aside and walked through the portal alone. At the sight of Mirren's High Lord, all but the Soldatian jumped to their feet in a show of deference. Mikale noted that the Barraidi male leaned down to hiss at the Soldatian, probably to prompt the man to rise, but the Soldatian only looked at Mikale with weary curiosity.

Interesting. His demeanour did not seem disrespectful in any way, but he'd made no effort to humble himself either, a trait he and his countryman, Lord Sheftu, had in common.

Mikale tapped a finger against his thigh as he stared down at the man. Then he looked over at Estalla.

"I would have a private word with you, Mistress," he told her. Mikale strode to the long table at the other end of the Great Hall.

Estalla's eyes widened in alarm. She looked at Randide for succour, but her husband only shrugged helplessly. She rose and nervously followed the Mirren High Lord. Seren wriggled out of Randide's grasp and ran after her mother. Estalla clasped the little girl's hand, taking as much comfort from the contact as she was giving.

"My lord," Estalla said. She wasn't certain how to address Mirren's ruler and hoped she would not give offence. She bowed politely then peeked up from her bent over position to see if she'd done correctly.

Mikale smiled at the young mother reassuringly. He looked down at Seren whose round little eyes looked like saucers in her tiny face.

"I have questions," Mikale told Estalla.

"Me, too," Estalla murmured, then blushed to her roots. She tried an apologetic smile but only half succeeded. She did *not* want to over-step her bounds with a man as powerful as this one.

"And what is it you would ask of me, Mistress?" Mikale asked her.

Did he mean it? Did he really want to know?

"Well, why *me*, my Lord?"

"Why have I drawn you aside and left your man to wait?" Mikale smiled again at Estalla's nod. "Because, Mistress, when men are present women are often, foolishly, left in the background. And because some women don't expect their opinions to be noted, they will often offer them without the politics of forethought, and without deceit." He paused a moment.

"That, and my wife tells me that women are keener observers of human nature and as a result can often read others better than can we men."

Estalla grinned. She was surprised by the Tania's candour and said so.

Mikale leaned back in his chair. "Now, Mistress, why are you and your family here and why are you traveling with an injured Soldatian?"

Estalla glanced behind her quickly to see Randide and Provos staring at her intently. She turned back to face the High Lord.

"I will speak with equal candour, my lord. If that is what *you* wish?" she added hastily.

"It is, Mistress."

Estalla took a deep breath. "We have heard that an army, a *Soldatian* army, has crossed the Barraidi border."

Mikale brows shot up in astonishment. "Where have you heard such a thing, Mistress?" he demanded.

"Word had traveled and there was talk of it, much talk, in the village near our home. Perhaps it is untrue, my lord, but my husband did not believe it to be so, and he was afraid for our family." Estalla looked into Mikale's eyes willing him to understand.

"Do not think him a coward, my lord," she told Mikale. "My husband is a brave man and he has fought in defense of Barraid many times against Soldat. He fears we will be destroyed this time and he thought to save his family if he could." Estalla hesitated a moment.

"Can you understand that?" she finally asked.

"*Ashaii*," Mikale said quietly. "I can." He also imagined that their own countrymen would not look kindly on them for helping the injured Soldatian, particularly in the circumstances.

"And what else do the villagers speak of, Mistress?" he asked, his expression intense.

"They say the army has been traveling up-country in the direction of our home. They say that they have not engaged our people in battle as yet. No one seems to know why, my lord, or what they are doing in Barraid. I only know that it bodes ill for our people who were devastated by the last war and cannot afford to defend themselves again."

"And the Soldatian you travel with? He has information on the army's destination and purpose?"

Estalla threw another glance over her shoulder in the direction of her husband.

"No, my lord. I don't think he is even aware of them. He has never spoken of it and we have not mentioned it to him."

"Then why is he here, Mistress? With you?"

"We found him," Estalla explained. "Provos. That's the Soldatian's name. He was lying wounded in the woods near the creek we often fish. Randide didn't want to help him at first. My husband has no fondness for Soldatians, you see. Well, neither do I, truth be known. But I was able to convince Randide to help him just the same." Estalla said this last with a grin meant to persuade Mikale that such an occurrence was not uncommon.

She looked at a nearby high-backed chair and wondered if she should pull it up. The High Lord was already seated behind the long table. She moved it into position and deposited herself into it, lifting Seren to her lap as she did so. She fervently hoped the High Lord would not be offended. He didn't look it. He looked, in fact, slightly amused.

"And *why* did you convince your husband to help the man?" Mikale asked curiously.

"I told Randide that I'd seen Provos and another Soldatian the day before. They were with a young Mirren girl." Estalla registered the High Lord's surprise at this statement.

The kinsman, Mikale thought. *This "Provos" was Lord Sheftu's kinsman.*

"She spoke Barraidi, this girl, and said the two Soldatians were taking her home to Mirren-Bar. She told me not to fear them, that their hearts were kind and that they would not harm my children or me. They didn't. And then *that* one," Estalla said, jerking a thumb over her shoulder in the direction of Provos, "pulled me out of the water when I fell in with our babe strapped to my chest. Notel could have drowned!

I felt I was in his debt," she said of Provos. She nodded to herself at the rightness of the statement.

"When we found him," Estalla continued, "it was clear there had been a terrible fight. There were bodies, Barraidi bodies, all over the headland. Randide recognized some of them. They had been very bad men, Randide said, men who'd do anything for money. Anything at all! *He* figured they'd attacked Provos and his kinsman. We never did find the little Mirren girl," Estalla said sadly.

"And then we heard that Mirren soldiers had taken the *other* Soldatian away with his hands bound. We realized the soldiers must not have known he'd tried to *help* the girl. We figured *they'd* found her, and that she must be dead, else she would have spoken for him."

Not dead, Mikale thought morosely, *drugged. I'd had her drugged to allow her to heal for a time free of the nightmare she'd endured.*

Her first words had been for the Soldatian, Mikale suddenly remembered. *He'd* told her Lord Sheftu was dead. In her grief, she'd said nothing more about what had happened.

I was a fool, Mikale thought. *Blinded by rage and sorrow, I didn't allow myself to see what had really transpired there on the Barraidi headland.*

"We knew they hadn't found Provos," Estalla was saying, "or if they had, they'd thought him dead; *we* did at first."

Mikale shook himself mentally to clear his mind and to listen to the Barraidi mother's words.

"So, you see, Randide wanted us out of harm's way to protect our family, but we *both* wanted to come, my lord. It was the right thing to do! And..." Estalla blushed.

"Continue, Mistress," Mikale prompted.

"And Randide hoped that your Captain of Guards, who Provos said was the little Mirren woman's father, might wish to reward us for bringing him information as to what *really* happened on the headland that day."

When Mikale only stared, Estalla rushed on. "Randide is not a greedy man, my lord. Far from it, but he worries for our future, especially *now*. It will no longer be a secret that we took in a Soldatian. Even if the rumoured army does *not* materialize, Randide thinks we might be cast out of the village we've lived in all our lives! Or worse," she muttered. "Soldatians are not well-tolerated in Barraid, you see."

"So I have heard," Mikale assured her.

Seren was growing restless and began to squirm in Estalla's lap, trying to make good an escape.

When Mikale remained silent, Estalla grew nervous again.

"Provos would have come here with or without us, you see," she said. "He was determined to find his kinsman."

Mikale nodded thoughtfully and glanced over Estalla's head to see the other Soldatian. Provos met his eyes fearlessly from across the Great Hall.

"The Mirren girl you spoke of," Mikale said quietly, his gaze on Estalla once again, "is my daughter, Mistress. She is the Saharani Laran Tania.

"She was injured there on the Barraidi headland you spoke of and my soldiers brought her home to us."

His daughter! Estalla looked horrified. "That's why *you* wanted to talk to us! I… I did not know." She was quiet a moment. "I hope she survived her injuries, my lord," she offered in a small voice.

"She did," Mikale confirmed. "Thank you."

"And… I am very sorry our people hurt her. Though I wouldn't really consider *those* horrible men *our* people, you understand."

Mikale nodded that he did.

Estalla sat erect. "But if the little Mirren girl… If your daughter," she amended, "survived, she will already have spoken for Provos' kinsman and you will already know what really happened on the headland."

"So I do, Mistress, though that truth has only recently come to light."

"Then…" Estalla began. She paled.

"Continue," Mikale urged once again.

"Then we have traveled all this way and have delivered nothing of value." She felt her stomach clench. If the Mirren turned them away now, what would become of them?

"On the contrary, Mistress. If the information traveling between Barraidi villages is correct, if a Soldatian army has indeed crossed into your country, you will have brought great value." He glanced at Provos once again. "Perhaps the young Soldatian you have healed knows more than you believe."

314

Estalla turned to look at Provos as well. Fear for his life suddenly kindled in her chest.

"What… what will happen now?" Estalla whispered.

"Now, Mistress, you and your family will be given quarters to rest from your long journey and you will be made comfortable. You may assure your anxious husband," and here they both glanced at Randide who shifted nervously in his seat, "that he need not worry for the future of your family. All will be well."

Estalla blinked. "Thank you," she said sincerely. "And thank you for hearing me, for *actually* hearing me."

Mikale smiled, rose and walked around the long table to stand beside Estalla's chair. He reached his hand out to her.

Estalla stared at it, then tentatively placed her own within his grasp. Burdened as she was with a wriggling five-year-old, she allowed the ruler of Mirren to help her from her chair.

"My name is Estalla," she told him, suddenly shy.

Mikale bowed slightly. "I am Mikale Tania." And then he remembered the murmured words and the seat taken without invitation. He raised a brow at Estalla. "Only my wife has leave to call me Mikale, Mistress Estalla."

Estalla giggled, and then clamped her lips shut, embarrassed. "What about Provos, my lord?" she asked him.

"I will have to think on the Soldatian, Mistress."

"He is a good man, my lord. I know it to be so. And so did your daughter! It was *she* that convinced me first!"

Mikale inclined his head, then called for his guardsmen. He issued a quiet command in his own language. The Barraidi family was escorted out of the Great Room.

"Only *you* could charm a king, Estalla," Randide whispered, a combination of shock and affection evident in his voice and barely heard as the family passed through the entrance arch. They disappeared down an adjoining corridor with the guardsmen.

JS MURPHY

Estalla glanced behind her once, eyes wide with apprehension over the fate of the wounded Soldatian they were leaving behind in the Great Hall.

Provos pushed off the tabletop with his palms to support his rise to a standing position. He was frowning in confusion as he watched the Barraidi family being led away from him. The Tania was approaching.

He turned his bewildered expression on Mikale.

"Why are you here?" Mikale asked Provos. Tall for a Mirren, Mikale had nevertheless to look up to meet his eyes. As black as Lord Sheftu's, they were devoid of artifice.

"I have come for my kinsman, High Lord," Provos explained. He tried to repress his mounting fatigue and concern for his cousin. "His name is Sheftu, Lord Sheftu, second son to the Morrow Lord of Soldat."

Mikale said nothing to this. "And you? Who are you to this Lord Sheftu?"

Provos elevated his chin. It was a familiar gesture. Mikale had seen Sheftu do the same when faced with upset.

"I am Provos Morrow, cousin to Lord Sheftu. My position in the Morrow House is a minor one. I did not come to impress upon you my own importance, or lack of importance, my lord. I have come solely for my kinsman."

Mikale stared at Provos, then seemed to come to a decision.

"It is my understanding, young Provos, that you and your kinsman, Lord Sheftu, brought my daughter out of slavery in Soldat and into Barraid on your way here to Mirren-Bar. Is this so?"

But Provos heard nothing at all after 'my daughter'. "Laran is your *daughter*, High Lord?"

"*Ashaii*. Would you have me believe that you did not know this?"

"I did not," Provos said. "Neither of us did. She told us Tishane, Captain of Guards, was her father."

"And you believed this?"

Provos shook his head. "No," he said slowly. "I didn't."

316

"And Lord Sheftu?"

"He suspected otherwise but didn't press her to tell him."

This, too, was interesting, Mikale thought.

"I thought he should," Provos added. *No wonder she hadn't wanted to tell them!*

Provos didn't know whether what he was feeling was anger or relief. Laughter bubbled up in his chest unexpectedly and he grinned widely.

Stupefied. That's what he felt.

"Pray share what you find amusing, young Morrow."

"Amusing?" Provos considered the concept. "Laran is the daughter of the ruler of her country. I should have guessed. We both should have guessed!" He grinned wider yet.

Aey, Provos thought, *her carriage alone should have hinted at her lineage. She carried herself like the queen she will one day be! And those imperious commands of hers!* Provos laughed softly.

And then there was Santago's kneeling deference. That bastard had known, that much was certain.

Mikale watched the range of emotion pass over Provos' face. The young man hid nothing. By the Holy Ones, it was refreshing!

"Where is he, my lord?" Provos was asking of Sheftu. "Does he live?"

Mikale nodded.

Provos sighed in relief.

"And Laran? Is she...?" Provos looked down at his booted feet dreading the High Lord's answer. "Does she also live?" he asked gently.

"She does."

Provos' head snapped up and he grinned again, this time in evident pleasure. "That is well," he said. He looked down at the High Lord. "I am happy to hear it. Now, my lord, will you bring me to my kinsman?"

Mikale raised a brow. "I think you will want to heal, young Provos, before you march off in search of your kinsman, *ashaii?*"

317

"No," Provos told him. "I have come far and endured much. I would see Sheftu *now*." His voice grew cold. "Where is he?"

Mikale's patience ebbed away. "You will be reunited soon. Does this meet with your satisfaction, young Provos?"

Provos nodded, aware of the irony in the High Lord's voice. He'd spoken injudiciously, even rudely. But by the Seven Layers! He just wanted to see his cousin for himself! Still, it wouldn't hurt to use a little diplomacy.

"Perhaps my fatigue has overshadowed my manners, my lord," Provos said, inclining his head. "I meant no disrespect."

Perhaps? Mikale met his eyes, clearly irritated now. These Soldatians appeared to have high opinions of themselves—*this* Soldatian in particular.

"You would do well," Mikale said softly, "to remember in whose country you now find yourself. Breaches of manners and exhibited lapses of respect can be foolhardy at best." He paused a moment to make his point. "Lethal, at worst."

Mikale was silent a moment to allow his words to take root, but the Soldatian's indiscretion was not the most pressing matter he needed to address. Estalla believed Provos knew nothing of the reported Soldatian invasion of Barraidi territory. She likely gave Lord Provos too much credit.

Or too little.

He signalled the remaining guardsmen to his side. Another quiet command sent two of them back to Provos. The young man eyed them warily.

"I have had word, Lord Provos, that a Soldatian army has entered Barraid and appears to be heading into its heart. Will you enlighten me as to its purpose?"

"What?" he demanded. *A Soldatian army!* "I know nothing of this, my lord," Provos told him.

"Think hard, young Morrow. You will be given motivation and time to do so." "What do you mean?" Provos demanded. He was thoroughly alarmed now.

But the Tania gestured with his arm, and Provos' escort drew weapons and closed in on him, moving him forward.

By the Seven Layers! "Wait!" he said to the guards. He tried to twist to look behind him but was restrained.

"I know nothing of its purpose!" he repeated, but his words went unanswered, and he couldn't be sure the High Lord had heard them regardless.

That he knew nothing of the army was true, but he could guess who was responsible, who'd sent the army in his cousin's absence: Du-kar, that greedy bastard!

Provos looked into the grim faces of the guards marching him forward and felt his courage falter.

Am I to be imprisoned?

The pain of his wounds seemed to intensify as his fears escalated.

The Mirren ruler had confirmed that Sheftu still lived. Provos hadn't thought to ask if he were *free*! He hoped to the Seven Gods that he was.

Come for me, Cousin. If you can, come for me now as I tried to come for you.

CHAPTER FIFTY-SEVEN

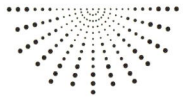

J ODPUL STOPPED WARILY on the landing, his hand on the short sword sheathed at his hip, his eyes straining through the gloom. He was nearing the last of the stone steps leading to the highest level of the palace. He'd been aware of another presence for some time, though he could swear he'd heard nothing at all.

"Come to kill me, Viscount?" a voice asked softly from above.

"No," Jodpul said, his voice just as quiet. *Let that simple assertion be enough,* he thought. By now Lord Sheftu must be feeling a powerful urge to do him violence and he had no wish to be attacked on the steps of his own home.

Jodpul continued to speak into the shadows. "Seems to me that it's *you* with motivation for murder, Lord Sheftu. Will you try?"

"Maybe," the voice said darkly.

Jodpul conjured up an image of the Barraidi headland. He'd heard what the Soldatian had done there, how many men he'd killed. He was capable of killing in self-defence and in the defence of others, that much had been proved, but would he kill to attain what he wanted? Was the Soldatian lord capable of *murder*?

Laran was convinced otherwise, but she was in love with the man.

The Soldatian was large and powerfully built and his skill as a fighter was obviously considerable. Still, Jodpul was himself a consummate swordsman. True, he'd never before killed anyone, but he knew he could if he had to.

By the Holy Ones, he hoped he wouldn't have to! He did not want *this* Soldatian's blood on his hands.

Now, he was alone with the man in an uninhabited part of the palace under cover of night. Ascending the stairs as he was, he knew he was an open target.

"I'd hoped *not* to have to kill anyone at all tonight, Lord Sheftu," Jodpul said evenly as he continued his climb. "Or ever," he muttered under his breath.

The muffled foot treads above led Jodpul to believe that the Soldatian had moved away and was allowing him to pass unmolested. Cautious relief washed over him.

"What are you doing here, Viscount?" Sheftu asked over his shoulder. He was barely visible leaning against the stone balustrade in the dim light. He was looking down at the city below, his back to Jodpul in an apparent show of either confidence or bravado.

Jodpul stood silently a moment evaluating what he should say.

"I'm not entirely sure," he admitted slowly. "Perhaps I've come to see what kind of man you are."

Sheftu grunted and turned to face him.

"Why?"

"It would appear that the Saharani Laran has a fondness for you."

Sheftu stiffened. *Fondness. That word again!* "Does it?" he asked noncommittally.

"*Ashaii.*" Jodpul settled himself comfortably against the balustrade beside Sheftu. He crossed his arms, leaned against them and looked over at the black silhouette of the mountains beyond.

He prayed the Soldatian did not have it in mind to throw him over.

"And this 'fondness' you speak of bothers you?" Sheftu inquired innocently.

"A great deal," Jodpul admitted.

The viscount swung the pouch he wore on his back over his shoulder and dug inside. He produced from within a glass bottle sheathed in leather. It may have been blue, but starlight had robbed it, and everything around them, of colour. Jodpul uncorked it and took a healthy swig. He handed it to Sheftu.

Sheftu looked down at the offered bottle in his hand in surprise, then over at Jodpul, but Jodpul seemed to think nothing of the gesture and continued looking out at the view. Sheftu raised it to his nose and sniffed its contents.

"I wouldn't..." Jodpul began.

Sheftu snorted explosively, his eyes watering, and his throat burning with the fumes.

"What in the Seven Layers is *that?*" he demanded of Jodpul.

"Perhaps Soldatian sensibilities are too demure for strong Mirren drink," Jodpul grinned. He took back the bottle and downed another swallow.

"*Aey,*" Sheftu croaked, wiping his eyes with the back of his hand. "Perhaps so."

He eyed the bottle dubiously, then put out his hand, retrieved the bottle, tipped it to his lips being careful *not* to breathe in, and swallowed. The fumes were worse than the drink, he thought, but still it burned the back of his throat and heated what felt like the entire path right down to his stomach.

He'd been chilled, dressed as he was in the sleeveless Mirren shirt, and his legs were bare in the knee length *talom*. He took another drink, forgot he'd ever been cold, and stomped one foot in appreciation. Or shock-induced stupor.

"By all that is sacred!" Sheftu croaked again. "What *is* that?"

"*Sloan,*" Jodpul told him. "Give over." He tipped the bottle back once more then handed it amiably to Sheftu who, not to be outdone, did the same.

"Is this wise?" Sheftu murmured.

"Depends," Jodpul said. He turned to Sheftu now and looked up into his black-velvet eyes. "Are we to kill one another tonight?"

"Maybe not tonight, then," Sheftu agreed. He placed his back to the pillar he'd rested against earlier and slid down to the cool, white stone. He patted the stone beside him in invitation.

Jodpul unfastened his cloak from his shoulder and dropped it into Sheftu's lap.

Sheftu looked up at him. "You proposing we *share?*" he asked, his tone incredulous.

"Not in this life," Jodpul said, grinning down at him. "I've just climbed several hundred stairs and have no need of the thing. I do not intend to spend the night here. I'm thinking that maybe you do."

Sheftu nodded thoughtfully. "*Aey,*" he acknowledged agreeably. "I had thought to."

Especially now, he thought, aware of the alcohol as it hit his bloodstream.

"Hmmm," Jodpul said, and he, too, slid down the pillar. He sat beside Sheftu in companionable silence for a moment.

"You don't feel like an enemy, Lord Sheftu," he said quietly.

"*Aey.* I see what you mean. I wish it could be different," Sheftu told him. "Will you try to win her, despite our Promise to one another?"

Sheftu nodded. He bent one knee and rested a long bare arm over it. "I will."

"And do you imagine a marriage between a foreign lord's second son and the eldest daughter of Mirren's High Lord will meet with approval? Even *without* the existing Promise?"

"I don't see how," Sheftu answered bleakly. "But I must try, Jodpul." *I must succeed!* He took another swig of the seemingly lethal *sloan* but forgot his edict not to breath in. "By the Seven Gods!" he wheezed.

"Then your craving for the wealth and power of the Mirren throne is worth the probable humiliation of defeat?"

"What?" Sheftu's sinuses were on fire and he blinked back tears from eyes that felt all but melted from the fumes. He shook his head.

"In truth," he rasped, "I have had no great ambition for power, though I could rise to the challenge if I had to. Laran was a slave when I met her: a *slave*, Viscount. I didn't know who she was until *you* told me in the cells."

"And yet you loved her."

"I did. I do."

Sheftu turned to Jodpul, his focus a moment or two behind. "You left me there to die," he accused Jodpul once again.

But Jodpul was shaking his head.

"Put on the cloak," he grumbled. "You are big enough without gooseflesh raising you that much higher."

Sheftu was still staring at him, all semblance of good humour vanished.

"Why would you have done such a thing?" he demanded. "I would not have wished such a fate on my worst enemy let alone the man who brought someone I loved out of slavery."

"You acknowledge that I could love her then?" Jodpul asked softly.

Sheftu nodded. He was beginning to feel vaguely sick to his stomach. "Laran told me as much."

"And would you have told me that she loved me in return had you realized she still lived?" Jodpul asked.

"Probably not, though you must have known."

"*Ashaii*. So I did. And so I do. We love one another. Always have." He took a long, deep swallow of the noxious drink and Sheftu marveled at his ability to tolerate it.

"But," Jodpul continued, "her love for me is not *like* her love for you. Do you understand?"

"I think so," Sheftu acknowledged. "Are you *in* love with her?"

Jodpul hesitated. "*In* love? Perhaps not."

I am in *love with another*, he thought but did not say. He tried, and failed, to stifle his longing for the woman he would never have.

"But I love Laran in my own way," Jodpul continued. "I *will* protect her from harm or unhappiness if it is within my power to do so."

He rose clumsily and stood above Sheftu, swaying slightly. "And I have a great *deal* of power, Lord Sheftu," he said, the threat clear.

Sheftu nodded. *And I have none here. None at all.* He handed the cloak up to Jodpul, but the viscount shook his head, then put his two hands to either side of his skull as though to stop it from ringing.

"Keep it until the morrow. I have no need of it tonight."

And with that, he turned and began to retrace his steps.

"Have a care for your footing, Viscount," Sheftu called out.

"*Ashaii.* These stairs will be no mean feat now." He laughed quietly at his own swaying ineptitude but continued his descent just the same.

When he reached the landing, he pressed his hands flat against the wall for balance and turned to shout up to Sheftu.

I did not leave you there to die! But he changed his mind. It didn't matter what Lord Sheftu believed. He turned and nearly stumbled down the next stair. *Take care, Jodpul,* he told himself, *else the death you feared at the hands of the Soldatian will be caused by your own sloan-induced clumsiness!*

Death by sloan. Not unheard of.

He began to laugh and continued on his way.

* * *

"SAHARANI," JODPUL SAID. He looked around at the garden entrance to his chambers as though surprised to find himself there. Certainly, he was surprised to see *Laran* there. "What are you doing out here in the middle of the night?"

"I would ask you the same, Jodpul! I've been waiting for you. Where have you been? You went after Sheftu, didn't you? Have you seen him? No one knows where he is! Even the watcher and the guard my father assigned to him have…"

"The Soldatian's a wily one," Jodpul interrupted good-naturedly.

Laran stepped closer and narrowed her eyes at him. "Have you been drinking? Are you *drunk?*"

"Oh, *ashaii,*" Jodpul agreed. He grinned widely. "Been drinking *sloan*. With your Soldatian. I don't think he liked it much at first, but he got used to…"

"*What?* With Sheftu? Where is he?"

Jodpul put a hand out to steady himself against the trunk of a cherry tree, missed and tried again. The movement caused a cascade of white cherry blossoms to flutter all around them. He swiped a hand over his shoulder and swept off several, then reached out for Laran's hair to dust them inelegantly from her curls.

"You look like a fairy, Laran, flitting about in the flowers."

"Jodpul," she said softly. "Did you really drink with Sheftu? Is he all right?"

"*Aey,*" he said mimicking Sheftu's language. "Your Soldatian is fine, Saharani Fairy. He will spend what remains of the night in the highest reaches of the palace. It's a fine place to think, *ashaii?*"

Jodpul shook his head vigorously to displace a shower of white petals from his curly hair, and nearly lost his balance once again.

"I need to sleep," he told her. "Promise me you won't go up there unescorted, *ashaii?* I need my bed, Laran," he almost pleaded, "but I won't sleep if I worry for you."

Laran looked thoughtfully in the direction of the palace heights though they were invisible behind the garden walls. She didn't respond.

"Good," Jodpul said as though she'd promised wholeheartedly. He leaned in to kiss the top of her head. "I *do* love you, you know."

"I know," Laran whispered miserably.

"And I will release you from your Promise if that is truly what you want."

Laran stared at him dumbfounded. "You will?"

Jodpul looked deeply into her eyes. "*Ashaii*. If that is truly what you want," he repeated. He blinked heavily. "But, Laran," he finally said. "I do not think your family will find the Soldatian suitable." He continued looking into her eyes. "Do you?" he asked quietly.

"I don't know," she said. *I don't see how. But there must be a way. There must!* "Jodpul, is this the *sloan* speaking? Will you still feel this way in the light of the new day?"

"*Ashaii*," he said seriously. "It was as you said. I knew the Soldatian lived. I believed his innocence must be proved before *you* learned it as well. If he was not worthy of you..."

Jodpul sobered a moment as he looked down at her. "I did what I thought I must to protect you. If he was the one who hurt you, if he proved unworthy of you..." He didn't finish the thought.

"You would have kept your knowledge of him to yourself and married me regardless?"

"*Ashaii*, Saharani. And I will, even now, if Lord Sheftu is not deemed suitable. I *will* protect you and your child, and I *will* see you happy. Understand?"

Tears sprang into Laran's eyes. "And that's also why you will release me. Thank you, my friend," she whispered. She stood on her toes to kiss his lips. "Thank you."

Jodpul closed his eyes briefly then opened them again when dizziness threatened to topple him. He concentrated on what he must say.

"I was wrong to do what I did." Jodpul sighed loudly. "You were hurt and angry," he continued. "I *know* how you feel about the Soldatian. I *know* what is at stake. I'm not likely to forget."

Laran reached out to touch her life-long friend's face and felt the coarse bristles of a new beard beneath her fingertips. *Unshaven.* When had Jodpul *ever* appeared in public unshaven or unkempt? Or swaying with drink? *Her* life was clearly not the only one in turmoil.

His family! The Degeres would be outraged by the dissolution of the Promise between them. There must be a way to appease them.

Jodpul bumped the tree once again and another cascade of pale petals fell around them in the night like fragrant snow. Speaking intelligently *and* remaining upright were proving to be a tricky combination.

He grunted.

This was going to go badly for him; he knew that. His family, his connections, his fortune, his very status in the court had hinged on the long-awaited marriage to Laran Tania. So had his happiness. At this moment, Jodpul had no idea what he would do or where he would go if their Promise to one another were dissolved, *especially* when it became known that he'd released her. His family would be furious, that much was certain. There would be no forgiveness.

On the other hand, if Laran was denied the union she wanted with the Soldatian lord, as he imagined she would be, he would keep her secrets and marry her regardless. He would be forced to endure the public humiliation of being second choice in marriage to the Saharani and worse, of appearing to have been cuckolded if the life she carried inside resembled the Soldatian, but he *would* endure it. For Laran and the babe, he could endure anything.

"Jodpul?" Laran was asking. "Had *you* planned to try to prove Sheftu's innocence?"

Jodpul nodded. "Five men." He was mumbling now. "I sent five men to find the sailor, Santago, and bring him back here. Another five were sent to find the Barraidi hunter who fled the headland in the wake of the killings." He could no longer think. "I couldn't ask *you*, Laran. If I did, you'd know he'd survived. I needed to be sure he deserved to have."

"I go to my bed," he said abruptly. The viscount stumbled off in the direction of his chambers but stopped at the entrance portal. "Laran," he said, "*don't* go up there alone, *ashaii?*"

Laran brushed handfuls of white blossoms from her clothing and hair and smiled beatifically at her life-long friend.

"G'night," he mumbled.

"I love you, too," Laran whispered to his back.

CHAPTER FIFTY-EIGHT

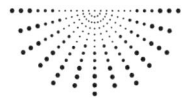

L ARAN LOOKED BEHIND her apprehensively. She hadn't been up to the heights for many years and never alone—certainly never at night.

Here there were no torches burning brightly to light the corridors, no candles glowing softly in the niches to dispel the shadows. Here seemingly endless corridors linked endless stairs angled up and forever up into the continuing darkness beyond.

The voices of the few Mirren living or working so high above the Great Hall were heard infrequently and then only as murmured syllables, though once a frightened cry caused Laran to stop on the stairs, her hand to her throat, and her heart beating wildly in her chest. She strained to hear what would come next, to try to ascertain where the cry had come from, but the sound did not split the night again and the never-ending staircase seemed to resonate with tomb-like silence.

Jodpul's words began to repeat themselves in Laran's mind like a mantra: "Don't go up there alone," he'd said. She swallowed, the sound audible in the hush. She wished she hadn't been loath to awaken Tishane. *He* would have accompanied her, no questions asked.

Turning back now, though, was not an option. She was more than halfway to the top and the black, empty corridors below frightened her no less than the unknown shadows above.

"Foolish!" she admonished herself, the word whispered out loud. There were no horrors here! These heights were a part of her home. She'd considered them a great adventure in the past. She straightened and pulled her shoulders back. She would consider them an adventure *now*. And at the climax, Sheftu would be there. She'd have a chance to be with him at last!

Please let him be there still!

* * *

"SOMEONE'S COMING," TYLLERD said quietly. "There. One person. Hear the footsteps?" He grinned nastily. "Now who else do you suppose would be rash enough to come up here at this time of night?"

"Huh," his companion scoffed. "You nearly knocked the last one off his feet before you recognized him. What were you going to do to him anyway?"

Tyllerd looked down at his massive fists. He'd *wanted* to beat the last wayfarer to death before he'd realized who he was. Killing the Viscount Degere would have been disastrous. *Never mind*, he'd thought. He knew another opportunity for violence would present itself eventually, if not here, then somewhere else. All it took was a little patience.

"I'd have bled him, just a little," Tyllerd answered, his voice a ghoulish combination of menace and callous glee. "Or a lot." He laughed softly, the sound ghastly to Allane's ears. *I'd have had my fill,* Tyllerd thought wistfully, *at least for the night.*

Oh, *ashaii*. He'd wanted to feel the man's blood spraying into his face. He'd wanted to feel it slick against his palms. He'd wanted to rub it on his arms.

And then he'd have wanted a woman.

Tyllerd's companion stared at him in revulsion and not a little fear. Allane had climbed halfway to the heights in order to win back the money the man had won from him in the cells the night before. The other three card players, all prison guards like the two of them, hadn't materialized and he'd found himself alone with Tyllerd. Allane had heard the man was dangerous but he hadn't realized the extent.

Well, how could he have?

He scratched at his scalp. He'd seen what Tyllerd was capable of, though. He'd seen what the man had done to the Soldatian prisoner they'd held. He'd witnessed Tyllerd's evident pleasure in inflicting pain.

He should have known.

Now he wondered if Tyllerd was even sane.

Tyllerd held up his hand, then looked a warning to be quiet at Allane. The bigger man bent to peer out of the slit in the door behind which he stood.

"It's a woman," Tyllerd hissed as though he couldn't believe his good fortune.

Allane hunched his shoulders nervously. Tyllerd was considerably larger than he was himself, and armed. As soon as Tyllerd dragged the woman in there, Allane would take off down the stairs.

Nothing he could do for her anyway.

He stood silently and waited for her to come closer, then tensed his muscles readying for flight as her footfalls sounded right outside the door.

Tyllerd threw open the door and lunged at the woman, knocking her onto her side on the stone. As soon as Tyllerd reached down to yank her to her feet, Allane rushed around him and began to run.

"Hey!" Tyllerd shouted at his fleeing back. "Come back you little bastard!"

When Allane judged himself to be a safe distance away, he stopped on the staircase and turned toward Tyllerd. Yellow light from the room they'd occupied spilled out of the now open doorway and onto the stairs.

The woman, he saw now, was young and slim. Her hair was strangely short, and her clothing finely made. A noble woman, perhaps. *No matter!* It was a shame about what Tyllerd would probably do to her, but by the Holy Ones, he wasn't about to get in his way. The man was *definitely* dangerous.

Allane watched the woman struggle in Tyllerd's grip for a moment, then turned away. He hoped she wouldn't suffer too much before Tyllerd killed her. He continued down the stairs.

He glanced behind one more time. The door to the room was banging shut and the light that had illuminated the stairs shrank to a sliver and was withdrawn in an instant. All above him was cloaked in darkness once again.

There was no sound. It was as if Tyllerd and the woman had never existed at all.

Allane moved a couple of steps closer to the door. *What am I doing?* He wanted, no, he *needed* to run in the opposite direction! But his feet carried him back to the room, slowly, one step at a time, and seemingly against his will. *No, no, no!* he told himself. *Run!* But still he continued to climb.

* * *

LARAN SPRANG TO her feet to face her attacker. Her leg hurt abominably from her collision with the steps, and so did her arm where the man had grabbed her, but she pushed the pain aside to study her adversary.

He was a big man. His coarse features were twisted in cruel contempt and something else, something she recognized immediately. Sadistic pleasure. She'd seen it on Du-kar's face many times. Fury coursed through her and with it the absolute certainty that she could defeat this man. She would *not* be a victim tonight!

"You will not have me," she said, certain. Her voice was calm, controlled and she appeared absolutely confident.

Tyllerd bared his teeth in what might have passed for a grin. His teeth were stained and one in the front was missing altogether. Laran glanced down at his hands. Clenched into fists, the knuckles were white with tension. Muscles bunched in his forearms.

"Coward," she taunted. She could see the anger in the man's eyes, not, she imagined, at the insult she'd hurled, but at the fact that she was neither cowed nor begging for mercy.

He charged Laran abruptly and roared out his fury as he did so, the sound sending a shard of ice down her spine, but still she kept her feet, and still she watched his eyes. When she saw his intent, she dropped suddenly to a low crouch, then dashed between his legs, unbalancing him. She ran for the door.

He was fast for such a big man. He whirled around and tackled her as she reached the portal. Both of them thumped heavily into the solid wooden door then fell to the floor. Tyllerd crushed Laran with his weight, and then raised himself above her to jeer in her face, his weight slightly to the side.

The door opened suddenly and the edge struck Tyllerd square in the temple, stunning him momentarily and knocking him further off balance.

"Get off her," Allane shouted, his voice high and tremulous. His knees felt like butter and threatened to give way at any moment. "I said, get off!"

Tyllerd glared at the intruder unconcernedly, a ridge of red and white beginning to swell grotesquely on his forehead. Distracted, he hadn't noticed Laran's newfound ability to raise one knee. She brought it up into his testicles with as much strength as she could muster.

Tyllerd screamed in sudden agony, and Laran pushed and wriggled her way out from under him, wrenching his knife from his scabbard as he curled involuntarily. She aimed another kick at the man, this time in the ribs. He shrieked again, crazed with pain and wrath, and reached for her leg, but Laran jumped back out of range.

She looked about for a better weapon than the knife she held, careful to keep the second man in her peripheral vision. She snatched up a heavy metal ring, its original purpose unknown, and angled the knuckles of her right hand through it.

"You planning to try your luck with me, too?" she demanded of Allane.

"What? No!" Allane said. By the Holy Ones, how had she gained the upper hand so quickly? He gulped.

He should kill Tyllerd right here and now! If he didn't, he'd come after him, he'd come after them both. He'd kill them sure.

"Then let me pass!" Laran ordered.

"What? Pass. *Ashaii.*" Allane was still staring in obvious terror at Tyllerd. "*You* should kill him!" he urged Laran abruptly. "Kill him. With the knife!" He finally glanced up at her and his face turned a sickly grey.

The Saharani, Allane thought. Nausea rose up in his throat. Laran's eyes widened. "I… I cannot," she whispered.

"Then…. You'd better run!" he said. No amount of gambling debt was worth this, he decided. "We'd both better run!" And with that Allane turned on his heel and tore down the stairs two at a time.

And then I'll keep running, Allane thought. *The Saharani! By the Holy Ones, this night kept getting worse and worse.*

Inside the room, Tyllerd had raised himself to a half-bent crouch. His eyes were red with pain and rage and his lips were pulled over his yellowed teeth in a snarl.

"Bitch," he hissed.

He lunged at her once again, and Laran swung her metal clad knuckles at his head, connecting solidly. She shot out of the door and slammed it shut in his face. She heard the satisfying thud and subsequent grunt as some part of him, possibly his forehead, rammed into the wood at full speed.

She eyed the stone steps. *Up or down?* She debated the wisdom of each, but wanted Sheftu more than ever now. *Please, please, please be there!*

She sprinted up into the shadowy darkness of the stone staircase and resumed her climb, this time with her heart banging against her ribs and the rasping sound of her breath chafing the renewed tomb-like silence of the night. If the door had reopened, if footsteps pounded up the stairs behind her, she didn't hear them.

And if Sheftu were no longer there when she reached the apex, if the man in the room had followed her, she'd be trapped there alone. The highest reach of the palace was a dead end. If the steps were blocked, there was only one avenue of escape left to her, a precarious climb over the balustrade to the precipitous trail on the mountainside beyond. The path to the caverns was dangerous in the full light of day, nearly suicidal in the darkness.

If, if, if! Keep your mind sharp and your feet swift, Laran admonished herself. One more corridor, one more set of steps and she'd be there, and all the "ifs" of her upward flight would be resolved one way or another. Her calves burned, her thighs ached, and her breath tore out of her lungs in ragged gasps now. *No matter! Nearly there. Nearly...* There!

The deep black of the steps coalesced into pallid grey structure, the pale stones of the last terrace floor and the paler pillars and balustrade standing at the edge. Beyond it all, the inky silhouettes of the mountains loomed against a myriad of stars glimmering in the night sky. Laran knew that Mirren-Bar stretched out below, its torch-lit streets and illuminated windows as glittery a sight as the starry skyscape above.

But this final terrace was empty!

She looked behind her at the shadowed steps she had just ascended, but neither saw nor heard activity there. She took a few cautious steps forward onto the stone terrace, the knife clutched hard in her fist.

* * *

SHEFTU HEARD THE staccato clip of racing feet on the steps below him. Rising swiftly, he tried to will away the residual effects of the *sloan.* He positioned himself out of sight behind the massive pillar he'd been resting against and listened carefully.

The clip of rapid footfalls ceased. Movement was stealthier now, slow and wary. He pressed his back to the pillar and silently slid around it to catch a glimpse of the man who now shared the heights with him.

A knife, clutched in a small hand, gleamed dully.

Sheftu leapt from behind the pillar, grabbed the wrist holding the knife and jerked downward with his left hand, dislodging it. His right pushed hard on the man's chest, smashing him against the pillar, and holding him there.

"Sheftu!" the man said.

Not a man. A woman. Laran. *Laran!*

Sheftu stared at the woman he held against the pillar in disbelief. He dropped his imprisoning hand from her chest and stepped back in surprise.

"What...?"

But Laran launched herself against him, her arms reaching for his neck, her upper body pressing hard against his torso. She hung onto him fiercely.

By the Seven Gods, it felt good! He returned her embrace just as fiercely. He murmured into her hair.

But she was already pulling away to look up into his raven eyes.

"Sheftu, there is a man!" she told him. She glanced behind her at the steps. "A man down below! He... he wanted to kill me, I think!"

Sheftu's eyes widened and he, too, glanced at the steps. He released Laran and moved to stand in front of her. He strained to hear movement but heard nothing at all.

"Where?" he asked grimly.

"There was a room, a single room off the steps nearly halfway down. It's the only one before the final set of corridors and terraces. Do... do you know it?"

"I remember seeing it."

"He was in there. He grabbed me off the staircase and... I may have killed him!" she whispered. "But I don't know for certain." She bit her lip anxiously and glanced once more at the steps. "I was afraid he'd followed me."

Sheftu swung Jodpul's cloak off his shoulders and placed it around Laran's. "Stay here and out of sight, Little Elf," he said quietly. He turned on his heel and started down the dark stairs. His tread was soft, his every sense attuned to the possible presence of another.

The steps remained silent and Sheftu remained the only one on them. When he reached the door to the single room, he approached it carefully. Turning the latch, he pushed it open gently, stepping back and to the side as he did so.

No one challenged him. He cautiously stepped inside.

A man lay on his back on the floor, crumpled and unmoving. He was large for a Mirren and his nose appeared to have been broken. Even so, he looked familiar. A guard! He'd been one of the guards in the cells below. A large swollen ridge of red decorated his forehead and a grisly, bloodied abrasion covered much of one ear. A long, thin knife lay on the floor by his outstretched hand.

Sheftu stared at the man's chest. It appeared to be rising, falling, and rising again. *Alive.* The bastard was still alive. He felt an unreasoning desire to kill him as he lay, but he reluctantly tamped it down. He glanced about the room.

Chain. Short lengths of chain hung neatly from pegs on the back wall above a series of alcoves containing all manner of metal hardware. Sheftu lifted two lengths of chain off the wall and bound the man's feet and hands. The chains were tight but Sheftu cared little for the man's eventual discomfort.

"Sheftu," Laran whispered from the doorway. She held a burning torch aloft with both hands, her posture suggesting she'd meant to use it as a weapon. She slowly lowered it and stared at the man who'd attacked her. She looked up into Sheftu's eyes, her own huge.

"I… I couldn't let you come alone," she told him. When he only frowned, she elevated her chin. "I told you once I would protect you," she added. "I would have!"

"Hmmm," he said.

He didn't sound angry, but he looked it. Perhaps he'd only been worried for her, as she'd been for him.

"We'll leave him here until morning. Come," Sheftu said, holding out his hand.

Laran extended one of hers towards him. He encompassed it warmly in his big palm. Despite the terrors of the last half hour, she felt both a wash of relief and a small thrill of anticipation at his touch.

Sheftu reached for the burning torch and together they began the arduous climb to the upper reaches of the palace once again.

CHAPTER FIFTY-NINE

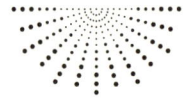

"**I** TOLD YOU, I know nothing about it," Provos said through clenched teeth. He was angry. He'd spent a sleepless night in a filthy cell below the palace not knowing what would become of him or whether he would again see the light of day. The injustice rankled.

"Nothing!" he ground out once more.

"You pass through Barraid and shortly thereafter a Soldatian army crosses the Barraidi border. Shall I believe this is sheer coincidence, Lord Provos?"

"*Aey*," he said. "Coincidence." *Though perhaps not entirely.* He wondered how much he should share with Mirren's High Lord.

"All of it," Mikale said and Provos met his eyes, startled.

Could the man read his mind? He hesitated a moment.

"I know only this: my kinsman, Lord Sheftu, has been Morrow Lord in his father's absence these past months," Provos began. "A powerful noble from a neighbouring house, Lord Du-kar, put forth a well- financed bid to re-invade Barraid despite the existence of a treaty. Lord Sheftu lobbied for and won support from the majority of noble houses to oppose Du- kar's plans."

"Why would he have done this?" Mikale asked.

Provos looked surprised. "There was a treaty," he repeated. "It wasn't right."

"And Lord Sheftu felt this sufficient motivation to make an enemy of a powerful opponent?"

"*Aey*, he did." Provos answered simply. "And undoubtedly it cost Du-kar a great deal of money. He will have lost status as well, a result even less forgivable. He promised retribution against my kinsman."

Provos paused, watching the Tania's reaction to his story carefully. He appeared interested, absorbing every word. He wore a frown between his brows.

So young Lord Sheftu knows his way around the political arena, Mikale thought. This, too, is interesting.

If Provos' words were true, Lord Sheftu was motivated by a sense of fairness. Then again, if there were darker considerations, it might explain why the two Soldatians had risked their lives to return Laran to Mirren-Bar. Lord Sheftu insisted his only motivator had been love. Was it power he really sought? Was his agenda political?

Provos claimed that the two of them had had no idea who Laran was. Tishane believed that.

By the Holy Ones, Mikale thought, so did he. "Continue," Mikale said impatiently.

"Now that Lord Sheftu is no longer in Soldat and the influence of the Morrow House has been withdrawn, perhaps Du-kar has launched the invasion he planned all along." Provos shrugged. "It is an educated guess, High Lord. Nothing more. As I have said repeatedly, I have *no* knowledge of the whereabouts or intent of the Soldatian army save what you, yourself, told me."

Mikale rose slowly and looked down at Provos. He had been forced to kneel. The man looked pale and exhausted. Likely the night in the cells had exacerbated the pain of his wounds and now he was angry and afraid.

That had been the intent.

Still, as unlikely as it seemed, Mikale was inclined to believe this Soldatian's assertion that he had no knowledge of the approaching army.

He would like to have put the question to his kinsman, but Lord Sheftu had yet to answer his summons.

"He is not to be trusted," Provos added.

"Lord Sheftu?" Mikale asked with a raised brow.

Provos frowned. "Lord Du-kar! It was to him that Laran was slave."

"So I have heard," Mikale said. He betrayed no emotion at the information. "My kinsman, High Lord? I'd like to see him."

Mikale looked down at Provos once again. "In due course," he answered, his growing concern outweighing his inclination for kindness.

He glanced up at one of his guardsmen. The man was bowing.

"Those you requested attend you await without," he told the Tania discreetly.

Mikale raised his hand to indicate that the guard was to wait before admitting the men.

To Tishane he said in Mirren, "Install Lord Provos in quarters appropriate to his status in Soldat."

Tishane bowed low. "*Ashaii*, High Lord." *Thank the Holy Ones*, he thought. This Soldatian seemed no more possessed of guile than his kinsman. That he spoke the truth seemed almost certain.

* * *

"WHAT DO YOU *mean* you don't know where he is?" Mikale demanded.

The watcher assigned to Sheftu and the guard who had been posted at his door stood awkwardly, their eyes downcast.

"When?" Mikale said grimly. "When did you last see him?"

"Last evening, High Lord," the watcher said. "After your audience with Count Degere and his family. He lost me not far from the Great Hall," he admitted, ashamed. "Purposely," he added under his breath.

"And he did not come back to his sleeping chamber last night?" Mikale demanded of the guard.

"He did not, High Lord."

"Go," Mikale said tiredly. Lord Sheftu would have to be found.

"Ah, High Lord?" the guard said, bowing. "May I relay a message from the Lady Tania?"

Mikale frowned and indicated his affirmation. *What now?*

"The Lady Tania bids me to tell you that Saharani Laran is... ah, also missing." The guard flushed, his face taking on an alarming colour. He swallowed audibly. "She bids me tell you she did not go missing at the same time as the Soldatian lord."

That the guard believed the disappearances were connected, though, was written in his face.

"Ah... The Lady Tania bids me tell you that she believes she knows where both the Saharani and Lord Sheftu are."

Mikale said nothing to this. He turned on his heel and left the two men glancing apprehensively at one another.

CHAPTER SIXTY

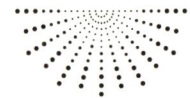

S HEFTU RE-DRAPED LARAN in Jodpul's cloak. Ironic, he thought, that he'd be using his rival's cloak to warm her. She was still disturbed by what had happened and had begun to shiver as soon as they'd reached the final terrace, though the climb itself should have heated her thoroughly.

He sat down with his back to the now familiar pillar and drew her down to the stones to sit beside him. She nestled in close and Sheftu wrapped a strong arm around her.

"I love you," she said after a time. Her voice was muffled against his chest. "You believe that, don't you?"

Sheftu sighed and nodded. *"Aey.* I do."

She buried her face deeper into his shirt. "And do you believe that I Promised to Jodpul before I knew you still lived?"

Before? Sheftu stared out at the seamless sky. Emeldra and Shell had said nothing of a Promise. He'd seen Laran at dawn the day he was brought up from the cells, and again only a few hours later. Had the Promise been made in that short span between?

"How could that be?" he asked.

"Jodpul has made it a habit to stop by the garden just after dawn each day." Laran hesitated. "Truth is, I was anxious to see him that morning, anxious to tell him I would marry him. It was only a few hours later that I learned you still lived."

"You *wanted* to marry him?"

"*Ashaii*," she admitted softly. "Because... Sheftu, it was because..." She placed her hand against her flat stomach. *What is the matter with me? I am afraid to tell him!*

"He.... he insisted we wait for two weeks before marrying. I didn't understand it then."

Sheftu stiffened. Two weeks! *Time was running out.* He felt his anger stir as he thought of Jodpul. The viscount had known Sheftu was alive and imprisoned when he took Laran's Promise. He'd said nothing!

He'd done nothing.

"That son of a bitch," Sheftu muttered angrily.

Laran pulled away to look up at him. His expression had hardened.

"Sheftu," Laran said. "You don't understand. Jodpul *delayed* the wedding to two weeks hence. He meant to prove your innocence in that time!"

Sheftu frowned, dubious. It was not in the viscount's best interests to exonerate his rival of guilt. Sheftu shook his head angrily. *Not that it would have mattered!* It had been the Tania's intention to kill him that day. He looked down into Laran's earnest golden eyes.

She didn't know.

Perhaps, Sheftu thought, just perhaps, Jodpul hadn't known either.

"It was Jodpul who told me where to find you tonight!" Laran told him.

Sheftu registered surprise. "He did?" He was silent a moment as he pondered that.

"And he let you come after me alone?" he suddenly demanded.

Laran narrowed her eyes and moved away slightly. Cold air rushed between them. "He requested I *not* come alone. He thought I had agreed."

She raised a brow. "I hadn't. And," she added, "no one *lets* me or *forbids* me to do anything, *Lord* Sheftu," she said coolly.

Sheftu cocked his head and looked down at her in amusement. "Is that so?" he asked softly.

"It *is* so!" she insisted.

"Hmmm. Come warm me, Little Elf," he said. "If it pleases you to do so," he added grinning.

"As it happens," Laran told him slowly, "it does." She smiled at him, her cat's eyes glistening like amber in the dim light. She snuggled against his side and tried to spread the cloak over both of them.

Sheftu frowned as he contemplated Jodpul. Had he really tried to prove his innocence? He'd said nothing at all about it. And *Jodpul* had been the one to tell Laran where he was? He must have known she would come to him! Rather than insisting she not do so, he'd insisted that she not come *alone.*

He didn't understand the viscount at all.

"Bare legs and arms," Laran was saying. "You must be freezing."

Sheftu mentally shook the image of Jodpul away. "*Aey,*" he said quietly. "But the warmth I seek from you does not come from a cloak." Strong fingers lightly caressed her jaw and lifted her chin. He dipped his head and angled his lips softly against hers.

The thrill shot down her spine and weakened her limbs. She pressed her lips against his with considerably more ardour as the urgent sensation she was feeling quickened and became nearly unbearable. Sheftu deepened the kiss immediately.

By the Seven Gods! He felt desire course through his body. His blood heated and his breath grew ragged. As the kiss grew deeper yet, he was aware of the pounding of his heart and he could have sworn he heard the drumbeat of Laran's as well. He pulled her onto his lap and she straddled him, moving against him. He was rock hard beneath her.

Laran broke away from the kiss and placed her hand behind her where she rested her weight on Sheftu's thighs. She stroked the rigid muscles so accessible beneath the *talom* and raised her buttocks slightly to move her fingers up, up toward that part of him that strained for her.

When he gasped, she bent forward to fasten her lips to his once again, and Sheftu grasped her buttocks and positioned her over him until she felt him, solid and unyielding beneath the cloth.

Sheftu pulled the cloak away from her shoulders, lifted the diaphanous fabric and touched her breasts lightly with his palms, teasing the tips to hardness beneath the form-fitting sheath she wore. Laran arched her neck and Sheftu rose up, carrying her with him, to run his tongue along the length of that long column before dropping his head to suckle at her nipples through the thin fabric.

"By the Holy Ones!" Laran breathed. The sheath felt too tight, too confining, and her body strained to be rid of it, all recognition of the temperature on the terrace gone. She tried to tear it off, but Sheftu intervened.

"Do not rip it, Little Elf," he laughed softly. He pulled it over her head and pushed it aside, his eyes filling with the sight of her.

Completely naked now in the starlight, she was squirming against him with need and her chest rose and fell with the heavy inhalations of lust, the nipples taut against the ripe fullness of her breasts. Her narrow waist flared to the generous camber of her hips and her buttocks were full and pliable in his hands once again.

Sheftu thought he'd never seen a sight more beautiful.

"Sheftu!" Laran panted. Her hands stroked his chest and traveled the lightly-furred route to the muscled ridges of his stomach. She raised herself once again, this time to reach beneath her. She took him in her hand and he drew his breath in suddenly.

"No!" Sheftu pleaded, his passion nearly blinding him. "You," he whispered. "Only you." He placed his hands on her waist and lifted her as though she weighed no more than a child. He pushed her to the stones gently and rolled on top of her, taking care not to crush her with his full weight.

He dipped his head once again to feast on her lips. The feel of her hands as they roamed his bare back beneath the loose shirt inflamed him and he tore it off and over his head; tore, too, at the *talom*, but Laran yanked it up from between them and then he too, was all but naked in the cold light of the stars.

"Now," she whispered urgently. He moved against her and she guided him into her. He entered her slowly and slowly, slowly she felt him inside of her, moving deeper and deeper yet, and then he withdrew. Slowly, slowly he penetrated her once again until she cried out in ecstasy, her buttocks beating a pulse against the cool stones of the terrace. He continued his slow dance over and inside her until she could bear it no more.

Laran thrust her hips up, sheathing him to the hilt, once, twice and then again until it was he who cried out. He stiffened, clenched his strong white teeth, then gave up control and spilled his seed inside of her.

She felt it, hot and liquid, leaking down her thighs, and her final thrust after the fact brought her to climax and she cried out his name.

Sheftu grinned, satiated. He rose slightly and put his finger to her lips.

"Shhh, Little Elf," he said, though he'd enjoyed the sound. "I do not wish to be imprisoned again, *aey?*"

"*Aey*," she mimicked him sleepily. She wrapped her arms around his neck happily.

"I love you," she told him again.

Sheftu collapsed against her, forgetting this once not to allow his full weight to crush her. She felt warm and soft beneath him and her hands pulled him down into the comfort of sleep.

Beneath him, Laran smiled tenderly. He was too heavy, of course, and she would soon have to wake him but for just a little while she would savour the feeling of his big body warm against hers once again.

She wanted to keep him with her. There had to be a way! And when he learned of the child she carried? Would he be happy?

What if he were not?

And if her family would not accept him? What if the pressure from the Degere family was too great? What if Jodpul changed his mind about releasing her once the effects of the *sloan* had worn off?

If, if, if! Have I come full circle?

She was with The Smiling Man once again. For now, that would have to be enough. She poked at his big form.

"Sheftu," she whispered. "Roll off." She nudged him again. "You're too heavy."

"Oh, *aey*," he said sleepily. "Sorry," he mumbled. He rolled to his side, gathered her into his arms, and resumed his slumber. Laran closed her eyes and tried not to let her fears for the future taint the joy she felt in the present.

* * *

THE MUTED LIGHT of dawn played against Sheftu's closed eyelids. Something had awoken him—Laran, stirring and now moving away from his side. Cold air washed over him as she drew the cloak aside and rose to her feet. Believing him to be asleep, she arranged Jodpul's cloak over him with care. He heard the sound of her bare feet padding softly toward the balustrade. He opened his eyes and turned his head to see her.

She was standing completely unclothed in the soft light. A shimmering crescent of the new sun appeared as a halo over the adjacent peak, painting her body with a soft yellow patina. Laran was wrapping her arms around her as she watched the awakening city below.

Sheftu rolled to his feet, rose and stretched out his muscles. Lying on the cold stone all night had been reminiscent of his many nights in the cell and he'd awakened a few times in the night in dread of being confined. Now, though, he felt strong. And happy.

Happy!

He had a hard road ahead. Here, right now, his path was simple. He would enjoy these few, precious moments with the woman he loved and try not to think too far ahead.

He pulled the *talom* into place and moved behind her. Wrapping strong arms around her, he nestled his chin on the top of her head. Laran leaned back against his naked chest with a little sigh.

"Cold," she murmured.

Sheftu swung the cloak around his shoulders and enveloped Laran in it as well.

"Sheftu?" she asked quietly. "Could you live here in Mirren-Bar?"

"*Aey*," he answered just as quietly. "I could."

She twisted to look up into his face. "You could leave your family and your country?"

"My brother's wife and their son..." Sheftu hesitated. "That would be a loss. Other than that, there is little left to hold me in Soldat. If you were at my side here in Mirren-Bar, Little Elf, I would have no regrets."

Laran faced forward again and leaned harder against him. Sheftu strengthened his hold on her, and Laran covered as much of his big hands as she could with her own.

"Your father and your brother? Would they not mourn your absence?"

"My absence would not impact on their daily lives with any significance."

Laran was silent a moment as she digested the hurt Sheftu must feel that this was so. Growing up as she had with the unconditional love and support of *her* family, it broke her heart to consider the boy Sheftu had been growing up without the same.

There is little left to hold me in Soldat, he'd said.

Provos! Provos had given him the support and the love he'd undoubtedly craved, she suddenly realized. Sheftu's grief over his cousin's death must have been, must *still* be, crushing. He hadn't said a word about it. Perhaps he felt he couldn't.

"Sheftu," she began again. "How... how would you feel about a child?"

Our child!

Sheftu laughed and kissed the top of Laran's head. "You fear that our coupling has conceived a child, Little Elf?"

Laran heard the smile in his voice, felt the rumble of his laughter against her back.

"Let's hope not!" he said, grinning. "A pregnancy now would not strengthen our case and would *definitely* not endear me to your family, *aey?*"

Laran twisted to look into his eyes, but he was looking over the balustrade to the precipitous trail directly below.

"Where does that lead?" he asked.

Let's hope not! By all that was sacred, this was not the response she'd hoped for.

"It looks to be no more than 100 feet long," Sheftu was saying, his eyes still on the narrow path. "It seems to disappear into the wall of solid rock beyond."

"Caverns," Laran answered as steadily as she could.

Perhaps this was not the time to tell him about the child she carried after all. She took a deep breath.

"Our Grandmother told us about them when Shell and I were children. She said one could hide there for years without being found, that there was fresh water and plenty of fresh air. One only needed to bring food." She smiled at the recollection of her often stern-faced Grandmother. "Our father was angry with her for telling us about them for much longer than he was angry with us."

"Why was that?" Sheftu asked curiously.

"Because while it was true one could hide for years without being found, it was also true that one could get *lost* with the same result. Naturally Shell and I wanted to find out for ourselves."

"Naturally." Sheftu smiled at the daring little girls Laran and her sister must have been. "Sounds like something Provos and I would have done."

Laran turned to study the gleam of interest in Sheftu's black eyes.

349

"Would *still* do, you mean," she grinned. There was no doubt that The Smiling Man enjoyed a good adventure. She continued looking up into Sheftu's beautiful eyes.

"Is it possible?" Laran murmured. A sense of desperation slid over her. "Could we really be together?"

Yes! Sheftu bent slightly to kiss her forehead. *The answer has to be yes!* The threat of impending loss enveloped him like fog.

"I will fight for you," he replied softly. "With words, with action, with everything I am, and with whatever it takes. I will not leave you willingly."

"Sheftu, I must tell you…"

But he jerked his head around.

"What is it?" Laran demanded.

"Someone approaches." No. Not someone. *Many* feet thumped up the last approach to the heights. Soldiers. It must be Tishane's guards! *If they discovered him here with their Saharani… By the Seven Gods! Had they already discovered the man wrapped in chains in the room below? He needed a chance to explain.*

"Laran," Sheftu began. His raven eyes were intense. "If I am imprisoned again…"

"Come!" She slipped out of his embrace and scooped up her sheath and its filmy covering, his shirt and their sandals. Clutching the lot, she climbed up on the balustrade and swung her feet over the edge.

"What…?" His eyes widened in alarm. *Oh. The caverns.*

Sheftu threw a quick glance behind him. The sound of a deep male voice shouting a command in Mirren sounded from the steps, not thirty feet away.

When Sheftu looked back, Laran had disappeared over the edge. Sheftu threw one leg over then froze. *What new hell is this?* The path below was even narrower than it first appeared. The drop appeared to lead straight into the Seventh Layer of Darkness, so steep and unrelenting was it. One misstep…

But Laran was already halfway across, naked, glorious and running the terrifying path. *Running!*

The sounds of a great many men grew louder as they reached the last steps to the terrace. Sheftu jumped, landing on the path below. Unbalanced, he teetered precariously for a moment. His eyes were drawn against his will to the sheer drop below.

"Don't look down!" Laran hissed. She'd reached the other side and was hurriedly donning the cerulean sheath. She looked over his head and he saw her eyes widen in dismay. She ducked out of sight and into a hidden opening in the wall ahead.

And still Sheftu was frozen. A life on the Soldatian plains had not prepared him for the heights. *Move,* he demanded of himself.

A head thrust over the edge of the balustrade searching the ground, such as it was, below, and then disappeared from sight. A hurried conversation ensued and then another head appeared.

Sheftu did not look up. Adrenalin pumped ferociously through his veins and his limbs began to feel disconnected.

"What are you doing?" a familiar voice asked. The tone was mild.

Sheftu swallowed from a mouth gone dry as the rock dust beneath his feet. "Out for a stroll, Captain," he answered conversationally.

"Like a hand up, would you?"

Yes! By the Seven Gods, yes! "No. Why?"

"Just wondered," Tishane replied. He'd noted Sheftu's bare chest and feet. He looked across the path to see a small patch of cerulean blue, there and gone, disappear behind a rock. *Laran.* He breathed a sigh of relief.

"Found a dead man down below, wrapped in chains. Did you kill him?"

"Maybe," Sheftu said. *Dead? He was dead?* His own body was rigid and seemingly paralyzed. His eyes still stared straight ahead and down the path, and he most certainly hadn't raised his head to look at Tishane. "He wasn't dead when I left him."

Tishane was silent above. "Why was he bound?" he finally asked.

"He attacked Laran. Bruised her up some, scared her badly."

Tishane's brows shot up. He looked again down the path where the flash of cerulean blue had appeared. He sighed.

"I give you one hour, Lord Sheftu. If you are not back by then, if you have *both* not returned by then, I will send my men over to retrieve you. If that happens, it will not go well for you. Do you understand?"

"Oh, *aey*," Sheftu said calmly. He'd still be *standing* there in an hour, frozen with fear of the precipice below. And just when had he become a *coward*?

He heard Tishane move away, heard a murmured command; heard the clanking sound of well-armed men retreating.

CHAPTER SIXTY-ONE

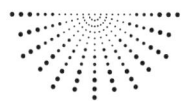

"SHEFTU," LARAN CALLED softly. "Don't look down. Come to me." She stood in plain view now, the cerulean blue sheath pressed across her slender body by the breeze. She held the diaphanous covering in one hand, and it flew from the mountainside like a gossamer banner.

He willed his feet to move, one step at a time. At the halfway point he had an inexplicable urge to weep. *What in the Seven Layers is wrong with me?* When he reached Laran, he released his breath explosively, unaware he'd been holding it.

"This is where I will live now, Little Elf," he told her, trying for levity in the face of his embarrassment. "Right here. I cannot cross that chasm again." He looked back at the terrace. It looked impossibly far away. His throat felt as though it would turn itself inside out. "Water," he said. "You said there was water?"

"Oh, *ashaii!*" she smiled in delight, though she darted an anxious glance at the terrace as she did so. It was empty of soldiers now.

Tishane had known to look for them here. Did her parents know as well? Likely, she thought glumly.

She glanced at Sheftu's wide, naked chest despite her self-admonishment not to do so. She reached for his hand and tugged. "Come. I'll take you to it."

Sheftu grabbed at the dangling leather laces of his sandals as he passed the little pile of clothing Laran had deposited on a rock ledge.

"You won't need those," she said.

Sheftu raised a brow, but dropped them just the same.

Laran ducked through a stone archway and he bent double to follow her through. When he straightened, his eyes widened in astonishment and his head swiveled to take it all in at once.

"It's lovely, *ashaii?*" Laran asked. She was looking into his eyes to enjoy his reaction.

"It's amazing, Laran." And it was. The cavern was a rounded dome encased in milky calcite with the delicate, drooping patterns of stirred cream. A large hole at its zenith let in the pale rays of the early morning sun, which glistened on a canopy of hundreds of opaque and white stalagmites, some as long as he was tall. A tiny, sparkling drop of moisture hung suspended from each long column like a blessing.

Below the canopy lay a nearly perfectly round pool. The top layer of liquid shone as blue as Laran's sheath, but the layers beneath were darker and darker yet until the colour disappeared entirely. It must have been very deep. A filmy haze of smoke skimmed across the surface like a living entity.

No, Sheftu thought. *Not smoke. Steam.* He looked at Laran in wonder.

She was grinning at him, clearly taking pleasure in his delight. She tugged on his hand once more. "Come swim with me, Sheftu," she said softly.

Sheftu watched as she pulled the narrow sheath over her head once again. She shook her short curly hair like an animal—a stunningly beautiful animal, he amended to himself. He smiled in pure pleasure. When she moved to the edge of the pool to look in, the angled light of the sun bathed her naked skin, her soft curls and, he saw when she turned to him, her lovely cats' eyes, in liquid gold, and liquid gold caressed the curves of her breasts, the flare of her hips and the smooth lines of her thighs.

Sheftu felt the rise of an erection beneath the *talom* and he reached for the fastening and dropped the garment to the stone floor of the cavern.

Laran stared at him, fascinated. *Big,* she thought. *Impossibly so.* And yet... and yet he hadn't felt too large the night before. On the contrary. She felt a thrill of anticipation race down her back. It spread its tendrils through her abdomen and down into that part of her that ached for his touch.

"You are quite beautiful," she told him, admiring the curve of muscle across his shoulders and chest, the bulge of his biceps and the slight camber of muscle on hip and groin. Her fingers itched to touch him there, to touch him everywhere.

Sheftu grinned at her, his teeth strong and white. Desire had turned his black, black eyes to velvet and they were closed to half-mast.

Laran felt a surge of lust at the sight. Her lips parted and her breath quickened. Her heart pounded with urgency.

"An hour," Sheftu murmured. "We have an hour to be together. It will have to be enough."

"Enough," she nearly groaned.

They came together then, warm skin against cool, breasts flattened against hard broad chest, and four hands stroking, stoking, touching.

When Sheftu slipped a strong finger inside of her, Laran cried out and tried to pull him down to the cavern floor.

He picked her up off her feet, ducked at the entrance to the cavern pool, and with one hand swept the clothing off the stone ledge. He positioned her there carefully, her legs to either side of his hips. He kissed her then, gently at first then deeply as their passion mounted to nearly unbearable limits. He moved his mouth down, down until she writhed and moaned in ecstasy.

When he straightened again, he plunged into her, wringing from her a startled cry. She grasped him tightly and fought to remain still as he pushed into her again and again until finally she arched her neck and stiffened, Sheftu's name escaping on a gasp. Sheftu cried out inarticulately.

They clung to one another, slick with sweat and the juice of their coupling, satiated. Laran began to weep.

Sheftu pulled back slightly to look into her face. "I've hurt you," he said, his voice heavy with self-recrimination. "I didn't mean to, Laran. I didn't…"

But Laran was shaking her head.

"No," she sobbed. "You didn't. I just… I just feel… good. That's all."

Sheftu put both hands on her hips and lifted her down off the ledge. He looked dubious at her statement. "Forgive me," he said. His eyes were filled with his distress.

Idiot! he chastised himself. *What in the Seven Layers is wrong with you?*

Laran reached up to place her hands on either side of his face.

"Listen to me!" she said. "You didn't hurt me! I was just… overwhelmed. It was wonderful. I never expected… I just didn't know."

"You are not hurt?"

Laran shook her head.

Sheftu took a deep breath. "Ah," he said uncertainly. And then all at once he relaxed. "Oh," he said again, smiling.

Tell him!

"Swim with me," she said instead.

Ducking under the stone again, Sheftu looked at the deep pool. The darkening depths that had at first looked forbidding now appeared welcoming.

But that sense of impending loss was back. They'd soon have to leave this wondrous place. They'd have to travel the narrow path once more. *He'd* have to place his trust in Tishane once they reached the terrace.

Sheftu was aware that his life rested in the Tania's hands once again. He had to hope that the High Lord did not throw him back into the cells, or worse, for having spent the night with his daughter.

356

He'd be angry. Sheftu knew that. But no matter what happened, he *wouldn't* regret the time he and Laran had taken. He couldn't.

And if he wasn't imprisoned? Sheftu would have another abyss to traverse. He'd have to prove to the Tania and his family that he belonged with the Saharani and she with him, that he was the right choice for her husband, and a valuable asset to Mirren-Bar. And all of this in the face of an existing Promise.

It appeared an impossible task! He laughed at the enormity of it all in spite of himself, then swung one bare foot across the surface of the pool.

Warm.

"*Aey*, let's swim." He clasped Laran's hand and together they jumped.

* * *

"OH, MY," EMELDRA murmured.

Ten of Tishane's men, with their captain looking grim-faced and worried at their head, escorted Laran and Lord Sheftu into the Tania's private receiving room.

Emeldra, seated beside her husband, watched their daughter as she returned from the palace heights. She could see that Laran's eyes reflected the same level of anxiety as did Tishane's and she was biting her full lower lip, a habit in times of stress she shared with her mother. And yet… and yet she looked happier somehow. Could that be so? Was Emeldra reading her correctly?

The young Soldatian lord walked at her side. *His* expression spoke of carefully schooled calm but his raven eyes… *Ashaii*. She saw something there that hadn't been present before, some deep emotion he did not wish to display.

Though they were not touching, their body language spoke of intimacy and… something else. Comfort? *Ashaii*, Emeldra thought; a kind of comfort in one another. She glanced up at her husband.

Mikale was angry and *his* eyes were narrowed in displeasure. When Laran and Sheftu drew closer and stopped, he ground his teeth together in an

357

effort not to shout. He looked over his daughter's head to address the Soldatian.

"You have disrespected my daughter, Lord Sheftu," he said coldly. "You have disrespected me."

Sheftu inclined his head in a gesture meant to appease, but it only added fuel to the Tania's ire.

"That was not my intention," Sheftu said gravely.

Laran looked from Sheftu to her father in dismay. "No!" she cried in Soldatian. "You don't understand! I *followed* Lord Sheftu to the heights. He did not *ask* me to go with him. And then I was attacked and…"

"What?" Emeldra whispered, aghast.

Laran aimed an apologetic look at her mother. She hadn't meant to blurt that out and she hadn't meant to upset her. Any more than she had already, that is.

"There was a man," Laran began. She darted a glance at Sheftu and continued in Soldatian. "He wanted to hurt me, but I fought him. I knocked him out!" She said this with such obvious pride that Sheftu nearly smiled.

Mikale aimed a questioning look at Tishane and the captain nodded grimly. Mikale closed his eyes a moment to compose himself. *Later,* he told himself. *We will speak of this later.*

The man was dead, Sheftu knew, though Laran obviously wasn't aware of that. She'd be upset when she…

"I was unnerved," Laran continued omitting the details. "Sheftu made sure the man was restrained, he calmed me, and… uh… we must have fallen asleep." She said this last in a small voice and avoided meeting her parents' eyes. Her cheeks were suddenly suffused with colour.

So much for pretending innocence of action, Sheftu thought resignedly.

"And Jodpul?" Mikale asked. "Did you give any thought to him?"

Laran straightened and elevated her chin. Anger flashed in her golden eyes. "I have given Jodpul a great deal of thought," she told her father icily.

Mikale's eyes widened at his daughter's tone.

"Would you disrespect me, too, daughter?" he asked Laran quietly.

Laran's eyes dropped to the stone at her feet, ashamed. "No, my father. Not ever. Not purposefully." She looked up into his eyes. "You have my utmost respect," she said sincerely. *And my love.*

Mikale regarded her silently a moment and read the unspoken sentiment in her face.

"Then why have you done this thing, Laran?" he asked her in Mirren.

"I seek happiness, father," Laran told him, reverting to her own tongue. She looked deeply into his eyes, willing him to see in Sheftu what she could see. "Jodpul understands this."

Sheftu was listening intently, trying to decipher what had just been said. He met Laran's eyes and held them a moment, before moving his black-eyed gaze to Emeldra.

He bowed to her then, the gesture courtly, and again to the High Lord. "Laran has no blame in this matter. I have been indiscreet," he admitted. "I know that. Truly, I meant no disrespect. You are Laran's parents and for that alone I would honour you."

Oh my, Emeldra thought again. She cocked her head to the side waiting to hear what would come next.

Mikale crossed his arms on his chest and jerked his chin at Tishane. "Dismiss your men, Captain," he said.

To Sheftu, he said, "Did you miss your time in the cells, Lord Sheftu?"

Sheftu stiffened and something flickered behind his eyes. A small muscle moved in his jaw. He heard Laran's sudden intake of breath and the horrified words she spoke to her father in Mirren, but he remained silent.

"What did you hope to accomplish?" Mikale demanded of him.

Sheftu's eyes widened. *Accomplish?* "I wished only to be reunited with Laran," he said truthfully. He looked over at her and swallowed audibly.

"Reunited?" Mikale asked. His frown intensified. "And did you, young lord? Did you *reunite?*"

"Father!" Laran cried again, appalled. Her complexion deepened to red.

"Mikale," Emeldra murmured. "Surely you do not mean to imply such a thing?" She exchanged glances with her husband. *And even more surely, you don't wish to know the answer!*

"I wish to petition for marriage," Sheftu told them. He saw Laran's startled glance in his peripheral vision.

"My daughter is Promised!" Mikale all but roared.

"She belongs with me," Sheftu said. He straightened to his full height and elevated his chin.

"I love her. I will care for her. I will protect her with my life," he said.

Mikale stared at Sheftu incredulously. He swung his gaze to Laran, and it rested hard. "What have you to say to this, daughter?"

"I Promised to Jodpul before I knew Sheftu still lived. It was a mistake, Father." She looked into Sheftu's eyes and echoed his words, though in Mirren.

"I love him," she said. "I will care for him. And I will protect him with my life. To me, he is The Smiling Man, the bringer of joy. He *is* the happiness I seek."

"And Jodpul?" Emeldra asked. "What of him?" The young man had waited for Laran's return and grieved her likely death with the rest of them.

"He has offered to release me, Mother," she said. She looked up at her father. "He is my friend," she told him. "He wants my happiness. He *has* offered to release me!"

The two stared at their daughter in stunned disbelief. "And Lord Sheftu knows this," Mikale observed.

"In truth, no," Laran said. "I have not yet told him in deference to Jodpul."

"Jodpul would do this for you?" Mikale asked softly. When Laran only nodded, he thought of the Degeres. There would be hell to pay for dissolution of the Promise.

"No," Mikale said abruptly. "The Promise stands." Mikale rose from his seat and held his hand out to his wife. Emeldra placed her hand in his, her swift glance at her husband inscrutable, and the two of them began to walk away.

"High Lord!" Sheftu called after him. "I have more to bring to a marriage than first appears! Will you hear me?"

Mikale turned slowly and stared at Sheftu. He bit off the urge to retort that there was *nothing* the Soldatian could offer that might warrant breaking the Promise. The Degeres were a powerful family and their influence was great.

"High Lord?" Tishane interrupted respectfully from the doorway. "A messenger has arrived from the border."

Mikale held one hand up, palm forward, to forestall the flow of Sheftu's next words, and with the other signalled Tishane to allow the messenger entry.

Emeldra observed Sheftu's understanding that Mirren's High Lord was being distracted. She saw his quick grasp of Laran's hand and the equally quick release. The Soldatian's handsome face was serious, and he looked resolute enough to follow through on his intention to petition. The prospect must be daunting, though, especially in the light of Mikale's less-than-subtle threat to re-imprison him.

Emeldra knew her husband would not do so, but young Lord Sheftu clearly did not.

Laran, on the other hand, looked almost desperate, and heart-breakingly hopeful. Her love for the young man at her side was plain to see.

Laran's cerulean sheath, her favourite, was soiled now and the diaphanous covering appeared to be ripped along the hem. Her sandals were dusty. Emeldra's eyes rose to her daughter's face. The light brown curls framing it looked, strangely, darker. Damp? Were they *wet*?

361

For the first time she noted that Sheftu's sleeveless white shirt, dirty now in spots, was nearly transparent across his broad shoulders where the ends of his long, straight, *wet* hair had dripped.

The cavern pool! These two had been to the cavern pool, the very place she and Mikale had professed their love for one another, and the very place they were Promised! *Against* the wishes of their parents, she recalled ruefully.

Oh, my, she thought once again. And isn't *this* an interesting turn of events.

"...now approaches our border and appears intent on marching into Mirren-Bar," the messenger was saying. Emeldra jerked her head around to see the man who'd delivered the message. A soldier, she noted, one of Tishane's guards. Had he been sent on reconnaissance?

Mikale and Tishane exchanged glances.

"This does not bode well," Mikale murmured to his captain.

They both glanced at Sheftu, their expressions wary and Sheftu's brows shot up. He noted the tension in Lady Emeldra's body; saw the shock in Laran's face.

"What is it?" he asked.

Mikale moved to stand in front of him and crossed his arms over his chest, ignoring his question and seemingly changing the subject.

"And so?" he said softly. "What is it that you bring to your marriage petition that is 'more than first appears', young Soldatian?"

"Soldat!" Sheftu said quickly before the Tania could turn away again. "The Great Houses are often at odds with one another, but by law, they must align for matters of national interest. Each House has its own sizable army. *All* are a force to be reckoned with." He paused for a moment to let his point sink in. "Soldat makes a *persuasive* ally," he added, the understatement clear.

"And you believe, Lord Sheftu, as second son to the Lord of one of those Houses, that *you* wield enough authority to influence national policy?"

"A marriage into your family would secure that influence, High Lord." Sheftu paused at the look on the Tania's face. "I have some experience rallying the Lords of the other noble Houses to a cause," he hastened to add. "Though, I will not go against my conscience to do so."

"So I have heard," Mikale said wryly.

He'd heard? How could he have heard? Sheftu looked a question at Laran, but she was shaking her head. He glanced back at Mikale, bemused. *Had the Tania made inquiries of him with the Soldatian court? To what purpose?*

Mikale reacted to the unasked question on Sheftu's lips unexpectedly.

"Your kinsman told me," Mikale informed him. "I heard the story from Lord Provos." He watched Sheftu's reaction carefully.

Sheftu paled. "Provos?" he asked quietly. *He is dead.* Sheftu looked at the Tania, bemused. Grief guttered in his chest. "I don't understand. You spoke to him on the Barraidi headland? Before he died? But how…"

"Yesterday," Mikale answered. Sheftu was absolutely still. *Yesterday.*

"He lives?" he asked softly. *That can't be. I grieved for him. I still grieve for him. Aey,* and hadn't he mourned Laran's death as well? His eyes widened in sudden revelation.

Provos lives! Or did.

When Mikale did not answer immediately, anger sparked in raven eyes.

"*Does* my kinsman *live?*" Sheftu stepped close to Mirren's High Lord and looked down at him menacingly. "Where is he?" Sheftu snarled. "Does… he…live?" he demanded.

"He lives. Now step back."

Sheftu stared at the Tania in disbelief. He moved back a step and then another. He looked at Emeldra and Tishane in turns.

"Where? Where is he?"

"He will be brought to you," Tishane interjected at a nod from the Tania.

"And was he also tortured for information he did not have?" Sheftu asked, his fury beginning to own him. He moved once again to within inches of Mirren's High Lord.

He registered Laran's gasp from somewhere outside of himself. She hadn't learned all that had befallen him in the cells. Or perhaps her dismay was for the physical threat he now posed to her father.

"Step back, young lord," Mikale said quietly, "or I *will* have you thrown back into the very cells you detest. Is that quite clear?"

"*Aey*," Sheftu said, though he remained in place. He heard Tishane's muffled curse as he was forced to withdraw his sword.

"He was not tortured, Lord Sheftu," Mikale told him evenly, "though he did spend a long night in those same cells in the hope that he would mellow enough to answer my questions. He did not."

"Perhaps he did not have the answers," Sheftu said through bared teeth.

Mikale nodded. "*Ashaii*. Perhaps." He looked up at Sheftu, seemingly unconcerned by his proximity and willing, for now, to allow it despite his threat to the contrary.

"Your kinsman tells me you single-handedly put an end to one of your countrymen's ambitions to reinvade Barraid despite the existence of a treaty. Is this so?"

Aey," Sheftu answered slowly. His mind was whirling. He wanted to believe Provos was alive. He *needed* to believe it.

"What was your purpose in doing so?"

Sheftu looked at the messenger, still standing to the side. He was watching the interaction carefully, his understanding of Soldatian clearly sufficient to understand what was being said.

He wanted to see his cousin. *Concentrate,* he instructed himself.

"It was the right thing to do," Sheftu answered simply, chagrinned at the lack of political sophistication his answer seemed to imply.

"You risked the enmity of a powerful lord simply because 'it was the right thing to do'?"

Sheftu frowned. *"Aey,* though this particular lord was no particular friend at any rate. The Houses of Morrow and Du-kar had been... at odds since before I was born."

"And why is that, Lord Sheftu?" Mikale asked him.

"Philosophies of conduct, High Lord. They differ on personal, social, and political levels. Always have."

Conduct? Mikale nearly sneered. Du-kar! This was the name given the man who had enslaved his daughter in Soldat. Inquiries made had cemented the man's reputation as brutal and sadistic. Mikale looked over at Laran. That she still feared the man, even now, was evident in her expression.

His heart sank. He should have conducted this line of questioning out of earshot of his daughter. He had no wish to dredge up her terrible memories of that time.

Mikale glanced up at Sheftu once again. *This* Soldatian, no matter what his motive, had rescued her. Mikale resolved to keep his own anger curtailed and to remember that simple fact. Lord Sheftu *had* taken her out of Soldat and he *had* intended to deliver her to Mirren-Bar and back into the arms of her family. That it seemed the young lord hadn't known who her family actually was, spoke well for him.

"Tell me, young lord, about the Soldatian army now approaching Mirren."

Sheftu's brow shot up once more. *A Soldatian army!* "I know nothing of this." He shook his head in disbelief. "Are you certain?"

"Ashaii," Mikale said. "It is said they have not engaged the Barraidi. Its purpose is unknown, but I believe it must be connected to you and your kinsman."

"I don't see how," Sheftu said frowning. *Du-kar! That bastard, Du-kar.* He wasn't killing the Barraidi. Why? Was his intention to cross into Mirren in search of Laran and himself? Could he be that obsessed with reclaiming her and exacting revenge?

Aey, Sheftu thought, he could. Then again, the riches of Mirren-Bar were significant.

Mikale regarded Sheftu through slitted eyes.

"And if I were to allow your petition," Mikale said, abruptly changing the subject once again, "just what would you expect in return?"

The sudden change from a matter of national security to the personal matter of the marriage petition gave Sheftu pause. Were they now connected in the Tania's mind?

Sheftu stared fearlessly into Mikale's golden eyes.

"I wish to make my home here, in Mirren-Bar, High Lord," Sheftu said, "with Laran as my wife."

Mikale carefully constructed his reply. "An outsider, a *Soldatian*, will never possess the power of the Mirren throne, Lord Sheftu."

Sheftu frowned at the assertion. "And so be it," he told the Tania. "That has never been my goal, though I could rise to the challenge if I needed to."

Mikale registered this with a grunt.

"As well," the Tania continued, "young Morrow, a Promise is not entered into lightly and once done, is considered sacred.

However," he added, sighing tiredly, "I will take your petition and all it entails into consideration."

Sheftu only nodded. *It was a start.*

"In the meantime, you will be given an opportunity to show me the 'expertise' you have described when the Soldatian army comes knocking, *ashaii?*"

"*Aey*, High Lord. I will do what I can." A deep sense of foreboding tingled down his spine. *What in the name of each of the Seven Gods am I to do with an invading army? This is more of a test than I had dreamed.*

"Father," Laran said quietly. "I understand that something is happening, something disquieting. I understand the threat this army may pose for our people. But I beg you, please do not throw Sheftu's petition aside."

"I have said I will consider it, daughter. I will."

"Please call Jodpul to you now," Laran asked, "to clarify what has happened between us?"

Mikale turned to Tishane. He spoke to his captain in the language of their country. "Gather what information you can from the border lands. Secure the name of the leader of this army and confirm its numbers. If you are able, find out if it represents a particular Soldatian House or whether it is nationally driven."

Tishane bent low. "*Ashaii*, High Lord. It is done." He straightened. "As the Soldatians near the border, other messengers have been dispatched. Another should arrive within minutes," Tishane said.

Mikale only nodded.

"Send for Viscount Degere, Captain," he told Tishane. "Have him brought here immediately."

Emeldra smiled her approval. She moved close to speak into his ear. "Well done, Mikale." She moved closer still. "Listen and I will tell you something that has transpired that may give you more to think on yet."

Mikale looked down at his wife curiously. "What is it, Emeldra?"

Emeldra stood on tiptoe to speak into his ear. "Laran and the young Soldatian have been to the cavern pool. They bathed in its waters only this morning."

Mikale swore softly under his breath and turned to stare at his daughter and at Lord Sheftu. And then his eyes narrowed at a sudden recollection.

Emeldra's paintings! In all that had transpired since the night he'd searched for his wife in the garret, he had forgotten that last painting! *Forgotten?* In truth, he'd blocked it from his consciousness. He studied Laran closely.

His daughter looked the same.

No. *She didn't.* Her cheeks were fuller and her golden eyes sparkled with life. Was it her love for the Soldatian lord that animated her so? Or was it something else?

By the Holy Ones, *was* she with child?

CHAPTER SIXTY-TWO

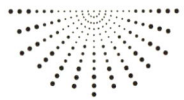

S O, IT BEGINS, Jodpul thought morosely. He was standing before the Tania, his usually immaculate attire rumpled and looking as though he'd slept in it, which he had. His hair was loose of its usual neat queue and curled wildly about his face and shoulders with a softness that might have looked feminine on another man. He bowed low but it was Laran's eyes he met when he straightened. He looked away from her with some reluctance.

"High Lord, Lady Tania," he said with deference. "You wished to see me?"

"*Ashaii,*" Lady Tania answered for both of them. She was quiet a moment contemplating how to begin what she needed to say. *Best to plunge right in,* she decided. "Jodpul, despite the existence of your pre-existing Promise, Lord Sheftu has petitioned marriage to the Saharani Laran. Laran has asked us to bring you here."

Jodpul stared at Laran intensely, trying to gauge what she would like him to say.

"The Saharani Laran and I spoke late last night," he said softly, his eyes never leaving Laran. "We have both agreed that the Promise made between us is invalid. The Promise would not have been made at all had the knowledge that Lord Sheftu still lived not been withheld from her."

"Did *you* know he was still alive when you made it, Jodpul?"

"*Ashaii.* It was my intention to prove him innocent before letting the Saharani know. It was a decision made with her best interests at heart, truly." He bowed to Laran then. "It was a mistake. I should never have accepted nor given the Promise knowing what I did."

He glanced at Sheftu, who stood silently, fists clenched, brows knit in concentration as he tried and failed to understand what was being said.

"I believe Lord Sheftu to be a good man, Lady Tania," Jodpul said. "And only last night my men brought the betrayer, the sailor Santago, across the border into Mirren-Bar. He can be made to acknowledge Lord Sheftu's innocence if there remains any doubt."

Sheftu stiffened as he heard Santago's name on Jodpul's lips. *What does it mean?*

"And the lone survivor of the attack on the headlands? The Barraidi hunter?"

"Dead. Killed in a tavern brawl not three days later."

Jodpul looked at Mikale and tried to swallow the humiliation he knew he would feel with his next words.

"High Lord," he began, "if Lord Sheftu's petition of marriage is rejected, my own petition will stand once again." Red crept up Jodpul's neck and flamed the tips of his ears with colour.

A furious eruption of noise sounded outside the door of the private chamber and a harried guard stepped inside with an apologetic bow.

"High Lord, Lady Tania: Count and Countess Degere respectfully request admittance to this audience."

Jodpul closed his eyes a moment. When he opened them again, they were resigned.

But Mikale was shaking his head.

"This audience is closed," he informed the hapless guard, who managed to look both dutifully respectful and reluctant to convey the Tania's message.

"*Ashaii*, High Lord," he said bowing. He stepped outside and the eruption of noise began again.

Mikale looked at Jodpul closely.

"Jodpul, you have set yourself on a difficult path."

Jodpul nodded. *"Ashaii,"* he said miserably, but he looked down at Laran and tried to smile. "My path would be no less difficult if the Promise stood. It is not my wish to stand in the way of your daughter's happiness."

"Jodpul," she whispered. Tears gathered in her eyes and one rolled down her cheek. She left Sheftu's side, wrapped her arms around the viscount's neck and kissed him lightly on the lips.

Sheftu's eyes widened in surprise. He stood stiffly, uncomprehending. Emeldra took pity on him.

"Viscount Degere has agreed to release Laran from her Promise if your petition is allowed," she told him. "If it is not allowed, his own petition will be renewed."

Sheftu stared at Emeldra in shock. His astonished gaze slid down to Laran, whose arms had remained around Jodpul, then over her head to meet Jodpul's golden eyes. Sheftu read no agenda in their depths and saw, instead, an open appraisal of himself. The viscount had one arm around Laran and Sheftu tamped down the unwarranted thread of jealousy that bloomed in his chest.

Aey, unwarranted. *Probably.* He frowned and Jodpul grinned slowly, and widely, at his discomfort.

The viscount lowered his head to whisper into Laran's ear, "Now, Little Saharani, see what you can do to break tradition, *ashaii?*"

Laran broke away from the embrace and nodded solemnly. *"Ashaii,"* she told him. She looked back at Sheftu and smiled beatifically.

The door to the private audience chamber opened again and another messenger stepped inside at Tishane's bidding.

"High Lord," the young man panted, a sense of urgency written in his face. That his message was being delivered after a run was obvious.

"The Soldatians have crossed the border," the young man blurted out without being given leave to do so. "They are five thousand strong. Their leader has not been identified." He hesitated, breathing hard.

"Continue," Mikale urged, his own sense of urgency escalating.

"They have not engaged the Barraidi at any point in their travels and the only deaths reported have been those few Barraidi who attacked them first. Apparently, request for safe passage through Barraid was sent to the Barraidi sovereign. It was denied."

Mikale frowned at this.

"And still," the young messenger said unnecessarily, "here they are."

Ashaii, Mikale thought. *Here they are.* He glanced at Sheftu once again, evidently deciding on his next move.

"Captain," Mikale directed Tishane, "see that Lord Provos is brought to me in the Great Hall. Rally the guardsmen you have readied and send them out to meet the approaching Soldatians. Escort only their leaders through the gates of the city. I will meet with them there."

Tishane bowed his acquiescence and, turning on his heel, ran for the door, collecting the winded messenger as he did so. Sending his guardsmen to the gates of the city was his first priority. Collecting wayward Soldatians and delivering them to the Great Hall dropped to nearly incidental on the mental list he silently checked as he ran.

"I will bring Provos, Tishane," Laran called after him. He was moving swiftly and merely grunted his response, though his feet slowed at the realization that he had been impolite.

"Go!" Laran said, dismissing the breach of manners. "I will do the same."

Tishane turned slightly, inclined his head gratefully, then resumed his run.

"Attend me," the Tania ordered Sheftu as he strode away. "I have questions. When we are done, you will meet me in the Great Hall."

Sheftu threw a quick glance at Laran, who was already on her way to Provos.

"*Aey,* High Lord," he said.

CHAPTER SIXTY-THREE

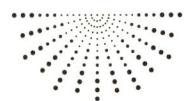

PROVOS ROSE SLOWLY from his bed, wincing as he did so. His shoulder was finally beginning to heal, but the chest wound still robbed him of sleep at night and of coherent thought for much of the day.

Now, though, he was roused not by the lingering pain of his wounds, but by the staccato clip of hooves in the courtyard below—hundreds of them by the sound of it, and by the shouts of men. And was that the clank of weaponry?

He crossed to the window of the room he was being detained in and stared at the scene below in astonishment.

There were, indeed, hundreds of horses in the courtyard. Their riders appeared to be well-armed Mirren soldiers. One voice could be heard above all others. Tishane's.

The Captain of Guards was himself mounted and shouting orders to the horsemen, who turned as one and immediately pounded out of the courtyard. Moments later, another hundred or so mounted soldiers assembled and once again Tishane shouted orders and once again the horsemen dispersed. When Provos figured five or six hundred men and horses had arrived and then departed the courtyard, Tishane finally prepared to ride off himself. He was still issuing orders, this time to the several remaining soldiers who had remained on foot.

With the captain's final command, both Tishane and the soldier he addressed raised their heads to look directly at Provos. He resisted a childish urge to jump back from the window.

What now? Provos thought, dread churning in his stomach. Something was happening, that much was clear. What? And why would Tishane have looked to *him?* Was it something to do with his cousin? *Sheftu! Where in the Seven Layers are you?*

Provos stared at the barred door of his chamber and willed it to open.

When he heard the bar on the outside of the door being slid out of place, he *did* jump back a pace. He cast about for something to use as a weapon, but nothing came to hand. Instead, he concentrated on standing tall and proud. If Tishane had ordered his death, they'd not find him cowering in the corner! And, wounded or not, they'd not find him easy prey, either.

Two soldiers stepped into the room, one to each side of the door. Provos saw two more on the outside of the room, again one to each side. But it was Laran Tania walking through them!

Provos laughed aloud in relief and Laran grinned at him in delight, though both his pallor and his relative thinness gave her pause. He looked almost as bad as Sheftu had when she first saw him again. She crossed the room to take his hands in her own.

"Provos!" she said. "I am happy to see you! We thought you were dead! But how did you survive the chest wound you suffered?"

"You knew about that?"

"*Ashaii,*" Laran told him. "Sheftu saw you lying on the ground with an arrow through your chest and your blood spilled in a pool around you. And," she added softly, "so did I."

Provos grinned, almost against his will. "Remember the Barraidi mother?" he asked Laran. "Estalla. Her name is Estalla. She and her husband nursed me back to life." He paused a moment. "They are here, Laran! Estalla and Randide and their children! I was separated from them when we arrived and I haven't seen them since." Provos' smile had disappeared with this last statement and worry reappeared in his eyes. "I hope they are all right," he said quietly.

He removed his hands from Laran's and brought one up to touch the soft curls of her short hair. "It's grown," he murmured. "You look well. You look beautiful!" he said.

Laran laughed. "Must you sound so surprised?"

"My cousin, Laran?" Provos asked, his expression serious now. "Does he live?"

"He does! And he, too, is well, Provos! My father has called for him, and for you! You are to be brought to the Great Hall where my father is assembling his nobles. You can see Sheftu for yourself then!" She took hold of his hand once more and tugged him toward the door. "Come!"

"*Aey*," he said. "I will!" He laughed again and started out the door behind her, moving cautiously past the guards, his hand still clasped in hers. "Your father…" he began. "He is the *ruler* of Mirren," he said accusingly.

"Oh. *Ashaii*." She glanced at him, shyly. "So he is."

Laran stopped in the centre of the corridor, her face registering dismay. "You are still injured!" she said.

"*Aey*," he answered slowly, bemused.

"But why were you not healed, Provos?" She stepped up to him, her hand poised to touch his chest, but she held back. *No. There is no time!* "I… I promise I will heal you as soon as I can. Can you manage the long walk to the Great Hall?"

"*Aey*," he said again. "Slowly. What's happening here, Laran?"

"Soldiers!" she told him. "Soldatian soldiers. Five thousand of them. They've marched across Barraid and have crossed the border into Mirren. It appears they are heading here to Mirren-Bar!"

Provos stared at her. This was the army the Tania had spoken of. "Why?" he demanded.

"No one knows yet. But my father thinks it must have something to do with you and Sheftu."

Provos grasped her arm. "Have you considered Du-kar, Laran? Could it be Du-kar?" He felt her shudder.

"I don't know," she said quietly. *Please, please, by the Holy Ones, don't let it be he!*

* * *

THE RAISED VOICES of a great many men and women emanated from the Great Hall, but there was a noticeable lull when Provos and Laran entered. She held his arm as they walked as much to show support for him as to actually support him. He clenched his teeth against the pain of his wounds, but his expression and posture gave no hint that he was suffering. Heads swiveled to watch their progress through the crowd and Provos felt the weight of accusation in golden eyes.

A deep voice shouted his name and Provos stopped to search the crowd, though the man he searched for towered over all of them.

"Sheftu!" he replied. His grin nearly split his face at his first sight of his cousin. Sheftu's straight black and white streaked hair hung below his shoulders now, as did his own. Sheftu's though, swung against the sleeveless white Mirren shirt he wore. His powerful legs were bare in a knee length wrap of white cloth, and his feet were shod not in the leather boots common to Soldat, but in leather sandals tied with thongs to mid-calf. He wore a grin duplicating Provos' own.

When they reached each other, they embraced mightily.

Provos gasped. "Leave off, Cousin." He stepped back, his grin erased and sudden pallor flooding his face.

"Sorry," Sheftu mumbled, contrite, but he continued to grin just the same. "I thought you were dead, Provos."

"*Aey*, and I imagined the same of you," Provos assured him. His happiness at seeing Sheftu alive and well began to light his eyes once again and his smile followed.

They grasped each other's arms, but the open stares and occasional murmured hostility finally broke through their euphoria.

"Cousin!" Provos said. "These Mirren believe we have something to do with the army now approaching Mirren-Bar."

"*Aey*," Sheftu replied grimly. "I know."

"Du-kar?"

Sheftu shrugged. "Perhaps," he said doubtfully. "We'll know soon."

There was a sudden ripple of sound as the Tania made his way through the crowd. It was parting like torn paper before him.

"Ride with me, Lords Sheftu and Provos," he instructed as he passed. Sheftu and Provos exchanged startled glances.

"I will also ride with you," Laran said.

"No!" Both Sheftu and Mikale spoke emphatically, the latter having turned to deliver the edict. Laran straightened with a stubborn frown.

"No," Sheftu repeated, more gently. "If it *is* Du-kar, he should not be given the gift of seeing you here, *aey*?"

Laran nodded reluctantly and watched him follow her father out of the Great Hall, her concern for his safety clouding her golden eyes.

"You *can* ride, young lord?" Mikale inquired of Sheftu.

Sheftu smiled. "*Aey*," he replied. "Though Provos is not yet healed…"

"Meet me at the stables. You are expected. Horses will be saddled and ready for you."

Sheftu nodded, then looked at Provos, a question in his eyes. "I'll manage, Cousin." Provos told him.

Sheftu thrust his shoulder under his kinsman's arm to support him and propelled him toward the stables. Mikale watched them go, and then turned away to conclude his own business. He wished to see his wife before he rode out.

CHAPTER SIXTY-FOUR

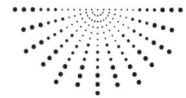

L ORD SHEFTU RODE like a man who'd spent his life astride a horse, Mikale noted. He sat erect but appeared at ease. His kinsman was clearly in pain yet rode competently just the same. The horses the two Soldatians had been given were headstrong young stallions, large, to accommodate their greater weight. Both were tan with jet-black manes to match one of their riders' stranger attributes. Strange, at least, to Mirren eyes. The five thousand men they rode to meet would not find it so.

He watched with interest as Lord Sheftu raised one hand to his brow to shield his eyes from the glare of the morning sun. Mikale appreciated for the first time the breadth of the young man's shoulders and chest and the muscled curve of his biceps, exposed in the sleeveless shirt he wore. He glanced down at Sheftu's legs, bare beneath the *talom*. Long and powerful, he noted. The young lord was big and his strength evident. If he were to lose his temper with his daughter…

Mikale wrenched his mind from Laran and back to where it needed to be. Here, nearing the gates to the city. Both Soldatians were squinting now to better see the banners displayed at the head of the approaching army.

Sheftu shook his head. "Can't make them out yet," he murmured.

Tishane rode to Mikale's right, Jodpul to the right of him. Sheftu and Provos, each on an outside edge, made up the fourth and fifth riders in a small but formidable line in front of the six hundred of Tishane's guards that had been rallied. On alert, out of sight, and awaiting the outcome of this meeting, were seven thousand warriors of the Mirren army.

Sheftu reined in abruptly, a look of shock written in his expression. "What is it?" Tishane demanded.

"The banners," Provos answered for him. "They bear the colours of the House of Morrow!"

"But… that cannot be!" Sheftu said, clearly astonished. He was still staring at the Soldatian army, assembled now behind the city gates. "The Morrow House does not advocate war, nor does it act as aggressor!"

"And yet it holds an army five thousand strong," observed Mikale wryly.

"*Aey*," Sheftu agreed. "Not an aggressor, but it has the capability of defending itself, or its interests, when called upon."

"And would you consider yourself an 'interest', young Morrow?" Mikale asked softly. "Would either of you?"

Provos stared at his cousin, but Sheftu was shaking his head.

"No," he answered, certain. *Was it a trick? Had Du-kar stolen Morrow colours?*

Tishane was raising his hand to halt the guardsmen behind them. He nodded respectfully to the Tania, then started forward, alone.

"Wait," Sheftu insisted. If it *was* Du-kar…

Mikale lifted a restraining hand. "Hold, young lord," he said. "See there?"

The Soldatians had stopped and a single rider had been dispatched through the city gates to meet Tishane.

* * *

"WHY HAVE YOU come?" Tishane asked the rider when they'd both traveled halfway. The Soldatian was a tall man and looked strong. He was, perhaps, thirty years of age. His shoulder-length hair shone blue-black in

378

the sunlight. His expression was serious, his raven eyes intense. He resembled the young Lord Sheftu.

"You have someone we want," the rider said.

Tishane raised a shaggy brow. "*Ashaii?* And who would that be?"

"One of our own: a Soldatian," the rider answered. "Lord Sheftu Morrow."

Tishane remained expressionless and did not answer the implied question.

"Who are you?" he asked instead.

"I am Lord Tyson Morrow, first son to the Morrow Lord and elder brother to Lord Sheftu," he answered growing impatient. "Where...?"

But Tishane cut him off. "And you've brought five thousand men. Do you plan to fight for him, Lord Morrow?"

"*Aey,*" Tyson said. "If we have to, we will. Does he still live?" "What do you want him for?"

Tyson looked surprised. "He is my brother," he said simply.

Tishane eyed the man curiously a moment, then turned his horse and rode away, back to the head of the Mirren guardsman.

He inclined his head to Mikale, then jerked his chin toward Sheftu. "He wants this one," Tishane told the Tania succinctly. "They are prepared to declare war to have him returned."

Mikale raised his brows but looked neither surprised nor disturbed by this news.

Sheftu was both.

"*What?*" he demanded. "And who is it that carries the colours of the Morrow House? Who is it that demands my return?" *Du-kar, that duplicitous son of a bitch!*

"He called himself Lord Tyson Morrow, Lord Sheftu," Tishane informed him. "Your brother."

Sheftu went absolutely still. He shook his head in disbelief. "This is something of a trick," he said, still certain that his family would not cross

Barraid and enter Mirren to reclaim him. His brother had always been indifferent, his father...

Sheftu raised his eyes to stare at the Soldatian rider. He rode a magnificent chestnut mare. *Tyson's mare.*

"By the Seven Gods," Sheftu murmured. The rider was staring at him as well and clearly recognized him. He nudged the chestnut mare forward, then thought better of it when a less than subtle shifting of Tishane's guardsmen caught his attention.

"Sheftu!" he called out.

Tyson. It was Tyson!

Sheftu suddenly urged his own horse to speed and crossed the distance between them at a gallop, insensible for the moment of the reaction he might cause.

"Wait!" Mikale shouted. He glanced at Tishane, who was swearing under his breath.

And if the Soldatians decided to reclaim the young lord forcibly?

Mikale took a deep breath. What in the name of all that was sacred was he to do then? *Nothing,* he told himself. *For now.* What unfolded next would lead him to his next decision.

* * *

"TYSON," SHEFTU SAID, reigning in beside his brother's mare. "What in the Seven Layers is going on?"

"We've come for you, Little Brother," he said.

Sheftu's eyes widened. *For me? You've marched across Barraid and into Mirren, risking war, for me?*

"We?" Sheftu murmured, dumbfounded.

"*Aey,*" Tyson said. "Our father and myself." He nodded toward the head of the army clearly visible on the other side of the open city gates. Sheftu saw the Morrow Lord moving back and forth in front of his men as his war

380

horse danced with only partially restrained enthusiasm to run. Perhaps his father felt the same urge. He was staring at his sons, his head swiveling to keep them in sight while the horse turned and pranced.

Sheftu looked back at the four men behind him at the head of the Mirren guardsmen. As he did so, Jodpul left the line to approach them. His expression, Sheftu saw, was wary.

Tyson watched the Mirren draw near. He was smaller than he and his brother were, as appeared common to his countrymen, but taller than most of the Mirren he'd seen so far. He looked... capable. He was well armed but kept all armament sheathed. He wore unusual clothing, as did Sheftu—a sleeveless shirt and a knee-length wrap of cloth fastened somehow at the waist. The Mirren's was snow white and immaculate. A crimson sash draped from one shoulder to the man's waist. His curly hair had been tied back.

Tyson eyed his brother. Sheftu's clothing was just as finely made but was soiled and rumpled. He was thinner than he had been but seemed just as robust. His hair had grown longer than was fashionable in Soldat, certainly longer than was apparently the custom for Mirren men, save perhaps the one drawing near, and it was windblown and tangled. And, strangely, streaked with white! He sported the shadow of one day's growth of beard.

Jodpul nodded to Sheftu and Sheftu returned the gesture.

"Tyson," Sheftu said by way of introduction, "this is Viscount Jodpul Degere, a particular friend to the Tania family and a trusted advisor to Mirren's High Lord. Apparently."

Jodpul shot a swift glance at Sheftu at the addition of the final word. A fleeting grin flashed across his face. He looked at Tyson and inclined his head in greeting.

"My brother, Lord Tyson Morrow," Sheftu said, continuing the introduction. Tyson returned the greeting, taking care not to incline his head a fraction more than the Mirren viscount had. Sheftu resisted the urge to roll his eyes.

"The Tania and his family invite you to dine with them this evening, Lord Morrow," Jodpul told Tyson. "Whoever you most wish to join you, will be welcomed. Your men," and here he eyed the seemingly endless columns of men with dislike, "may either retreat to a more favourable location or may make camp where they stand, so long as they remain outside the Gates of Mirren-Bar. The City Gates will be closed until you are sent for."

Tyson looked irritated by Jodpul's instruction but diplomatically refrained from voicing his displeasure.

He inclined his head once more, again not a fraction more than Jodpul had.

"We are grateful for your hospitality," Tyson said as though the words choked him. He stared at Sheftu, waiting for his younger brother to intervene. When he did not, Tyson turned his horse to rejoin the Morrow Lord, but reigned in again after only a few feet to face his brother once more.

"Do you not wish to await the... ah... Tania's invitation with your family, Sheftu?" Tyson asked quietly. He was staring at his brother again, clearly trying to fathom whether Sheftu was captive to the Mirren or whether he had the freedom to choose his own path.

Sheftu shook his head. "All is well, Tyson," he assured his brother quietly. "We will meet you in the Great Hall in Mirren-Bar." He looked down at himself briefly, smiling. "I wish to dress. It was a long night, brother." He aimed a vicious grin at Jodpul, who frowned.

"We?" Tyson asked.

"*Aey*," Sheftu answered with a smile. "Provos and myself."

"Provos," Tyson breathed. "I should have known he'd be here with you."

"Brother," Sheftu said when Tyson turned away again. "I *am* pleased to see you. Pleased to see *both* of you, though there is much I do not understand. We will speak this evening, *aey*?"

Tyson looked over at his younger brother, nodded, and rode away bemused. He was already going over in his mind what he would say to the Morrow Lord. How could he tell him the son he'd traveled through three countries to see was well, but wished to "dress" for dinner rather than cross the field to see him, though it appeared he was free to do so?

Had they been that unresponsive to his younger brother's needs over the years? *Aey,* he answered himself. They had. It was some time before he'd even been aware that Sheftu was missing, and he could swear his father had been just as unmindful of his youngest son.

And then news reached them that he was presumed drowned in the wreck of a ship. Tyson could scarcely believe Sheftu was dead from drowning. He'd been an excellent swimmer: *that* Tyson remembered, if little else, from their childhood.

The ship had been bound for Barraid. *Barraid!*

Provos had been spotted on the wrong side of the border. Barraid was a dangerous place for Soldatians, particularly two alone. *If* Sheftu had also survived the wreck, neither Tyson nor his father expected the two cousins to last a fortnight in the hostile country.

Their father had grieved. Lord Morrow's sorrow over his youngest son's death was notable in itself.

News of the wreck had, at last, been the impetus for interest in Sheftu's life. *Aey,* and they'd learned Tyson's younger brother had been... busy in the absence of the Morrow Lord.

Sheftu's apparent intention to cross the Barraidi border en route to Mirren- Bar gave them pause. Tyson hadn't even known of the country's existence, though he'd heard the myths. They all had.

And then came the response to his father's message. Sheftu was alive. And about to be executed.

And yet there was his younger brother, riding at the front of a line of Mirren guardsmen with the ruler of Mirren himself. *What in the Seven Layers was happening here?*

Tyson reined in and met his father's eyes.

"Tonight," Tyson explained. "We are to dine with Mirren's High Lord, the Tania. Sheftu obviously believes that he and Provos will be there for the meeting."

The Morrow Lord lifted a brow at the inclusion of his nephew's name with his son's. "But you have doubts?" he asked.

383

Tyson shrugged. "It would *seem* all is well and Sheftu said as much." He hesitated a moment. "*Aey.* I think they will be there, though I don't pretend to understand any of this."

His father nodded, but betrayed neither his doubt nor his disappointment in the outcome of the meeting between brothers.

In truth, he hadn't expected to find his youngest son alive. He'd *expected* to find him long dead; he'd *expected* to demand both retribution and the return of his body. He'd fully expected to have to fight for both. Learning now that Sheftu still lived brought Lord Morrow a sense of relief that nearly overwhelmed him.

One way or another, he'd force a return. He wanted his son back. He would have what he wanted.

He always did.

CHAPTER SIXTY-FIVE

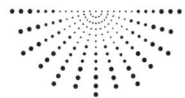

PROVOS STOOD BESIDE Sheftu as he had most of his life, this time on the steps of the white stone palace of Mirren-Bar. He raised his face to the sky and closed his eyes a moment to better savour the sensation of mist, cool and nearly insubstantial, upon his skin. Clouds had obscured the sun and drifted in ominous strands across the mountaintops. To the south, the sky was dark and bruised with rain. The rootless mist was undoubtedly a prelude to the coming deluge.

He was standing straight and whole, his wounds healed, his strength restored and his mind whirling. His immediate interest lay with a beautiful little Mirren noblewoman. Attired in a form-fitting saffron sheath, she had smiled at him both beguilingly and often.

A throng of her countrymen lined the stone steps and filled the courtyard below, waiting for a glimpse of yet two more Soldatian lords, this one with a substantial military entourage, to pass through the palace gates. Mirren voices, musical with the lilt of the language, rose and fell as conversation ebbed and flowed.

Beside Provos, Sheftu appeared at ease, his arms folded on his wide chest, his legs braced slightly apart. Though outwardly relaxed, Provos felt the tension emanating from his cousin in waves as he awaited the appearance of his father and his brother.

The timbre of Mirren voices changed, hushed, and an excited undertone began to hum through the crowd. Provos glanced at his cousin, saw the small muscle move in his jaw, and frowned.

That his cousin should feel tension at what should have been a joyous reunion cemented his usually ambivalent feelings for his uncle, the Morrow Lord, into anger.

Provos clapped Sheftu on the back, breaking his cousin's obviously troubling train of thought. Sheftu turned to glare at him but relaxed at his reassuring smile.

"*Aey,*" he said as though answering an unasked question.

* * *

THE MORROW LORD strode confidently into the courtyard, his eldest son beside him. Behind them an escort of thirty Morrow soldiers stoically attempted not to gape at the sights around them, but now and then a pair of black eyes drifted to the impressive architecture of the palace or over to the scores of Mirren nobles in their beautiful and unusual clothing.

Sheftu's father's step faltered at the sight of his second son, standing in the centre of the wide stone steps with Provos. The Morrow Lord's usually grim countenance softened slightly but he did not smile. He raised his arm to call a halt to the men behind him and began to climb the steps alone. Sheftu left Provos' side to meet his father halfway.

They grasped each other's forearms in greeting. Lord Morrow looked deeply into his son's eyes.

"What is happening here?" he asked, his voice lowered for Sheftu's ears only. "Are you in trouble?"

Sheftu smiled, bemused. The grasp on his forearm was fierce, the look on his father's face intense. He appeared to be deeply concerned for Sheftu's welfare.

"All is well, Father," Sheftu replied steadily. "It's good to see you both. But what brings you here?" he asked, mystified.

"We've come to bring you back!" the Morrow Lord said, frowning in return. "And what do you mean 'all is well'?" he demanded, before Sheftu could respond. He released his grasp on Sheftu's arms.

"All is *not* well!" Lord Morrow's voice had risen suddenly in agitation as his eyes swept the unfamiliar scene before him. "What in the Seven Layers were you *thinking?*"

Sheftu straightened, elevating his chin, as he waited for the onslaught he knew was coming.

"You were given leave to act as Morrow Lord in my absence, and *this* is how you conduct yourself?" Lord Morrow accused. One arm swept out to seemingly encompass all of Mirren-Bar. "By *shaming* the Morrow House? By *stealing* a slave woman from the House of Du-kar?" Lord Morrow snorted derisively. "Did the Morrow House not have enough slave women for your expansive tastes?"

Sheftu kept his face impassive, but that same muscle moved in his jaw and a slow red flush crept up his neck to singe the tips of his ears.

"And then you *abandon* the Morrow House to march into *Barraid?* Barraid! Alone!" He shoved a finger into Sheftu's chest. "Men were sent to retrieve you. They did not return." He glared at his youngest son. "I've never known you to be foolhardy!"

You've never known me at all, Sheftu thought furiously. He kept his mouth shut.

"And now *this!*" Lord Morrow said, gesturing widely, apparently at Mirren once again.

Sheftu felt the red heat of anger rise into his face.

"How did you know to look for me here, Father?" he finally asked, his voice as toneless as possible.

Lord Morrow grunted. "Reedin. Talked about surviving a shipwreck. Knew where you were headed and why."

Reedin had survived! *Thank the Seven Gods!*

"The High Lord of a country I did not know existed responded to my inquiry!" Lord Morrow continued.

Sheftu raised his brows, stunned into silence. *The Tania had responded? Just what had the High Lord told his father?*

"He said," Lord Morrow explained coldly, "that you were to be executed." He shook his head in disbelief. "For *rape*, Sheftu. And murder!" He poked a finger into Sheftu's chest. "Are the charges true?" he demanded.

Sheftu took a step back and the distance between father and son grew cold.

Lord Morrow's face reflected his displeasure. *Displeasure?* Was it only that? Was he merely *embarrassed* by the charges? *Aey.* After all, if it became known, it would not reflect well on the House of Morrow.

That his father might believe him capable of rape and murder distressed him more than he cared to admit, even to himself.

But perhaps the truth didn't matter to his father so long as the Morrow name was not besmirched. Sheftu moved another step back, putting more space yet between father and son.

"The matter was resolved, Father," Sheftu told him, his voice chilled.

Lord Morrow was silent a moment, noting that his son had neither confirmed nor denied the truth of the indictment against him. He continued to stare at Sheftu, then raised his eyes to glance about at the waiting Mirren.

"We need time," he grumbled.

Always did. Sheftu had an unreasoning desire to reclaim the stallion he'd been given earlier and ride away, *far* away from this meeting.

"What is to happen here?" Lord Morrow asked, his voice resigned.

"You will be escorted into the Great Hall where you will be received for dinner," Sheftu told him. "If you will excuse me." Sheftu bowed slightly to his father, turned and walked away into the crowd of Mirren nobles still gathered on the stairs watching the exchange.

His second son's manner, Lord Morrow noted, had become heavy and formal. His departure was unexpected. The older man frowned.

"Let's get on then," Lord Morrow muttered. He turned to wave Tyson forward.

Tyson eyed his brother's retreating back with dismay.

* * *

LARAN LEANED OVER an inner balustrade, a storey up, to watch the two Morrow nobles and their escorts enter the Great Hall. Provos accompanied them inside, but, strangely, Sheftu did not. Straight-backed and proud of bearing, the three Soldatians' great, dark stature alone made them an imposing sight.

Their soldiers were attired as Soldatian custom dictated: long, belted tunics worn over loose-fitting trousers tucked into knee-high leather boots, the clothing travel-weary but presentable. As a sign of respect, they hadn't had their weapons confiscated, though Laran knew it was a serious breach of etiquette for guests to carry weapons into Mirren's Great Hall.

Only the backs of the Morrow Lord and his first son were visible from Laran's line of sight now. *Their* clothing was immaculate, the tunics constructed of crisp, white linen. Long, black hair swung straight and shining against their broad shoulders as they moved. Swords rested in leather scabbards at their hips, and sheathed knives were strapped to their thighs. Their faces, quickly glimpsed, were both nearly as handsome as Sheftu's.

This was Sheftu's family! He'd been certain the army crossing into Mirren could not be for him.

And yet, they'd come for him.

From what little she had gleaned from Sheftu, his father and his only brother had given him little thought over the years. It was not remarkable then that he'd grown up believing that they did not care about him to any great extent.

And if that were true, perhaps there was another motivation for their presence.

Laran narrowed her golden eyes and prepared to descend the wide stone staircase with her family. They would enter the Great Hall together, *after* their Soldatian guests were seated.

* * *

TYSON LOOKED AROUND the Great Hall in astonishment. Mirren- Bar was nestled into a setting of immense beauty and this structure mirrored it all. Every second window set into the white stone walls had been opened to the magnificent view. The clean air scent of high mountain snow carried on the breeze and drifted inside. It mingled deliciously with the scent of the feast being prepared behind the scenes.

He elbowed his father gently to draw his attention to Mirren's High Lord, who was entering the hall. The man looked every inch a warrior. Well-muscled forearms were exposed beneath a sleeveless crimson shirt. Like many of the Mirren nobles present, his legs were bare beneath a wrap of pure white cloth fastened at the waist. What had he heard it called? A *talom*? A jeweled pin ornamented the *talom* at his waist and it sparkled in the yellow stripes of sunlight spilling through the long narrow windows. It appeared to be his only adornment.

On the High Lord's feet were leather sandals and his calves were wrapped with the leather thongs that held them. His light brown hair was short as was the style for Mirren men, but it curled silver around his face. Like his people, his eyes were slightly slanted and golden, the brows above a slash of light brown.

The moment the Tania set foot in the Great Hall, the entire assembly rose to their feet, bowing. Tyson stood as well, unsure of protocol. He looked down at his father.

The Morrow Lord had remained seated, apparently disinclined to show respect for their host until it was proven warranted. Tyson looked about for his brother but didn't see him. Provos, who had been seated with them, was standing and had yet to notice his seated uncle. He was facing the Tania and his family as they entered but his eyes scanned the room, presumably for a glimpse of his cousin.

Another glance at his father started an uneasy thrum in Tyson's chest. The Morrow Lord was overt in his display of disregard for the ruler of Mirren.

Tyson looked over at the Soldatian soldiers lining the entryway. Completely outnumbered by their Mirren counterparts, they, too, looked on edge. The men shifted and spoke quietly among one another trying to comprehend the unspoken message being exhibited by the Morrow Lord.

Tyson glanced now at the scarlet-clad Mirren guards stationed discreetly inside the Great Hall. Their features remained impassive, but their eyes had hardened at this insult to their leader.

Tyson swallowed and turned his attention back to the High Lord and his family.

A beautiful woman walked beside him, and two more, younger, presumably his daughters, walked directly behind them. Though small in stature, the three women looked every inch the royalty they were: proud of bearing, but graceful as well. Their floor-length sheaths were the colours of the jewels sparkling at the Tania's waist and were covered by some sort of filmy material so fine as to be transparent. Two of the women had waist length hair, but one wore her hair short like a man's, though there was nothing masculine about her.

Unlike the noble women of Soldat, they were not laden with jewelry, but wore instead a single jewel, albeit a large one, tucked into the light brown curls of their hair.

The Tania continued up the aisle to the head table but stopped when he reached Tyson and his father. He met Tyson's eyes and looked into them as though trying to take his measure. Then, without moving his head, he looked down his nose at the Morrow Lord, who suddenly found himself at a psychological disadvantage, seated as he was. The Tania continued to look down at Lord Morrow, his expression cold.

The room was absolutely silent.

Mirren's High Lord looked once again into Tyson's eyes, then bent, to speak into Lord Morrow's ear. Lord Morrow looked startled at Mikale's words. His bronzed complexion paled. He stood slowly, his expression defiant, but his bow no longer mirrored his apparent disrespect and was, in fact, lower than was warranted.

Tyson remained standing, showing no outward signs of fear, but his legs were threatening to buckle.

When the High Lord and his family passed them, the older of the three women, presumably the Lady Tania, hesitated a moment, looking up at Tyson and deeply into his eyes as her husband had done. Gold dust glittered in the depths of hers. There was meaning for him there, but he couldn't fathom what it was.

She did not glance up at his now erect father and Tyson instinctively understood that the slight against her husband had been returned to the Morrow Lord. When the younger women passed him, they too, looked into Tyson's eyes, curiously it seemed, though in the eyes of the short haired one was some strong emotion he didn't understand. Then they, too, passed by without acknowledging or even looking at his father.

The Morrow Lord had made a tactical error.

A muscle worked at the back of Tyson's jaw as he clenched his teeth in dismay. Where in the Seven Layers was Sheftu? *We're in trouble here, little brother!*

When the High Lord's family was seated at the long table, Mikale rose to speak. The Great Hall grew hushed once again. He looked over at Jodpul seated with him at the long table.

"Viscount," he said quietly. "Will you translate my words for our Soldatian guests?"

"*Ashaii*, High Lord." Jodpul bowed politely and moved to the table occupied by Provos, Tyson and his father.

"Please be comfortable," Mikale told his nobles, smiling. Around the room, chairs were pulled out and the gathering was seated once again.

"You will have heard of the Soldatian army on our borderlands," the Tania said, his voice carrying to the back of the Great Hall. "And you will have seen our Soldatian guests who have traveled far to be here."

Jodpul's voice was discreet as he interpreted and could barely be heard beyond the Morrow table.

Mikale looked directly at the Morrow Lord now and noted the insolent stare in return. Mikale removed his gaze and set it upon Tyson.

"You will know, as Lord Morrow may not, that his second son, Lord Sheftu, and his kinsmen, Lord Provos, brought the Saharani Laran Tania back to us at great peril to themselves. Both were wounded in so doing. Both have exhibited compassion and great courage.

We are honoured to receive the kinsmen of Lords Sheftu and Provos into our midst."

Tyson's eyes widened and his head snapped around to seek out his younger brother once again. *The Saharani? The High Lord's daughter?* He looked over at the Tania family, took in once again the short hair of one of the daughters. *Short hair! The mark of a Soldatian slave!* His brother had rescued the daughter of the Mirren ruler!

Tyson glanced at his father and saw that the Morrow Lord had come to the same conclusion. His father's face mirrored his surprise.

Provos looked bewildered at the words spoken in his honour. He hadn't expected recognition for his role in returning Laran to her home. He sat back in his chair, a pleasant sensation stirring in his belly. Satisfaction? *Aey.* He was satisfied. After all he and his cousin had endured, the Tania's words were agreeable to his ears.

A small hum of murmured voices sounded among the assemblage both at the import of their High Lord's words and at the appearance of Lord Sheftu within the Great Hall.

"These two young lords are a credit to Soldat," Mikale continued with a glance to the back of the hall where Sheftu stood. "If their courage, loyalty to one another, and their sense of justice are echoed in the Soldatian people, then Lord Sheftu and his kinsmen carry the goodwill of Mirren with them.

And," Mikale added, this time in Soldatian, "Soldat's inclusion in Mirren sensibilities will be considered. What was it Lord Sheftu said?" Mikale feigned a lapse of memory, though he was unlikely to forget Sheftu's words. "Ah, *ashaii*. 'Soldat makes a persuasive ally.' While Mirren does not engage in territorial war, we have many allies, some very powerful. This, too, will be considered."

Lord Morrow and Lord Tyson exchanged quick glances. Was the High Lord of Mirren *threatening* them, threatening *Soldat*? Or was he making an offer?

Perhaps both.

Mikale's gaze rested a moment on Sheftu, still standing at the back of the room, his brow furled in concentration as he tried to interpret what was being said. He'd certainly comprehended the last of it. His brother and his father looked dazed.

"We welcome the family of Lord Sheftu and Lord Provos," Mikale said in conclusion. He inclined his head toward the table the Soldatians occupied.

Lord Morrow rose to his feet.

Tyson stared at his father in dismay. *Now* he rises when all others were seated? He glanced to the back of the Great Hall and caught his first glimpse of his brother that evening. *Sheftu!* He was standing just inside the entrance portal, his feet braced as though weathering a storm. His arms were crossed on his wide chest, and his expression was a study in determination.

Mirren dissatisfaction hummed throughout the Great Hall at this second breach of etiquette by the Morrow Lord.

"Father," Tyson hissed. "What are you…?"

"Mirren *sensibilities* aside, High Lord, you know well why we have come," Lord Morrow's voice rang out. He hadn't yet seen his second son.

What the Morrow Lord lacks in diplomacy he makes up in raw courage, Mikale thought. *Apparently a family trait.* His second son, though, standing at the back of the Great Hall, had stiffened, Mikale noted. He was frowning at his father's words.

"*Ashaii*, Lord Morrow," Mikale answered reasonably in Soldatian. "So I do. Your motivation is clear to me, though my guards may not see it in the same light."

Lord Morrow resisted the urge to look over at the stationed guards though he sensed their heightened readiness for action.

"You have come far to see justice done," the Tania acknowledged. "And so it has been," he confirmed.

Lord Morrow finally caught sight of his second son and registered Sheftu's nearly imperceptible nod. *It has been resolved,* he'd said. Sheftu looked grim, though, and not well pleased with the situation. Lord Morrow looked more closely. *No. Not the situation. He is not well pleased with me!* Well, so be it. He'd done what he'd thought best in the circumstances.

He glanced swiftly at Sheftu once again, then, hesitating only a moment, the Morrow Lord executed a bow aimed at the High Lord. When he straightened, he looked to the Tania's family and bowed once again.

"Our presence here appears to have been predicated upon a misunderstanding. High Lord, Lady Tania, Saharanis: your pardon."

"I extend my own, Lord Morrow," Mikale said politely. He looked at Tyson. "And to you, Lord Tyson. That the justice you sought did not come sooner is an omission we have attempted to redress."

Tyson let out an audible sigh of relief and, feeling foolish about it, grinned in Sheftu's direction, though his brother did not notice. *Honoured by all of Mirren, was he?*

He watched as the viscount crossed the hall to speak quietly to his brother. The two of them left for places at either end of the Tania's head table, clearly a tribute to them both.

You have acquitted yourself well, little brother! Tyson thought in wonder.

Great platters of the prepared feast were brought into the Great Hall and dinner was commenced.

CHAPTER SIXTY-SIX

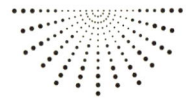

SANTAGO STRETCHED OUT on the filthy floor of the tiny cell he resided in now. He placed one hand beneath his curly hair to cushion his head from the stony surface on which he lay. He stared at the grimy ceiling, his golden eyes narrowed by the direction of his thoughts. Hatred churned in his stomach and threatened to choke him. *The Soldatian,* he thought. *He is to blame for this! He is to blame for all of it.*

Once again he resolved to punish the man, though this time he would accomplish the task himself.

With me in here, Santago reflected, *he probably imagines himself safe.* He grinned nastily to himself.

He is not. And neither are those he cares for.

He raised his head, reached out with his free hand to crush a large, black spider between his fingers, and then settled back to refine his plans.

CHAPTER SIXTY-SEVEN

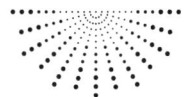

"**S**EREN!" PROVOS LAUGHED, pleased to see the Barraidi child. "What are you doing here by yourself, little beauty?" He looked around at the crowded hall. "Where are your mother and father?"

Seren didn't understand, but she climbed happily into Provos' lap just the same, leaving a small grey footprint on the white *talom* he wore. Provos supported her with one arm and rested a hand on her back to keep her steady, then he stood, scanning the Great Hall. *There!*

He grinned at Randide's panicked expression as he searched for his daughter here amid the Mirren. Little Alam was firmly in hand and trotted alongside her father good-naturedly.

"Randide!" Provos called.

Randide's head snapped up at the sound. He grinned in relief and evident pleasure at seeing Provos there, alive, whole, and with the recalcitrant Seren in his arms.

He approached and extended his hand. Provos shifted his burden to safely grip it in his own.

"It is good to see you, friend," Provos said in halting Barraidi. Randide's grin widened.

"And you, friend," he answered, his Soldatian heavily accented. "Will come you?" he asked, thinking hard of the correct words to use in the unfamiliar language. "Estalla like see you now, *aey?*"

Provos nodded with pleasure. He inclined his head to the Morrow kinsmen seated with him and took his leave.

* * *

"ESTALLA." PROVOS GREETED her warmly and her smile for him was affectionate. She shifted her own burden, the babe Notel, and standing on tiptoe, she drew his head down in order to kiss his cheek in welcome.

"You are well?" Provos asked her. She looked to Randide to interpret.

"*Aey,*" she answered, using the Soldatian term. "Well."

Provos winked at Alam. "Will you meet the Saharani Laran once again?" he asked Estalla, looking toward the head table.

The Tania family and their honoured dinner companions, Sheftu and Viscount Jodpul, he saw, were conversing among themselves, though an occasional dinner guest stopped by the head table to speak to one member of the family or another. He noticed his cousin leaning toward Laran's sister, evidently listening intently to her words. His eyes, though, wandered often to his father's table. Sheftu looked ill at ease and unhappy. Provos frowned.

Estalla was nodding shyly. Provos tore his gaze away from his cousin to concentrate on the Barraidi family who'd saved his life.

* * *

"LARAN," PROVOS BEGAN. There was a smile in his voice.

Laran turned from her surreptitious study of Sheftu and spied the Barraidi mother they'd met so long ago on the headland. In her arms was the babe that had been strapped to her chest in the carrier that day. A Barraidi man, presumably her husband, stared at her with unabashed curiosity. He held the hand of a little girl. Provos had the other in his arms.

Laran laughed spontaneously. These were the people that had cared for Provos when, it would seem, most of their countrymen would have left him to die. Or hastened his death. The little Barraidi family had doubtless risked a great deal in helping the wounded Soldatian.

Estalla bowed awkwardly and straightened quickly, seemingly in a hurry to see the Mirren Saharani once again.

"Do you remember me, Lady? I mean, Saharani?"

Laran grinned. "*Ashaii*! I do! And I am happy to see you now." Her eyes sought Sheftu again. He would take great pleasure in meeting the family that had saved his cousin's life.

Sheftu looked over Shell's head to lock eyes with Laran. She was smiling at him and he smiled back though he still looked troubled.

Was it the proximity of his family? Laran wondered. *Why wasn't he happier to see them?* She signalled with her chin to attract his attention to the family she spoke with and his eyes lit at the sight of them. She watched as he excused himself to her sister, who turned to look at Laran and the Barraidi family as well. Sheftu strode around the table.

A fine-looking man, Laran thought. She stifled a surge of jealousy. It seemed that he, and his cousin, had the eye of every woman present.

But Estalla took in a sharp breath as Sheftu approached and alarm, not appreciation, registered in her face. Though she knew now for a certainty that they were in no danger from the two Soldatians, old fears ran deep.

This Soldatian was bowing low. *To them!* When he straightened, he pinned Estalla with his raven eyes and smiled warmly. When Randide shifted uncomfortably, Sheftu grinned and bowed to him as well.

"I am in your debt," he told them sincerely. "For the life of this reprobate." He jerked his thumb at Provos and Provos laughed.

"Reprobate, is it?" Provos winked at Estalla, though Laran had stopped translating in surprise at the harsh word. "If that is so, perhaps you will excuse me. I am having immoral thoughts as we speak."

"She's married, Provos," Laran said softly to his retreating back.

Provos stopped dead and turned a wounded expression towards her.

"Now why did you have to go and spoil his evening, Little Elf?" Sheftu said, grinning evilly. "He was happy in his ignorance."

"Here in Mirren, ignorance can get a man killed," she told them seriously. "After all Estalla and Randide have done, that would seem a shame."

"*Aey*," Provos said woodenly. "A shame." He looked so disappointed that Sheftu laughed again and slapped him on the shoulder.

"You would do well to remember, Provos," Laran began, "that Mirren has a different set of social mores than does Soldat."

"And you address this statement to me, alone?" he said, trying and failing to look insulted.

"I did not think it necessary to mention it to your kinsman." She smiled up into Sheftu's eyes and he smiled back, settled and happy once more. At least for the moment.

Estalla and Randide exchanged glances. The bond between the Soldatian and the Mirren Saharani was heated and strong. Estalla wondered what the Saharani's family thought of *that*. She looked up at the Soldatian and for the first time, felt sympathy for the big man. That he was in love with the Saharani was clear. That his love was returned seemed certain.

"Mistress Estalla," a deep voice said from behind. She spun in surprise and then smiled in pleasure.

"Mik... High Lord," Estalla amended with a grin. She bowed and straightened with a wink at Mirren's ruler.

Mikale laughed, delighted with her.

"With your permission," he said to Randide. "I would like to introduce your wife to mine."

"As you wish, High Lord," Randide mumbled, alarmed. He shot Estalla a parting glare that seemed to say, "Don't say anything foolish". He gritted his teeth when she stuck her tongue out at him.

"Are your accommodations to your satisfaction?" Mikale was asking her as they turned away.

"Wonderful!" she exclaimed. "I could never have imagined such beauty! And the city! But I am curious, High Lord." Estalla pretended not to hear her husband's urgent whispered admonishment *not* to exhibit curiosity.

Mikale stopped and raised a brow. "Oh?" he prompted.

"I've wondered," she began with a covert glance. "The Soldatian, the elder Lord Morrow. He was rather disrespectful, I think. Everyone saw that he was. I notice your own people did not care for the display overmuch."

Randide turned away from their conversation with a wince. *Estalla,* he thought at his wife desperately, *stop!*

"And then suddenly," Estalla said, snapping her fingers, "he was on his feet and paying you homage." She eyed the Tania sideways. "Surely you didn't *threaten* him, High Lord?"

"Of course not, mistress," Mikale answered smoothly. "I merely admired the handsome features of his two sons. Surely you don't think Lord Morrow misunderstood my comment?"

"Hah!" Randide heard his wife exclaim as they walked away. He hunched his shoulders up around his neck as though to protect it.

"And if I *hadn't* given the High Lord permission to lead her away?" he muttered in his own language.

Laran shook off the shock of overhearing her father's remark. He could be ruthless, she knew, but she also knew him to be fair. He would never allow harm to come to an innocent for sins committed by another. And she knew, as Sheftu's father apparently did not, that her father had gambled on Lord Morrow having the same powerful urge to protect his progeny as *he* did.

It appeared that he did.

She glanced at Sheftu but he hadn't understood the Tania's comment, spoken as it was, in Barraidi.

"Asking for permission was merely a polite formality," Laran told Randide in his own language, though it was clear he realized it. From his expression, it was also clear that he hadn't meant to be overheard. "But do not fear," Laran continued. "Estalla will be safe with my father."

"It's not *her* safety I worry about," he told her, though that was only half true. "Trouble follows my wife around and her tongue invites most of it." He sighed worriedly then straightened and looked about him.

"Now here's a scenario I could never have imagined," Randide said dazedly. "My family and I, Barraidi all, standing here among the Mirren nobility talking to Mirren royalty," and here he bowed to Laran, "with two *Soldatians*, at least one of whom we call Friend." He scrutinized Sheftu. "Perhaps two." He shook his head and laughed. "If I were to tell anyone from home of this, they would call me a liar."

Home. Here was a Barraidi word Provos understood. "Will you be able to return home?" Provos asked Randide. "Safely?" He looked to Laran to translate.

Randide shrugged. "In truth, we have been offered a home and work, here, in Mirren-Bar. Seems the Mirren value their horses and the High Lord keeps a very fine stable. There is work for me here. Or so he says. Perhaps he is being kind. Either way, if we decide to stay, these little Mirren will soon recognize my value." His resolute expression dropped off to be replaced by chagrin.

"Forgive me, Saharani," he said worriedly. "I meant no insult."

But the Saharani looked distracted. She was watching Lord Sheftu as his eyes returned time and again to his father.

"Sheftu," Laran said when Randide bent down to speak to Alam. Her voice was very quiet. "How long will you avoid going to him?"

Sheftu turned to her in surprise.

"Will you meet them?" he asked her.

"*Ashaii*. With pleasure."

He put out his hand and she clasped it with her own. Heads turned and murmurs started as they crossed the Great Hall together.

"Father," he said. The Morrow Lord rose swiftly to his feet. Of a height with Sheftu, their eyes met and held a moment, before both men lowered their gaze to Laran.

"My Father, Lord Morrow," he said to Laran by way of introduction. "Father, this is the Saharani Laran Tania, first daughter to the High Lord of Mirren."

"I am honoured, Saharani," the Morrow Lord said politely.

"Your son saved my life, Lord Morrow," Laran told him. "Not once, but many times. He was wounded in so doing, even imprisoned. It is I who am honoured, my lord."

The Morrow Lord looked at his son curiously. He turned to call Tyson to his side. "May I introduce Lord Tyson Morrow, my first son and Sheftu's brother?"

Laran smiled. "Lord Tyson," she said.

Tyson was staring at Laran in open appreciation. She was a beautiful young woman, and elegant of manner. The cerulean sheath she wore hugged her lithe figure and the transparent covering made one imagine... He straightened suddenly, aware of his lapse in manners and colouring faintly at the direction of his thoughts.

"Saharani," he said bowing. He looked down at her small, pale hand clasped in his brother's.

"The Saharani and I..." Sheftu hesitated. "She is Promised to another. But she belongs with me," he told them.

Three sets of eyes widened at the statement, including Laran's. "What are you saying?" Lord Morrow demanded.

"That I have petitioned for marriage."

"Sheftu," Laran whispered, her gaze sliding to those Mirren who stood nearest. "Perhaps this is not the time for this conversation."

"*Aey*," Sheftu asserted. "It is. My family is here now. I have their full attention. It is an event unlikely to be repeated." His voice sounded bitter. He released Laran's hand.

The Morrow Lord stiffened. "What are you...?" he began.

"Lord Morrow?" A scarlet-coated guardsman waited respectfully a few paces away.

Three Morrow heads turned toward him.

"Lord *Sheftu* Morrow," the guard amended. He bowed. "The High Lord requests you attend him."

"You will excuse me," Sheftu said politely. His father and his brother stared at his retreating back.

When they glanced down at Laran, it was to read anger in her lovely golden eyes.

"You," she hissed, one finger poking into the Morrow Lord's chest. "Have hurt him. And," she accused Tyson, "so have you!"

Tyson's face turned red.

But Lord Morrow looked dumbfounded. "What are you talking about?" he demanded.

"*Why* did he not suspect the Soldatian army approaching Mirren was yours?" Laran poked Lord Morrow again. "Not for a moment did it occur to Sheftu that it might be coming for *him*!"

Lord Morrow looked down at Laran's finger in disbelief.

"He told me that his absence from Soldat was unlikely to impact you significantly," Laran berated him. "*Significantly*," she said, emphasizing the word.

"What have you done with your lives that your own *son* and your only *brother* could have come to such a cold conclusion?"

Tyson was no longer looking at her. He searched the Great Hall for his brother. Head and shoulders taller than the Mirren gathered there, he was not difficult to spot. He executed a hasty bow and left Laran with his father.

She was right! The little Mirren Saharani was right. He'd paid his younger brother no attention at all throughout their lives together. It was *he* being groomed to take over the affairs of the Morrow House, *he* that was to manage the estates and the fortunes of the family, *he* that had basked in the attentions of their father, the Morrow Lord.

The child Sheftu had been *had* faded into insignificance in their eyes. The man he had become was *anything* but insignificant.

And Tyson didn't know him.

When he reached his younger brother, the Tania was walking away. Tyson grabbed Sheftu by the arm and jerked him around. Sheftu glared at him and wrenched his arm free.

"Hear me, Little Brother!" Tyson said. He tried to ignore the scandalized stares of the nearby Mirren at this rough gesture. "I have been a fool," he rushed on. "I was too caught up in my own life, too full of my own importance to see you standing there.

"I have heard what you've done from many tongues now. You have courage; that much is clear. And integrity. You are twice the man I am, Little Brother. And I didn't see it! Well, I see it now! I see *you* now. And I hope you can forgive me."

Sheftu stared at Tyson in disbelief. Was his brother *apologizing*?

"Look," Tyson said. "The future seems a little…" He looked around the Great Hall. "…uncertain," he finished. "You are my brother. I don't want to lose you now, not *now* when I've finally come to my senses, *aey*?" He grabbed Sheftu's arm again and squeezed, trying to bully his way into his brother's consciousness.

"Leave off," Sheftu muttered, looking down at his brother's grip on his arm. "I see you, too," he said reluctantly when Tyson released him. "Always did."

"And… you can forgive me?"

"Only if you stop blathering about it, Big Brother." He grinned at Tyson suddenly and Tyson laughed in relief. He sought a lighter topic.

"Your clothes," he murmured. "Interesting choice." Sheftu smiled. "I like the freedom," he said.

"*Aey*," Tyson said dubiously looking down his brother's bared legs. "It's colder than the Seventh Layer here at night. These little Mirren must be tough."

"They are that," Sheftu agreed.

* * *

"LOOK AT YOUR sons," Laran said to Lord Morrow. She was smiling. He looked over her head, over *all* the gathered Mirren heads, to see his sons, tall, dark, straight and proud, standing together. Tyson was touching Sheftu's streaked hair, presumably commenting, and Sheftu grinned in response. When Tyson draped a strong arm around his shoulders, Sheftu stiffened, then relaxed into the embrace, wrapping his own arm around his brother briefly, and then pushing him away, laughing.

Laran saw Provos standing a short distance away, a look akin to approval on his face. It appeared that he, too, had been troubled on his cousin's behalf. She wondered about *his* family. If it was true that the two cousins had been together continuously since childhood, did that mean that Provos no longer had a family with the exception of his uncle and his cousins? If that was the case, it reflected well on Provos that he could take pleasure in his cousin's reconciliation.

Provos glanced at Laran across the room and smiled. He jerked his head slightly to the left of him and Laran's eyes followed.

Shell! She was sitting beside Jodpul, still seated at the head table, and talking earnestly. She looked happy. *Very* happy. And Jodpul looked… besotted!

Shell and Jodpul?

Ashaii. There was symmetry there! She noticed that her mother's gaze rested thoughtfully on the two as well.

Laran put her hand to the base of her throat in wonder. Why had she never seen it before? Perhaps Jodpul hadn't allowed himself to see Shell for the woman she had become. Or had he stifled his attraction because of the long-expected marriage to her sister?

And Shell? Jodpul's future had always belonged to Laran. Had she kept her affection for Jodpul hidden because of her? How it must have hurt her!

If they were in love, if they grew to be, here was an answer for Jodpul and the Degeres! Jodpul would retain his pride and, though he'd been willing to let it go, he would also retain the status he had always imagined. He'd know great happiness in Shell for Shell was as kind and as loving as she was beautiful.

Shell would, in turn, have as her husband as fine a man as ever lived.

And Degere aspirations would be satisfied, thereby relieving her father of the burden of guilt over promises made.

Her father! He *must* allow Sheftu to Promise to her. He'd been speaking with him. *What about?* Though his back had been toward her, she'd noted the serious nature of her father's words by the set of his shoulders. His hands had moved as he spoke as though for emphasis. Sheftu had leaned in, his face expressionless but his eyes intense.

How did he *do* that, Laran wondered? *Her* thoughts were always written in her face. What *had* they been talking about? Both men's eyes had moved to the Morrow Lord.

Now Sheftu was taking his leave, his eyes on his father. His steps seemed reluctant.

Laran hurried to the point she'd meant to make all along. "Lord Morrow," she said, reclaiming his attention, "I love Sheftu. Do you?"

Lord Morrow looked down at her in shock, both for her admission of love and for the question put to him. He opened his mouth to protest, but Laran forestalled him.

"He believes you do not," she added. "*If* you do, tell him!"

"Tell me what?" Sheftu asked as he drew near.

"You will return with us," the Morrow Lord said, ignoring Laran's plea. "We leave tomorrow." It was not phrased as a question.

Sheftu shook his head. "No, Father," he answered succinctly. "My future lies here, in Mirren-Bar."

"And do you really imagine the High Lord of this country will allow his own *daughter* to wed the second son of a foreign lord?" Lord Morrow demanded. Impatience was written in his features. He looked about for the Saharani Laran, but she had moved away and was conversing now with a young Barraidi woman. Though her eyes followed their every move, she was out of earshot.

"*Aey*. I do," Sheftu answered. *I have to believe!* "And you will help me," he said.

"What?" Lord Morrow raised a brow at his son's tone. "And how do you propose I do that?"

"By giving me your assurances that the Morrow House will come to the aid of Mirren if it is required and by lobbying for the inclusion of *all* of the other houses in this aid. I will take authority over all matters pertaining to Mirren in Soldat. And," he added, "to Soldat in Mirren." Sheftu was silent a moment letting that sink in.

"And what," Lord Morrow asked, "would be the benefit to Soldat of such an arrangement?"

"Even without its many allies, the Mirren army numbers seven thousand mounted soldiers. They are the best-trained, best-equipped military unit I have ever seen," Sheftu told him. "If Soldat is attacked, Mirren will dispatch its army. It is capable of protecting Soldat's eastern flank and will prevent its enemies from gaining a stronghold through Barraid."

Lord Morrow nodded thoughtfully. On the surface the arrangement sounded useful. He stared into his second son's eyes. "I will require thought on the matter, *aey?*"

Sheftu nodded, satisfied.

"And you believe Soldat's protection will allow you access to the ruler's daughter in marriage?"

"No," he answered truthfully. "I believe it to be of little leverage. Still, it benefits both countries and gives the proposition of marriage better optics."

Lord Morrow looked bemused.

"It renders the marriage more understandable to the average citizen, *aey?* That can be important," Sheftu explained. "Especially since the man Laran is currently Promised to has an extremely influential family. They have much to bring to the marriage beyond the mere joining of man and woman."

His father raised a brow at that. "And you and I?" he asked.

"You are a formidable force in Soldat, Father. It is your influence I ask for now."

"And *you and I?*" he asked, his voice elevating a little. "Did you not see your little Saharani poking, *poking,* her finger into my chest in chastisement?"

"No," Sheftu answered slowly. A grin flashed across his bronzed features in spite of himself.

Chastisement?

"She tells me that I've hurt you."

Sheftu stiffened and colour suffused his face. "Did she?" he asked carefully. His grin faded away.

"That was not my intent," Lord Morrow muttered. "It was never my intent."

When Sheftu remained silent, the Morrow Lord shifted uncomfortably.

"Perhaps I was not there for you," he allowed. "Perhaps I did not heed your needs."

"Perhaps," Sheftu said, still looking wary.

"It was not my intent," the Morrow Lord repeated. He sounded defensive. And a little lost.

"I know," Sheftu finally acquiesced. "And, strangely, that neglect no longer… rankles. I've reached manhood without your support, Father. I ask for it now."

Lord Morrow grunted noncommittally.

Sheftu straightened to his full height and elevated his chin. There was another matter he wished to discuss before his father returned to Soldat. *"And you and I?"* his father had asked.

"I am your son," Sheftu began slowly.

"And yet?" Lord Morrow grumbled, reading the disquiet in his son's eyes. "And yet you must *ask* if charges of rape and murder are true."

Lord Morrow was silent a moment. "And you are insulted."

"That you'd put my honour to question? *Aey*!" he shouted abruptly. "I take insult!"

Sheftu glanced back toward Laran, seeking a measure of solace. She'd been speaking to Jodpul and Shell and Shell had thrown her slender arms around her sister in a joyous outpouring of emotion Sheftu didn't understand, wasn't even capable of understanding at this moment. When he'd raised his voice to his father, the sound had carried across the Great Hall.

He'd inadvertently displayed the anger and the hurt he felt in his tone and Laran, Shell and Jodpul had turned toward him, as had most of the nobles assembled there.

By the Seven Gods he wanted out of there! He turned on his heel and left the Great Hall in what he recognized as a childish desire to outdistance the deep ache hollowing his chest.

Laran began to follow him, but Emeldra stopped her with a hand on her arm.

"Allow me," she told her daughter and Laran reluctantly assented.

On the other side of the hall, Lord Morrow swore under his breath. *Had* he actually believed the charges? The truth was, he hadn't known *what* his second son was capable of. He'd learned more of the young man who bore his name in the past few hours than he had in two decades.

Aey, he thought sourly. This had been a day for enlightenment. Societal conventions aside, he'd obviously been a fool to have marginalized Sheftu's place within the Morrow House.

CHAPTER SIXTY-EIGHT

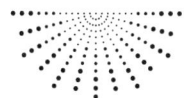

S ANTAGO SAT UP quickly at the sound of footsteps in the corridor between cells.

"Allane!" he whispered. "That you, man?"

The guard looked behind him fearfully as he stepped near the bars. *"Ashaii,"* he said unnecessarily. *Am I making a colossal mistake?*

Santago saw the doubt in the man's face and panicked. His plan rested entirely on his success in duping the gullible guard.

"Well done." Santago hid his concern and spoke confidently. "You will have the undying gratitude of the Saharani, Allane. You will be honoured by the Tania and his family, honoured by all of Mirren for what you are doing. You," Santago added slyly, "will be a wealthy man."

Allane closed his eyes briefly to savour the thought. What was it his mother used to say? *Do not let avarice overshadow common sense. Ashaii.* Was he doing that now?

"The Saharani," he told Santago slowly, "already *has* cause to be grateful to me."

"So you've said." Santago rose to face the guard. "Your place of honour at the Tania's table is assured," he told him seriously. He held out his hand.

Allane stared at it. He pushed his hand into the pouch at his waist and grasped the key to the cell. His doubt appeared to be fading but traces still lingered in his face.

Maybe I should try to talk to her first? he argued with himself. *She will want to thank me! She will want to...*

"Allane!" Santago snapped. "Time grows short!" Allane stepped back. He was shaking his head.

Santago snorted, apparently in disbelief, and silently cursed himself for his impatience. He took a deep breath.

"Will you leave the Saharani to be murdered in her marriage bed by the Soldatian?" Santago asked. "She is the eldest child of our High Lord." His voice was low, calm now, and intense. "When he finds out you could have stopped it..." Santago shook his head gravely.

"You have a choice, Allane," he continued. "Honour and untold wealth, or torture and death here in these cells you protect. Which will it be?"

"She will see me," the guard told Santago defensively. "She will remember me. I will remind her that I am the man who saved her, saved her from rape and probably murder in the palace heights. Tyllerd was insane, you know! I didn't have to come back, but I did! I saved her! I will talk to her. Explain what you've told me. Let her know you are here. *She* will see that you are released." He was nodding to himself. He was beginning to move away.

"No!" Santago nearly shouted. Allane jerked his head around in surprise. Both men looked up and down the long corridor. It wouldn't do to be overheard.

"No," Santago said again, evenly. "Why do you think Laran Tania was running to the heights that night? *Why?* Think, Allane! The Soldatian holds her captive. I've told you how devious he is. She was trying to run *away* from him. He won't allow her to see you, and he definitely wouldn't allow her to tell anyone else what you have learned regardless! The Mirren throne is within his sights!"

Santago paused to better emphasize his next words. He leaned into the bars of the cell, snaked his hand through, and grabbed Allane's wrist.

"Would *you* have a foreigner sitting upon it? No," he said resignedly. "No. This is the only way."

Allane wasn't a clever man; he had learned that of himself. And he knew he often made errors in judgment. Gambling with Tyllerd had been one, climbing up into the palace heights with him had definitely been another. This time, though, *this* time he'd do the *right* thing.

Santago had explained how the Saharani had been enslaved in Soldat, and he'd heard that before. What Allane hadn't known was that her so- called rescuer, the Soldatian lord, was a Soldatian spy. He *hadn't* known that the Soldatian was forcing the Saharani to marry him so he could acquire the power of the Mirren throne.

Allane's eyes widened. *He* knew the real story now. Only *he* could prevent it. Santago had told him so! Soldat was a powerful country and it intended to take over Mirren. Thousands of his countrymen would die, along with the Saharani and her family. He could stop it.

I will! I will be a hero! He smiled to himself, delighted with the notion.

He reached into the pouch he carried and handed Santago the key to the cell.

CHAPTER SIXTY-NINE

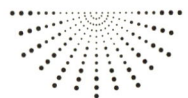

S HEFTU HADN'T GONE very far. He was standing at the edge of the first garden and appeared to be staring at features too indistinct to make out now that the light had fallen. Rain fell now, too, and the deep, foreboding echoes of thunder reverberated in the darkness, the slash of its companion lightning unseen in the mountain reaches.

"Lord Sheftu," Emeldra said softly from behind him.

He whirled, startled, though he'd only been standing there a few moments.

"You wish to be alone," she said. "I understand the need for solitude. I have a place, a special place I go to when the need arises. Come. I will show it to you."

When Sheftu began to shake his head, Emeldra took his arm.

"There, in my place, we will have no need to speak. The silence will bring you peace. Come, young lord," she said again. Her voice was quiet, soothing. It felt like velvet on his nerves. "You can return to the Great Hall with your fears for the future, and the wounds of your past, when we return."

Wounds of my past? Is that what they are? Sheftu asked himself. *Aey, perhaps.* He looked down at Laran's mother. *Fears for the future...* The Lady Tania was a gentle soul, like Laran and Shell. And like Laran, she seemed to have an uncanny knack at getting to the heart of a man.

He nodded, still silent, and allowed her to lead him away from the garden and into the white heart of the palace, climbing, always climbing.

"It's a garret," Emeldra finally explained. She opened the door to the room she painted in and preceded Sheftu inside, lighting the lamps as she did so.

Sheftu looked around the room in astonishment. Architecturally, like the rest of the palace, it was a wonder, but here the details were either hidden beneath or usurped by the sheer quantity of paintings, some very large, others small, all leaning haphazardly against the windows or the walls, on tabletops, or heaped upon one another. The quality of the work was astounding.

As he wandered through the garret he noted six, presumably the most recent work, on easels. They appeared to be a series, and were not large, but even here halfway across the room and in the muted light of the lanterns he could discern the beauty depicted in each.

As he drew close, he saw that the subject was Laran. He glanced over at Emeldra, who watched him serenely, her gold-flecked eyes full of knowledge and the power only women seemed to possess.

He looked back at the first canvas. In it Laran wore a pure white sheath, this time without the ubiquitous diaphanous covering. Her feet were bare. She was kneeling amongst a small sea of tiny blue flowers at the foot of an overhanging tree. Her head was bent and her short, light brown hair curled softly over her face, hiding her features. The arch of her delicate neck and the slope of her shoulders depicted great sorrow. Grief? *Over him?*

He looked at Emeldra again, but, though she still watched him, she offered no comment.

In the painting, Little Dog lay in the shadows, her big shaggy head upon her paws, and her large, soulful eyes alert. The impression of having been there, watching over Laran, for a very long time was a strong one.

As Sheftu moved past the paintings, one by one, he was immeasurably moved by the grief Laran had suffered on her return to Mirren-Bar. She loved him. He'd known that. But this...

He swallowed, his own eyes suddenly shining with moisture.

In the fourth painting, a shadow lay over the sea of flowers she'd knelt upon in the first and Laran had turned to look up at the source of that shadow from the bench upon which she sat, one hand on Little Dog who stood, tall and fearless, at her side. She was smiling faintly at last, though her eyes still reflected her sorrow. She held out a hand to the shadow and it was apparent the shadow man, for it had to be a man based on the height, had given her hope.

Jodpul! It must have been Jodpul. Sheftu felt a surge of jealousy and tried to tamp it down. Jodpul also loved her. He'd said as much. He'd offered to release her from her Promise. Wasn't it *because* he loved her that he'd done so?

Sheftu squeezed his eyes shut. He glanced once again at Lady Tania. *What are you trying to tell me?* Her hands were clasped behind her back in a posture of openness and her face was still serene.

In the second to last painting, Laran was alone once again. She was standing now, still in the garden, Little Dog still keeping vigil. One arm rested along the gentle curve of her hip, and her hand rested on her stomach. The other was placed over her heart. She looked... fragile.

In the final painting, she was facing forward bathed in a shaft of pure, white sunlight. Her slanted eyes were large and luminous, her features resigned. Both hands rested on her stomach now as though protecting...

Sheftu turned swiftly to stare at Emeldra. He looked again at the final painting, then over at Emeldra again. Her expression had not changed.

"Is...?" But he didn't finish the sentence. He couldn't.

By the Seven Gods! Was Laran with child?

She couldn't be. He would have known. She would have told him. *Wouldn't she?* Emeldra's silence suddenly sounded deafening.

The silence will bring you peace, she'd said.

"Peace?" he asked incredulously. He felt anything but peaceful!

He turned on his heel and ran, *ran,* through the garret door and down the long staircase. Rain hammered against the white stone structure and soaked him through within seconds. He pushed wet hair out of his eyes and stumbled through the dark garden, hoping he wouldn't lurch into a pond.

His ankles caught in the clenching fingers of a vine, and he fell headlong to the saturated ground. He half-heartedly brushed himself off as he continued his run back to the Great Hall.

Music drifted out into the courtyards but Sheftu heard none of it. As he reached the entrance portal, he was prepared to dodge the ubiquitous scarlet-clad guardsmen who stood on either side. He wanted nothing to delay him now.

But the doorway was empty. No guardsmen stood without. Sheftu stopped abruptly and frowned at the unguarded entrance. Why would the entrance portal to the Great Hall have been left unguarded when the High Lord and his family were within with the entire Mirren court? And surely the presence of foreign nobles, nobles who'd been accompanied by an army five thousand strong, warranted at *least* the usual security?

He stared at the guards' customary station to the right of the portal. Was that *blood* on the wall? *Aey, it was!* And, there, a thin rivulet of red ran diluted across the white stone in the rain.

Sheftu's eyes widened. He looked down at his legs where he'd brushed the soil and the mud away after his fall in the garden. *What* had he tripped over?

He glanced once at the black depths of the garden he'd just traversed, then began to run once more.

This time he thrust rudely through the throng of Mirren nobility in their jewel-coloured attire in the Great Hall. He scanned the hall anxiously. *Tishane!* he thought. *Where in the Seven Layers is Tishane!*

Laran stood near the head table, close to Jodpul, both hands upon his bare arms. He was bending down to hear her, a strange look upon his face. Hope? No. Not hope. Not quite.

Sheftu didn't care what it was. Or why. Not now. He crossed the room at a run, ignoring his father as he called out his name. He pushed a florid noble out of his way in his rush to reach them.

Behind him, clad in the scarlet jacket of a palace guardsman, Allane entered the hall. He looked for a signal from Santago who waited within.

There!

Allane was excited. He was about to become a very wealthy man. He was about to become a hero! He was the saviour of Mirren-Bar! He leapt to a tabletop.

"Seize him!" he shouted loudly, pointing at Sheftu. "Seize the Soldatian! He plans to kill the Tania!"

The hall, already abuzz from Sheftu's flight through the crowd, suddenly erupted. A woman screamed, nobles jumped from their seats sending their chairs crashing behind them, and those with family tried frantically to gather loved ones in order to quit the place at speed.

The Soldatian guards stepped forward, their hands on their weapons, desperately trying to make sense of what was happening. Their Mirren counterparts silently melted from sight as they regrouped, then burst into the commotion from all sides of the hall.

"Laran!" Sheftu was calling. He'd momentarily lost sight of her in the chaos.

"Sheftu!" Laran could see him pushing his way against the stream of the crowd toward her. "What's happening? Is my mother…?"

Mirren hands clutched at Sheftu's arms and someone threw a punch, effectively doubling him up in surprise.

"No!" Laran yelled. She was jumping now, trying to see over the heads of her countrymen, trying to keep him in sight.

"What are you doing?" she called to the guards. "There has been a mistake!"

Sheftu shook off the restraining arms and plowed through the crowd toward her.

Jodpul placed his arms around Laran to protect her from the mindless scramble of the crowd. Sheftu saw him searching the crowd anxiously. *For Shell?* When the viscount turned back, he stared at the dark smudge on Sheftu's legs and *talom* as he neared.

Was that blood *on the hem?* "What...?" Jodpul began.

Sheftu was grappled from behind by two palace guardsmen. He fought his way out of their grasp but two more dove at his legs and the original two took hold of his arms once again.

"Listen to me!" he cried as he struggled. "Guardsmen! The entrance portal is unprotected..."

Jodpul had a hand out, but was listening to another scarlet-clad guardsman, his face serious. When he turned to Sheftu, his eyes were wide with apprehension.

He turned on his heel, releasing Laran and leaving Sheftu restrained and impotent.

"Protect her," he called to the guardsmen as he disappeared into the surging throng.

"Laran," Sheftu rasped as he thrashed about trying to secure a release.

"My father," she whispered, horrified. "I must find my father!"

In the ensuing tumult, Sheftu lost sight of her when she turned, then saw her again not six feet away being pushed along by the crowd.

No. Not by the crowd. She was being escorted to safety by a Mirren guard. As the man steered her behind a column and out of the way, his scarlet clad back was completely visible.

The waist-length scarlet jackets worn by the palace guards were form fitting. *This* one was loose.

It wasn't his!

By the Seven Gods! Who was this? If he hurt her...

Fear clutched at Sheftu's guts. "Stop him!" he shouted to his captors, but his cries went unanswered and his struggle to free himself began taking its toll on his considerable strength.

From the back of the Great Hall Provos had seen Sheftu's flight across the stone gallery. Though he didn't understand the impetus, he understood that something was occurring, something dangerous. He raced across the stone floor toward his cousin, disarming his startled uncle as he passed him and shouting for help as he ran.

Tyson raised his sword and started after his cousin, swearing and nearly sick with dread.

The two cousins sprinted through the remaining nobles. Provos leapt up and off a table to avoid the clumsy maneuvering of a particularly rotund couple trying to negotiate the chaos. As the crowd thinned and he saw what lay ahead, Provos skidded to a halt so abruptly that his booted feet slipped out from under him and he crashed down onto his buttocks between the tables. Tyson rounded the last table simultaneously and stopped just as abruptly though he kept his feet beneath him.

Six guardsmen were holding Sheftu, two with their arms around his legs, two restraining his arms. Two more held weapons at the ready and one was endeavouring to keep the point of his sword centred on Sheftu's chest though Sheftu still thrashed about in an effort to free himself. As Provos climbed to his feet, Sheftu caught sight of him.

And so did the Mirren guardsmen. One shouted an alarm at the sight of the armed Soldatian nobles.

"Laran!" Sheftu gasped, pointing with his chin. "He has her, Provos!"

"Who?" Provos demanded, but he didn't wait for an answer. He followed the direction of Sheftu's frantic eyes and raced around the nearest column before more guardsmen could arrive.

Tyson hesitated a moment, wondering if he should fight the guardsmen for his brother's release, but decided to follow Provos' lead. Only steps behind him once again, he nearly crashed into his cousin's back as all forward motion halted suddenly.

420

Tyson's eyes widened. The Saharani Laran was caught in the grip of a knife-wielding Mirren guardsman.

The Mirren guardsman was going to kill her. Tyson could see it in his eyes. He glanced behind him in Sheftu's direction but his brother, and his captors, were hidden from view behind the column.

"Santago," Provos hissed.

He knows the man, Tyson thought.

Provos' voice had betrayed his loathing, but that emotion was clearly returned ten-fold by the guard holding the Saharani.

Guardsmen seemed to materialize from every direction, with the Tania himself and his captain among them.

All movement came to a standstill, though, as the scene played out before them.

Shell had appeared behind Santago, her eyes bright with both fright and determination. She kept moving, always at Santago's back, clearly hoping for the element of surprise. Now that Santago's attention was being diverted to the newcomers, she lunged at the sailor, wrenching at his knife hand with both of hers. She pulled, leveraged by what there was of her slight body weight.

Santago swung his knife arm to knock her off balance and Laran wriggled free of his now one-handed grasp. She whirled and struck him with her fist, her blow landing on the side of Santago's head. It numbed her elbow painfully but did no more than elevate his anger.

Provos, forced to inaction by the proximity of Santago's knife to the Saharani, now saw his opportunity. He pushed Laran out of the way and attempted to drive his uncle's sword through the sailor's shoulder but the guardsmen, infuriated that one of their own was being attacked, lunged at the Soldatian, disarming him.

As Jodpul manhandled an astonished guardsman, relieving him of his sword, a knowing, light-hearted grin was spreading across Santago's features. He was eyeing Provos' chest, exposed and vulnerable now that the guardsmen were effectively rendering him defenseless.

He tightened his grip on his knife and prepared to strike.

Jodpul leapt between them. He deflected the descending arc of Santago's knife with the hilt of the sword he'd wrested from the guardsman, then launched himself at the smaller man, riding him down to his collision with the hard stone floor. When he rolled off the sailor's prone body, preparing to reposition himself, Santago leapt to his feet like a cat, his eyes on Jodpul's neck. He tensed his muscles to strike, rebalancing his blade.

But Tyson was faster. He plunged his sword into Santago's abdomen, and just as quickly withdrew it.

Santago looked down at his bloodied shirtfront in disbelief, then up into Tyson's eyes accusingly. *Soldatian.* He mouthed the word, though no sound left his lips.

The Mirren sailor slowly collapsed to his back on the stone floor, his expression still reflecting amazement. His golden eyes remained open and became opaque.

The grip on Provos' arms slackened and fell away. He wondered abstractly if Tishane had ordered his release or whether the guards had finally realized their mistake. They must have released Sheftu as well.

Through the confusion Provos could hear his cousin's deep, anguished shout as he was finally able to round the column.

Stopping suddenly, Sheftu stared at Santago's body, then looked up at his brother who stood, dazed, his bloodied sword still in his hand and dripping on the white stone floor.

Tyson had killed the bastard.

There were people all around them now. Sheftu wrapped his arms around Laran and her arms encircled his waist. The two of them stood apart amidst the turmoil, eyes closed, locked in relieved embrace, and swaying slightly.

Provos watched Shell tentatively place her hands on Jodpul's arms. The viscount looked sick to his stomach. He was speaking to her in a low voice and shaking his head. *Probably berating her for her foolhardy attempt to save her sister.*

Foolhardy or not, she likely had.

Provos sighed deeply. His uncle had come up behind him. The Morrow Lord would not have been pleased at being so summarily disarmed, but he stood at his nephew's back now and placed a big hand on his shoulder. Surprised at the gesture, Provos turned his head to look at him.

As he did so, a scarlet-clad guard buried his sword halfway to the hilt in his uncle's chest.

* * *

ALLANE HEARD THE inarticulate yell of the Soldatian nearest the elder Soldatian lord, saw him turn, catching the wounded man as he fell to the stone floor.

Though he didn't understand what had happened to Santago, he shook off the shock of his own unaccustomed act of violence and allowed himself a brief moment of euphoria.

I am a hero! He would dine in a place of honour at the High Lord's table.

But guardsmen were surrounding him. They disarmed him, and roughly grasped his arms.

"Wait! What are you doing?" Allane protested, struggling. *They didn't understand.* "I saved you!" he tried to explain. "I am a hero!"

He was hastened from the Great Hall.

* * *

PROVOS CRADLED HIS uncle's head, staring in dismay at the rapidly spreading stain, which crawled across the front of the Morrow Lord's pristine tunic. From somewhere outside of himself, he'd heard Tyson's horrified shout. And then Sheftu was kneeling by his side.

* * *

LORD MORROW DREW breath in an agonized bubbling wheeze. People were rushing toward him. He thought he recognized his sons. Someone was wrapping his arms around him, but he wasn't sure who it was. He couldn't feel them. Couldn't feel anything but the cold of the stone beneath him: cold all around him. He must have fallen to the floor. He must have....

Conscious thought spun off into the void.

CHAPTER SEVENTY

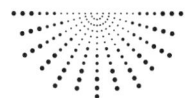

T HE SOLDATIAN WAS barely visible through the mists of pre-dawn, but Jodpul could make out his large form at the edge of the garden.

He approached him cautiously.

Sheftu sat on a boulder, his elbows resting on his knees and his head in his hands. His fingers were threaded through his straight, black hair and those digits, grimy with dried blood, had discoloured one of the strange white streaks in his hair with a rust-coloured stain. Distress was written in the slope of the broad back as clearly as though his expression had been visible.

Ashaii. And no wonder, Jodpul thought. His father lay within the chamber opposite, his life's blood spilled over the white stone floor of the Great Hall by a would-be assassin.

The angle of the assassin's sword had torn through Lord Morrow's lung and pierced his heart. Even the Lady Tania's formidable skill at healing had been unable to revive the man, though he was still alive and no longer unconscious. He appeared, instead, to be deep within healing sleep. Jodpul hoped, for all their sakes, that he would eventually awaken.

"Soldatian," Jodpul said quietly from a few feet away.

"Go away, Viscount," Sheftu mumbled without lifting his head.

Jodpul deposited himself on the damp ground, sat, his back against the rock Sheftu sat on. He was silent.

"Jodpul," Sheftu finally acknowledged.

"*Ashaii.*"

"Laran…"

"She still sits vigil with her mother and your kinsman at your father's bedside."

Sheftu hesitated. *Ask,* he demanded of himself. *I need to know! Ask!* He took a deep breath. "Was she raped, Jodpul? There, on the Barraidi headland? Did they…?" He closed his eyes to block out the image that came unbidden to his mind.

Jodpul took a deep breath. He'd wondered. Of *course* he'd wondered. But she'd been absolutely certain the child she carried was Sheftu's. Surely if she'd been raped, she would have questioned the child's patrimony? "I do not think so," he finally said.

"She is with child," Sheftu murmured. He dropped his hands and raised his head, though he didn't look over at Jodpul. Instead, he stared unseeingly into the grey darkness of the garden.

Beside him, he could hear the rustle of Jodpul's clothing as he reacted.

"*Ashaii,*" he agreed softly. "So she finally told you."

"No," Sheftu said. "She did not. She has said nothing to me about it. And yet *you* knew." He lowered his head and stared at the palms of his hands as though trying to divine an answer to that which troubled him most.

"The only conclusion I can come to is that the child is not mine."

Jodpul twisted to stare up into Sheftu's face. He rose in one fluid motion and stood silently, anger twisting in his gut.

"What are you implying, Soldatian?" he said, his voice chilling.

"She thought me dead," Sheftu began. Then he stood as well, only inches away and towering over Jodpul. "But *you* knew the truth!" He bunched his fists. "Did you take advantage of her grief, Viscount? Did you *bed* her?"

Jodpul swung his fist and connected solidly with Sheftu's jaw. The bigger man went down, sprawled across the damp grass. Jodpul stood over him, seething.

"You question my honour and not for the first time, Lord Sheftu. You do so again, and I will show you what a smaller man can do to a larger."

Sheftu picked himself up off the ground and rubbed his jaw. He wanted to pound his own fists into Jodpul's face. He wanted to hurt him. He wanted to…

He wanted to understand. "Then why…?" Sheftu began.

"The child is yours," Jodpul told him icily. He was still standing in an aggressive posture, still waiting to see if he had need to defend himself. "And you are a fool to have thought otherwise!"

"Then *why*?" Sheftu asked again. He felt lost. The urge to do violence was gone as quickly as it had surfaced. "*Why* has she not told me?"

Jodpul lowered his fists, relaxed his stance.

"I don't know," he admitted, puzzled. "Perhaps," he said slowly, "she is ashamed."

"*What?*"

"In Mirren, both men and women come to the marriage bed as virgins. It is considered a sign of respect to their eventual spouse. To bed another outside of marriage is both disrespectful and a grave insult."

Sheftu shook his head. "But *I* am the 'other'! I cannot believe…"

Jodpul interrupted, thoughtfully. "Could it be that she is afraid to tell you? Have you given her reason to believe you do not *want* this child?"

"No! I would never…" But his memory stirred. She'd asked how he felt about a child. He'd laughed! '*Let's hope not,*' he'd said. Sheftu turned on his heel to walk a few feet into the misty garden, then returned abruptly to stare at Jodpul.

"*Aey*," he said horrified. "Maybe."

"And is it so, Lord Sheftu?"

"Is what so?" he asked, distracted. He needed to talk to Laran. Now. He would seek her out at his father's bedside. He felt a spear of guilt that fear for his father's life had been shoved from his consciousness by the mere thought of the babe.

"Do you *not* want the child?"

"No! Yes." Sheftu stopped moving altogether. A grin was beginning to assert itself on his handsome face. "I want the child, Jodpul." *By the Seven Gods! I will be a father!* He laughed and grabbed Jodpul by both arms. Suddenly euphoric, he planted a kiss on the viscount's forehead.

Jodpul tried to dodge it uttering a single syllable that managed to convey his disgust, but Sheftu had already released him and had turned away. He strode out of the garden toward his father's chamber but turned back before he reached the door.

Jodpul still stood in the garden, wiping his forehead and grinning to himself, though he smoothed the grin from his face when he caught Sheftu's eyes on him.

"You knew," Sheftu said quietly.

"*Ashaii.* We've already been over this, Soldatian."

"You *knew* Laran carried my child and yet you would have married her. What about Mirren traditions, Jodpul? What about the child?"

The viscount shrugged. "Would I have preferred that Laran come to the marriage a virgin? *Ashaii.* I admit as much. I would also have preferred she had never been abducted. But that was not to be." He took a deep breath.

"I care for her," he told Sheftu as he drew near once again. "I wanted to help her. She was deeply troubled. I knew she had been ill-treated. I suspected then that she might have been raped. It would have been both selfish and cruel to take insult over an act of violence. I am a better man than that.

"No," Jodpul continued, shaking his head. "My difficulty, Lord Sheftu, was accepting that she had allowed *you* to bed her."

Sheftu frowned.

"I have tried to do the right thing, Soldatian," Jodpul said. "But I am only a man, after all."

A good one, Sheftu thought.

"And the babe, Jodpul?" he asked.

"The child is an innocent," the viscount said. "There was room within my heart."

One of the finest men I've met, Sheftu thought.

But Jodpul was suddenly grinning evilly. "Not the child's fault his father is a great, hulking, black-eyed Soldatian."

Sheftu snorted but his grin reasserted itself. *A baby!* The grin grew wider yet.

Jodpul took a step back. "Kiss me again, Soldatian, and I'll knock your teeth out."

CHAPTER SEVENTY-ONE

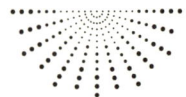

"SHEFTU, I HAVE something to tell you, something wonderful!"

"Aey?" The child! His heart seemed to lift.

He strode across the garden toward her. She took both of his hands in hers.

"Come," she said. "Come inside."

She led him into the anteroom at the entrance to the room she had referred to as the Healing Room.

"*Aey?*" Sheftu asked again. He glanced involuntarily at her flat stomach.

Tell me, Laran! Tell me about the babe you carry! "What is it?"

"Your father has awakened. He's asked for you. He's going to be all right!"

She was smiling into his eyes, certain of his response, and once again Sheftu felt the spear of guilt. And a sudden release of tension he hadn't realized he carried. *He will live. My father will live!*

He looked at the door to his father's chamber.

The Morrow Lord had asked for him. *And what new torment will be thrown at me now?* Sheftu shook his head, ashamed at the direction of his thoughts.

Laran was tugging at his hand and he followed her inside.

His father lay as he'd last seen him, stretched out on a bed within airy, sunny chambers. The room, like the rest of the palace, had been constructed of the white stone ubiquitous to Mirren-Bar, but unlike others he'd seen, this one was round. Light streamed in through tinted windows in the curved ceiling and a small red bird sang cheerily in a cage in one of the deep window wells.

Aey. A Healing Room, and appropriately named.

Lord Morrow's eyes were open and aimed at Sheftu. His expression was intense. His colour was good. He looked... well.

Sheftu glanced at the Lady Tania and she nodded her reassurance. He felt another wash of relief.

Provos was standing back in the room, his arms folded on his chest. He'd been at his uncle's bedside all night. He nodded to Sheftu tiredly.

Tyson, on the other hand, had only been ushered into the room in the past hour, his duty to the Morrow contingent having taken precedence over his desire to remain with his father. A number of their men had witnessed the attack on their lord, and it hadn't taken long for word to spread all the way to the city gates, where the bulk of the army waited. Though Tyson's heart was heavy with the sure knowledge that his father had suffered a fatal wound, he had calmed and reassured their men before hastening to the Morrow Lord's deathbed.

Tyson was seated now, his eyes wide, his bronzed complexion pale with shock.

Aey, Sheftu thought. *He understands the miracle that has taken place. He has seen the healing first-hand.*

"Father," Sheftu said as he approached his bedside.

"Son," Lord Morrow said. "Something has happened."

Sheftu nodded. *"Aey,* Father. You were wounded. And now you are healed."

The Morrow Lord stared into his son's eyes. His voice dropped to a whisper. "I don't understand," he said.

"You have been given a great gift, Father." Sheftu looked up at Tyson. "We all have." He extended his arm to draw his brother closer and Tyson rose shakily to join him. "With this gift comes great responsibility," Sheftu told them. "No one outside of Mirren-Bar must know."

Lord Morrow frowned his confusion.

"As strong as Mirren is, as mighty as its defenses may be, as powerful as its allies are, it *will* fall if knowledge of this reaches the outside world through Soldat."

Tyson nodded soberly.

"*Aey*, brother. You have my word. I will never speak of it." "Father?" Sheftu asked.

Lord Morrow looked up at the woman who had returned him to life. Her beautiful gold dust eyes were shadowed with fatigue and her usual upright posture was slumped in exhaustion. Laran held her arm as though to help her remain upright. *The healing had exacted a toll*, Lord Morrow realized.

He noted Lady Tania's attention to his youngest son's words. Her face reflected surprise. And... approval. *Aey, that's what it was. Approval. Sheftu hadn't been prompted, then.*

Lord Morrow elevated himself to a seated position experimentally. He stared down at his chest in renewed amazement, and then fixed his raven gaze on Emeldra.

"And what will the High Lord think of your work here this day, Lady Tania?" Lord Morrow asked. "Will he order it undone? Will we be allowed to leave Mirren-Bar alive?"

Emeldra returned the Morrow Lord's gaze steadily.

"The life of our beloved daughter, Laran, was gifted to us by your son and your kinsman. In return, we have given your family the gift of your life, Lord Morrow."

Lord Morrow said nothing as he pondered her words. *My life as a gift to my sons and my nephew? Aey, and that was something to ponder.*

"You may leave Mirren-Bar when you wish. Until then, as kinsmen of Lords Sheftu and Provos, you and your first son are our honoured guests."

Emeldra made a visible effort to shake off the appearance of fatigue. She moved away from the support her daughter offered and straightened her spine. Her voice firmed.

"But gift or no, grateful or not, we will have your word that you will speak of this to no one outside of this room just the same."

Lord Morrow took a deep breath and looked down at his now undamaged chest once more. "*Aey*," he said. He looked up into Emeldra's eyes. "You have my word."

Lady Tania nodded. "I go to my bed, my lords. We will speak of this no more except to say that Lord Morrow's wound was not as dire as first thought. *Ashaii?*"

"*Ashaii*, Lady Tania," Sheftu agreed for all of them. He placed one hand over his heart and reached down with the other, placing it on Lady Tania's chest.

She looked startled and stared at him in shock. He jerked his hand away just as Laran had when she'd made the same gesture to him all those months ago.

Forgive me, she'd said then. *I only meant to show my gratitude. It is a common custom where I am from.*

Had he done it wrong? Sheftu glanced quickly at Laran for succour, but her eyes were on Provos, who was bending to speak quietly to the Morrow Lord.

"Forgive me my clumsy attempt to show gratitude, Lady Tania. I understood the gesture to be a common one in your country. I thought..." *Stop talking,* he told himself desperately. The Lady Tania was still staring at him. She hadn't moved. *Idiot! You've offended her.*

And then she smiled warmly. She placed her palm against Sheftu's stubbled cheek for a moment. If she noticed the fresh bruise upon his jaw, she gave no indication.

Sheftu took a deep breath and tried again. "My kinsmen and I thank you for the life of my father."

Emeldra inclined her head once, then took her leave.

CHAPTER SEVENTY-TWO

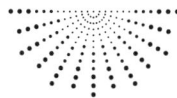

W ITH THE DRAMA of the attack on the Soldatian Lord Morrow a day behind them, life in the palace of Mirren-Bar was returning to normal. Tishane tried to block out yet another discussion of the attempted assassination as he awaited the High Lord. The Tania was attempting to take his leave of the noble who'd claimed his attention as he left the Great Hall after dinner.

"How long must I suffer your silence on the matter?" Tishane blurted as the Tania strode toward him.

Mikale looked over at him in surprise. There was no need to clarify his question. His captain had paled and looked away now, obviously ill at ease for having brought it up. That the possible repercussions of Tishane's actions regarding the, then, Soldatian prisoner still weighed heavily upon him had not occurred to the Tania. It should have. It had definitely weighed upon his own mind.

He put his hand upon his captain's arm and spoke gently.

"No longer," Mikale told him. "You will make reparations now. Tonight." Tishane only nodded and managed to look even more miserable.

"You questioned my judgment, Captain," Mikale told him. "You acted against my orders. That you were right has no bearing on what must follow. You understand this, *ashaii?*"

"*Ashaii*," Tishane said quietly. He swallowed audibly.

"Understand this, too," Mikale said. "I take neither pleasure nor pride in what I am about to order." He looked at Tishane a moment, and then sighed deeply.

"This night's work will be difficult," Mikale continued. "The ramifications afterward will be no easier." He hesitated again. He drew one hand through his curly, silvered hair. *Get on with it,* Mikale instructed himself.

"When you are asked to account for your actions tonight, and you will be, I will take responsibility. I will personally make it known that what you do tonight, you were ordered to do, and that those orders were issued in answer to your previous imprudence."

Tishane opened his mouth, could not find his voice, and nodded his understanding instead.

"This task may be dangerous, Captain," Mikale finally added. "I ask it of you just the same."

"It will be as you wish," Tishane said, relieved to see an end to the waiting at last. It was time to have it done. It was time to get on with his life.

Or his death.

CHAPTER SEVENTY-THREE

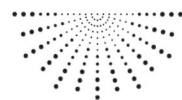

"**S**OLDATIAN," TISHANE SAID. His voice was quiet, light. He was grinning good-naturedly. "A word."

Sheftu turned from his conversation with his brother. The Great Hall was nearly empty. He smiled spontaneously at the sight of the captain.

"You've met my brother," Sheftu began. "Allow me to introduce my cousin, Provos."

"Lord Provos and I have met," Tishane said bowing to all three kinsmen. "Lord Tyson. I am honoured." He looked directly into Sheftu's eyes, still grinning.

Sheftu raised his brows and cocked his head. "What is it?"

"Will you attend me?"

"*Aey.*" Sheftu smiled his apology to his brother and to Provos, then followed Tishane out into the garden.

"The Saharani," Tishane began, his smile fading. "She has made it clear, as have you, that the two of you wish to wed, *ashaii?*"

"*Ashaii,*" Sheftu mimicked, though his sense of levity suddenly plummeted. He waited for Tishane to make his point.

"Permission to do so is not entirely within your control, would you concur?"

"I do." Sheftu was beginning to frown.

"Then it makes sense," Tishane continued, "to take every avenue that might weight the cubes in your favour, *ashaii?*"

"What are you getting at, Captain?"

Tishane grinned widely once again.

"Wolves," he said. "Black wolves." He laughed at the bemused look on Sheftu's face.

"They are elusive creatures, seldom seen in the mountains of Mirren. It is said," and here Tishane raised a brow, "that to see one in the presence of the one you love cements the bond between you and bestows a rare blessing on the marriage." He paused a moment. "The Blessing of the Black Wolves is given great credence, young lord, by the Mirren people."

"And you tell me this because…?"

"Because," Tishane said, a conspiratorial glint in his golden eyes, "there has been a sighting, a pack of nine or ten individuals hunting in the hanging valley to the east, a journey of less than an hour. The rain has left us, the sky is clearing, and a full moon rises. It is a good night for a blessing. What do you say?"

Sheftu shook his head at the timing and looked behind him at the portal to the Great Hall. His brother and his father would not remain in Mirren-Bar for long.

"*Aey,*" he heard himself saying. "If we are back before morning. Provos has an affinity for wolves—I will bring him along."

But Tishane was shaking his head. "This is a journey for you and the Saharani to make alone. I will accompany you with a few of my men until we are in within range of the pack. And then we will leave you. You will find us waiting on the trail when you are done. Agreed?"

"All right," Sheftu answered slowly. He smiled. Even if they didn't spot wolves, the ride into the mountains in the moonlight would bring him peace and an opportunity to think. It would be beautiful. With Laran? Even better. He smiled wider. This evening's endeavour had all the markings of an adventure, albeit a milder one than the last few he'd undertaken. Thank the Seven Gods! He looked behind him wondering where Laran was.

"The Saharani felt certain you would be agreeable," Tishane said, guessing his train of thought. "She is changing into riding clothes. She will join us at the stables."

"As will I," Sheftu said. "I must take leave of my family. I won't be long."

Tishane inclined his head, turned on his heel and walked away, presumably in the direction of the stables.

* * *

LARAN LOOKED OVER at Sheftu riding tall and proud beside her. She'd never seen him on horseback, hadn't been certain he could ride. He could! The huge stallion he straddled was brimming with strength and power and Sheftu looked as one with the animal.

He was at ease, laughing at something Tishane said, one hand relaxed on the reins, his knees exerting pressure on the stallion's sides in silent communion with the animal. Every now and again, Sheftu's free hand slid down to the arching neck to stroke the horse, and his voice when he spoke to the animal was gentle.

Watching the beast, Laran knew this particular horse had not been chosen for its meekness. She wondered if Sheftu had been given the stallion not merely because it was large enough for him, but also as a kind of test.

The thought angered her, and she frowned.

"What troubles you, Little Elf?" Sheftu said, his black eyes glistening like obsidian in the moonlight. Even in the silvered light she could see the smile crinkling the corners of those beautiful orbs. He looked happy and Laran felt a surge of pleasure that it was so.

"I hope we see the black wolves," she said, skirting the thought that had prompted his question.

439

"And if we don't?" he grinned. "Then we will have had a ride in the moonlight together." He looked at her straight-backed posture and the small, sturdy horse she rode. "You ride like you were born to it, Laran."

"Tishane taught me when I was a child," she told him. She glanced over at the captain fondly, but he jerked his gaze away when their eyes met. He stared ahead intently, a strange expression on his face.

"Is something the matter, Captain?" Laran asked him quietly.

"Nothing," Tishane muttered. He dug into the deep pocket of the long coat he wore and produced a silver canister. He uncapped it, tipped his head back, and took half a dozen long, slow swigs of the liquid within. Sheftu watched the muscles of Tishane's throat contract with each swallow. When he lowered the canister, he grinned at Sheftu sheepishly.

"*Sloan*," the captain told him.

He passed the canister over, but Sheftu shook his head, declining. If several gulps of the noxious substance had intoxicated Jodpul and reduced a man Sheftu's size to near drunkenness, what would six do, gulped down all at once, by a man much smaller? He looked at Tishane in amazement. The captain appeared unaffected.

The prospect of another evening spent in genial company with a bottle of *sloan* had its attractions. But not on this one.

Tonight he had Laran with him. Tonight they sought a blessing.

The trail had narrowed, and Laran rode slightly ahead now. Her buttocks, neatly outlined in the split skirt she wore, rose and fell with a nearly inaudible *plop* against the leather of her saddle as she moved, and Sheftu watched, fascinated. He shook his head to dispel the fantasy about to take over his thoughts. He grinned, though, in spite of his self-admonishment to keep his mind on the trail where it belonged.

He breathed deep of the cool mountain air. It was lightly scented with pine and rain-washed rock. Beyond the creak of leather and the soft clack of horses' hooves against the pebbled path, the night was utterly silent.

He glanced behind him. Twenty paces back, four of Tishane's men brought up the rear. They rode two-by-two and did not speak to one another, though Sheftu saw one dart a worried glance at his companion. Perhaps they thought the night's mission foolish. *Aey*, it probably was.

But it was also a great pleasure. The mountain trail they rode was exhilaratingly precipitous but not terrifying as the narrow path to the caverns had been. Moonlight washed the rugged land with silver and cast the shadows of its jagged contours into impenetrable blackness. The ridges of white rock glowing in its half-light looked like the skeletal structure of the mountain itself.

It was a stark sort of beauty, and the steep land was dangerous. Perhaps it was a trick of the light or the splendour of the surroundings, perhaps it was the company of the woman he loved and the presence of the man he had come to think of as a friend, but Sheftu was filled with a sense of calm.

"There," Tishane instructed, pointing. He took another swig of *sloan*. "The hanging valley lies ahead." He swallowed another. "We'll split up here." He signalled to two of the soldiers.

"Accompany the Saharani Laran to the ledge, there," Tishane told the two men, indicating the rock shelf just below them. "Lord Sheftu and I will ride up onto the bluff above." He signalled the remaining two soldiers. "We can see in both directions from up there," the captain explained. He turned to Laran. "If you spot wolves below, Saharani, signal silently, waving your arms. We will be able to see you from above."

"Keep an eye to the bluff," he told one of the men instructed to stay with Laran. "We will wave you up if we see wolves on the other side, *ashaii?*"

The soldier bowed.

But Sheftu was shaking his head. "Laran and I will stay together, Captain." "No!" Tishane said emphatically. "*This* is the way it must be done."

Sheftu frowned at him. Surely the myth of the black wolves' blessing did not extend to *how* they were sighted?

Laran put her hand on Sheftu's arm and smiled up at him. "We will be able to see one another," she assured him. "All will be well." She looked down toward the foot of the escarpment.

"If I were a wolf," she told him happily, "I'd live there," she said pointing below. "The valley on this side has a stream that flows even in the heat of summer."

She turned away from him with a wave and started down onto the flat ground at the edge of the stone shelf, her double escort only steps behind her.

"Bet I see the black wolves first!" she called over her shoulder.

Sheftu hesitated a moment, his sense of peace dissolving around him. He was inexplicably uneasy. *Ridiculous,* he thought. His time in the cells, alone, injured and grieving, had made him jumpy. It was natural not to want to part from Laran after all they'd been through, but it was also unreasonable to try to keep her within arm's reach at every moment. She was an independent woman.

Besides, she'd be in sight every step of the way.

Sheftu turned to follow Tishane and his men, who were already climbing the trail to the bluff above. The path was clearly illuminated in the moonlit night. He watched as Tishane sloshed *sloan* into his mouth once more, then swiped the back of his hand across his mouth. When the captain raised the canister to his lips again, Sheftu frowned, his sense of unease intact.

And escalating.

CHAPTER SEVENTY-FOUR

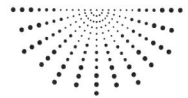

"HERE," TISHANE SAID as they reached the bluff. He gestured a little too widely with his arm, then slung himself awkwardly out of his saddle. When both feet were on the ground, he stood, swaying a moment, before he seemed to gain a sense of control.

Sheftu walked to the edge of the bluff. He saw Laran below them lying on her belly, looking over the edge of the white rock shelf into the valley. She must have sensed his gaze, because she twisted to look up at him. He couldn't see her face, but he imagined her smile. She waved and mimicked searching with a hand to her eyes as though to shield them from bright sunlight. He waved back, his own smile unseeable and fleeting. When he turned to Tishane, the captain was staring at him, his expression inexplicably grim in the circumstances.

Sheftu glanced at the two soldiers with them. One avoided his gaze entirely, but the other, a thin-faced man, looked up and into his eyes with something that looked like... malice.

He'd seen that look on the faces of the prison guards when they wanted to do him harm.

The silvered night and the thick silence, both so rich with promise only moments earlier, seemed ominous now.

Sheftu glanced at Tishane again. He was drinking deeply of the *sloan* once more. He watched Sheftu through narrowed eyes over the canister.

It didn't seem like Tishane to allow his senses to be dulled like this, especially not in the presence of his Saharani. But then again, perhaps Sheftu didn't know the man as well as he'd thought.

"Captain?" Sheftu asked warily. "Have you not had enough?"

"*More* than enough, Soldatian." Tishane strode to the edge of the bluff unsteadily and looked down at Laran and the two soldiers guarding her. When he looked back at Sheftu, his expression was contemptuous. He stepped close to the larger man, looked pointedly at his shoulder-length black and white-streaked hair, then up into his eyes.

"*Raven Seeker!*" Tishane snarled suddenly. It sounded like an accusation. Or a curse.

Sheftu took a step back, confused.

Tishane drew himself up, his tone oddly conversational now, his words slightly slurred once again. "But perhaps you haven't heard?" he continued. "The Barraidi sometimes refer to your countrymen as *Raven Seekers*."

"That so?" Sheftu asked guardedly.

"It is," came the answer. "The Barraidi legend of the *Raven Seeker* describes a man who cannot be trusted, a Soldatian imprisoned for treachery and murder. In the story, he escapes."

Tishane lifted the cannister of *sloan* to his lips once more, then seemed to think better of swallowing more of the noxious liquid.

Sheftu stood silently, trying to understand what was happening.

Tishane was looking around him. He gestured widely with his arm once more, this time to indicate their surroundings, or perhaps all of Mirren-Bar.

"*Here*, we have no such legend, Lord Sheftu. *Here*, treachery does *not* go unpunished."

"What are you...?" Sheftu began. But Tishane forged on.

"Did you know that *here,* in Mirren," Tishane said, his finger pointing, stabbing, at the ground beneath their feet, "your people are sometimes referred to as *Black Wolves?*"

Sheftu nodded. He'd heard as much. Though the black wolves they sought tonight were apparently revered, being described as one was not entirely complimentary.

"You, *Soldatian,* are the only *Black Wolf* we will see here this night."

"What in the Seven Layers is the matter with you, Tishane?" Sheftu asked. He glanced again at the soldiers.

"*You* are the matter, foreigner. You think a Soldatian, a *Raven Seeker,* can take the throne? You think a *Black Wolf* can *bed* his way into the ruling family of my country? Think again."

Sheftu shook his head. Was this the *sloan* talking? Did Tishane actually think Sheftu was a threat to Mirren rule? He kept his eyes on Tishane's face, kept his voice even and calm. He felt anything but.

"That's not the way it is," Sheftu said quietly. "That's never been the way of it." But Tishane must *know* that!

Was Laran in danger? Surely Tishane wouldn't hurt her? Or permit her to be hurt? She believed he loved her!

He does. Sheftu had seen it in the older man's eyes many times. Tishane wouldn't allow anything to happen to her. Sheftu was certain of it. Sudden revelation widened his eyes.

No, not Laran. Him. *He* was in danger.

That was why Tishane had split the two of them up. Here, high on the bluff, Sheftu was about to have an accident.

Tishane and his men were going to kill him.

Sheftu tensed, readying his muscles to defend himself. Coming straight from the Great Hall as he had, he'd brought no weapons.

The captain was already issuing terse commands in Mirren and one of his men, the youngest, swung a bow off his shoulder. The other became a blur of movement in his peripheral vision as Sheftu sprinted toward the bay stallion.

He took hold of the inky mane and vaulted onto the big animal's back. He swung the horse's head around and prepared to lunge.

Down. His first instinct was to protect Laran. *No!* Doing so would endanger her. *Up!* He'd follow the path up into the heights and try to lose Tishane in the darkness above. The captain would not allow harm to come to his Saharani.

But the arrow nocked tight now in the strung bow was not pointed at Sheftu. It was pointed below!

At Laran.

Sheftu pulled back on the reins, stopping all forward motion. The startled stallion reared, then danced sideways, and Sheftu instinctively stilled him with a soft word and a hand on the arching neck. He stared in horror at the bowman. Tishane jerked his chin toward the ground, indicating a dismount, and Sheftu slid slowly from his saddle to the heather-clad earth, one hand still wrapped in the jet-black mane. His chest was tight with fear.

"Tishane," Sheftu all but whispered. "What are you doing?"

"I have to kill you, Soldatian," Tishane said. His words were beginning to slur again. "And I have to kill Saharani Laran. The Mirren throne must remain unpolluted by foreign ambition."

Sheftu looked helplessly at the soldier holding the nocked arrow. If he charged the man, the arrow would release. He couldn't take the chance.

He swallowed audibly. "What… what do you want me to do? Do you want me to leave Mirren: to renounce my interest in marrying Laran? I will! I can arrange to leave with my father. Tomorrow. Laran needn't die. She will marry the viscount as planned. Is that what you want? Is that what you need?"

"Kneel."

Sheftu stared at Tishane in disbelief.

"Kneel, foreigner!" The thin-faced soldier, the man who'd looked with malice at Sheftu, approached him with his sword drawn.

Sheftu looked wildly back at the bowman still holding the taut bow, still aiming directly at Laran below. *She didn't know! She still thought they were seeking a blessing!* A blessing. The irony made him want to weep.

Seeing no recourse that wouldn't put Laran in further danger, Sheftu dropped to his knees in the heather. He could feel its coarse texture against his bare legs, felt a sharp stone digging into his shin.

"By all that is sacred, Tishane! Think what you are doing! It's the *sloan, aey?*

The *sloan!* You wouldn't hurt Laran else!"

"Oh, *aey*, Soldatian," Tishane mimicked Sheftu nastily. "'Tis most definitely the *sloan.*" He stared at Sheftu for a moment, blinking heavily as he attempted to clear his blurring vision. "Perhaps we'll make this a game, *ashaii?* Perhaps only one of you needs to die tonight after all."

Not Laran! It couldn't be Laran.

The babe! Jodpul knew about the babe. Had the viscount had his hand in this night's betrayal? By the Seven Gods, did he want Laran dead because of the half-blood child she carried? Did he want the way clear to marry Shell? The throne would be back within reach then.

"I'll take Laran away with me if that is what you want! I'll leave with her! If I am gone, if we are both gone, the blood of the ruling family of Mirren will remain pure, *aey?*" Sheftu glanced desperately at the bowman once more. "Is that what Jodpul wants?"

"Jodpul?" Tishane looked puzzled. He shook his head, the movement causing him to stagger slightly. "Kill her," he ordered the bowman, raising his hand.

Time seemed to slow. When Tishane's hand dropped, the arrow would release.

"No!" Sheftu cried. He sought desperately for a diversion. "The game!" he yelled. "What about the game?"

447

Tishane hesitated, his hand still poised in mid-air, then, the decision made, he dropped it in signal to the bowman.

No choice! Sheftu gathered his legs beneath him and dove at the bowman, his momentum rolling the young man onto his back. The arrow flew, clattering against the rock on the stone shelf beside Laran. Sheftu heard her startled cry. He didn't see her jump to her feet.

"Sheftu!" she was shouting up at him. "*Sheftu!*"

He glanced over the edge. One of the soldiers on the ground beside her had leapt up and had taken hold of her arms. "Tishane!" she cried as she struggled.

"By the Holy Ones!" Tishane roared at the soldier who'd loosed the arrow. "What have you done?"

The man stood shakily, his face chalk white in the moonlight. Sheftu rose beside him, tensed for battle but confused. The soldier hadn't fought back. He wasn't even looking at him. He wasn't chagrinned that he'd missed his target. He looked horrified that he'd loosed the arrow at all!

"What is happening here, Tishane?" Sheftu demanded, his voice unsteady. He shuddered at the near death of the woman he loved.

The captain sat heavily on a boulder, his head in his hands. He muttered incoherently, his language a slurred mix of Soldatian and Mirren. Then he stood as abruptly as he'd sat and nodded to his men.

The thin-faced man attempted to take hold of Sheftu's arms from behind, but Sheftu spun out of his grasp and swung his fist hard. It connected with the soldier's jaw and the man fell. As he did, the man scissored his legs against Sheftu's knees, knocking him off his own feet.

Before he could regain them, Tishane brought his sword down to Sheftu's throat in a lightning-swift move. It should have been impossible under the influence of *sloan*.

"Rise slowly, Soldatian," he ordered. The captain's voice was clear and steady now.

Sheftu climbed to his feet. The man who'd scissored him pressed the point of his blade into his spine. Tishane's sword bit into his throat now.

I trusted you! You son of a bitch!

Sheftu watched Tishane's eyes, saw them slide sideways to the young bowman. The captain jerked his head toward the edge of the bluff once more, and the bowman lay back down on his belly and repositioned himself. He nocked another arrow, pulled his bow taut and aimed down toward the shelf below.

"Tishane!" Sheftu gasped. "Don't do this."

"The game," Tishane began, his smile magnanimous now. It did not light his eyes, which were narrowed with intent once again. "I will grant you a chance to change your fate, Soldatian." Alcoholic fumes seemed to drift in the air around him and the captain's breath was redolent with it. "A chance to live, *ashaii?*"

Tishane dug the blade into Sheftu's throat, breaking the skin. Blood rolled down the young lord's neck, a hot trail against his cool skin. He could feel it soaking into his shirt.

Sheftu sucked in a breath. "What is it you want?"

"*One* of you must die tonight, Soldatian." The captain nodded to himself. "*Ashaii.* One will be enough." He took a deep breath and looked down into Sheftu's face.

"You may choose. Shall I have my bowman release the arrow?" Tishane asked him. "Death will come to her quickly, *ashaii?* She will not suffer. And then I will let you go. You can return to Soldat with your family tomorrow."

"No!" Sheftu rasped. The blade pressing against his neck was making speech difficult, but it was terror closing his throat. "No," he repeated.

"*No,* Soldatian? Then *you* would prefer to die instead? I put it to you again: *you,* Soldatian? Or Laran? Which will it be?"

"Me!" Sheftu panted. "It must be me! Swear you will let her live! Swear you will deliver her back to her family unharmed! Swear it, Tishane!"

"*Ashaii,*" the captain whispered. He could no longer meet Sheftu's eyes. "I swear it."

449

"Do it, then," Sheftu croaked. He squeezed his eyes shut.

No! He opened his eyes to stare directly into Tishane's. He'd watch the golden depths of his killer's eyes as he died; he'd watch his own murder at the hands of a man he thought was a friend.

"Sheftu!" Laran's voice rose up in a sob from the shelf below. "Tishane! What is happening? Tishane?"

Was she struggling? Were Tishane's soldiers *hurting* her?

The pressure of the blade at Sheftu's throat lessened as Tishane turned his head to hear.

"Reassure her," the captain instructed softly.

'Laran," Sheftu called. He tried to keep his voice even. "It's all right. It's…"

But the pressure at his throat returned. Sheftu tried to see the bowman without turning his head and imbedding the point deeper. Was the bastard still poised to shoot? *Aey.* He could see him now.

He was!

* * *

ON THE LEDGE below, Laran relaxed suddenly in the grip of her captor. She elevated her chin.

"I am ordering you to release me, soldier," she said, her voice as imperious as she could make it. "At once!" She refrained from casting a panicked glance at the bluff above.

"We *have* our orders, Saharani," the man replied. He tightened his grip on her arm painfully.

"Surely an order from the Saharani takes precedence over that of our captain, Halley," the other man said.

"It does not!" the man referred to as Halley barked. "We are to keep her restrained for her own safety."

Laran twisted wildly in an attempt to loosen Halley's grip on her arm, but his hands were like iron bands.

Use your head.

She feigned a dead faint and crumbled to the ground. *It's worked before! It could work again!* She repressed the memory of the Barraidi hunters and concentrated on remaining absolutely still, though she hung like a rag doll from the grip of the soldier holding her.

"Halley!" the second man cried. "By the Holy Ones! Can you not see that she's fainted? Release her!"

Halley callously let Laran fall to the ground. Her head struck the hard surface and bounced slightly but, though slightly dazed, she willed herself to remain limp.

She heard Halley grunt and had the impression the man was bending over her, perhaps to ascertain that she still breathed. Praying that her impression was right, she opened her eyes and jerked her head up, striking the soldier in the nose and sending him sprawling backwards onto the ledge. He swore loudly, a hand held fast to his face. Blood seeped between his fingers.

Laran sprang to her feet and raced away, her eyes casting about for something, *anything,* to use to her advantage. *Rocks!* Here on this wild ledge, there were only rocks. She could see Halley in her peripheral vision. He was already on his feet and moving swiftly toward her. His face was a furious mask of blood and pain. *The horses were too far!* He'd have her by the time she reached them.

Laran bent, pulled a rock from the surface that, she realized belatedly, was nearly too heavy for her. She straightened, wrenching away from Halley's grip as she did so, then half-fell onto the rocky ground. She rolled, clutching the rock hard against her. When she regained her feet, she raised the rock to chest height with both hands, then thrust it out forcibly against the soldier's legs. It struck him in the shin.

Halley shrieked and went down a second time.

Laran rounded on the second soldier and began backing away.

"Will you try to stop me, too?" she demanded. But the second man was shaking his head.

"No, Saharani!" He was a young man and solidly built. He appeared sincere. He executed a swift bow and glanced at Halley who was floundering in an attempt to rise, his face bloodied, and one hand behind him on the rocky ground, the other pasted to his damaged shin.

"I am Reeshed," the second man told Laran. "I will accompany you to where you'd like to go, *ashaii*? If there is danger for you there, I will protect you."

Laran nodded gratefully.

"Although…" Reeshed began, then fell silent. He looked over at the Saharani with respect as they mounted. She'd handled herself well. He shook his head in wonder and a slight smile crinkled his golden eyes. It appeared this delicate-looking Saharani did not really *need* his protection, at least not against the likes of Halley.

Laran leaned out of her saddle to grab the reins of Halley's horse with a backward glance at the fallen soldier. He had succeeded in rising and was hobbling toward them painfully. She squeezed her thighs together in communion with her own horse and galloped up the trail leading Halley's mount. Reeshed moved in directly behind her.

CHAPTER SEVENTY-FIVE

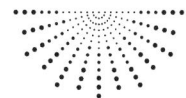

"SO IT IS to be *you*, then, Soldatian?" Tishane confirmed.

"*Aey*! I've already said as much! How many times will you ask? You've sworn not to harm her, Tishane. Don't let *them* hurt her!"

"They will not." Tishane said. His voice sounded strained. He looked like he wanted to vomit but his grip on the sword remained true. He nodded to the man behind Sheftu, the gesture curt and quick.

The soldier withdrew the point of the sword from Sheftu's spine. Tishane withdrew his blade from Sheftu's throat but kept it close.

Sheftu turned his head to see the bowman still holding the strung bow. The man's hands were beginning to shake with the stress of keeping it taut. *By the Seven Gods!* He wouldn't be able to hold it much longer!

Sheftu dropped to his knees once more. His gaze kept returning to the bowman. If the man lost control...

"Get on with it!" he growled at Tishane.

But Tishane had stepped back. The man behind him moved away. The young bowman was easing back on the bowstring. He climbed shakily to his feet once again and stared at Sheftu, his face still chalk white. The bow hung loose from his hands now.

What...?

A commotion on the trail behind him had Sheftu surging to his feet. *Laran!*

Her horse pounded onto the heather-strewn bluff, spraying rock and vegetation at its sudden stop. Laran held the reins of a second horse and it, too, skidded to a standstill. One of her guards thundered into view right behind her. He swung his leg over his saddle and dropped to the ground immediately. Laran remained astride. Her eyes were wide with apprehension as she took in the puzzling scene before her.

Sheftu had been kneeling near the edge of the bluff but had jumped to his feet at her arrival. His entire body was tensed for flight. Or to fight? Something dark and wet stained the front of his sleeveless shirt from his neck to his chest. He was moving swiftly now, toward her, and angling his body as though to shield her from his assailants. One of his arms was outflung in a defensive position.

But these were not his enemies, Laran thought. This was Tishane and his men!

Tishane stood eight or nine feet away, a sword in one hand. *A sword?* His grip was white knuckled. The biceps on his sword arm bulged with strain though the weapon he held pointed at the ground. He looked as though he'd just witnessed the death of a friend.

Two guards stood to either side of Sheftu, also eight or nine feet distant. Even in the wash of moonlight she could see that one, younger than the other, looked upset. The other looked afraid. He was trying, and failing, to hide it.

By the Holy Ones! What had happened here?

Fear coursed through Laran's body and she began to tremble. Had violence played out here? Was it over? What *had* happened? She slid off the little mare's back and moved cautiously, closer to Sheftu.

"Sheftu?" she was asking softly. "What…?"

The last guard, Halley, sprinted onto the bluff. He was on foot, limping and gasping for air after his frantic run up the steep trail. Twin trails of blood spilled from his nose and he swiped at them irritably.

Laran turned away from the sight of him.

Sheftu glanced at this last man. *Good. All in sight now.* Without looking down at Laran, he wrapped one strong arm around her. The other he still held out as though to ward off an attack. He, too, was breathing heavily.

He swiveled, moving Laran with him, as he tried to keep Tishane and his four men in view at all times.

But none made a move against him. None made a move at all. All stood still and silent in the moonlit night.

Laran felt a sob rise up in her chest. Whatever had happened had been terrible. She could feel Sheftu's despair as it rolled over him.

He moved toward the bay stallion, still wary, still tensed to fight for his life and for Laran's, one arm still wrapped around her shoulders.

Laran's golden eyes were huge in her face. He lifted her, practically *threw* her onto the stallion's back, before turning back to Tishane.

"Why?" he asked, his voice low and dangerous.

The captain tried to read Sheftu's eyes. Though they were as dark as the mountain's shadowed places, he thought he saw anger simmering in their depths. *And no wonder,* he thought.

Tishane opened his long coat, shrugged it off and let it fall to the heather at his feet. He took hold of his own shirt and ripped it down the middle, baring his chest as though in invitation.

"I have wronged you this night," the captain said quietly. "I know it." He hesitated, and then straightened to his full height. He put his shoulders back and waited, waited for what he felt he knew would come next.

"Kill me, Lord Sheftu, if that is what you will."

Laran was aghast. "What are you *doing*?" she asked Tishane. She looked at Sheftu, who was staring at Tishane, violence in his eyes.

"Sheftu, what...?"

Tishane tossed his sword to the ground at Sheftu's feet and braced his own.

Keeping Tishane in view, Sheftu bent to pick up the fallen sword. He tested its weight and balance in his hand. He stared at its lethal tip a moment, then wiped it against his *talom,* leaving behind a smear of his own blood. He looked deeply into the captain's eyes.

"Sheftu, no!" Laran slid off the stallion's back. *Holy Ones protect us!* "Don't hurt him, Sheftu!" She placed herself between the two men, one hand on each wide chest.

"Why?" Sheftu asked Tishane again, his gaze still locked on the older man. He was no longer worried for Laran's safety. He was looking over her head. "*Why* did you do it?"

"What?" Laran demanded. "*What* have you done?"

"I did it for Mirren," Tishane answered slowly. "And for the High Lord."

Does he truly see me as a threat to Mirren rule? Sheftu asked himself.

"Explain yourselves!" Laran demanded. "Do *not* ignore me!" She looked from one man to the other in desperation.

"I could have refused," Tishane continued to Sheftu. "I did not." He shrugged.

The High Lord. Sheftu's eyes widened. "The Tania ordered you to do this?"

Tishane finally looked down at Laran.

"*Ashaii,*" he whispered.

Sheftu shook his head. "Why would he…?" *The Tania would not have ordered his own daughter to be put at risk.* Sheftu turned to stare at the bowman. He was still pale, still shaky. He still looked horrified.

The bowman hadn't been aiming at Laran at all!

Sheftu had charged the man. It had been Sheftu, then, who had changed the course of the arrow. It had been *he* who'd nearly caused her death! *By the Seven Gods!* Nausea twisted through him. So did revelation.

He'd been asked to choose between his life and Laran's. "It was a *test*?" Sheftu asked incredulously.

"Ashaii." Tishane sighed heavily. "So it was." He didn't want to die. His wife...

"You bastard," Sheftu whispered. He stared at the tip of the sword he still carried in his hand. He imagined driving it through the captain's chest.

"A *test?*" Laran demanded, thinking of the stallion Sheftu had been given. But the men's reactions had been far too strong for that. "I don't understand! What do you mean? Tishane! What do you *mean?*"

Tishane looked down at the Saharani once again. He loved her like a daughter. Always had. She'd be lost to him now. Sorrow rose up to burn the back of his throat. He knew he must not display it.

"Lord Sheftu," he told her quietly, "was given a choice, Saharani: his life for yours. He chose well."

By the Holy Ones! "You threatened to *kill* him?" She looked into Tishane's face. "You threatened to kill *me?*"

"Ashaii," Tishane said. "I did."

Sheftu swept Laran aside with his sword arm. He fisted his free hand and punched the older man in the stomach. When Tishane doubled over, he hammered his fist against the side of his face, once, and then again, bloodying him and sending him careening to the ground.

"No!" Laran cried. *Oh no. Please don't hurt him. Please!*

"I trusted you, you son of a bitch!" Sheftu ground out.

When the thin-faced soldier moved to defend his fallen captain, Sheftu turned on him.

"Try it."

The Soldatian's voice had been low and ominous and a quick glance into his raven eyes stopped the soldier mid-stride in a stance that would have been comical at any other time. He balanced precariously for a moment, then brought his feet together with an audible *thwack.*

"You," Sheftu told the man with barely restrained fury, "were able to put hands on me once because I believed your captain to be a friend." Sheftu glanced over at Tishane, who was staggering to his feet.

"I will not make that mistake again," Sheftu vowed.

He turned back to the thin-faced man and didn't see Tishane close his golden eyes briefly in misery.

"Touch me again, soldier, and I…will…kill…you."

"A…*ashaii*," the thin-faced man finally stuttered. "My lord," he added deferentially. He executed a quick and cautious bow. But Sheftu was staring at his captain once again.

"I will take what provisions you have," Sheftu said. "Now. The Saharani and I will travel up into the heights. Do not follow."

"What?" Laran demanded. "I can't just *leave*, Sheftu! Tishane is…"

"Then you, too, have a choice to make," Sheftu told her roughly. He felt nausea roll over him again, this time gaining more than a foothold.

Laran fell silent. She stared at Sheftu in dismay.

He turned, doubled over and retched into the heather.

By all that is sacred, what have they done to him? How much more can one man endure?

Tishane put a hand on Sheftu's shoulder, but Sheftu shrugged it off angrily.

"Take this," the captain said stubbornly. "Wash your mouth with it. Don't inhale." Tishane handed the remains of the canister of *sloan* to Sheftu, who did as the captain suggested.

"Did you really drink the stuff?" Sheftu finally asked him. His eyes were watering with the fumes.

"How else could I have done what I felt I must?" Tishane admitted. He watched silently as Sheftu regained his composure, watched, too, as rage reclaimed his bronzed features.

Sheftu turned to Laran. She looked as though her heart had broken in two.

"I did not mean it," he murmured to her. He looked into her eyes. "Will you come with me?"

"*Ashaii*," she said tearfully. "Where you go, so will I."

458

"It is my duty, my lord, to accompany..." Tishane fell silent. Even in the dim light, the violence implicit in Sheftu's expression was clear.

His last "duty" had been like smoke, Tishane considered. Executed there on the mountain, the trial of Lord Sheftu had been dark and dangerous with a bitter scent that was not likely to fade away soon. If ever. The thought depressed him.

"As you wish," Tishane finally agreed. He wiped blood from his nose and mouth with the back of his hand, then nodded to two of his men, who began unstrapping blankets, and the water cannisters and food rolled within, from their saddles.

Even if Lord Sheftu didn't kill him in the next few hours, Tishane thought, the Tania might very well do so. True, he'd completed his task and had therefore exonerated himself in the Tania's eyes, but forgiveness for allowing the Soldatian to take the High Lord's daughter up into the heights alone would undoubtedly come hard.

So be it! One way or another, Tishane's time in hell was coming to an end. One way or another.

* * *

SHEFTU LIFTED LARAN up to the stallion's back once again and stood looking up at her a moment. She appeared small and fragile against the sheer mass of the powerful animal, but he knew she was not. Despite her diminutive stature, Laran Tania had strength and determination. She had courage.

She'd endured Du-kar and escaped Soldat. She'd survived the shipwreck, Santago's betrayal and violence at Barraidi hands. She'd endured pain and terror and uncertainty and grief. And tonight, she'd bested the guards assigned to her, winning one over and wounding the other. She'd ridden up from the shelf below to defend him.

He'd die to protect her. He'd thought he'd been about to.

Sheftu tied the provisions to his saddle, then vaulted onto the huge animal's back behind the woman he loved. He urged the stallion away, up into the mountains of Mirren-Bar.

459

CHAPTER SEVENTY-SIX

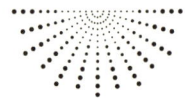

PROVOS LAID A calloused palm against the rough bark of a gnarled tree. It was heavily laden with fragrant blossoms, its twisted arms spread wide as though seeking permanent embrace. Provos felt unexpectedly comforted there under its ancient canopy. He also felt a strong sense of communion. He, too, felt rooted to the spot.

He was watching Jodpul's retreating back through the moon-dappled garden. Though his crimson sash had been robbed of colour, the last flash of the viscount's white shirt blazed briefly through the hanging boughs and then disappeared as the man strode out of sight.

Provos shook his head. He'd just learned firsthand of the viscount's intention to release Laran from her Promise.

A favourable outcome for his cousin with the little Mirren Saharani had been an outside chance from the start. Still was, Provos reflected, even *without* the dark spectre of the Promise weighting the air like a charged thunderhead.

He'd had time and opportunity to consider all outcomes for Sheftu's petition for marriage, but now the viscount's withdrawal of the Promise had torn a hole in the seeming certainty of rejection.

With the first hurdle toward that goal removed, Provos expected to feel delight for his cousin, but instead, he felt.... bereaved. That it was so shamed him.

He and Sheftu had walked life's paths together since they were boys. That was about to change.

It will never change. How many times through the years had Sheftu quietly uttered those words?

"You are my kinsman and my friend, Provos," he'd said only yesterday. "Though I hope to make my life with Laran now, though I hope to make my life *here* in Mirren-Bar, you will always be among the first in my heart." He'd placed his hands on Provos' shoulders.

It will never change.

Provos had shrugged away from Sheftu's hands, embarrassed.

"Leave off, Cousin," he'd grumbled. The Seven Gods knew that Sheftu would always be among the first in his heart as well, no matter what happened in the uncertain future.

But no matter the outcome of his petition, Sheftu's life *would* change. It already had. So had his own.

Well, he'd always thrived on change in the past. They both had. He resolved to thrive on it now.

Sometimes life changes for the better. Or so he'd heard.

Provos spread his fingers wide against the rough texture of the bark, and then leaned against the primordial tree.

Perhaps he'd stay here, in Mirren-Bar, for a while. *Aey.* That sounded right. Perhaps their journey together was not over yet. Provos felt something in his chest, something tight, let go suddenly.

It was not over!

He would make Mirren-Bar his home for a time. Sheftu and Laran would be here. Randide, Estalla and the children would also be here. He would not be alone. And in the unlikely event that the Tania accepted his cousin into his family, Provos would learn to find his way without his cousin's constant companionship.

He looked around him at the exotic structure of the palace, at the magnificent scenery glimpsed from open rooms and through floor length windows. He breathed deep of the scent of cool, mountain air and high snow. He nodded to himself.

He would find meaningful work to occupy himself and when he wasn't working? Life held adventure here. He could feel the very thought of it tingling in his veins.

A moon-washed shimmer of colour in his peripheral vision had him turning his head to admire two Mirren noblewomen who, in turn, had been admiring him.

He smiled at them, and his raven eyes crinkled at the corners.

Oh, aey, he thought. Adventure. Though his cousin endeavoured to embark on his own, Provos imagined he felt the same thrill of anticipation.

CHAPTER SEVENTY-SEVEN

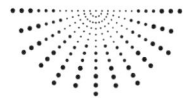

"ARE YOU HURT?" Sheftu finally asked.

He rode with one arm around Laran's waist and had pulled her against him, shielding her from the cold with his big body. As his upset began to fade, his awareness of the slight movement of her hips against the muscles of his parted thighs became more acute. He splayed his fingers so that his thumb brushed the underside of one breast. He glanced up at the firmament.

Wisps of cloud wafted now across the diamond sky and drifted across the full moon. The silvery light dimmed. To the south, lightning flashed over the mountains once more, illuminating the snowy peaks in staccato bursts of light. The rumble of accompanying thunder was quiet; the storm was evidently far away.

Laran relaxed against him. She'd been utterly silent as they made their way ever upward. They were riding higher and higher, the air was growing bitingly cold, their supplies were few, and those that could offer assistance if they required it, were now far below. And yet, she thought, she felt secure and unafraid. Sheftu had that effect on her, she realized. Always had.

She was home now, in Mirren-Bar. Sheftu was literally at her back. She closed her eyes briefly.

I cannot lose him!

"There," Sheftu said, indicating a level plateau. Three flat-edged boulders, each as broad as Sheftu was tall, and as high as Laran herself, would provide both shelter from the rising wind and a vantage point from which to watch the distant storm.

He pushed backwards and off the stallion's rump, then moved to help Laran down, but she was already sliding down the big animal's side. She landed on her feet. She still hadn't spoken.

Once again despair rushed over him like water.

"I... I'm sorry," he told her again. He'd not really meant to demand she choose between him and her familial loyalties and childhood ties. He wouldn't.

Laran looked over at him and he saw the glint of tears on her cheeks in the dimness. He felt his chest tighten as his own surge of emotion threatened to overwhelm him.

"I..." He shrugged. There was nothing more he could say, not now.

Laran was desolate. *Father,* she thought, *how could you have done this to Sheftu? To us? I love him!*

But her father knew that.

By the Holy Ones, that must have been the reason! Her father had ordered this "test" to either prove or disprove the depth of Sheftu's love for *her*!

She took a deep, shuddering breath, then covered her face with her hands. She couldn't look into his beautiful eyes, not now. She was responsible for yet another wound to his heart! By the Holy Ones, these were her people, this was her home: she'd known Sheftu's place within it would be uncertain at first, but she'd hoped...

It is my fault.

She dropped her hands. The wisps of cloud drifting across the glittering sky had thickened. Complete darkness was beginning to reassert itself.

She steeled herself to look as deeply into his raven eyes as she could in the diminished light.

"The sea," Laran finally said, clearly struggling to steady her voice. "Do you still want to see it, Sheftu?" She hesitated. "With me?"

In his peripheral vision the white crests of faraway peaks flickered briefly in and out of existence. He thought about her words. The Mirren Sea had become a symbol to them both.

"*Aey*," Sheftu whispered. "I do."

"Oh." Laran stifled a sob. "I thought maybe you had... that you had..."

"Changed my mind?" he asked quietly.

He placed his big hands on her arms and looked down into her golden eyes, platinum now in the faded light, and spilling over with tears. He watched one roll down the soft curve of her cheek.

He shook his head resolutely.

"I want to be with you, Little Elf," he told her softly. "I will always *want* to be with you. Nothing, no one, can change that."

She nodded and tried to smile at him, but his expression did not speak to her of levity.

"I'm sorry, too." She dropped her head against his chest and murmured into the bloodstained shirt. "I'm so sorry, Sheftu."

"It is done," he said. *Nearly done. That bastard, Tishane...*

But strangely, here, high on the mountain, where there were only the two of them, his ire at what had been done was beginning to wilt. He released Laran's arms and wrapped his own around her. He lowered his chin to rest it upon her head. He closed his eyes briefly.

A test! Had he *passed* this "test" by choosing Laran's life over his own? If so, was there benefit? Would it propel his petition of marriage forward?

And if I'd pleaded for my life at the expense of Laran's, would I be dead now? Would Tishane have driven the sword at my throat through my neck? Had the Tania's orders extended to execution?

This line of thought was not helping. Laran pushed away from him slightly and looked over at the now invisible view. Sudden pulses of far-off lightning brought it to life, there, and then gone.

"Here there are only the two of us," she began. She glanced up into his shadowed face. "Only you and I now."

Sheftu nodded slowly. "You and I."

Laran placed the flat of her hands on his chest and stood on her toes to reach for his lips with her own. He bent his head and kissed her gently.

* * *

THE BOWMAN TOOK careful aim. He resisted the natural sway of his tensed arms under pressure and concentrated on holding the bow true and straight. The stag was in his sights. It was a magnificent animal with an antlered rack so heavy its thick neck was corded with muscle. The bowman released the arrow.

He didn't normally enjoy the killing but this time the swish and hiss of the arrow slicing the air thrilled him. The final satisfying thwack *as it pierced its target was, strangely, exhilarating.*

Blood.

He could see it pouring from the stag's side, could see it staining the rock and pooling into the heather. The stag dropped onto its front knees, then, and top-heavy under the great weight of its antlers, collapsed headfirst onto the ground.

The bowman nudged the animal's body with a booted foot, then looked down at his own leg in surprise. Where were the laced sandals he'd worn? Now, calf-high leather boots, Soldatian boots, encased his lower legs. He glanced down at his chest. Gone was the sleeveless Mirren shirt he'd worn to the hunt. Now, over loose-fitting trousers, he wore a white Soldatian tunic. It was stained with tiny droplets of blood as though the shot that killed his quarry had caused arterial blood to spray across both landscape and hunter.

But that wasn't possible.

He bent down to examine the stag more closely, inexplicably blinking blood out of his own eyes. He could feel it streaming down his face, could hear it splattering against the rocks like rain.

By the Seven Gods! It wasn't a deer at all! It was a woman!

"Sheftu! Sheftu, wake! You are dreaming!"

He could hear her voice.

He looked down at his hands. They were slick with her blood. It began to slide up his forearms.

No!

"Sheftu!"

The dead woman reached out to him, shook him. She was staring sightlessly into his eyes.

"Wake!" she said. "It's only a dream. A nightmare."

It was a nightmare!

Her face! There was something about her face. He couldn't look at it. He was afraid. Laran. Was it Laran?

Terror gripped him by the throat. He pushed the dead woman away and cried out in anguish.

"Ow!" Laran cried. Sheftu had pushed her against the rock they'd sheltered near. He was sitting up now, his chest heaving with the exertion of his dream. He blinked in confusion. He looked down at his hands, and then over at Laran, sprawled against the boulder.

"Dreaming," he mumbled, still breathing hard. In the orange embers of their fire, Laran could see the sweat glistening on his brow. His raven hair was slicked with it and damp strands were plastered against his neck.

The Smiling Man looked as though all joy had been driven from him. He was muttering. "I didn't mean to, Little Elf."

What was he talking about? The fact that he'd practically thrown her against the boulder? Or was it a residual of his dream?

He placed his head in his hands.

"I nearly caused your death," he said. "On the bluff."

She moved to his side and let him talk.

"Tishane wouldn't have hurt you. I knew that," he said. "I *thought* I knew it, but the *sloan:* he'd had so much to drink. He was angry. Talked as though he believed I had bedded you to reach the throne. Talked about the dissolution of Mirren blood in the ruling family. He ordered the bowman to kill you. I charged the man. The arrow he'd aimed above your head nearly killed you. I didn't know it wasn't aimed *at* you! By the Seven Gods, I didn't know it was a 'test'!"

Nausea surged over him and he climbed to his feet, doubling over once again, though this time what little remained of his stomach contents stayed within.

He straightened slowly, his gaze fixed on Laran, who was barely discernible now in the red glow of the embers. Their visible world had shrunk to no more than a few feet from the finished fire. The night had become black and thick around them. A cold breeze caressed the back of his neck with icy breath.

"Come back to the blankets," Laran said softly.

But Sheftu was shaking his head. "If we join now, I will not be gentle, and I have no wish to hurt you."

"You will not..." Laran began.

"Or the babe within," he added softly. Laran froze. "You... you *know?*"

Sheftu nodded. He suddenly felt absolutely alone.

"Why did you not tell me?" he asked, his voice giving away the hurt he felt. Laran stood slowly, letting the blanket slide away.

"I... I had already given you the gift of my virginity. Knowledge of the babe was meant to be my gift to you on our wedding day." He couldn't see her expression, but she sounded aghast. "Oh, Sheftu. I didn't want you to find out from someone else! I can't believe Jodpul would have..."

But Sheftu was shaking his head. "Not Jodpul. Your mother."

"My *mother?*" Laran felt the blood drain from her face. "She knows?" *Oh no!* And her father? Surely, *he* didn't know? No. No, if he did, he would have confronted her with what he would consider her disgrace.

468

Disgrace. The child was a treasure of immeasurable value to them both!

"And if we aren't given permission to marry?" Sheftu asked. *Would you have kept the knowledge of our child from me?*

Laran took a deep breath. She wrapped her arms around herself. "If we are denied, I… Well, we cannot *be* denied. Don't you see?" She sounded almost desperate.

Sheftu nodded slowly. *Where you go, I go,* she'd said.

"I do *not* want you to have to choose between me and your family and home, Little Elf."

"And yet I would have no choice."

"Because of the child…" he began.

"*Ashaii,*" she agreed, "because of our child, but also because I will not find happiness without you, Sheftu. It is as you said: I belong with you. And you belong with me."

From across the embers of the dying fire, Sheftu absorbed her words. He shook his head resolutely. He *could* not take her away from her family and her home. Even, he thought glumly, if he was given opportunity.

"But Sheftu," she was saying. "The babe… Are you… are you happy? You said…"

Sheftu relaxed suddenly. His heart expanded in his chest.

"*Aey*, Laran," he said. "*Aey!* I want the babe! I *want* you both! I *want* your happiness. I want my own.

But, Laran," Sheftu continued, "what about Jodpul? If we are denied, he will…"

"He loves Shell."

Sheftu nodded. "*Aey.* I believe he does."

"You and I," Laran said. "You and I belong together."

"*Aey,*" he repeated. "So we do." She was barely visible across the glowing coals. "And so we will be."

Laran smiled, though her expression was lost to the night. She dropped her coat to the ground, then lifted the hem of her shirt and pulled it over her head. It, too, dropped to the stone at her feet.

Sheftu watched her from across the embers. His heart still felt seared, but the curved undersides of her bared breasts were faintly outlined in orange light and he felt himself growing hard despite the turmoil within.

He imagined warming his cold hands on her soft flesh. He imagined her nipples, rigid with chill, firm against his palms, and the ripple of gooseflesh that must be moving across her half-naked body now.

His breath caught as he watched, fascinated. She was pulling off her riding skirt, letting it slide down her legs to pool at her feet.

When she stepped out of the fabric, he saw that her bare legs, too, were outlined in orange light but that the junction was still bathed in darkness.

He wanted to touch her there. He wanted more than that! He wanted to take her hard, right there on the frigid stone! He wanted to claim her as his own. She was *his*! Only his.

And he was hers, body and soul.

"I do not need you to be gentle tonight, Sheftu," Laran said quietly. "The babe is protected within."

"What *do* you need, Laran?" he asked her gruffly.

"You," she answered. "Only you." She held out her arms.

"That you have," he murmured. "And so will you always." He stepped over the smouldering embers and walked into her embrace.

* * *

DAWN GRADUALLY REAWAKENED the mountain. Somewhere in the distance a hawk screamed and much closer, two jays called to one another companionably from the stunted trees. The rain foreshadowed by the distant lightning storm hadn't materialized, but dew sat heavily on the sparse vegetation. It beaded on the blankets and in the softly curling hair of the woman sleeping beneath them. Another, a larger unmistakably male figure, was wrapped around her as though to give, and take, heat as they slept.

The black wolf watched them silently, his head down, his eyes and ears alert. He looked a signal at the rest of his pack and one by one they appeared, eleven in total including two yearlings and a cub. They padded quietly along the game trail in front of the boulders sheltering the sleeping humans, each glancing cautiously at the intruders in their territory and on their hunting grounds, as they passed.

One of the yearlings huffed its annoyance and Sheftu opened his eyes to see the young wolf staring down at him from four feet away. Its jet-black fur shone in the morning light and its amber eyes glowed from a face as black as the night had been. Its body was slender and lithe, and its paws were huge. Already large, it would be a formidable size when fully grown.

Without moving overtly, Sheftu nudged Laran awake with an admonishment for silence. But sudden apprehension had her jerking her head up to see what held Sheftu's attention so raptly.

The yearling padded away uneasily at the quick movement then turned and trotted back, lowering its head but keeping its amber eyes fixed in fascination on Laran and Sheftu. It lifted its lips slightly in menace.

Another of its pack, this one enormous with a scarred muzzle, loped into view and growled softly at the recalcitrant yearling. The yearling trotted after its leader, throwing a final swift glance at the humans before rounding the bend and leaving their view.

Sheftu released his breath explosively.

"Black wolves!" Laran said. She pushed away the blankets and stood looking down the trail the animals had taken. "Black wolves, Sheftu! We saw them! I knew it was meant to be. I knew it!"

Sheftu looked up at her curiously. She was climbing the boulder behind them to get a better view.

"You hold with this myth?" he asked, looking up at her. "You really believe we have been blessed?"

"*Ashaii!* Did you not *feel* it? It was wonderful!" She smiled beatifically.

471

Sheftu nodded slowly. It *did* feel as though they'd been given a powerful gift. A *gift*. He warmed at the reminder of the child Laran carried.

"*Aey*," he answered. "Perhaps I did."

Laran looked down at Sheftu from the flat top of the boulder. *He* wasn't smiling. His generous mouth was set in a grim line, giving him an almost frightening aspect, and his raven brows were drawn together over eyes shadowed by sleeplessness. The nightmares of the previous night, both real and imagined, had taken a toll.

Fear trickled down Laran's back.

"Sheftu," she whispered. "Do you…? Are you all right?"

He looked up at her once more, noted her apprehension. It fueled his ire.

He climbed to his feet.

"No." His voice was very quiet and simmered with barely restrained fury. "I am not!" he suddenly erupted.

Laran wasn't certain which was worse, the quietly uttered denial or the shouted one.

Laran glanced down the trail to see the retreating backs of the black wolf pack, then clambered off the boulder. She placed a small hand on Sheftu's forearm.

"My father…" How could she rationalize what he'd done? "He had my best interests and the interests of Mirren-Bar in mind, I think. He…"

"This must end," Sheftu interrupted. "Now. This morning." He bent to scoop up the blankets. He movements were jerky and quick.

He was angry and it showed.

Ashaii, she thought. *This* will *end. Before any more damage is done.*

"Let's return home," she told him quietly. "I will speak to my father."

"Oh, *aey*?" Sheftu asked grimly. *So will I!* High Lord or not, there would be words between them. And perhaps more.

He hoped Jodpul had had nothing to do with the 'test.' He hoped his father and Tyson had not returned to Soldat. Most of all, he hoped Provos was still in Mirren-Bar. He wanted his cousin's counsel, if only to gather his own thoughts, and more selfishly, he desired the continuity only his lifelong friend could provide.

And Tishane? The man was likely below at the bluff awaiting their return, waiting to resume his "duty". Sheftu felt hostility swirl up in his chest at the thought of seeing the captain again.

"Ordered" to betray him? Sheftu welcomed another opportunity to demonstrate what he thought of the previous night's work. The captain of the king's guards was going to have reason to question orders regarding Lord Sheftu Morrow in the future.

CHAPTER SEVENTY-EIGHT

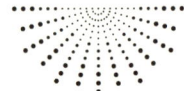

MIKALE RESUMED HIS pacing.

He'd spent a sleepless night agonizing over the task he'd demanded of Tishane. He agonized, too, over its possible outcomes. Had *death* been one of them? On the Barraidi headland, the young lord had proven his ability to fight against greater odds than Tishane would have presented. Had Lord Sheftu *killed* the captain and his men? As skilled a warrior as Tishane was, that outcome seemed unlikely and yet…. None of them had returned from the mountain. *None* of them.

"Perhaps I've made a mistake," Mikale confided to Emeldra. The Holy Ones knew it wouldn't have been the first he'd made where Lord Sheftu was concerned.

Perhaps? Emeldra kept her thoughts to herself. Criticizing her husband now would do nothing to amend the situation. Besides, he was clearly on edge and tormented by uncertainty.

But what *had* befallen their daughter? Why was she not here, furious with her father for what he'd done, and railing against the injustice of it all?

And it had been unjust.

The young lord had been made to suffer. *Again.* The choice forced upon him would not have been easy to bear and the imagined consequences of his decision, either way, would have been torturous.

By all that was sacred, Emeldra *had* to believe that her daughter was all right, that the young lord had not been harmed, and that Tishane and his men had survived the ordeal.

But if all had gone as planned, where *were* they? *Why had they not returned?*

"I cannot bear this another moment, Mikale. Let us ride into the mountains in search of them."

Mikale stopped pacing to stare at her.

"And how do you propose we do that? The Morrow Lord and his kinsmen have been demanding to see Lord Sheftu since dawn. His kinsman, Lord Provos, has been particularly insistent. How will these Soldatians interpret the High Lord and his lady leaving Mirren-Bar without giving answer as to his whereabouts?"

"We will do so quietly, husband. No one will know. Anything could have happened up there. We *must* discover for ourselves what it was."

Mikale frowned. He knew the trail along which Tishane had led the group the previous evening; he knew the bluff where the test was to take place. He also knew it to be a precipitous and potentially dangerous passage.

He reluctantly nodded his agreement. When he opened his mouth to forestall Emeldra, she interrupted him abruptly.

"I *am* coming with you, husband," she told him in no uncertain terms. She looked down at herself to evaluate her clothing. Instead of the figure-hugging sheath Mirren women normally preferred, she had dressed that morning in an emerald-coloured floor length gown, which, though snug in the bodice, hung full to the floor from the waist. It was split for riding. *Ashaii,* Emeldra thought. *I am ready.*

She slipped off her flimsy sandals and pulled on a sturdier pair. Mikale went down on one knee before her, lifting the twin hems of her split gown one at a time and tying the laces around her calves. He looked up at her but refrained from commenting on the fact that she was already wearing a riding dress though the decision to ride had only been made moments ago.

Ashaii, he thought ruefully. *It is* my *decision that is only moments old.* Obviously his wife had made the decision to go hours earlier.

So be it. He hoped her considerable skill at healing would not be necessary.

He rose, thinking about the best way to leave the palace undetected. Surreptitiously, but not foolishly, he decided. They'd bring ten armed soldiers with them.

CHAPTER SEVENTY-NINE

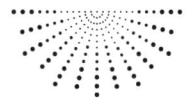

"**S**END FOR YOUR wife and your son, Tyson," Provos was saying. "She and your brother had a fine relationship and he is very fond of both of them. Did you know they visited Sheftu every morning while you were gone? Sheftu told your boy tales, took him riding, taught him many things."

"So I have heard," Tyson said dryly. He was ashamed of the surge of jealousy he'd felt, *still* felt, on hearing about his younger brother's attention to his wife. Truth be known, his own *in*attention had brought him guilt for all the months he'd been absent from Soldat. And here he was, gone again.

"*Aey*, perhaps I will, Provos," Tyson answered. "If I can be assured safe passage for them."

"It can be arranged," Lord Morrow said gruffly. *Aey*, he thought. *By all means, bring what remains of the Morrow family from Soldat. Perhaps a show of familial solidarity will help Sheftu's petition. This would seem to be a marriage worth promoting.*

"Invite the Lady Justice to accompany them, Uncle. Sheftu owes her a debt and Laran owes her an explanation."

Lord Morrow and his first son, Tyson, had been at breakfast in their shared chamber when Provos found them. Now the older man swung his chair around and away from the table. He redeposited himself on it and leaned forward, deep in thought, his big hands resting on his knees. His expression was serious, but his eyes were alight.

"Does he?" he asked.

He'd come to Mirren-Bar to either extricate his son from prison or to visit retribution upon the purveyors of his death! Instead, he was given an opportunity to both resurrect his relationship with Sheftu and further his own power within Soldat by bringing back with him an agreement of alliance. He snorted his disbelief.

His second son had petitioned to marry the eldest daughter of the ruler of a potential and powerful ally.

This union between Sheftu and the Mirren Saharani could greatly expand the already not inconsiderable sphere of influence wielded by The Morrow House. The dishonour visited upon it by Sheftu's prior actions now paled into relative insignificance.

"Where is Sheftu?" Lord Morrow demanded abruptly. "I would have a word with him."

Provos raised a brow. "I do not know, Uncle," he said grimly.

Mid-morning and his cousin had yet to return from his nighttime foray into the mountains.

The wait had been excruciating.

CHAPTER EIGHTY

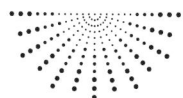

"RIDERS!" LARAN SAID, reining in. She'd retrieved her own horse from the captain and the sturdy little animal slid to a halt on the pebbled path. Sheftu, astride the bay stallion, towered over the smaller horse and its rider. He, too, reined in, squinting against the morning sun to make out the riders in the distance.

"Soldiers?" he wondered aloud. He looked behind him at Tishane, but the captain's brow was furled and he looked as unsure as Sheftu felt.

"Perhaps," Laran said uncertainly. She was shielding her eyes with a hand to her brow. "There appear to be a dozen of them. No, wait! Two of the riders look like... But that's not possible!"

Behind them, Tishane, having apparently come to the same conclusion, swore under his breath.

"Who?" Sheftu demanded. "Who is it?"

"My parents!" Laran told Sheftu. "To have left the palace with so small an escort, they must have disguised themselves!"

She urged the little mare to speed.

Sheftu clenched his jaw and touched his heels to the stallion's flanks to catch up.

The stallion's enthusiasm for speed outweighed the urgency of the command given and the animal reared and danced sideways on the trail. "Go easy," Sheftu murmured to the bay. "A broken ankle, or worse, here, will cost us both."

But by the Seven Layers, he wasn't ready to confront the Tania yet. Not here! He felt the anger he'd expended on Tishane begin to well up inside once more.

When he finally drew abreast of the High Lord and Lady Tania his jaw was sore and strained from clenching it tightly.

"Mother!" Laran was exclaiming. "What are you doing out here?" She looked at her father, who was raking his eyes over her as though searching for injury. "Father," she began, but he held up his hand to halt the flow of words he knew would follow. He dismounted slowly.

Sheftu did the same. Emeldra looked a warning at Laran and Laran squeezed her eyes shut a moment. When she opened them again, she glanced down at Sheftu.

"Sheftu," she pleaded. "Don't…"

He looked up at her and nodded. "*Aey*," he said vaguely. He bowed respectfully to Emeldra, and then produced an obviously reluctant bow for Mirren's High Lord. When he straightened, he nodded faintly at Mikale, then passed him by, continuing down the path and out of sight.

Mikale watched him walk away, a frown between his eyes, and then he turned to Tishane. The captain was dismounting awkwardly. When he turned, Mikale saw that his nose had been broken and one eye was bruised and swollen nearly shut. Both upper and lower lips were split and had recently bled. He was holding himself carefully, one hand over his ribs and Mikale wondered if one or more had been cracked or broken.

"Captain," Mikale said softly. "What happened here?"

Tishane licked his split lower lip.

"It has been as you instructed," he told the High Lord. He avoided any mention of the violence that had ensued. His voice was strained. "Lord Sheftu did not hesitate. When he saw no option, he chose the Saharani's life over his own. He did not beg. The only bargain he made was to ensure that I bring her safely home to her family after he was dead."

Mikale nodded. He did not look happy.

"Your debt to me has been fulfilled, Captain," he told Tishane quietly. "And," he added so his soldiers could hear, "I now find myself in yours."

Tishane tried to execute a bow but failed, grimacing in pain.

"Father," Laran began again. She swung her leg over the little mare's back and dismounted. "I wish to…"

But once again her father held his hand up to silence her and Laran felt her temper spike. She *would* be heard! And she had much to say! Her father's expression, though, silenced her for the moment. While not exactly repentant, it was deeply regretful.

Mikale had noted Laran's pallor. "Forgive me, daughter," he said. His voice was quiet and sincere. "Your heart is warm. I will pray to the Holy Ones that you soon find room within for pardon. I felt I had no choice."

Laran stared at him bemused. Though his words had diffused her anger, they had fueled her upset. She looked up at her mother in despair.

"Where have you been, daughter?" Emeldra was asking. She shifted in her saddle. "Why did you not return last night? Did Lord Sheftu…?"

"His heart, too, is warm," Laran interrupted quickly in Sheftu's defense. Her words, although spoken to her mother, were meant for her father's ears as well. She cast an anguished glance at the captain's battered face. "Though Tishane may have cause to doubt it now," she added quietly.

Emeldra looked over at Tishane for a moment and her eyes were filled with sorrow for what had transpired. It would seem the young lord had not taken this last injustice lightly.

"I am sorry for your suffering, Tishane," Emeldra told the captain. She turned back to Laran.

"The warmth of the young lord's heart has been well demonstrated, Laran," Emeldra added. "Particularly where you are concerned."

Laran darted a glance at her father, but he was standing silently watching his wife, his head cocked slightly to one side as though waiting to hear what she had to say.

"That Lord Sheftu's heart is capable of warmth, loyalty and great love, we have seen," Emeldra continued. "That he is capable of diplomacy we have heard. Though," she mused, almost to herself, "he might exercise that particular asset more often. And," she continued, "that his patience is at an end I think we can surmise.

Would you not agree, Mikale?"

The Tania raised a brow in question.

Emeldra paused a moment and looked out at the magnificent view of the mountains she loved. She elevated her chin. If she had been dressed in her finest gown and seated upon a jeweled throne she could not have looked more like the queen she was.

Laran swallowed, enthralled. She didn't notice the absolute silence of the men behind her as they waited for the Lady Tania to speak once again.

"He has also demonstrated immense courage. He has the heart of a warrior and is not overburdened by ego, though he has enough to feel pride in himself and in the people he bestows love upon.

That great heart was broken at least once, I think," she finally added, thinking of Sheftu's strained relationship with his father. "Would you not agree, daughter?"

"Perhaps," Laran said miserably. Her own heart felt on the verge.

"Lord Sheftu is clearly a man to be reckoned with. A heart broken in childhood is difficult to mend. That he found the strength within to do so is no mean feat. I think perhaps the pieces may not yet be cemented. Would you not agree to that as well?"

How could her mother have read The Smiling Man so well? How could she *know* what lay at the core of him? *She did!* Laran nodded, her own patience suddenly at an end as well.

Sheftu waited below on the trail. *Alone.* That he did not wish to walk his own path without her was also clear, at least to Laran.

"All he has asked of us," Laran said, her voice neither soft nor reasoning, "is to be allowed to make his life here, with me. With *us*! He's *never* asked more! Don't *you* agree?" she demanded of her parents looking from one to the other.

She saw that she had their full attention.

"He trusted us! Trusted Tishane!" She glanced at the captain once again, and then looked directly at her father. "He trusted *you*."

Mikale looked down the path in the direction Sheftu had taken, then back at his daughter.

Let her have her say, he told himself. *I owe her that. I owe* both *of them that.*

"Last night that trust was betrayed," Laran said. "He… He has not smiled since it happened, not even when he learned…" She swallowed, appalled at what she had nearly divulged. "Not even in the presence of the Blessing," Laran amended.

Laran let her gaze rest on Emeldra. "Sheftu had no wish to return to Mirren-Bar last night, preferring instead to spend the night here, under the stars." She took a deep breath. "And I had no wish to suggest otherwise."

She straightened her spine and willed herself to be as courageous as Sheftu had been.

"Tishane will tell you that Sheftu did not beg for his life." She forged on, her voice growing stronger with each syllable. "But I stand here before you begging for mine.

Please, listen well," Laran continued. "I love you. I love Shell and Jodpul and Tishane and all of Mirren so much sometimes I think my heart will burst with it." She took a deep breath.

"But I tell you now what I told Sheftu last night."

"And what is that, Daughter?" Emeldra asked softly.

"Where he goes, so do I," Laran told them.

Silence grew, until even the horses became edgy and shuffled their hooves against the stones on the path. Mikale and Emeldra glanced at one another.

Their daughter had just threatened to leave Mirren-Bar.

"Then," Emeldra said softly, "we shall have to see that Lord Sheftu has reason to stay here, *ashaii?*"

"*Ashaii*," Laran whispered. Relief washed over her in a warm wave. "It is my greatest wish." She glanced at her father furtively. His expression was solemn, but he was nodding slowly.

Hope rose higher yet in Laran's chest.

Emeldra straightened suddenly in her saddle, her gold-dust eyes wide as her memory stirred.

"The *Blessing!*" she exclaimed. "You saw the black wolves?"

"*Ashaii.*" Laran's golden eyes lit now with wonder. "Eleven there were, all told. One stopped to watch us and stayed with us for a minute or more."

Emeldra nodded to herself. "The bond between you and your young Soldatian has been blessed. That, I think, is as it should be."

Laran wiped suddenly moist eyes with the back of her wrist and willed her voice to remain even.

"And will that bond be permitted, Mother?"

"I believe it will. Is that not so, Mikale." Emeldra said. She hadn't phrased it as a question.

Mikale continued to watch his wife, his golden eyes nearly glowing with love and admiration. The corners of those eyes had crinkled in an inward smile.

Emeldra looked down the path in the direction the young lord had taken and looked a message at her husband. Mikale raised both brows in unspoken response. He set out after Sheftu.

"High Lord!" Tishane called after him. He signalled his men to accompany their ruler. "I don't believe the Soldatian's temperament is, ah... all that stable at the moment."

"Then so be it," Mikale called back to him before he, too, disappeared around the bend.

The young Soldatian had been kept waiting long enough. That Lord Sheftu wished their meeting to be unobserved did not bode well, but Mikale would have to trust that the young man had the self-control and the prudence to choose his next move wisely.

And if he does not? Mikale shrugged to himself. He would meet that challenge as it came.

"He must go alone, Tishane," Emeldra told the captain quietly. "Keep your men with you."

Tishane shot Lady Tania a troubled glance. He reversed his order and turned to stare down the path worriedly.

Emeldra remained serene.

She smiled at her daughter, and her eyes were rich and warm with the promise of happiness.

"Your Soldatian's heart will heal, Laran. You will help him find his smile once more," she told her.

But Laran only nodded. She felt as though she were being torn in two. Euphoria over her mother's words warred with dread as she stared down the path. Sheftu had been so *angry*. Surely he wouldn't... When goosebumps peppered her arms, she started down at a run.

"Wait!" Emeldra called, but Laran kept running.

* * *

SHEFTU TURNED SWIFTLY as the crunch of feet on the path sounded behind him. The wait to confront the Tania was finally over. He visualized his hand against the man's chest, could almost hear the satisfying thump of his body as he pushed him against the wall of rock at his back. Sheftu resisted the urge with some difficulty.

"This ends now," he told the Tania instead.

"*Ashaii*, young lord," Mikale answered reasonably. He watched Sheftu's expression for an indication of danger and saw the quick desire for violence blaze, but as quickly as it had flashed across the bronzed face, it

485

was suppressed. It seemed the young lord had retained a measure of wisdom.

"Laran belongs with me," Sheftu told him in no uncertain terms. His raven eyes were narrowed. "She will be my wife with or without your permission."

Mikale raised a brow as though to dispute the statement. He waited to hear whether Lord Sheftu would be foolhardy enough to threaten leaving Mirren-Bar with his daughter. He could remain silent when Laran had intimated as much but he'd not countenance the Soldatian threatening the same!

"She is with child," Sheftu told him instead. "*My* child," he said bluntly.

Mikale flushed with shock. Red climbed high on his cheekbones in outrage.

Ashaii, the Tania thought. *I knew! Deep down I knew but did not wish to consider it.* He tried to quell the burn of righteous anger, fueled, he thought, by hearing that which he'd suspected blurted out so ingenuously. *Or is it the fact that the young man admitted it at all that galls me so?*

Mikale clenched his jaw in an effort *not* to picture the Soldatian rising over his daughter in lust. He felt his face grow hotter. And redder.

Laran practically skidded around the corner, saw the umbrage in her father's face— saw, too, the resolute set of Sheftu's jaw.

Both sets of eyes swiveled towards her. One set, as black as the night had been, glittered with determination, the other, golden as the evening sun, was furious.

"You are with child, daughter?" Mikale accused her.

Laran blushed to the roots of her hair. She looked at Sheftu as though she could not believe her eyes.

"You... You *told* him?" she whispered.

"*Aey,*" Sheftu said. "I did." His voice was hard. He turned back to the Tania.

"Deny me, High Lord, and I will persevere," he told him. "Kill me, and your daughter will never forgive you. Give in to me, and I will never give you or Laran cause to regret it." Sheftu paused. "Never! This I swear."

"Those," Sheftu continued, "are *your* choices, High Lord. Easier than the two I was given, *aey?*"

Mikale looked from one to the other and back again and tamped down his rage. It would do no good to give in to it now.

"*Ashaii*. An easier choice, Lord Sheftu," he finally acquiesced. *Now that I know your heart*, he thought to himself. He watched Sheftu's eyes harden further at his own reminder of the "test".

Mikale held his right hand out for Laran and she stared at it a moment, then took it in her own. She looked into her father's eyes, her expression almost desperate.

"I have thought long and hard about your petition," Mikale said addressing them both. His gold-eyed gaze landed on Sheftu.

"For dishonouring my daughter, Lord Sheftu, for dishonouring *me* by taking my daughter to your bed without the sanctity of marriage..." Mikale began. He looked into his daughter's troubled eyes, then up into the raven gaze above him.

"For these things and more, I have an almost irresistible urge to feed you to the very wolves who have blessed you."

Sheftu lifted his chin and frowned. He heard Laran's quiet intake of breath.

Mikale looked deeply into the raven eyes above him. "That you have disrespected me by your admission, that you have disregarded our customs, that you *both* have, will be overlooked, *this* time. It will *not* be forgotten," he added.

Sheftu swallowed. It was clear that he'd narrowly escaped reprisal— clear, too, that what the High Lord saw as disrespect would not be tolerated again.

"You are Laran's choice," Mikale continued to Sheftu. "Emeldra has spoken in your favour. Tishane, a man whose counsel I have learned to respect, believes you to be a good man. Jodpul has honoured you by releasing Laran from her Promise. All of this, in conjunction with your willingness to trade your life for my daughter's, speak to me of your character, Lord Sheftu.

Your reputation for fairness and justice with your own people," Mikale continued, "and the exhibited wisdom to rein in your anger when you must —these, too, speak to me of your worth."

Sheftu's eyes had widened in surprise.

"That you have demonstrated the ability to defend yourself and have the strength and the will to defend my daughter, that you have courage but, as my wife pointed out, are not overburdened by ego: all these things and more have given me the answers I sought."

Mikale took a deep breath. His grasp on Laran's hand tightened. He looked into her eyes as he placed it, palm down, against his chest. When he looked up at Sheftu, he placed his left hand, palm open, over Sheftu's heart.

Sheftu looked down at the Tania's hand in astonishment. Laran had placed her hand just so once. He'd been startled by the gesture then. He was startled now.

"I grant your petition to marry my daughter, Lord Sheftu. It is with pride that I include you within my family. And it is with humility that I ask you to look into your heart to forgive me for that which was done to you last night."

Sheftu felt at a sudden loss. He'd worked out the various outcomes to his demand but hadn't really known what to expect.

Not this!

No, not this.

He looked down at Laran, who was gazing at him with love in her eyes. He looked at the Tania, who regarded him carefully as he watched for his reaction. He looked behind him and up the path though Emeldra and Tishane and his men were hidden from his view.

He grinned widely.

"*Aey,*" Sheftu said and laughed, the sound surprising even himself. "*Aey,* High Lord." He couldn't seem to *stop* grinning. He bowed deeply.

"It is with honour that I accept a place within your family. I am proud that Laran will become my wife."

He glanced down at her and Laran saw that light had returned to his raven eyes. She clasped his hand almost shyly.

Sheftu looked down at her hand and enclosed it in his own. He looked back at her father.

"I will work on my own humility, High Lord," he said honestly. "Though forgiveness for last night's work will not come easily."

"It was a cruel test, Lord Sheftu, and no fault of Tishane's," Mikale said. "But I defy you to have done any differently if the situation were reversed."

Sheftu frowned and Mikale forestalled his sudden flare of indignation.

"Imagine, young lord, your own beloved daughter, a great beauty with the immeasurable wealth and power of her ancestral family behind her. Imagine, too, that one day she comes to you with a tale of love for an impoverished foreign noble, a noble who *claims* not to have aspirations for the Mirren throne and all it entails. Imagine a noble who *professes* to desire only the love and companionship of your daughter, but who is without resources or holdings of his own. You want to believe him.

"But, young lord, *will* you take a chance on your daughter's very *life*? Will you take a chance on the lives of your family, on the very safety of your adopted country and its people, that this stranger speaks the truth?

"Will you be able to *afford* to believe him *unproven*?"

Sheftu dropped his eyes as the truth of the Tania's words hit him hard.

"There must have been a different..."

"I could think of none as definitive, Lord Sheftu."

Sheftu nodded, understanding at last.

He tried to glower as ferociously as he could as he recalled the High Lord's words. *Imagine...your own beloved daughter...*

"And if the child Laran carries is a son, High Lord?"

"Sheftu!" Laran said. *Do not provoke him!* Her face had reddened once again and so had her father's.

"Then," Mikale answered slowly, reining in his temper, "we will rejoice, for surely life must be easier with sons." He saw Laran flinch from the corner of his eye, and felt immediate remorse.

"But perhaps," he said quietly, his eyes on Laran now, "it would not be as rich or as filled with happiness. Who am I, as the father of daughters, to say?" He frowned suddenly and glared at Sheftu.

"And there will be no more talk of the babe until you are married, young lord."

"*Aey*," Sheftu agreed. His grin reasserted itself, wider yet.

He followed Mirren's High Lord up the trail and back toward their horses. Laran, walking hand in hand with her father, turned to bestow on him a radiant smile.

Black wolves be damned, Sheftu thought. *Now* he felt blessed.

CHAPTER EIGHTY-ONE

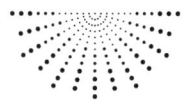

"WHERE WERE YOU?" Provos demanded as his cousin swung off the bay stallion. He looked at Sheftu carefully. "You look like you've been dragged through all Seven Layers by a team of horses." He eyed the procession of mounted guards behind his kinsman in confusion.

"*Aey*, and so I was," Sheftu answered him. "Is my father still here, Cousin? Is Tyson?"

Provos nodded. "*Aey*, and on edge. Thought you'd been kidnapped and murdered for your inflammatory statements."

The Tania appeared on an enormous black gelding, Laran and Lady Tania beside him, both on the sturdy little mountain horses unique to Mirren. Tishane and the remainder of his men brought up the rear.

Sheftu snorted, his back to the procession. He didn't notice the direction of Provos' eyes or the shocked expression on his face. "Oh, *aey*?" Sheftu said. "Which one?"

"Very likely the one in which you suggest in front of many witnesses," the High Lord said dryly from behind him, "that though my daughter is promised to another, she belongs with *you*."

Provos' eyes slid over Tishane and then returned immediately, astonished. The captain looked as though he'd been badly beaten.

"High Lord," Provos said quickly, bowing low. He glanced over at his cousin worriedly.

But Sheftu was smiling at the Tania's comment. Grinning. He was beginning to laugh! By the Seven Gods, what sort of lunacy was this? The High Lord would have him thrown back into the cells below! Provos watched Mirren's ruler warily.

A smile was tugging at the corners of the High Lord's mouth as well, though he looked as though he'd like to stifle it.

"Pray enlighten your kinsman, Lord Sheftu," he said. He turned his ebony gelding toward the stables.

Provos stared at Sheftu. He saw his cousin's gaze travel to Laran, where it lingered and locked. Laran looked happy, very happy, and when she tore her own gaze from Sheftu, she winked at Provos before following her father to the stables. Lady Tania smiled down on both of them before continuing on her way.

Sheftu grabbed his cousin's shoulders. "It is done!" he told him. "We are to be wed!"

"*What?!* When? No!"

"*Aey.* Soon. You will walk beside me at the wedding?"

"I would be honoured, Cousin," Provos said sincerely, but he was taken aback.

"How in the Seven Layers did you make this happen?" he asked.

"It's a long story, Cousin, and one best left for another time. Come: I am meeting Laran at the entrance to the Great Hall in thirty minutes to relay the news to Shell and Jodpul. Let us find my father and Tyson first." He grinned again, handed his horse to a groom, and then strode off, turning only once to urge Provos to speed.

* * *

SHEFTU REACHED THE Great Hall first. His meeting with his father and his brother had gone as he'd expected. Tyson had been both shocked and delighted at the news, while the Morrow Lord's enthusiasm for the marriage appeared to have little to do with his son's happiness, and everything to do with the perceived platform for power and elevated status it presented. The Morrow House would benefit. Therefore, his father was pleased.

And so be it, Sheftu thought. He'd hoped his father's experience in Mirren-Bar would have helped him to see, truly *see* the gift he had been given.

And perhaps he would in time.

Time. It no longer loomed ominously in front of him but stretched out purring before him like a cat on a hearthrug. Sheftu was content.

He walked to the entrance and cast his gaze inside in case Laran awaited him within.

To the side and far back in the hall sat a slender young woman, her curly waist length hair turned golden by the sunlight streaming through the window behind her. The dazzling backlighting hid her features and those of the young man who sat at the table across from her, though Sheftu thought he recognized the slope of those broad shoulders.

The couple leaned toward one another across the width of the table as though trying to get as close to one another as they could without actually touching. Both sets of hands lay flat on the table, the tips of the fingers only inches away from one another. They were speaking quietly, intimately, and when the woman laughed quietly, Sheftu knew.

"Shell and Jodpul," Laran said from behind him.

"*Aey,* so it is, Little Elf," Sheftu said as he turned. He lowered his head to kiss her softly and Laran stood on her toes to brush her lips across his.

"Husband," she said, smiling.

"Soon," Sheftu agreed. He glanced back at the couple in the Great Hall and wondered how to broach the subject they had come to speak of. Surely

Jodpul would welcome the announcement? After all, it cleared his way to Promise to Shell.

And if he and Shell were Promised, Jodpul would escape humiliation over the broken Promise to Laran. His high status as a favourite of the Tania family would remain intact, and his own family's sense of outrage would be mollified. *Aey*, Sheftu thought. The viscount had much to gain. He frowned slightly.

Was Jodpul *using* Laran's sister for his own purposes?

No, Sheftu thought. He loved her. It had been clear in his eyes for some time now. That he had much to gain by the alliance was merely a benefit. That Mirren itself would continue to benefit by the viscount's presence and counsel was a bonus.

Laran tugged on Sheftu's hand, pulling him into the room, but instead of waiting for him, she suddenly released him and ran to her sister, laughing and calling out elatedly in Mirren.

Startled, Shell and Jodpul pulled away from each other guiltily, but when the import of Laran's words hit home, both rose immediately.

Shell threw her arms around her sister. Her exclamations in her own tongue were clearly those of joy. Jodpul looked over their heads and grinned at Sheftu.

"What magic is this, Soldatian?" he demanded good-naturedly. "How did you make this happen?" The intent of his words unknowingly echoed Provos'.

"Then you are truly not displeased?" Sheftu asked, his own grin fading.

Jodpul shook his head. "Laran is happy," he said simply. "As for me..." He glanced down at Shell and smiled. "Things have a way of working out for the best, *ashaii?*"

Sheftu grinned. "Be careful, Viscount. This little Saharani will soon be my sister," he said, winking at Shell, who smiled happily.

Jodpul laughed. "And when we Promise, Lord Sheftu? You and I will be brothers. There is irony there."

"Promise?" Laran asked looking from one to the other. "Then you *will* Promise to one another?"

"*Ashaii*," Shell said, suddenly shy. "Tonight. After you make your own announcement!" She looked up at Jodpul. "Is that not so?"

Jodpul smiled into her gold-flecked eyes. "If you wish it, it will be so," he said.

"From rivals to brothers, then," Sheftu mused. "*Aey*," he nodded. "I like it fine."

"*Ashaii*," Jodpul said, moving away from the table to clasp Sheftu's arms. "So do I."

At the entrance to the Great Hall, Provos leaned against the stone arch watching the exchange. *Sometimes life changes for the better. Aey*, he thought. Sometimes it does. Though he and his cousin would never again walk life's paths in the same way, their journey was only beginning.

CHAPTER EIGHTY-TWO

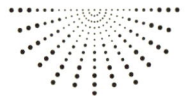

L ADY JUSTICE GLANCED once again at the carefully worded message in her hand. She raised her eyes to the astonishing beauty that was Mirren- Bar and carefully schooled her expression. Now, here in the Great Hall of the fabled city's magnificent white palace, it was her intention to reflect detached approval rather than the unabashed delight she actually felt. Ever mindful of the status she enjoyed in Soldat, she was determined to garner the respect of the Mirren people as well. The girlish exclamations of delight she was restraining would not further the serious image she hoped to portray.

After all, she had much to gain from this association, the least of which was an experience she'd never have dreamed possible.

Fate. She shook her head at the incongruity of it all and glanced down at the message once again.

Here was the invitation to the wedding she now attended. A marriage into the ruling family of Mirren-Bar by the son of an influential Soldatian lord. The union was without precedent and Lady Justice had a sense of being at a historical juncture.

The battered, courageous little slave girl and her idealistic protector: Lady Justice had never questioned the decision she'd made in releasing the two, though she'd endured considerable censure and the continued and uncomfortable political scrutiny of the Du-kar lord as a result.

The young Lord Sheftu had been tenacious. The Mirren slave girl had been extraordinary. Now, at last, Lady Justice understood just how tenacious and how extraordinary the pair was.

She smiled spontaneously at the sight of the wedding party moving slowly into the Great Hall. Lord Sheftu was dressed in a snow-white *talom*, the fabric fine and sweeping his bronzed thighs as he moved. His sleeveless shirt had been dyed a deep indigo blue and was constructed of the same delicate material, though the well-muscled young Soldatian looked anything but delicate in it. He was grinning in evident pleasure.

His kinsman, the young Lord Provos, walked at his side.

On his other side, the Saharani Laran Tania was dressed just as simply in the sheath traditional to Mirren nobility, but this one was uncovered. No transparent material softened the clinging lines of the garment, and its rich indigo colour was threaded through with silver filament. The result was very flattering to the Saharani's slim but curvaceous figure. Smoky kohl highlighted her slanted golden eyes and between her brows rested a single blue gem in the shape of a teardrop. It was held in place by a delicate silver band, which encircled her forehead. Her hair, its length doubtless an uncherished souvenir of her time in Soldat, curled softly to the base of her graceful neck.

She had clasped hands with a young woman who looked very much like her, a sister perhaps. A handsome Mirren nobleman with a crimson sash walked alongside.

The assembled guests heaved a collective sigh over the evident beauty of the bride and the groom and shifted closer, hoping to be bestowed with an opportunity to wish the couple well before they reached the front of the Great Hall.

Lady Justice glanced at the High Lord and Lady Tania who awaited them there, their expressions tranquil, their ceremonial garb simple but impressive.

Surely, they must have had reservations in allowing the union. The prospect of a marriage outside of the noble circles of Mirren-Bar, outside of the very *country*, could not have been taken lightly. She glanced over at the Morrow Lord. *He* did not appear troubled in any way, but then he had much to gain by the merger.

Lady Justice watched carefully for signs of discontent among the gathered Mirren but either they accepted the young Soldatian's marriage into the ruling family or the wedding guests had been carefully chosen from among those that did.

She blinked in surprise at the sight of the lone Barraidi family, plainly of less than noble birth, who numbered among the smattering of Soldatian and the scores of Mirren guests. She smiled inwardly. The presence of the Barraidi should come as little amazement in comparison to the unorthodox gifts requested by Lord Sheftu.

Unorthodox or not, she'd purchased the "gifts" he'd asked for: an ancient slave woman who, she saw now, could well be of Mirren descent, and a serving woman of middle years named Marid, both from, of all places, the House of Du-kar. They'd been given a new home within her own but were to be freed upon the Lady Justice's return to Soldat.

"Lady Justice." Sheftu's deep voice sounded both reverent and delighted as he approached. He executed a bow, then straightened with a smile. "We are honoured that you have come."

"Lord Sheftu," Lady Justice said, inclining her head. "I could not have refused so gracious, and so unexpected, an invitation. It is I who am honoured." She glanced at the beautiful Saharani at Sheftu's side and waited until she was spoken to.

Laran smiled, her regard genuine. "Lady Justice," she said softly in the Sowthern tongue. "Your presence does indeed honour us." She paused a moment, aware of the press of wedding guests waiting their turn to speak.

"I believe you have before you now the answers you sought on that long ago night in Soldat. Is that not so?"

"It is so, Saharani Laran Tania," Lady Justice acknowledged. She bowed her esteem. Laran placed her hand on the older woman's shoulder.

"You have our gratitude," she told her quietly. "If you hadn't done what you did, if you hadn't believed in us then..." Laran left the statement unfinished, but the implication of her words was plain. *None of this would have come to pass.*

"It was the right thing to do," Lady Justice declared, but the couple had already moved on. The venerable lady sighed. She'd made her choices and regretted none of them. Even so, she felt a touch of envy as she watched Lord Sheftu Morrow and the Saharani Laran Tania disappear into the throng of well-wishers. There in the Great Hall of Mirren-Bar, the promise of happiness and joy seemed to hang in the air.

Life was waiting.

AUTHOR'S NOTE

I hope you enjoyed reading The Blessing of the Black Wolves as much as I enjoyed writing it. I would be honoured if you'd take a moment to leave a review or rating.

I am currently at work writing the third novel in the Black Wolves series. Watch for

- **Raven Seeker** * Book 2 - *Available March 15, 2022*
- **The Road to Mirren-Bar** * Book 3 - *In progress*

The three novels of the **Nightfall Mountain series***, set in Montana in 1870, will also soon be available.*

If you'd like to learn about upcoming books or have a comment to share with me, I'd love to hear from you.

- WEBSITE - HTTP://WWW.JSMURPHY.CA,
- FACEBOOK - HTTP://FACEBOOK.COM/NOVELISTJSMURPHY,
- TWITTER - HTTPS://WWW.TWITTER.COM/JSMURPHYAUTHOR
- INSTAGRAM - HTTPS://WWW.INSTAGRAM.COM/NOVELISTJSMURPHY
- EMAIL - NOVELS@JSMURPHY.CA.

Thank you for reading Raven Seeker.

RAVEN SEEKER

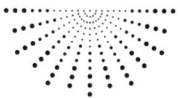

Special Advanced Preview

Black Wolves Series * Book Two

JS Murphy

CHAPTER ONE

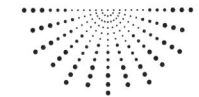

DEATH LAY, GRINNING, in her hands.

Terrin-tie drew the skull out into the light. The lower mandible had come away and one of the eye sockets bore the indent of tiny striations as though a mouse had nibbled there. The skull's teeth were those of a young person, straight and healthy. One, in the front, was slightly crooked. The rest of the bone was in excellent condition.

"Who were you?" she murmured. "Why were you buried *here*, so far from the original town?" She glanced over at the current village gate, only forty feet from where she'd discovered the tomb. The ancient town site was hundreds of feet away, upstream from Alusiat's present position.

Death had lessons to teach the willing.

"Teach me," Terrin-tie implored the skull. "I wish to learn."

The empty eye sockets seemed to stare back at her accusingly now.

"Fear not," she murmured. "You have my utmost respect. I will leave your place of slumber safer than I found it. This I promise."

She turned the skull over in her hands. It seemed delicate, smaller than she imagined an adult male skull would be. Could this have been a young woman? She felt a sense of solidarity with the person it used to be.

"Have you returned to the land as a shadow?" she asked it softly. It was an old folk tale, passed down through the ages, but many Barraidi still believed that shadows housed the images of the departed.

A male voice interrupted her reverie. "It seems you'd rather speak to dusty bones than to the living, Sister."

Terrin-tie glanced up, frowning at her brother.

"They don't speak inanely and at length of trivial matters," she answered crossly. "Leave me be, Sendall. I have discovered something of note here."

Sendall huffed out his impatience. "Groping in the dirt for the dry bones of the past," he said. "How could that be of import *now*? The sun is shining on *us*, Terrin-tie." He glanced back at the Alusiat gate where several villagers watched the exchange curiously.

Embarrassing. His sister had *always* been embarrassing. She was not interested in the traditional affairs of women, preferring instead to leave the village each morning to dig and stare at the dirt. Her evident delight in finding the remnants, however minuscule, of past lives was incomprehensible to him.

As it was to his friends and neighbours.

"Come," Sendall said. "Dust yourself off. Make yourself presentable. Our mother has sent me out here to collect you for dinner."

Terrin-tie set the skull down gently and stood, stretching her back and tipping her head back like a cat. It felt glorious.

"I've been here a long while," she admitted, looking up at the sky. The sun was low, but darkness was still at least two hours away. She was hungry and her water jug had long ago run dry.

"Please give my apologies to our mother," she instructed Sendall. "I cannot leave just now. I must make things right here first."

Plus, she was almost certain she could fit through the narrow opening in the rock to better view the tomb within.

She bent to rifle through her bag. There were candles and fire starter inside. She'd need those to…

"Terrin-tie!" Sendall protested. "People are watching you! Are you not uncomfortable? Do you not wish to be seen as 'normal'? What man will want you for his wife if you..."

"What?" Terrin-tie straightened and rounded on Sendall. "What!" she sputtered. "My life is my own! The gods did not put me on this world solely to be *wife* to some dull and uninteresting man!" She looked down at her work.

Tiny fragments of broken pottery stretched in an organized line down the short slope, the bound straw she'd used to carefully brush the dirt away lying beside it. Deerskin gloves, well-worn with torn thumb and index fingers, were balanced on a rock. A short wooden shovel leaned against it. The skull of the young woman lay on the ground beside it.

Terrin-tie glanced at the sky once more. She needed to hurry if she were to squeeze through the opening of the tomb and back out again before the light faded. She turned to Sendall but he was already half-way back to the Alusiat gate. He waved a hand at the watching villagers, likely trying to cushion what he probably considered social damage.

Terrin-tie sighed. *So be it.* She knelt on the hard ground to address the skull.

"I am going to visit your resting place now. Please, teach me what you can. Show me who you were. Why you are here. Tell me if you went to Death willingly or whether you fought him every step of the way. I would know your story. I will honour your life."

She shoved her bag in through the narrow opening and squeezed inside. The rock closed in over belly and back.

The passage remained narrow for the first four feet, just long enough to make Terrin-tie wonder if she'd made a serious mistake. If she became stuck, she'd have to be hauled out backward through the opening by her feet. She could admit to herself that she had enough ego to want to avoid such a spectacle.

The passage opened up into a small stone chamber, roughly square in shape, twice as long as she was tall and an equal distance across. It wasn't high enough to stand in. She struck the fire-starter on a stone and lit two candles, one of which she placed dead-centre on the closest wall. The stone in the hills of Alusiat was pale yellow in colour. It reflected light back into the chamber.

She lit the second candle and started toward the back wall. There, the headless skeleton of the young woman lay curled in a fetal position on the stone floor, the bones of a new-born baby cradled protectively in her skeletal arms.

Childbirth, she thought. The young woman and her baby must have died in childbirth.

"I am so sorry, Young Mother," she murmured. "So very sorry." She thought of the husband and the father of these two and wondered if he'd been grief stricken at the loss of mother and child. She hoped they'd been well-mourned in death and well-loved in life.

She looked toward the light at the entrance and wondered how the skull had travelled so far from the body. Dragged by a small animal, she supposed. She would reunite the skull with the rest of the body before she retired for the night.

She held the candle up to the walls to better see the paintings she'd glimpsed there. The dye used had been made from the earth and rock and were shades of browns and reds and charcoal with a few touches of startling blue. How had they made such a shade, Terrin-tie wondered?

The dead had much to teach.

The faded dyes had blurred over time. She squinted at the indistinct paintings, willing them to better focus.

Teach me, she thought again.

Toward the centre of the back wall, the paintings grew clearer. Red horses galloped across fields. A stream of water rushed down from the hills, dotted with what looked like fish. A strange animal stood sentinel and unmoving in the trees: *batheta.* Mountain lion. Terrin-tie shook off a tingle of fear at the illustrated presence of the predator.

Now people began to appear. A woman, her belly swollen in pregnancy walked hand in hand with a man. This must be her husband, the father of the child, Terrin-tie thought. He was considerably larger than she was. His hair was black. And straight.

Terrin-tie sat up straight.

Were there other paintings of the man? Yes, there, on the side wall! There were other men like him. They were tall, their hair straight and black. One was facing forward. His eyes were…. black!

These men were Soldatian!

Her eyes darted to the young woman with the baby. Death had lessons to teach the willing, she thought again.

"I am willing," Terrin-tie murmured, thoroughly shaken. "Teach me, Young Mother."

The men seemed to be working side-by-side with shorter, brown-haired men. Barraidi! Tall, black-haired women and shorter women with brown hair worked together at a mill, or well, of some kind.

Children of both colours played in a courtyard together with a toy, a square block, its purpose unknown.

Terrin-tie sat back on her heels.

This was not a frightening scene. It was peaceful. Barraidi and Soldatians working and living together!

It seemed impossible and yet…. Here it was! The scene would not have been painted on the tomb of the dead mother and baby if it were not true! This *was* day to day life in the ancient village. Day to day life with Soldatian neighbours!

How long ago had this been? It must have been a thousand years in the past, perhaps more! in the past, perhaps more! All memory of Barraidi/Soldatian cooperation had been erased, blurred into non-existence like many of the paintings inside the tomb.

Terrin-tie turned toward the entrance once more, lifting the candle as she did so. On one side of the entrance two small children were depicted running, a brown animal on their heels: a dog perhaps. The indistinct figure of a large Barraidi male, chest encased in some sort of armour, stood behind them. On the other side of the entrance a lone standing man was painted. His features had long since faded away, but his straight, black hair marked him as Soldatian. One arm was extended. Although the hand and the details of clothing were indistinct or missing, the raven perched on his arm was unmistakable.

Raven Seeker, Terrin-tie thought with a shudder.

But nothing at all in the painted gallery was anything but a cheerful depiction of everyday life in the ancient village. If this was indeed a *Raven Seeker*, he was benign.

Yes, she thought. Like the children, his was a peaceful presence there at the entrance of the tomb. And the raven? Was it a portent of the young mother's death?

Perhaps it was a guide to the place the young mother and her babe meant to travel. Who knew what the people of the ancient town believed?

Perhaps it was just a bird.

But Terrin-tie sucked in her breath and squeezed as far to the other side of the narrow passage as she could, trying and failing to avoid touching the painting of the raven as she passed. When her hair caught on the rough stone, she pulled it abruptly away, tearing a few strands and leaving them hanging from the arm of the painted Soldatian.

She needed to pass through the entrance twice more to reunite the skull with the rest of the young mother's body. On the morrow, she would seal the tomb to protect the resting place of the two, the baby eternally protected within the maternal embrace.

Tonight, though, she would ponder what she had learned. She couldn't wait to describe what she had seen to her family. She'd keep her findings from the people of Alusiat, for now, though. Cooperation with the warring nation of Soldat was unimaginable. Perhaps it always would be.

She feared the tomb would be desecrated if the villagers learned what was painted within.

CHAPTER TWO

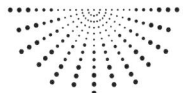

PROVOS WAS ALONE, in unfamiliar landscape, in a land not his own.

He glanced behind him for a final glimpse of the upper reaches of Mirren-Bar, but the natural, and massive, stone columns he led the mare through now hid the city from sight. Ahead of him the view opened up to the long reaches of the mountain pass and the magnificent snow-capped peaks all around him. Out of sight and beyond it all was his destination, the Mirren Sea.

He'd never seen the sea or the great oceans that bordered it, though he'd heard stories. They all had. Those stories had seemed... unlikely. And yet, since arriving in Mirren-Bar, he'd seen, and eaten, the strange and pallid creatures that had been transported from its waters.

He grinned to himself. *Aey*, the sea was real, just as Mirren-Bar had proven to be. Childhood tales of the mountain city, its otherworldly beauty, and the strange abilities of certain of its denizens, had been considered a myth by his countrymen. But it was as real as he was, as the warm animal at his back, as the smooth, hard stone beneath his feet.

The waves of wind-swept grass over the great golden plains of his Soldat home had been likened to the movement of the waters of the sea. He wanted to see that with his own eyes.

Provos contemplated re-mounting the sturdy mountain horse, but the path looked even more precarious ahead. No, better to lead the mare than to risk a fall here, he thought, where even a minor slip would mean a lingering and terrifying death as he plummeted to the rocks nearly a thousand feet below. He felt a tug of longing for his own horse, the stallion he'd raised and trained from a colt. The animal had been trained for war, though, to run, to withstand sudden turns and galloping starts during combat. The considerably smaller horse at his back had been bred to be sure-footed on the mountain paths. He stopped a moment, turning carefully to avoid unbalancing, and stroked the mare's velvet nose. He scratched lightly between large equine eyes. The movement caused the animal to close those eyes briefly in apparent pleasure.

Aey, he thought again. He'd see the Mirren Sea for himself. Though he sorely wished his cousin was there to experience it with him.

"Life changes," he murmured to the horse. "I know it. But, by the Seven Gods, I am not finding the change easy." His eyes re-traced the trail he traversed, back up through the stone columns to the hidden city beyond. His cousin resided there now, with his wife, his new family, and his responsibilities. He and his cousin had been inseparable since childhood. But things were different now. He didn't begrudge the happiness Sheftu had found with his Mirren wife, nor did he begrudge him the new life he'd begun.

Still, he missed his good-natured company. Provos was an adventurer, and his cousin with him. Together they'd left the Soldat capital to return the little Mirren slave woman to her family. Together they'd taken ship to Barraid, then traveled overland in that hostile country to Mirren-Bar. Together they'd suffered injury and deprivation, and together they had survived.

Sheftu hadn't wanted him to head off on his own. Provos knew his cousin worried for him, would continue to worry. But it had been time to begin an adventure of his own. And to let his cousin get on with his.

He turned around on the narrow path and continued down through the remaining columns, the mare's nose bumping gently on his back from time to time.

* * *

LANDEL STOPPED ABRUPTLY on the path, causing the entire line of heavily-laden, weary climbers to stumble into one another.

"What ails you now?" the man directly behind him complained.

"Look!" Landel said, pointing through a gap in the head-high boulders lining the path. "What is *that*?" He squinted harder, recognizing the figure approaching from above as a man. "By the Holy Ones, he's big! Is that *black* hair?"

"Skin's dark, too. Not one of us, then," his companion supplied. He glanced around him at his countrymen's curling, light brown hair and fair complexions.

"Soldatian, maybe," Landel guessed. "Though I've never seen one."

"*Black Wolves!*" his companion whispered. "That's what our people call them. The Barraidi call them *Raven Seekers*. I've heard Soldatians are dangerous!"

Landel made a disgusted noise. "You think *everything* is dangerous, Monne." He squinted at the stranger again. "Even so," he added, "I wouldn't be calling him '*Black Wolf*' or '*Raven Seeker*' to his face."

"He's a big one all right," one of the other climbers said. He was eyeing the man's great height against the height of the horse behind him. He automatically adjusted the large pack he carried on his back, and the rest of the climbers did the same.

"He sees us!" Monne hissed.

Landel broke through the cover of the boulder-lined trail into the open. He continued walking until he'd reached a wide spot on the trail where the Soldatian, or whatever the man was, could pass them by. To Monne's dismay, Landel raised his hand in greeting.

The Soldatian did the same. He was grinning at the group of them, teeth white against bronzed skin. The mounting breeze stirred his straight, black hair, lifting it off wide shoulders as he neared. The man was well-muscled, mid-to-late twenties in age. No weapons were evident with the exception of a hunting knife strapped to his waist. Low on his narrow hips he wore a *talom*, the knee-length wrap of white fabric common in Mirren-Bar. His sleeveless Mirren shirt was jewel blue. Judging by the way it covered his broad chest, the shirt had been made exclusively for him, as surely any other would have been far too small. Sturdy leather sandals were tied by leather thongs to just below his knees, as was common in the city.

He appeared relaxed and his smile stayed in place, but his eyes, black as the night, seemed to be assessing the approaching climbers.

As Landel, at the front of the line, drew near, the big man nodded his greeting.

"You… ah… you s…speak Mirren?" Landel asked. The night-black eyes were disconcerting and he heard himself stutter despite his best efforts to appear equally friendly and relaxed.

"*Ashaii*," the Soldatian said, his deep voice strangely accented. "But not well," he admitted.

"What are you…?"

"Your burdens are great," the Soldatian interrupted.

"Seafood," Landel offered. "We carry ice and shellfish to the Great Hall at Mirren- Bar. Here the path is too narrow for our horses." He eyed the Soldatian's mountain horse with interest, and some envy. "You will see where we have left them as you continue down."

Landel suddenly looked worried. He and his companions were fishermen, not warriors. Even outnumbered, if a man such as this decided to steal their horses while they climbed, there would not be much they could do.

"You wouldn't… ah… take them from us, would you?"

The Soldatian's smile dropped off. He'd had difficulty following the Mirren's conversation but believed he'd understood the gist of at least the last of it. He shook his head. "I will not," he assured them seriously.

Landel smiled up at the stranger in relief. Without the horses, the ice they carried on these trips to Mirren-Bar would melt halfway up the mountain, spoiling the seafood they carried, and their livelihoods with it.

"What are you doing here?" Monne demanded suspiciously.

"I am going to the sea," Provos told him.

"In Mirren. What are you doing in Mirren?" the man asked.

"I have been a guest of the High Lord," Provos answered. He was speaking slowly, trying to find the correct Mirren words for his answer. "But I have taken my leave to see more of your country."

A guest of the High Lord? Landel pondered what that could mean, but soon dismissed it. "Be wary," he warned as he passed.

Provos raised a raven brow.

"There are slavers operating near the border towns," Landel explained over his shoulder. "A man such as yourself would likely command a high price on the other side, in Barraid."

The words "slavers" and "Barraid" brought the warning to life.

"Thank you," Provos said sincerely. "I will." He passed the rest of the climbing party with a polite nod for each of them, noting the blinks of shock, presumably at his stature, but possibly at his eyes.

The Mirren were generally a pragmatic lot, Provos considered, but it seemed the colour, or rather the lack of colour, of Soldatian eyes gave them pause, stirring long-buried superstition.

"*Tulah!*" he called out as the last in the line of seven men was behind him. It was a greeting he'd come to understand meant both "hello" and "farewell".

Slavers, he thought with revulsion. He would, as the fisherman advised, be wary. He thought of Laran Tania, his cousin's Mirren wife. She'd been enslaved, carried across the border into Barraid, and then transported into Soldat. She'd been terrorized and abused by her captors. *Aey,* he thought grimly, he'd be wary. And if the opportunity presented itself, he'd drag the slaving bastards up to the heights, to Mirren-Bar itself, to answer to the High Lord.

CHAPTER THREE

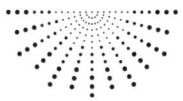

T ERRIN-TIE SETTLED COMFORTABLY into her saddle, enjoying
the early morning light. She stroked the coarse white mane of the
young gelding she rode and anticipated her race across the hills of her
Barraidi homeland. She'd been waiting all week for her turn to ride
Hanasta, and the gelding, in turn, was clearly anxious to run.

"See that you don't go as far this time," her mother chastised her. "It's past
mid-summer and the nights are growing colder. It isn't safe, Terrin-tie."

Terrin-tie pushed thick, wavy brown hair from her face and smiled down
at her mother. At twenty-five years of age, she was no longer a child, but
her mother evidently felt her parental ties as strongly as ever. Perhaps she
always would.

"Here," she said, handing her mother a small sketch. "It's the route I've
planned," she told her. "All the way to the foothills and back. You see? Here
is where I will make camp. Perfectly safe. No surprises. I know the way."

Her mother raised her brows. "And if something should happen? Will we
be able to find you? Using this?"

"Yes!" Terrin-tie laughed. "I will follow the route. I promise."

Her mother smiled in spite of her concern, secretly proud of her daughter's self-reliance. "Safe travels, then. Enjoy your time away."

"I will!" she called over her shoulder as she rode away.

Oh yes, Terrin-tie thought as she allowed Hanasta his head. The horse reared slightly in unrestrained enthusiasm, then stretched out into a wild gallop. The wind rushed past Terrin-tie's face. She felt the press of her clothing against her slim torso and her hair streamed out behind her. She grinned.

I will! I am!

ABOUT THE AUTHOR

JS Murphy takes inspiration for her novels from nature. Countless hikes into mountain wilderness, in every season of the year, spark her imagination in ways her hiking companions might be surprised to learn. The roots of an upended tree become a shelter from the

elements, a raging creek in full flood a fearsome escape route. An avalanche or encounters with wildlife become the impetus for acts of heroism or kindness. The silence of snow-covered forests, even the nightmare of forest fire, are catalysts for action.

Inspiration comes, too, from extensive travels. An appreciation for different cultures, customs, and music spur creativity and help bring life to her novels.

Above all, it is love that holds the ultimate power in her writing. Love drives the story of her own life, as well as the actions of her characters, ever forward.

Website- http://jsmurphy.ca

facebook.com/novelistjsmurphy
twitter.com/jsmurphyauthor
instagram.com/novelistjsmurphy

Made in the USA
Middletown, DE
16 February 2022

61065367R00314